CURSE BEARER

BOOK 1 IN THE RISEN AGE ARCHIVE

REBECCA P. MINOR

REALM MAKERS

For Riley, who is striking out on his own epic adventure

PART I

1

THE KNIFE

*S*omething unsavory was brewing outside Baledric's Apothecary and Alchemy shop.

Danae stared beyond the final customer of the day as he passed through the shop's front door. The bronze bell over the exit jingled the farewell she was too preoccupied to utter. Just visible through the rippled panes of the shop window, Danae's father huddled in hushed discourse with a handful of men—among them, the baker from across the way and the tanner from up the street. One man in particular piqued Danae's curiosity.

Despite the summer warmth, a stranger at Papa's side wore an ankle-length grey cloak with its hood pulled low over his eyes. He leaned on a clean-hafted staff of worn wood—perhaps cherry. His murmured contributions to the conversation pulled at her.

Papa's repeated glances up the street bespoke more than idle chatter with the neighbors, as did the tanner and baker's furrowed regard of the stranger beside them. A disquieting flutter in Danae's middle replaced her curiosity. She picked at already-short fingernails until the nail on her ring finger broke and peeled. A red streak seeped along the exposed quick, and she shook her hand against the sting.

But there was work to do, and Papa would likely take exception to her nosing into his exchange. She forced her attention away from the happenings outside and onto the vellum-paged ledger before her. A quick dip into the inkwell filled her quill with iron gall ink. Danae swept the instrument across the page's surface, penning the day's last sale in flowing script.

A few packets of Aconite Root and Henbane for pain, a flask of ginger and pippali, a bundle of matches. Sure, they added a few more gold pieces to the till, but did they make a difference?

Danae sighed and scattered a pinch of fine-ground pounce across the lettering, shook the excess back into the pounce pot, then closed the cracked cover of the book. The crumbling binding heralded the ledger's many years of service, but despite its dilapidation, it would continue to serve. After all, replacements for such luxuries came at a stiff price.

The beams of afternoon sun slanted through the front windows and kindled ever-present dust motes to an amber glow, a hint of the magical amidst the mundane. Danae sought her father beyond dancing specks of light. His jaw was tight and eyes narrow, but the men who remained with Papa had grown pale and careworn over the course of the conversation, especially Master Galen, the baker. The cloaked stranger had left their company.

She hesitated. Behind her, the cauldron burbled its demands for the next batch of ingredients. The dust in the air insisted the grime left about by customers and craft be swept. A savory waft of broth and bread reminded Danae that supper loomed too near for her to dally.

She shrugged off Papa's doings and hustled toward the laboratory at the rear of the shop. No use provoking both Mama *and* Papa's ire.

Just as she reached the laboratory doorway, to her left, the iron-bound door that set the boundary between the Baledric home and business burst open with a crash. She dodged the charge of a dark-haired brother, whose exact likeness barreled in after him.

"Would you two watch where you're going?" Danae said. "Honestly! Can't you take your sparring somewhere, anywhere, else?"

The coltish boys, too young to be reckoned men, but tall and lanky enough to encroach upon an adult's height, aimed slaps at one another's heads. A blocked punch, a kick to the shins. More of the usual, with the day's schoolwork likely done and idle time goading the boys into another of their intermittent scuffles.

Danae shook her head. *Brothers.*

Her glance flicked to the delicate composition that bubbled in the iron cauldron over the fire. How was she supposed to help their father with his work if her seven younger siblings kept popping in and out of the laboratory and shop like ground squirrels in a burrow? Tristan and Connall continually proved the worst of them.

The boys' skirmish raged past the laboratory, banging against the long counter and rattling the bottles, boxes, and tools that sat upon it. Danae dove to catch a tipping flask of lavender oil. Their small-scale war risked upsetting every stack or shelf of goods in range.

"Watch yourselves." Danae set the flask gently back in place. "Or else Papa will have you apprenticed now instead of holding off until next summer."

Tristan ducked his brother's swinging fist and dared a scoff in Danae's direction. "Wishful thinking. You know he can't—oof!"

Connall's knee connected with Tristan's side.

"Overconfidence strikes again." Connall laughed.

The brawl rumbled toward the center of the room, and Danae breathed a sigh. The breakables on the counter had survived. For now.

Was Papa coming in any time soon? Danae craned her neck to peer over her brothers who obstructed her view of the window. Just as she looked, the remainder of Papa's group dispersed. He raked his hands through short salt-and-pepper hair, making it stand on end worse than usual. The ruckus in the shop would surely draw his intervention now.

The twins' wrestling match ground to the floor, where Connall pinned Tristan's chest and shoulders to the floorboards.

"Mercy?" Connall leaned all his weight forward.

Tristan groaned.

Judging by past bouts, Tristan's groan closely preceded surrender, so Danae turned her back on the conflict.

She pulled a stoneware mixing bowl from a laboratory shelf. Her workspace brimmed over with supplies and raw materials: chemicals and shavings, ores and herbs that she surveyed with an adept eye. Danae's smooth script graced every front-facing label, each one an obedient soldier awaiting command. A pinch of powdered iron, a tiny scoop of sulfur, the bark of the mournbriar ... These and many more exotic ingredients made the journey from shelf to bowl. Danae blended them into a blue-grey slurry with even strokes of a wooden spoon.

As she stirred, Danae could just make out her brothers' shuffling feet and then their voices.

"You really shouldn't let me get you on the floor like that," Connall said.

"Let you?" Tristan snorted. A few more padding footfalls, followed by a pause. "What's this stuff in the cauldron today? Boy, does it stink. Do you think this one could explode?" His voice fell to an awed whisper.

"How should I know?" Connall hissed back. "Anyway, we shouldn't be messing with Papa's work."

Good. At least Connall had an iota of sense. Left to Tristan's sagacity, the twins might have long ago met a foolish end.

She wafted the scent of her concoction toward her nose. It needed more sulfur.

"What if we sloshed a little, just a tiny bit, into the fire?"

Danae dropped the mixing bowl and bolted for the shop. "All right, you two. I hear mischief in the works. Out!"

Connall frowned. "We weren't touching anything."

"Yet." Danae folded her arms.

Tristan sighed. "Fine. Was that Master Galen out front? Come on, Connall, let's go see if he has any leavings we can mooch today. I think I hear homeless pastries calling for me."

With a laugh, Connall rose and moved to the door. "Beats breathing in this stink-boil Danae's got going." The twins stepped into the street.

"Be back before the sunset bell, or Mama'll have your hides," Danae called after them.

She returned to the lab table and her mixing. Quiet reigned once again in the shop for a few, blissful moments.

The rattle of the latch on the door to the house her jarred her, and she juggled to keep from spilling her bowl of ingredients. Her heart hammered.

The door squeaked open. "Deklan, are you in here?"

"He's out front, Mama. At least, he was."

Mama poked her head around the door to catch Danae's glance. "I've got bread to pull from the oven, so could you go find him and tell him supper's almost ready? Then your brothers? I'm likely to have charcoal to serve if I get mixed up in tracking them all down."

"I'll see who I can herd to the table," Danae replied.

Mama smoothed her strawberry-blonde locks, tucked into a sloppy bun. "My thanks, dearest. Make sure he knows 'almost' means minutes."

Danae smirked. "Of course."

It was not unlike Papa to get up to his elbows in three projects, even though a meal had been declared nearly on the table. She passed through the shop and headed for the front door. When she opened the apothecary exit, however, she froze on the threshold.

A group of soldiers waited in the thoroughfare, seated upon three stout-legged horses with shaggy dun coats and coarse manes that stood straight up like long scrubbing brushes. The riders wore armor of overlapping scales of leather, boiled hard, and skullcap helms studded with short spikes. With them came a wood-wheeled cart drawn by a pair of oxen and driven by a soldier armored like the horsemen. The cart was half-full of anything from pelts to pig iron.

At the rear of the group, a bridled lizard as long from nose to tail tip as the street was wide surveyed the street with round eyes. Its sand-beige skin folded in thick creases at its throat and around muscular legs that scarcely held its belly clear of the street. A shiny black tongue flicked its forked way through a reptilian smile. The beast's saddle was empty.

Danae groaned. *A redistribution? Not now.*

Papa emerged from the baker's shop across the way, pointing back toward the apothecary.

"Tristan, Connall—get home," Papa said.

Her brothers scuttled into the street, but the soldiers assembled there fanned into a semicircle and barred their way. "Not so fast, boys," one of the grey-skinned soldiers said. "Captain Drex has something to say to you when he's done with the dough boy here, as I recall."

Tristan and Connall froze before the line of soldiers. Papa stepped to the boys' side and whispered something to them.

Not far behind Danae's brothers, Master Galen launched through his door and tumbled down the marble step in front of his shop, then sprawled in the street. Papa darted to Galen.

"Don't get in the way, Baledric," said the next person to step from the bakery. The hulking block of a man cradled a beaten copper helmet under his arm, doubtless to allow some air through the mass of dark dreadlocks that hung to his shoulders. Huge rectangular plates of armor broadened his already expansive shoulders. Upon these plates, intricate beading of dyed teeth and finger bones created a parallel linear pattern. Similar panels protected his legs.

How many victims had it taken for Drex of Cray to harvest so many embellishments? Danae shuddered. Papa still helped the baker to his feet, but then stepped back toward Danae's brothers.

"No bread, Captain?" the lead squad member said. "You mean this lazy lout isn't doing his part to see us fed?"

The baker dabbed a bloody nose with a handkerchief from his apron pocket.

"Baker!" Drex pulled a fat-bladed sword and rapped its pommel against his battered shield, which bore the telltale gargoyle device that heralded the soldier's loyalties. "You must remember how this works by now. My men are hungry, and it's your duty to render up anything that would better serve your benevolent leaders. Tell me I am seeing this wrong, and you have not emptied your bins for the day."

The baker trembled. Papa scanned the street and placed himself between the boys and Drex's men.

"Speak!" Drex bellowed.

"It's n-n-not customary to have goods left at the end of the day." The baker swept a pleading look across the group. "They would be . . . stale. Unusable for tomorrow's customers. Had you come in the morning . . ."

"We were not yet hungry in the morning." Drex gestured to the other riders.

They dismounted and encircled the baker, so they blocked Danae's view of the merchant from her vantage point at her own door. Drex remained in the bakery doorway, presiding over the bullying with his arms folded across his chest, his wide grin devoid of warmth.

Papa turned toward Tristan and Connall. He spoke to them, and they lowered their gazes, forcing them away from the baker and soldiers.

Drex's squad raised gauntleted fists and rained blows down upon Master Galen. Sickening thumps of armor against flesh assaulted Danae's hearing. The baker crumpled to the ground.

Danae gasped. The heat of fury surged into her cheeks. How could Papa just stand there, serving as nothing more than a human shield between her brothers' view and abject brutality? Why did he do nothing? Danae drew a long breath, tightened her lips, then marched into the street.

"Benevolent?" Danae said. "Your Western Tongue isn't nearly as good as it should be if you're going to insist Radromir is your new homeland."

"You dare address me?" Drex lowered a brow. "At least make sense if you open that flap of yours."

"I suppose I need to spell it out." Danae shook her head and heaved a sigh. "Seems to me you keep interchanging the words

'benevolent leaders' and 'violent invaders.' I thought the redistribu-
tions we supposed to be peaceable."

Danae's father whirled around to lance her with a sharp stare.
Her brothers' jaws went slack, though the shadow of a smile danced
on Tristan's face.

"No good will come of your sarcasm," Papa said through clenched
teeth. "Why don't you see your brothers home?"

"We're just going to slink home and hide while they beat non-
existent bread out of Master Galen's flesh?" Danae whispered. "That
makes us no better than them!"

Drex raised a gauntleted palm. The squad paused in their kicking,
punching, and jeering. "Congratulations. You have just elected your
father's pathetic potion brewery the next redistribution site. Van, take
a look."

One of Drex's underlings, a wiry man with a face like an opossum, brushed past Danae with a sneer on his lips. All the while,
Master Galen squirmed on the ground in a growing pool of his own
blood, moaning.

"And Ragshir, toss this blubbering bag of dung back in his own
flour bin." Drex spat at Galen. "Next time, you'll remember to have
bread aplenty on hand. Won't you?"

The soldier named Ragshir wrenched Galen to his feet by one
arm and half-dragged him back to the bakery.

Van slammed the apothecary door open with a wild jangle of the
doorbell. He snooped around the shelves, the sacks, and the corners
like a hog snuffling after truffles. Danae bristled as he lifted jars and
flasks, sneered at the contents, and then put them back—in the
wrong spots.

In a last gesture, the soldier scooped a line of matchsticks from
the counter and brought them with him on his return to the street.
Van held them out for Drex's appraisal. "This is all there was worth
taking."

Danae's father shot a hand out. "They're not dry yet! I don't
recommend—"

"Don't tell me what I should or shouldn't claim, Baledric. I ought to take your hide for your laziness!" Drex snatched the matches from Van and pored over them like a hand of cards.

"Laziness?" Danae blurted. "You haven't left us enough time between raids to remake half of what you plundered last time."

Drex's feral look lifted over the matches and settled upon Danae's brothers.

The wider their eyes grew and the more they cringed, the more an ugly sneer twisted Drex's ash-colored cheeks. The ritually-inflicted scars that crisscrossed his face crinkled grotesquely. "Perhaps Baledric would rather barter a deal that benefits us both."

Danae's father pushed his wild, dark hair out of the beads of sweat that glistened on his forehead. His glance flitted to his sons. "I have no interest in any sort of joint venture between you and me."

"So quick. And so testy," Drex said. "Your boys there. They're about old enough now to train for the enforcement squads."

"The only place those boys are going is in to the dinner their mother has prepared." Danae's father folded his arms across his chest. "Take anything—everything—from the shop. The lab, even. I won't negotiate with my sons as bargaining chips." He stepped closer to Drex, squaring his shoulders and stretching to his full height before a heavily armored adversary. Still, it would have taken two of Papa to rival Drex's weight and girth.

Drex swept a glance over Papa. "Really, Baledric. You could use the gold, clearly. And think of your sons' futures. Where will they prosper? Here? Brewing sad little cocktails for people stupid enough to trust in them?"

Surely Papa would never sympathize with the occupation, allowing Drex to muscle her brothers into a lifetime of beating down their own countrymen. Her father's lack of rebuttal skittered up and down Danae's spine.

She huffed. "You heard what he said, Drex. My brothers aren't going with you. You've got all there is! Take the matches." She muttered under her breath, "I hope they blow up in your packs."

"You going to let this hussy keep talking to you like that,

Captain?" Van cracked his knuckles and took an aggressive step toward her. The other squad member rested his hand on his hilt.

Drex withheld an immediate reply. In the intervening silence, the calculating intensity of his black stare drove to Danae's heart.

She swallowed. "Boys, Papa's right." Her glance flicked about the simmering threat. "Let's get you home for supper . . ." She clasped her brothers' arms.

"That won't really do." Drex's stare sparked to life. He sprang.

The street exploded into chaos.

Drex, his meat-hook hands flexed into claws, lunged for Danae's father. He shouted to his soldiers, "Get the boys!"

Tristan and Connall dodged past the soldiers, stumbling and scrambling over one another as they barreled for the shop's front door. Danae followed. The shabby sole of Tristan's shoe snagged on a cobblestone. He crashed onto his shoulder. Danae barely leapt over him and shoved Connall through the doorway.

Drex's remaining retainers wheeled and pursued. Before Danae could get back to Tristan, one of the soldiers yanked him up by the collar.

Danae's wild glance volleyed from the soldiers to Drex. Papa gripped Drex's wrists, holding them back from the choke hold Drex aimed for Papa's throat. Though Papa resisted for now, the Tebalese soldier's bulging strength would make a short match of that encounter.

"Get . . . in . . . the house!" Papa cried, his voice pitching higher.

Danae charged for the shop, but stopped short of passing through the doorway. She reached out, grabbed the door handle, and yanked it shut.

"Bar it, Connall!" she yelled through the wood. She spun and slammed her back against the heavy planking. Her limbs trembled.

Thunk. The crossbar landed on the opposite side of the door. At least Connall was safe. For now. She could not flee without Tristan and Papa.

"Not too smart, sweetie," Van said. He closed the distance between them on ponderous strides. Danae's eyes widened.

Van dove. Danae dodged to the side, but her pursuer snatched her ankle and sent her skidding on her side across the cobbles. She kicked his hand with her free heel. His grip faltered, but he swiped with the other hand. Danae flailed.

The other soldier wrestled Tristan, kicking and scratching, toward the redistribution cart. The boy sank his teeth into the soldier's arm. The assailant roared and delivered a solid rap to Tristan's temple, who ceased struggling and went limp.

Danae's ankle-height boot slipped from the foot Van gripped, setting her free of his grasp. She scrambled backward on hands and feet, when her palm landed on a loose cobble. Before Van could tackle her, she heaved the stone.

The round river rock struck Van full in the teeth. He recoiled with a curse, giving Danae just enough space to roll to her feet, then whirl toward Papa.

Drex had forced her father to his knees. Taut tendons banded across the hand Drex clutched under Papa's jaw. Papa gasped and choked and tugged at Drex's forearm, but for all his pulling, he might as well have sought to pry an iron collar from his neck. His face turned crimson for want of air. With his left hand, he scarcely restrained Drex's other hand from also clamping around his windpipe.

Tristan's abductor neared the cart. The paralysis of an impossible choice seized Danae's legs.

Van, bloody-faced, lunged again.

Papa's woe-stricken glance intercepted Danae's for only a moment. He threw his palm out toward her, mouthing words Danae could not hear.

A bright jet of flame erupted from Papa's hand, streaked through the street, and burst into a fireball against Van's back. The wave of heat swelled over Danae, and at the same time, an uncanny, sizzling shiver spread across her skin as well. She cringed from the blaze— but the fire retreated as Drex's engulfed henchman fell back from her. Flames licked over his clothes and hair. He howled like a crazed bull and batted at the fire.

The other soldier hauled Tristan into the cart, climbed aboard, and whipped the oxen into a run.

Danae uncurled from her protective ball, just in time to see Drex shake off a stupefied gape. He whipped a long, smoky-bladed knife from his belt. Drex brandished it above her father's head, and a sickening look of relish flooded his features.

Papa strained backward, his eyes bulging and chest heaving for air. In a surreal moment stretched by calamity, Danae's gawk shifted from Papa to the weapon, the lithe sweep of its curved blade, the glint of unwholesome light off the bejeweled gargoyle's eyes on its pommel. She sprang toward her father.

Papa twisted from Drex's fist—but not far enough.

Drex plunged the knife.

2

DARK REMINDERS

*D*anae pulled ten earthenware bowls—no, nine—from the doorless cupboard beside the wide slate and fieldstone fireplace in the main room of the Baledric home. A single bowl remained on the shelf. Four months, and still she had not grown accustomed to the empty place at the family table she must leave as a constant reminder of Tristan's absence. How close it had come to being two empty places.

From beyond the barred door that led to the apothecary, the echo of a cough mocked Danae. Two empty places? It may yet be. Danae squeezed her eyes shut against memory, the sting of guilt, and fearful projections of the future. She turned with the bowls and headed to the pine plank table in the center of the room. She immersed herself in the warmth and homey smells of the kitchen, pulling them close like a comforting embrace. A cauldron of butter beans, garlic, and onions steamed over the fire. Two loaves of fresh golden bread sat on the board, waiting to be sliced.

The family table bore the scars of many years of service, and continual wear had polished the benches on each side smooth. On either end of the table stood a chair, each appointed with a cushion, cornflower blue in Danae's distant memory, but long since faded to a pale blue-grey.

Danae placed the bowls around and sawed into the bread, making sure to cut it into uniform pieces that would spare everyone the vexation of brothers fighting over whose piece was obviously an inferior portion.

Beside the fire, Mama blew on a spoonful of beans. She took a thoughtful bite and propped her other fist on her rounded hip.

Danae drifted to Mama's side and took a deep whiff of the meal's aroma. She contemplated the combination of scents. "How about the winter savory, Mama? And just a couple leaves of the sage."

After a final sip of the dregs of broth on her spoon, Mama shot Danae a smile. "Savory and sage it is. Now please call your brothers to wash up."

Danae sprang up the narrow spiral staircase in the back corner of the living area. She poked her head into the upper room of the home, where her brothers engaged in a riotous smattering of activities, ranging from whittling a wooden spoon to fighting free of a headlock.

"Boys!" she said. "It's time to wash up for—"

A stampede of hungry young men thundered as one to the stairway. Only a single member of the tribe remained in place: the youngest of the bunch, sandy-haired Weylan. He hunched on his lumpy cot, fixated upon the pages of a small volume bound with cedar shingles and leather thongs.

Danae slipped to his side and sat on the cot. "What's this you find so interesting that dinner hasn't tempted you from it?"

Weylan traced a finger over before the page before him. "It's an explorer's journal. Full of maps and notes all about other lands. I don't understand a lot of it, but it's still fun to read."

Danae's attention lingered on the book for a moment, the flutter of a nameless dream arising in her stomach. How vast a world Weylan's little book implied. She forced a smile and ruffled her youngest brother's hair. "Always discovering something new. But if you don't come down now, all you'll discover today is that one of your brothers has eaten your portion."

One final scan of the page later, Weylan closed the journal, stashed it under his cot, and followed Danae down the creaking staircase to the first floor.

Their mother's voice greeted her. "Before you wash up, head back to the shop and drag your father in for supper." She reached out a small kettle and a cup to Danae. "Drop this on the table on your way, please."

Danae took the rag-swathed handle of the kettle and the cup. Peppery steam curled from the spout. Another day, another elixir. She hardly dared hope this one would yield better results than the last, which was to say, any results at all. After placing the vessels beside Papa's place at the table, Danae crossed the room and poked her head through the doorway that led to the shop.

She peered around the apothecary, but found it empty.

"Papa," she called. "Mama sent me to 'drag' you to supper." She tried the lab. Empty as well. "Papa?" she called again.

Quiet reigned. Mama wasn't going to be happy.

The soft murmur of voices caught Danae's ear and drew her glance to the side window of the apothecary. There he was, in the alley beside the shop. Again. He and another man conversed, shoulders hunched against the wind of a grey, autumn afternoon.

Papa's companion was about a hand span taller than he was, but owing to his deep hood and cobble-sweeping cloak, Danae could glean little else.

Danae eased into the corner between the front and side windows while Papa continued to speak. His back was to her. She pressed her ear to the window frame.

Papa stretched his palms toward the other man. "If I could tell you more, I would. But I have a family now, and their safety trumps whatever goose chase your people have you on."

"Has it deteriorated to this, Deklan?" The cloaked visitor said, his voice sonorous but accented. "What has happened to you? The years hang upon you differently than I imagined they would."

Papa scoffed. "Easy for you to say, since the years have left you largely unchanged."

"Will you hold that against me?"

"No," Papa said more softly. "But please, I have no idea if this rumor of the Underground has anything to do with what you are looking for. And I'm not in a position to risk showing you anything."

Danae gasped. Underground? That sounded promising. At any rate, it sounded like something that was not aligned with the Tebalese occupation, and Danae would take anything of that nature she could get.

"I simply ask that you consider passing along any information you have or might come across," the stranger said. "You cannot imagine how important it may be, how soon the time of need may be upon all your people."

"Danae! Deklan!" Mama's voice rose on the other side of the shop door.

Danae sighed. *Just when things were getting interesting.* She leaned from the corner and tapped the window behind her father.

The man in the cloak tipped his chin a fraction higher, though not high enough to reveal anything more about his features. But even without seeing his glance, Danae felt the stranger's eyes upon her, and a shiver swept through her limbs. Papa's posture stiffened. A few murmured words passed between the men, and the visitor turned to disappear down the alley, his tall walking stick clicking into the distance.

Papa mounted the shop steps and scurried in the door, shutting it with a firm shove. He turned the key in the lock. He shielded his mouth and stifled a cough.

Danae's lips tightened. "Who were you talking to? Not the nicest day to hang about in the street, with that cold wind."

Papa's glance flicked to the side. "Just an old business associate." He rounded the shop counter, then pulled a ladle hanging from its hook under the mantle. With long, slow, circles, he wound the ladle around the simmering concoction in the cauldron.

"Has he been around here before? He looked in a little bit of a hurry," Danae said.

"As any sensible person should be. We're nigh the bell-toll."

She gritted her teeth. Why the Tebalese occupying force thought it necessary to seal everyone up at sunset remained beyond her comprehension. She nodded toward the kettle over the fire. "Do those need bottling up? Mama's already in foot tapping mode, you should know."

"Bottling? No, not yet," Papa replied. "A little more time, I think. Don't rush them."

Don't rush them. Wait and watch. It's all we do anymore. "Very well, Papa. After dinner, then."

He nodded. "I'll put some tin sheeting over it while we eat." He stepped toward the laboratory.

"Save yourself the hunt. The sheeting's gone. I wasn't able to wrap the goldenseal root either."

"I almost—" A fit of coughing snatched away Papa's words. Only after much throat-clearing and pounding his fist into his chest did he continue. "Last week's raid."

The thought of raids thrust a white-hot needle into Danae's heart. "I'm still not convinced that cough is unrelated to—"

"A man doesn't develop a cough from a blade in the shoulder." Papa rubbed his chest near his collarbone. "The only physical ailment I'll be left with is some stiffness when the weather turns cold."

Even though the place Drex's blade had bitten had been fleshy, not vital, four months' time was hardly enough to hope for full healing. Danae sighed through her nose. "But nothing we've tried helps, Papa. Mama's got tea for you at the table, but if it's not a new formula—"

"It will run its course." Papa approached and wrapped an arm around her. "Don't worry."

She leaned her head against his shoulder for a quiet moment, but the groan of hinges begging oil whined behind them. Danae peered around her father.

Mama stood in the doorway. She folded her arms and frowned. "You were just on your way in, I'm guessing?"

"Of course, love." Papa chuckled. "Danae looks more like you every moment, I'm certain. Which means she's lovelier by the day."

A wash of pink rose in Mama's cheeks, but she lowered her brows despite the grin that overtook her lips. "That's enough of your buttering, Deklan. In we go before the boys eat each other, sitting at that table waiting on you."

Mama and Papa led Danae into the house, where the boys sat along the benches of the dinner table. The seat beside Connall, however, remained conspicuously empty. Danae sighed and plunked onto her end of the bench.

Mama turned to ladle beans from the cauldron.

Stifling another cough, Papa took his place at the head of the table and cast a sideways glance toward his wife. If she noticed the evidence of his nagging illness, she refrained from commenting as she served the family. He poured a cup of his tea.

Finally, Mama sat at her end of the table and nodded to her husband. Danae's father blew out a long breath.

"Creator of all things," he began.

Mama cleared her throat. "Deklan, do you really think—"

Papa's face hardened. "In the privacy of my own home, I will not be cowed by that cult." He bowed his head. "Almighty Creator, we thank you today for this bounty set before us, and for the loving diligence of my dear Fiona to prepare it for us all. We acknowledge every good thing we have is a gift to be managed with care and thanksgiving. May this meal bring us health and strength, and may the company of our family bring us joy. To you be the honor and praise."

As Papa closed off the last syllable of his prayer, the boys all dove wholeheartedly into their meals. There was little conversation for a few minutes while they shoveled steaming bites, aside from their mother's reminders to eat like young men at a dining table, rather than ravenous wolves.

After the boys had gobbled down the majority of the food in their bowls, the talk around the table resumed, ranging from the day's school lessons to her brothers' boisterous interjections about rocks in the courtyard and the slimy inhabitants beneath them. Weylan, however, remained quiet and mournfully studied the bottom of his empty bowl.

Danae reached across the table and patted his hand. "Why don't you tell me what's on your mind? I know it's hard to get a word in."

Weylan lifted his large eyes to his sister, then cast his gaze back down to the table. While Danae waited upon his response, the other chatter stilled.

"I'm still hungry," Weylan muttered, his voice barely above a whisper.

Danae met her mother's gaze. Sadness and long-suffering puckered her mother's features.

"Dear one," Mama said. "I know it's hard. But if I give you more now, there will be no portion for you at week's end. You may not feel full, but if I allow you to eat your fill, then in a few days you'll learn what it's like to go to bed with no supper at all." She scraped a pat of butter across her bread, giving the task an uncharacteristic level of concentration. She extended it to Weylan.

One of Danae's middle brothers, fifteen-year-old Anyon, slapped the table. "Curse the rationing! Our block has its own garden. We work hard to grow what we can there, and still we're forced to go on short supply. Why should foreign soldiers eat what we grow and leave us only with scraps?"

Papa fired a sharp glare at Anyon. "Mind your tongue, boy. You're quick to complain and ever a thrall to your temper. Speak your mind in the wrong company, and much worse shall befall you than suffering a small dinner."

Anyon narrowed his green eyes. "I suppose I'm finished with my meal. May I be excused?"

Papa offered a stiff nod. Anyon rose and headed for the stairs. He bounded up on lanky strides.

Danae's eldest brother, Farrell, rose. "If I may have your leave, Papa, I'll go after him."

"Do so." Papa sighed. "I have work to finish in the lab. Boys, help your mother clear up. Danae, I need you with me."

Danae followed Papa back to the shop, carrying the remainder of his tea in the kettle while he held the cup. He set the cup down on the counter and disappeared into the lab. She gazed out the window, where twilight left the street cast in the deepening hues of dusk. Motion outside startled Danae.

Although the curfew bell had long since tolled, someone tapped furtively on the apothecary door.

3

*D*anae crept over to the door and peered out the peephole —newly drilled in the stout wood since the occupation made it wiser to know who stood outside before lifting one's latch. Danae caught a glimpse of the curly-tressed baker's wife. She turned the brass key in the lock and ushered the older woman inside.

"Mistress Alaine." Danae pushed the door shut. "What brings you out?"

Alaine, her brow dewed with sweat, trembled and glanced repeatedly out the window. "Thank goodness you answered. It's Galen. I think he's got another bleed."

Papa emerged from the laboratory with an armload of glass vials and a rack to arrange them in. "Oh, I'm so sorry. Is it bad? Is his belly bloating?"

"Not that I can tell as yet." Alaine ducked her head. "Though given the shape a baker ends up from sampling his own wares, I'll admit it's hard to say."

Danae scanned shelves that were far too empty for good service to customers. She selected the last small bottle of geranium extract and lady's mantle.

Alaine cast the vessel a forlorn look. "I was mainly askin' after advice, if you have any to give. I can't afford even a little medicine with the way baking extra for Drex has tapped us out."

Papa shook his head.

"You can do us a good turn in better times," he said. "I won't send you home without that vial."

Danae pressed the medicine into Alaine's hand. "Truly. Take it."

Tears welled in Alaine's eyes. She covered her trembling mouth with her free palm. "The Patrons smile upon you—you're too good to us. None can afford to give away what little we've got." She tucked the medicine in her housecoat pocket.

Papa took Alaine's arm and led her back to the door. "None of us can afford to be so callous as to withhold what is ours to give. If we don't have our neighbors in these dark times, who do we have?"

Alaine thanked them both again with a hitching voice and bustled into the street. Papa locked the door again behind her.

"That was the last of it, you know," Danae said.

Papa drew a slow breath. "I know, but—"

A yelp in the street cut him short. Danae flew to the window. On the opposite side of the street, two of Drex's squad members held Alaine by the arms. Their heavily-accented words were muffled, but Danae was certain she heard 'curfew violation' in the string of angry speech.

One of the guards pulled hand and leg irons off his belt.

"Papa!" Danae cried. "Heaven and Earth. Do you think they were lying in wait to grab her? I swear the street was empty when you opened the door."

Papa paled. With trembling hands, he pulled the cauldron of tinctures from the heat and set them on the counter.

"Didn't you just get done saying if we don't have each other, what do we have?" Danae said. "We have to help her!"

"I've helped how I can, enough for one night. What do you think will happen if they realize we're her reason for being out after hours?"

"But we can't just leave her to their version of justice," Danae said. "Especially if Master Galen needs that medicine."

"It's too risky. Stepping into the middle of that," Papa jerked a thumb toward the window, "would probably earn us blood and bruises. If not our own trip to the pillory."

"Not if you'd use even a fraction of what you can do." Danae jabbed a finger toward the conflict outside, where Alaine pleaded against the locking of the shackles. "I'll bet you know enough incantations—"

Papa dodged eye contact. "You really shouldn't use that word. It implies things you don't understand."

"I'd understand better if you'd pull the shroud of mystery off the whole business. You probably know enough whatever-you-want-to-call-them to be sure no putrid Tebalese soldier ever troubles anyone on this block again. There was a time—not very long ago, I might add—when you would have—"

"It's different now." Her father dragged a stool beneath him and plunked down, his eyelids drooping and his shoulders sagging. "And there are certain talents that cause more problems than they solve." He took a breath to speak again, but another bout of coughing snatched away the remark. Every time he tried to get a word out, it lodged in his chest, and the coughing gripped him anew. With an unsteady hand, he lifted his teacup from the counter and took a long draught.

While he coughed, Danae's attention flitted between her beset father and the peril in the street, where the soldiers laughed and jeered as they led Alaine off.

Finally, Papa's hacking subsided.

Yes, things are different now. "The father I once had would have insisted on real justice." Danae propped a hand on her hip.

"Justice?" Papa rasped. "I'm not in a position to demand anything."

Danae thumped her fist on the wooden counter with a hollow

thud. The teacup rattled. "If not you, then teach me what you know. There must be something we can do besides capitulate. That's just as bad as sympathizing with the whole occupation."

"Teach you? How many times have we been over this? I don't know if you even have the necessary gifting."

"If I did, would you teach me then?"

Papa scowled. "I'm finished discussing this, Danae." He rose from his stool and began yanking corks from the vials, each stopper making a high-pitched pop as it emerged. He arrayed the vials in the pouring stand with his lips pursed and a refusal to meet Danae's glance.

Papa's silence sufficed as a reply, so she turned her pout back to the window. The street was empty once again.

"I need to go check on Master Galen." Danae reached for the door handle. Faster than Danae thought him capable of moving, Papa interposed himself between his daughter and the door.

"Don't, Danae." His shoulders sagged. "What can you do, other than tell him you're sorry he's still suffering from the beating he took? The medicine's spent."

"Medicine or no, we can't turn a blind eye."

"And if the next patrol catches you out? We can't risk another . . . altercation like we had over the summer."

Danae softened. No, that horrific day was not a misery she could bear to revisit. While the beatings, the bullying, even the disappearances had grown commonplace, the outright stabbing had taken everyone by surprise. That Papa survived the attack had garnered more awestruck murmuring.

Papa pulled Danae to his chest and kissed the top of her head. "I know it's awful, Danae. But I'm just trying to keep you safe. I can't fail my family in that again." He shuddered.

Tears prickled Danae's eyes. Was safe better than free? She couldn't answer that. She blew out a breath and dismissed the tears with it, then stepped back from her father. "Well, those vials aren't going to fill themselves." She pressed her palms to the outside of the cauldron. "The tincture still needs to cool."

Papa pressed the backs of his fingers to the cauldron as well. "Indeed they do."

Danae surveyed her father's face. The dark circles beneath his eyes and the faint whistle in his breathing caught her notice. "I can handle it. Get some rest."

"I brought you in for help, not to pawn the work off on you."

"It's not pawning it off when I offered to do it," Danae replied. She handed the teacup and kettle to Papa. "Mama will be glad to have your attention for an evening, for once."

Papa smiled. "If you run into any questions, come and ask."

Danae ushered Papa back home, then returned to the shop and hooked the door latch behind her. She could justify another couple hours' wait before transferring the tinctures to vials. For now, she had a compelling sense of how to pass the time.

4

———

AFTER CURFEW

*W*hile Danae labeled the vials Papa had set out, footfalls in the upper story of the Baledric home slowed, petered, and then finally stilled entirely. She slunk to the rear of the laboratory and leaned out the narrow window there. No lamplight filtered from her parents' bedroom window, about halfway down the building's façade. She checked the latch on the door that led to the house—still hooked from her side. The shop's front door—locked as well.

Danae settled onto the stool behind the counter and slid open the middle drawer to her right. Beneath a bundle of rags, a stack of unsent invoices that Danae knew would never find their way to the indebted, and a broken grater that no one had mustered the motivation to repair, she unearthed the pocket-sized book. She set it on the counter beside her own journal, the inkwell, and a pen.

Danae opened the stained hide cover of the book and leafed to a page about a third of the way in. She smoothed her fingers over the rough tooth of the paper. The book had once been Papa's, and by its worn look, must have also been one he kept close and used often, but as far as she could tell, it had been long forgotten. The exhilarating scents of hand-pressed pulp mingled with more exotic aromas: iron and copper, pungent leaf and peppery stem, and others she could not name. Lost in the mystery of the text, she drank in the syllables on the page with an unquenchable thirst, and here and there sorted some into words with meaning. So much of the odd language in this little book eluded her. The few notes scribbled in the margins filled her with a growing appetite to know more. If only more of the book's contents had notes. There was power here. Power to change her circumstances.

Calletumnis, she penned into her journal. *Callet... well, I know that means 'fire,' she thought. But what about 'umnis?' I'd venture a guess that 'is' functions as a suffix, but—*

Danae circled her fingertips on her temple. Visions of a helpless neighbor, slowly dying from internal bleeding, repeatedly swept away her ability to focus on her book study. After another handful of attempts to comb the text for meaning, she set the pages aside and instead ladled cooled tinctures into vials. She stoppered and sealed each small dose of remedy with gold wax.

A bell's single toll called from the distance. How had time flown so?

Danae glanced across the street in front of the shop, and found a fluttering glow alight in the baker's upper story window—the only light burning on a dark and silent block.

It's not right. Danae paced the space behind the shop counter. *Even if he's not dying of blood loss, he's got to be wracked with worry. Too many people just worry and whine while too few try . . . well, anything.*

That night, enough was enough. She'd try to help at least one person oppressed by insane edicts. Somehow, she'd get that vial of medicine from Alaine.

Danae returned the notebook of mysteries to its hiding place, slunk across the room, and tucked her journal into her satchel that hung on the back of the laboratory door. She exchanged the book for a sheathed dagger that she tucked into her belt.

With silent strides, she unhooked the shop door, eased her way from the shop, then glided across the lower floor of her home. She grabbed her cloak and a dark scarf from the peg. On cat-like tread, she slipped out the back door, vanishing into the shadows of the night.

The streets of Dayleston slumbered under a blanket of silence, the sliver of moon casting only the faintest glow upon the still city. Danae, now hooded and cloaked, stole through the narrowest alleys with hardly a patter of footfall or rustle of clothing, ducking from one dark corner to the next. Despite the piles of refuse, puddles of questionable origin, and the scrutiny of gleaming rat eyes, it was better to keep to the lesser-used byways whenever possible.

She rounded a corner and caught sight of a silhouetted figure sprawled across the tight easement. Danae jumped back a pace. The alley squatter's rattling snore checked her galloping heart. Surely he posed no threat of exposing her to anyone who might take exception to her late-night skulking. Even so, she dared not grow complacent. Rumors of the whippings, incarceration, and worse dealt to curfew breakers rampaged through her mind, and a twinge of raw guilt over Alaine's plight pricked at her. She fought the distraction to the back of her mind. If she did not want to join her neighbor in her misfortune, tonight's exploits would demand every ounce of her attention.

Stealthy steps carried her over the homeless sleeper, around a bend, and on to the end of a crooked alley. She stopped and wiped her sweating palms on her breeches.

Danae's glance roved over the antagonistic stillness before her: the wide expanse of Market Street, the broadest, most open avenue in the city. Long and straight, the road offered a clear view for many blocks. The silence dared Danae to breach it. She eyed her next milestone, the slim slice of black between the cobbler's shop and the silversmith's. After a deep breath, she lifted her foot to make the dash, but a flutter of motion in the distance sent her shrinking back against the wall of the alley. About two blocks to her north, a patrol of six Tebalese soldiers had turned the corner.

She backed farther down the narrow way in search of a place to hide. A mossy rain barrel offered the only refuge. Danae ducked behind it and waited. The steady footfalls of the soldiers grew louder with each passing moment. Panic lodged in her throat.

What if they saw me? What if they look down this street? They would have to be half-blind to miss me. Should I run? Is it too late?

Her heart hammered in her chest as the patrolmen grew closer. Her indecision had chosen for her. No time to run.

At the end of the alley, she caught a glimpse of armored figures. They marched past without even a glance her way. Danae heaved a silent sigh. She listened for a long time to the fading tramp of their ironclad feet, and only after her straining ears convinced her the soldiers were well beyond sight and hearing did she emerge. She crept back to the edge of the alley. Her legs trembled, and tension chilled her whole body.

This time, as she peeked out, not a soul moved on Market Street. Only lonely pools of lamplight and a handful of blowing leaves occupied the emptiness. With the blood pounding in her ears, she dashed across the avenue's oceanic vastness. She dove between buildings, clapped her body up against the wall, and rejoiced in the sanctuary of inky shadows.

There, that's the worst of it. After a momentary backward glance, she slinked onward. Danae slipped along, a mere vapor within the deepest shadows, putting one block behind her at a time. She traveled parallel Market Street, always sure to check for patrols before dashing between buildings.

She reached the rear of a three-story mercantile, where she lowered to a crouch to work her way along the side wall. Just beyond this building, the streets opened to the Market Square. The haberdasher, the vintner, the moneychanger—all the businesses supported by the few Tebalese sympathizers who seemed to also be the few Radromirians with money to spend— clustered around the cobbled square.

Danae disregarded the looming architecture. It was the dais at the center of the square that drew her focus.

The play water over the central fountain, crowded with sculpted maids and mythical horses of the sea, once captivated her childhood imagination. But once the Tebalese arrived, they chose to eclipse the city's pride with a display of justice. Most days, if she found a need to pass this way, she stared at her feet. But in the darkness, she dared to look.

The dark planks of a pillory and whipping post blocked most of Danae's view of the fountain. Hot frustration gripped her gut while the memories of too many battered friends scrolled through her mind's eye. Even so, she scoured the Rise of Justice, as the invaders called it. A mingled wave of surprise, relief, and consternation rolled over Danae as she found the dais empty of statute violators.

Probably didn't want to put Alaine on display until folks were out to notice. Danae ground her teeth. *Now what?*

Her gaze shifted to the ironworker's guild house two buildings down the block, where the front windows glowed bright. Being the stoutest building around, complete with iron bound shutters and doors, it had been confiscated by the Tebalese and now served as the city jail. If Alaine wasn't in the pillory, the jail was the next most likely place the squad had taken her. The Tebalese didn't exactly offer visiting hours, daylight or dark.

Danae drew a slow breath and let it stream out slowly through tense lips. Maybe, just maybe some opportunity to reclaim the medicines from Alaine still existed. Danae tiptoed to the rear corner of the jail house.

Once she drew close, loud conversation and the clanking of metal tankards reached her ears from inside the guildhouse-turned-jail. The voices spoke in the fluid Tebalese tongue, but what was normally a fast-paced and complicated language lumbered along, the drunkenness of the speakers defiling their speech. Danae picked through their bad diction to translate the words trapped within.

She slunk from one window to the next, her ears tuned to the men jibing within, while her eyes found only shuttered windows barred fast. Even if she knew which room housed the baker's wife, what hope did she have of reaching her? Still, Danae forged on.

The conversation in the front room rambled along, loud enough for anyone within ten paces of the building to hear. The scrape of a chair moving across the floor, the heavy footfalls of someone tromping about the room, and the clatter of dishware continued to punctuate the words.

"I wish we had a better district for the redistribution," a nasal voice complained.

"Maybe we'll get lucky this time," slurred another. "You never know when one of the lil' rats will have stowed away a trin . . . trinket worth keeping for your trouble." He struggled to form the syllables, and they dribbled from his lips, as an old, toothless horse dribbles grain.

"Hah!" bellowed a third voice. "Mind how much you keep, or the commander will take notice. I want no part of your noose if you get caught taking more than your share."

Danae's blood froze. The voice was all too familiar: Drex of Cray. As if it was not bad enough the man continually prowled her neighborhood, now she must endure him here as well? A tankard slammed with a slosh, and his loud, sloppy words suggested he was as drunk as the rest. The conversation paused, replaced by the groaning of floorboards and the shuffling of feet.

"Throw on another log, Ragshir," Drex said. "The next patrol should be here soon, and they'll start throwing punches if we let the fire burn too low." He cackled. "Maybe I'll just hold up Van here as a shield. He won't feel a thing in his state!"

"Pfah! The drinking's the only thing that makes this lousy night sitting here with you idiots tolerable," Van grumbled back.

A pair of feet clomped with an uneven cadence over toward the wall. A thump and a series of snaps and crackles followed.

"There. One log's enough?" Ragshir said in his pinched, nasal voice.

"For now," Drex said. "If we get cold, maybe we could organize a little bonfire down in the district. Some of these Rat-romirians are getting a little too headstrong for my taste."

"It's the . . . al . . . alchemist who puts 'em up to it." Van's words dragged slower with each syllable.

Drex snorted. "It's just a matter of time for him."

Danae stifled a gasp. *What does that mean?*

"He's been a lot quieter since our run-in with him over the summer," Drex continued.

"We going back for the other boy?" Ragshir asked. "The one we got's falling into line."

Danae's hands flew to her mouth to contain an outburst. Tristan! Where had those monsters taken him?

"Psh. I say we go back for the *daughter*." Van chuckled, and it echoed as though he laughed into his beer.

Drex guffawed. "That flap-trapped girl had better soon learn her place, or that family will pay the price of insolence. I've no patience for rabble-rousers."

"I'm sure we'd get some kicks finding ways to shut her up. Regularly." Ragshir said.

"Scrawny wench couldn't handle the likes of us," Van said. "She'd break too fast to be any fun."

"She's feisty," Drex said. "Who knows? But to get the boy or the daughter, better to wait until Baledric's taken care of before trying anything. But you'll have to get in line for her."

The men roared with laughter.

The thought of such threats sent a hot flush of nausea into Danae's cheeks. She swallowed hard against it to sort through what else she'd heard. Clearly, they had some threat in the wings for Papa, Connall was still in their sights, and Tristan was somewhere, maybe even within reach of rescue. She inched closer to the window.

"Throw in, you muck spout," Ragshir said. "You've been mulling your wager for an age."

"Ah, quit your blather. I'm out, or else I'm a fool . . ."

The conversation devolved into further grumbles and insults over whatever game of chance the soldiers played to pass the time. Beyond their ruckus, the mournful peal of the statehouse bell echoed through the night, marking the stroke of two.

The next patrol. Did they switch on the hour? Danae's heart skipped. *I've lingered too long—I better get out of here.* She clenched her empty fists as she gave the barred windows one last glance. Wherever Alaine was, the medicine would remain there as well. Galling, to say the least.

Danae slinked to the rear of the jailhouse, ready to take a cautionary look before crossing the alley behind it. She placed her back to the wall of the corner building, pulled her scarf higher on her nose, then leaned her upper body around the corner.

This time, her good fortune ran out.

_____

5

THE OLD CHURCH

*a*s Danae peered into the stillness of the gravel alley, the rear door of the jailhouse swung open, spilling lamplight into the street. Someone emerged. Her breath hissed through her teeth. She shrank back along the side of the building and flattened her body against the rough brick wall.

"'Night boys. Have another round for me!"

Drex's voice, without a doubt.

Heaven and Earth, he's leaving before the new patrol arrives? Danae held a breathless vigil over the pool of light in the street from the corner of her eye. The area of illumination narrowed and disappeared, and the clatter of Drex's squad members diminished to mutters.

Danae remained motionless while the moments trickled by. Her jangled nerves settled, and her breaths came slower and easier. *He's got to be well on his way by now. Just one last check . . .* She popped her head around the corner.

With the lighting-fast strike of a viper, a gauntleted fist shot out and caught her by the front of her tunic. The stench of smoke and cheap liquor stung Danae's nostrils as Drex twisted the fabric of her clothing and lifted her into the air. The bands of muscle on his arm bulged, visible even through his linen sleeve. When Drex held Danae at his eye level, her shoes dangled well off the ground, yet she still kicked and wriggled in a last, desperate hope of escape. Drex slammed her back into the wall and leaned in close. The hungry twinkle in his black eyes mocked her.

"What have we here, my boy?" he drawled. "A curfew violator, skulking in the streets? A serious crime, you know." A wicked smile curled his lips, and Danae shuddered at what cruel designs motivated it. "Did you have a fun night out, boy? I certainly hope so. Your little adventure has been dearly bought."

Boy? She may have been short, but no tunic and trousers could obscure all of her heralds of womanhood. If the light had been better, and Drex had not been so drunk, maybe he would have been in more command of his senses. For now, the mistake remained in her favor.

Drex raised his free hand to grab the scarf that hid her face. Desperation shrieked in her ears. Words of salvation, gleaned from Papa's book, sprang to mind.

Danae clapped her hand onto Drex's leather and steel-bound wrist, and a string of ancient words spilled from her lips. The sizzling energy the words evoked careened through Danae's flesh. Before Drex could unmask her, an arc of blue electricity entwined his arm and snaked about the metal ribbing of his armor. The captain barked. His face contorted. Thick fingers unclenched.

An instant was all Danae needed. She sprang from her aggressor and retreated into the solace of Dayleston's west side alleys. From the cover of darkness, she glanced back.

Drex stumbled a few circuitous steps, clawed at his gauntlet, and flung the still-sparking piece of armor to the ground. His infuriated glance searched the area but never lingered on Danae's position. He unleashed a string of curses that echoed against the lofty facades around him.

"Van, Ragshir!" he finally roared. "We've got a skulker to hunt."

Panic surged through Danae's body, nearly as electric as the incantation she had just unleashed. She ran a few paces, then skidded to a stop.

I can't lead them home.

Van and Ragshir staggered to Drex's side, cudgels in hand. Drex pointed down the street.

She bolted, into the twisting streets of the city, in the absolute opposite direction of home.

"Listen! He's on the run," Ragshir said.

Danae did not wait to learn if the squad followed, but pounded onward, heedless of her footfalls over the cobbles. While she ran, heat pulsed through her right hand, the one she had used to shock Drex. But it was in no way a pleasant warmth. More like being slow-roasted by spectres and angry glares. But there was no time to worry about that. It would diminish, just as it had the other times she had secretly experimented with the incantation.

She wound through the narrowest easements and any open gate she could find, but her countrymen's fear kept much of the back streets of Dayleston locked up tight. Shouts, not faint enough, echoed behind her.

"Lawless! Citizens, stop the criminal!" men yelled in accented Western tongue. "Rewards for those who apprehend the curfew breaker."

A growl rumbled between Danae's gasps for air. She pumped her burning legs harder, demanding more length from each stride. Yet another dirty tactic from the greyfaces—paying off any local desperate enough to turn a kinsman in.

Gotta get out of the streets. How? The current impoverished culture of scrimping and saving didn't even leave enough rubbish in the alleys to hide under. Danae scanned the rooftops—maybe there was time to climb?

Heavy strides pounded too close. Nope, climbing was definitely out of the current question. A dark spire, reaching into the star-dappled sky, grabbed her notice. She took a sharp corner and wound her way toward it.

A lantern swelled alight in a window beside her, and a pock-marked woman threw up the sash to lean out. "Criminal!" she shrieked. "This way!"

"Thunderation!" Danae said through her teeth.

Somewhere behind her, the unified herd of footfalls split into at least two groups of pursuers. Danae leapt broken barrels, dodged empty sacks, and set no fewer than four dogs barking as she skidded around cottages and storefronts. Finally, she found a towering wall of field stone ahead and to her left. The old church.

Fire raged in her lungs with every ragged breath she drew. Sweat plastered her scarf to her cheeks and made her neck bristle with itching. She hooked her arm around the lamp post at the church's front corner, swung around it, and launched herself to the third step at the building's double doors.

She staggered to the top of the stairs that led to the stone edifice and the sculpted overhang at the church doors. Danae grabbed the heavy iron ring of the front doors and leaned back.

Ka-thunk. The doors budged, but clearly met the resistance of a bar across the inside.

Tebalese shouts echoed in the streets behind the church.

No! She slammed her back against the doors and dug her fingers into her hair. Her frantic glance volleyed around the street ahead, where lights bloomed in a half-dozen windows.

"He went this way!" Drex yelled.

Were those running feet on the right or left of the church?

Both.

Panic locked Danae's legs. She cowered back against the doors, her vision suddenly blurred with mingled tears and sweat.

A *clunk.* Somewhere in the building behind her. The strides in the streets closed in.

The doors at her back gave way, and Danae fell backward into darkness.

6

*R*ight as Danae's rear hit the floor with bruising force, the moonlit street ahead of her vanished behind closing doors. They shut softly, muffling the shouts that multiplied outside. She blinked against the loss of light while she fumbled at her belt for her knife.

The church was silent. No singer lifted any song to the heavens, no faithful prayer warrior made supplication. No bell tolled in the tower to call worshipers to convene. The dusty smell of disuse hung in the air. Of course, much of that was owing the wee hour, but much more of it came from the way this cathedral, an empty shell, had the feel of a giant sarcophagus, not a place for the living to gather.

Her eyes finally adjusted to the scant ashen light that filtered through small windows at either side of the narthex where she sat.

A flutter ran up her neck and arms as a tall figure turned toward her from the doors, a mere silhouette of black against darkness. Danae wrenched her knife from the sheath. She shoved backward in a blundering retreat, still mostly on her rear.

"Stay back!" She pointed a shaking blade at the shadow.

"Hush," the shadow whispered. "Calm yourself and breathe, or they will hear you." His words were well spoken, but frilled with an exotic accent that rang of someplace other than Tebal.

Danae's head pounded. Her stomach churned bile into her throat. Her knees turned to jelly, and she toppled to the side.

A firm grasp took her arm, and the flutter over her skin increased. "Oh, no, no. You should walk this off unless you want to vomit, faint, or both." The stranger hauled Danae to her feet. "Go on."

"Who—?" A sharp clench in Danae's stomach cut off her question. She staggered a few steps toward the doorway to the main chamber of the building. *He's right, but no need to stick too close.*

The silence of the main meeting chamber demanded further silence, so Danae fought to quiet her labored breaths once she crossed the threshold. She shuffled beside row upon row of lovingly-tended, worn benches that filled the high-ceilinged room. Narrow, deep windows allowed moonlight through the opposing walls, and long slices of brightness and shadow cut across the space. She willed the tunnel vision misting at the edges of her sight to hold back, and instead focused upon the raised platform in the front of the room, where the image of a spreading tree in mosaic graced the back wall of an alcove. The tiles might once have been bright, but age and poor lighting washed them of all but the most saturated colors. Three thick candles beneath glass covers burned on a mahogany cabinet below the artwork.

She rounded the benches on the left side of the chamber, crossed the front, and turned to proceed up the center aisle, her heart rate finally steadying to a quick thump. Her queasiness ebbed.

The man who had pulled her up stood in the shadow of a buttress to the side of the chamber. He wore a floor-sweeping cloak, its hood still obscuring his head and most of his face. He held a tall walking stick in his right hand. Danae's eyes widened at the staff—perhaps it was just a coincidence.

He wasn't fur-clad or cross-gartered, to her relief. No warrior's armor or weapon on his back. Unassuming, really. But somehow, even under a hood, his attention both pierced and held her. She'd felt a gaze of this sort not very many hours earlier.

"I'm sorry," Danae said, though her voice came out dry and cracked. "I'm really not—um, are you the caretaker of this—uh, temple?"

"No," the cloaked figure replied. "Not of this place." His voice was fathomless, at once deep and light. It filled Danae with a simultaneous sense of longing and dread, even though he stood nearly ten yards distant.

"You shouldn't be in the building, you know," Danae said. "Creator worship is outlawed now."

"So it is. And yet, here we both are, in Creo's place of reverence."

Danae shuffled. The open talk of an illegal god piled an even heavier load of risk on her exploits. "Did you . . . pull me in here?"

The man nodded. He reached down for a pack at his feet and produced a water skin. He held it out to her but made no further move. "You look like you could use a drink."

Danae bit her lip. Her muscles tensed. Was there any risk here? Likely. Everything that transpired around her seemed to involve a calculation of risk anymore. But her throat was raw.

She drew a breath, squared her shoulders, and took hesitant steps toward the figure. The closer she got, the more needles of tension and wariness grew in her flesh. Once she stood within a handful of paces from the man, an undeniable needling spread all over her body. She shuddered.

The man's chin lifted a fraction. At this closer proximity, she could only glimpse his cleft chin and lower face—barely even the tip of his nose for how far he had drawn his hood. But his bearing, the cut of his hood, and that walking stick . . .

"No need to fear. It's just water." He straightened his elbow and pushed the skin a few inches closer.

Like a wave of heat from a bread oven, a wash of serenity smoothed away the prickling in Danae's skin. She narrowed her eyes at the man.

"Something amiss?" The probing in his voice further roused Danae's suspicion.

She cleared her throat. "No." She took the skin from his grasp. "Thank you." She unstoppered the skin.

She reached up to her scarf and hesitated. Did she risk pulling it down to drink, exposing her face to this odd stranger?

"You've nothing to fear from me," he said. "I *am* the one who pulled you in from the street and getting caught, am I not?"

"Not to be rude," Danae said, "but the past few years have taught me to look beyond the surface to test other people's true motivations."

The man shrugged. "No offense taken. Whether you believe I offer a way to quench your thirst is your own business."

Danae inched the scarf down off her nose and tucked it under her chin. She poured a mouthful of water. Its cooling touch on her throat was a relief and delight. After several large swallows, she cast the man a sidelong glance. "You look familiar."

The man's lip quirked.

"I saw you earlier today."

"Did you?" The man tapped his chin with a long index finger.

Danae faltered. Did this grey cloaked man have to be so evasive? "Well, I . . . could be mistaken." She held out the waterskin. "Well, thank you for the drink. I better get home."

"Home?" Greycloak said. "It seems there is a bit of a commotion out there you might want to avoid. Something about curfew violation?"

Danae laughed. "If I wait until dawn when I won't be violating curfew, it's my mother who will lock me up for the rest of my natural life."

The doors in the narthex rattled. Danae's insides jumped.

"—right through these doors, I saw it!" a hoarse voice said, beyond the doors.

Thump-thump-thump. A fist pounded on wood. "Open, in the name of Queldurik's Dominion!"

Thunderation. Danae shot a panicked look to Greycloak.

He nodded. "Follow me." He scooped up his pack and took off down the center aisle of the meeting chamber.

"Is there another way out?" Danae asked as she trailed the stranger.

"They'll have surrounded the building already, but yes. Your only job is to stay out of sight."

"What, why—?"

Greycloak glared at Danae, his shadowed eyes piercing from under his hood. She fell silent.

They had reached the mosaic end of the hall when a resounding *boom* rang through the building. Greycloak turned to the left and grabbed the latch on a narrow door, set into the side of the mosaic alcove. Another *boom* rang out, followed by a *crack*.

They passed through the door, which Danae locked behind them, and down a short flight of steps that ended in a tight room lined with bookshelves. Moonlight streamed through a single high window. Three cobwebby robes hung on hooks on the only open wall. Incense faintly spiced the air. Beside the robes, a dark doorway led to the unknown.

After unearthing a small lantern from his pack, Greycloak hastily lit the wick in some way Danae failed to understand in her nervous monitoring of the situation at the church doors. Another *boom* and she was sure those outside would have broken through. The much frailer alcove door offered little sense of security, even locked.

Greycloak closed all the side slats on the lantern to leave only a small slice of light peeking through.

"This way." He passed through the doorway.

Sure enough, the sharp splinter of wood and the clatter of timber hitting the stone floor echoed through the church.

Danae leapt after her guide.

Shadows danced against a fieldstone corridor, shifting erratically in the light thrown by the lantern. Danae tripped over crates and sacks leaning on the right wall. Greycloak turned back to her, his forefinger to his lips. He pointed to her, then the floor.

All right. Quiet. Stay here. Danae hugged her arms around her middle and hunkered down beside a sack stuffed with linens.

After slinking another fifteen paces down the hall, far enough that Danae could barely see the slightest contour of his arm and shoulder that the lantern highlighted, Greycloak reached out. An iron latch clicked. Hinges squeaked.

Danae winced. She shrunk into a tighter ball in the darkness.

A flurry of fabric rustled. Moonlight flooded into the corridor, startlingly bright. Three blinks later, Greycloak had lunged through the doorway. A grunt. The distinct *whump* of a body hitting the street.

Heaven and Earth, what's happened to him? Danae's ears throbbed with her pulse. Somewhere in the building, another door rattled against the jamb. She sprang to her feet.

Greycloak ducked his head back into the corridor, his staff gripped in tight knuckles. He jerked his head toward the street, and Danae was more than happy to fulfil his demand for haste.

She scuttled into the street and whacked her foot against a hard object. A boiled leather and iron bound skullcap helm spun away from her boot. To her left, a dreadlocked soldier lay face-down on the cobbles. She froze, agape, but for only a moment before Greycloak grabbed her arm and towed her across the street.

They broke into run, zig-zagging through byways until Danae saw the open stretch of Market at the next intersection. She closed in next to Greycloak.

"We can't go this way! There will be patrols," she whispered.

"It's the only way. You'll see." Again, he gestured for Danae to stay in place, a half block from Market.

Greycloak slunk toward the street corner. Danae's nerves thrummed and her insides shook. Even with her back to a wall, she felt too exposed, like at any moment the next group of captors would round the bend.

A soft grind of iron on stone drew Danae's glance. At the street corner, Greycloak knelt and set the grate from a storm drain aside. He nodded toward the opening. Danae suppressed a nervous laugh. What had she gotten herself into?

7

A LOSING BATTLE

*R*eaching to the ceiling of a rough brick tunnel, Greycloak lowered the storm drain grate back into its opening. Danae breathed only through her mouth while she waited. Storm drains carried storm water, sure, but storm water brought everything else from the street with it.

"You might want to put that scarf back over your face," Greycloak said. "The smell isn't going to improve as we go." He led her onward, into the darkness of a brick tunnel. They both had to walk hunched over to pass. Only occasional streams of moonlight glowed down from grates to light their sloshing steps.

Danae mentally inventoried the cleaning solutions they might still have in the apothecary that could expunge the pungent ordeal from her shoes. Papa's earlier conversation she'd overheard interrupted her train of thought.

"Is this . . . the . . .Underground?" Danae asked.

Greycloak chuckled. "Underground? No, this is mostly the sewer."

"But you know what I'm talking about."

Greycloak shrugged. "I only know that Dayleston wasn't the first city built in this spot."

"So, you're some kind of historian," Danae said. "That's why you're here?"

"After a fashion."

She huffed. Questions were clearly a waste of breath with this man, since she hadn't gotten a straight answer since she'd met him. Just as well, as they reached a point in their journey where the air grew so noxious and full of ammonia that Danae's eyes stung. She scarcely dared breathe, let alone talk. *We must be under the tanner.*

Thankfully, the choke-zone, as Danae named it after, only lasted for two bouts of breath holding before they returned to the merely putrid atmosphere. Soon afterward, they reached a four-way intersection of tunnels.

"If we're traveling along Market, then this must be Courthouse Way." Danae pointed left and right.

Greycloak nodded, and the cast of his mouth was appreciative. "An astute observation."

Danae cocked her head. "When only two of your hometown's roads have drains? Let's just say I'm no genius. But it does mean about three blocks to my street."

"Very good. Since you are oriented, I trust that you will gratefully not test your luck any further tonight and head straight home?"

Indeed, Danae had absorbed her fill of adventure for one night. She nodded. After a short bow, Greycloak turned down the Courthouse tunnel, and she slogged her way to the grate at the corner of Forge Lane. What a weird, concerning, confusing excursion it had been.

*M*orning came too soon, a morning of shop worked plagued with Danae's jumbled thoughts about the previous night's events—at least between queasy yawns, spawned by too little sleep. With her trousers, tunic, and boots confined to a bucket of lye soap in the courtyard, Danae had opted for a green frock and slippers for the day's attire.

When should she present her father with the evidence of more impending trouble? Was there such thing as a good time to do so? Or would he dismiss her, as he seemed to do so much lately, lost in his own fog of melancholy?

The late morning brought a lull in the day's flow of customers, leaving Danae a gaping opportunity for conversation. She shuffled to her father's side. Papa hunched over the ledger, his head in his hands and his eyelids drooping. She rocked on her heels.

"Papa." Danae lifted her gaze. "I think we need to seriously consider leaving the city."

Bewilderment splashed across Papa's face. His jaw fell slack. "Is *that* what you've been mulling all morning? I could practically hear the gears of your mind grinding from across the room."

"I know, but I can't let this fester until it's too late. Can't we make a run for it?"

Papa's expression soured like he had a mouthful of *balepetal* extract.

"And go where?"

"Mama's already talked about the idea of going to Aunt Moira's for the winter."

Papa shook his head wearily. "That idea came up merely as a panicked reaction to the mess over the summer. Mama and I agreed that running from our pain was no solution."

"It wouldn't be running, Papa. It's the best way of preventing more of the same."

Papa jabbed an accusatory finger at Danae. "Don't try and manipulate me. By running, and possibly getting caught, doesn't that simply ensure the very thing we're trying to avoid?"

"That's only if we get caught. People get out. I've heard about it."

"The Underground is a rumor, Danae. People who are desperate for hope have a way of embellishing."

Aha. The Underground again. So there was some meat on those mysterious bones. "What about the Donnallys? And that other family . . . the Coopers? Who's seen them over the past six months? It's not as if they just walked out the gate, and nobody's said anything about foul play."

"No matter what they chose to do, it doesn't apply to our family. Our choices. I can't condone law-breaking."

Danae sank her weight back on one leg and folded her arms.

"Even Tebalese law," Papa added.

A powerful urge to blurt everything she had heard the previous night reared up in her mind. She swallowed the words. If she posed her argument properly, perhaps her father would entertain different bait.

"What if they've taken Tristan out of the city? Wouldn't leaving put us in a better position to search for him? Wouldn't it be worth it to disregard their ignorant laws for the sake of finding him?"

"No, it wouldn't. We'd have access to no information at Moira's, in contrast to the little we can glean here." Papa's face remained impassive, though the expression struck Danae as carefully controlled, rather than unemotional. "And they'll likely bring him back once he's trained, and then we'll see what we might do."

"If they haven't completely broken his mind. He's the more impressionable of the twins. And who's to say they won't be back for anybody else they can make a grab for when circumstances allow?"

"If we keep our heads down, we'll fade out of Drex's view."

"Keep our heads down?" Danae gaped. "I can't believe that's the voice of a concerned father."

Papa recoiled. Wounded shock blanched his features.

She had overreached. Papa didn't deserve derision. "What I mean is, before we lost Tristan, you never would have said that. We need a change of venue. To heal. To give the family some reality besides fear and hunger. You heard Weylan at the table. Is it fair for a little boy to have to eat less than his fill?"

Fire sprang up in Papa's eyes. "None of this is news to me. What do you imagine plagues my mind as I lay awake at night? It's fine for you to nurse nothing but grief and discontent. Perhaps you don't think about some of the matters I must consider as a businessman. Such as, who will come to me so far in the country to buy medicine and matches?"

"We could work the farm to get by. That's what we've always done on other visits."

"With the seed rationing and Uncle Gavin off at war, you might be disappointed at what Aunt Moira's farm has become."

Danae brightened. "All the more reason she needs our help."

"Girl, you are being impossible. The answer is no. It's completely impractical."

Perhaps. Why could he not see the absolute necessity, nonetheless?

Papa prodded the logs in the fireplace. They showered glowing ash through the grate, and the wood sprang once again to flaming life.

"Papa?"

"I said no, Danae."

"One more detail for you to consider?"

Papa leveled a dark gaze upon her. "Make it good. It's your last tack before I send you out back scrubbing kettles."

Danae squeezed her eyes shut. "I overheard Drex's men that you encourage our neighbors to stand up to the occupation laws."

Papa groaned. "Is that why you're being such a nuisance? If providing medicine to our neighbors is conspiring, then I'm guilty. But I imagine they must mean something more than that—which of course, is hogwash."

A fierce fit of coughing suddenly clutched him. As the hacking forced Papa to one knee, Danae glanced around the shop for something he could drink, but found nothing. Just as she resolved to run into the house, the coughing ceased as abruptly as it had begun. He gripped the edge of the counter and hauled himself to his feet, his shoulders heaving as he struggled for adequate breath. Blue tinged his lips.

Danae gulped. "They also said something about it only being a 'matter of time' for you. What could they mean, or know?"

"That's a mystery . . . to me as well." Every breath he took wheezed through his tight airways. "Though it hardly sounds promising." Papa straightened and sat again on his stool. "How did you overhear these things?"

Danae winced at her father's question, swearing she saw a flicker of suspicion dance in his eyes. "Well, I heard the squad talking about it this morning. You know how they're always sort of looming around." After all, when Drex had caught her, it had been just this morning. Early this morning. No need to get too specific about where or when.

Papa rubbed his brow. "If the Tebalese think I'm up to something, then I must either prove to them that I'm innocent of wrongdoing, or flee their wrath, as you have been so persistently suggesting."

"Papa, if you want to try to clear the family name, that's one thing, but what if that goes awry? Drex isn't going to waste any time debating you on anything. If you rile him with your attempts at logic . . ."

"What, Danae? He'll just finish the job and manage to stab me properly this time?" His voice bit with a sardonic edge.

"Who knows? Maybe. But it's not just about you. Do what you like, but don't put everybody in range of the repercussions. Haven't we lost enough?"

"You have some gall to hurl my losses at me like shot." Papa took a long, hissing breath through his nose. "Can you really look me in the eye and accuse me of acting in anything but our family's best interest?"

Danae opened her mouth, but Papa's glare killed the words.

"Finally speechless, I see." Tears moistened his eyes, but his jaw muscles banded. He lowered his voice and delivered his words with restrained precision. "I'm going to do the books over in the house. Don't come get me unless there's an emergency." Papa stalked from the shop. The door slammed with jarring finality.

Danae thumped her back against the wall and slid down to plunk on her rear. She dropped her head into her hands. She had spent the ammunition of Tristan's rescue, the family's wellbeing, and even his own dimming fate. What tactics remained to shift her father's perception of just how desperate things had become?

8

MOUNTING WORRIES

The fall days wore on, and the last of the autumn leaves drifted to the cold ground, leaving the skeletal fingers of tree branches scratching at the night skies. The final remnants of brisk afternoons retreated ahead of the force of winter winds, and all of Dayleston hunkered down beneath the grey shroud that would envelop them for many months to come. Family life trundled on at its same, beleaguered pace, and as far as Danae could tell, her parents entertained no inklings of change.

Danae pulled the last basket of medicine bottles from the laboratory and carried them into the shop. She placed them on the counter beside the waiting cauldron. They had more elixirs than they did bottles to store it, but whatever she could package would still help a few of the families who had been stricken with the cough and fever rampaging through Dayleston of late. If only this formula, or the one they brewed last week, or the concoction from the week before that, had made any difference in Papa's condition. At least all their research was helping somebody, if not him.

She propped a small funnel in the mouth of the first bottle and ladled the steaming elixir in. By the time she had reached the second-to-last container, Papa shuffled into the shop. Danae's glance flicked to him, and she started. The ladle slipped in her hand and spilled medicine all over the counter.

"You all right, Danae?" Papa croaked, his voice hoarse.

Me? You're the one with the grey face and the ridge of bone around your eyes. How could you look worse after just an hour's nap?

"Just a clumsy slip up." Danae grabbed a rag to mop up the mess. "Did you get some rest?"

"A little. You're the one who should have taken the nap. You can't keep working here till after midnight and then come back before the sun. Probably why you fumbled the pour."

"I'm young, Papa. It's no problem. The work needs doing with as many panicked mothers we see on our doorstep the moment we turn the key each day."

Papa stepped beside her and rubbed a warm palm on her back. "I can finish this up, but would you run out to the alley and grab another armload of firewood?" He shivered. "That sad little fire could use it."

Danae frowned over her shoulder at the meager flames guttering in the drafts that blustered down the chimney. "Certainly."

She headed for the shop's front door, but paused and snuck another glance at her father. He hunched over the task of filling the vials like a man twenty years his senior. A wet cough rattled in his chest. The refrain that played in Danae's mind during every quiet moment echoed once again. *It's only a matter of time for him.*

Danae returned with the stack of wood and fed the fire. Sparks rained down from the nearly-spent wood on the grate.

"Papa, since that elixir is the last of things today, do you mind if I step out and hunt supplies at Market?"

Papa startled as if drawn from a half-dream. "What? Oh, supplies. Yes, we're running low on so much. You may go hunting, if you like. I only have a few silver to commit to the endeavor, however, so I'll be surprised if you have any luck." He handed his daughter a small pouch containing very few coins.

Very few coins meant fewer supplies. It would not be long before they could no longer offer remedies for even the most common injuries and ailments, and then people who might have been spared would start to die.

Danae bit off the thought. "Thanks, Papa. I won't be long." She swung her cloak over her shoulders and sprang out the door.

She hunched against the biting wind that roared through Dayleston's side streets, and rather than heading up to the carts and vendors on Market, she instead turned down Courthouse Way. New, better information out-valued any herb or ore she might find for sale. After shivering her way for two blocks, someone bumped her shoulder.

Danae turned, wide-eyed, only to find her brother, Connall, at her side.

"Papa let you out of the laboratory?" he said. "Are you sure you know what to do out here in the street?"

"Hey, brother," Danae gave him a squeeze with one arm. "Are you done deliveries for today?"

He rolled his eyes. "Finally."

"Will you come with me to the library?"

"Library?" Connall wrinkled his nose. "Papa lets you out of one crypt and you head to another? No, thanks."

"Come on, for Papa's sake. I've got to give research at least one more try. The librarian is creepy, and there's never anyone else there to take his insults." Danae hunkered down inside her cloak.

"Try not to make it sound like such a wonderful time." Connall laughed. "All right. Better than scrubbing floors at home anyway."

Danae and Connall rounded a corner to the crooked street where Dayleston's only library stood. It was a three-storied, narrow building of fieldstone, with dusty-paned windows and very few users.

"Are we going to be here long?" Connall eyed the library facade with a hint of suspicion.

Danae tossed him a playful mixture of smile and scowl. "I don't really know. Research isn't one of those things you can say is going to take a certain amount of time, like baking a loaf of bread. You could read something to pass the time."

"But it's so much easier for you to read and tell me the crux of it."

Danae punched his arm. "Don't act like that. You're not one of those kinds of boys, even if you pretend to be around your friends."

"If you wanted a reading buddy, you should have brought Weylan." Connall rubbed the spot Danae had punched.

Danae shrugged. She could not expect everyone she cared about to share her passion for the obscure. But today's venture was not about obscurities, but rather, a careful hunt for clues passed over in previous excursions.

Connall held the library door open for Danae, struggling to steady it against wind that swirled dry leaves into the building. They passed through the entrance, and the ticklish scent of ancient paper filled Danae's nostrils. She smiled. Paper, ink, leather. It all smelled of knowledge. When she cast a glance around the long, narrow room, however, her grin fled. So many bare spots on the endless shelves, as jarring as a mouth lacking half its teeth. Where scrolls had once been ensconced in meticulously crafted cases there were now only a few rolled parchments without even a ribbon to seal them. Sparse books lay on their sides with no comrades to stand at their shoulders and hold them upright. Too much bare, polished wood collected dust in places where tomes had once protected it.

A shriveled old man shuffled between the shelves, his back bent and the rim of white hair that wrapped the lower part of his skull sticking out in all directions. A syrupy cough burst from the deepest recesses of his chest, and when the hacking stopped, he spat a glob into a brass spittoon beside his desk. It landed with a wet-upon-wet splat.

Danae grimaced.

He turned bloodshot eyes to Danae, then creaked into a chair behind the desk. Knobby hands reached to pluck a sheet of parchment from a well-ordered stack on his work area.

"Maiden Baledric." His acrid voice bubbled through lingering congestion. "Back again?"

"Yes, Master Hawkspur. I need to search out more herb books."

"Well then, go search someplace else. You and your father have read all I've got. Some of them twice."

Connall blew a puff of air. "Well, that was quick. I guess we can go then."

Danae elbowed him, and then stepped closer to the librarian. "We haven't missed anything?"

"Beyond doubt," Hawkspur said. "It won't be long before the grey-faces have made off with everything besides fairytales anyway. Maybe then I'll finally escape your incessant 'Fetch this,' and 'Where do I find that?'"

"What's the point of running a library if you don't like helping people learn?"

"I like books. Not people."

"Fine." Danae's hope sunk like a millstone in the well. "If you can't help me, then I need to get someplace where there are more books."

Hawkspur guffawed, though this set off another round of coughing. He spat again. Though she did not want to scrutinize closely enough to be sure, Danae thought the expectoration carried a red tinge.

"It looks like you have a vested interest in my finding what cough remedies remain undiscovered," she said.

The librarian waved a dismissive hand. "Bah. I've given up on concoctions. Chicanery, I'm beginning to think."

Danae set her jaw. "Well, if it's any balm to your bitterness, we haven't had any luck with Papa's cough either." *Maybe he caught it from you.* "But anyway, you could be rid of me by telling me where I can find a bigger library than yours."

"Bigger library? This is as big as it gets in Radromir." Hawkpur's bony chest inflated, and his back straightened a fraction.

A nervous flutter rose in Danae's gut. "What about outside Radromir?"

Connall gaped. "What good would that do you?"

She met his incredulous stare. "I'm running out of options, Connall. I need to broaden my search." She rubbed her forehead. "Who are those people . . . lore keepers, I think. Elga . . . something? Confound it, I can't remember."

"The Elgadrim?" Confusion softened Connall's aghast pallor.

"So you do listen to what Mama teaches you." Danae elbowed him.

"If you two are planning on chattering, go outside and do it." Hawkspur smoothed his paper on the desk, dipped a white quill in some ink and scratched it across the paper.

"Now hold on," Danae said. "I may have something else to research here, since herbs are out." She looked again to Connall. "These Elgadrim. Aren't they those people whose remnant has recently re-gathered in the south? They had some sort of diaspora ages ago, if I'm remembering the right snippet from Mama's history lessons."

Connall laughed. "History aside, all I know is they're the chief target of the war, Danae."

Danae frowned. *Then why are we the ones who got invaded?* "But they're still supposed to be deeply wise, right?"

"As far as I know. Has anyone ever met one of them?"

Danae whirled back to the librarian. "Do you have any books about the Elgadrim?"

He looked up from his writing without raising his chin, so his bramble of brows shadowed his eyes. "One. I had others, but the greyfaces took them a long time ago. This one they missed because I was repairing it at home."

"Please, that's the book I want to see. Where can I find it?"

Grumbling, Hawkspur slid off his chair. "I'll get it. I keep it aside because it's fragile." He tottered to the rear of the room and ascended a wrought iron spiral staircase that led to a second-story catwalk and another series of shelves. He crept as though every step pained him.

Connall took Danae's hands. "What are you going to do with information about the Elgadrim?" His hazel eyes searched her face.

"I don't know yet. It's not like I can leave you to the wolves here."

Connall's facial muscles relaxed.

Wincing along, the librarian descended the stairs, a fat tome under his arm. Its cover was crafted out of chestnut-brown leather with tarnished bronze caps on each corner. The cracks and fissures in the hide testified it was likely far more ancient than the crotchety old man who bore it. He trundled back to his desk and set it down gingerly. As he did so, his sleeve bunched at the elbow, to reveal ugly black webbing that branched across his skin, deepest along his bulging veins. At the mark's center: a single white line of scar tissue.

Danae stared at the mark, despite more polite intentions. Hawkspur tugged his sleeve down to re-cover it. He pierced her with an accusatory glance.

"Uh . . . thanks," Danae said. "I'll just take the book over to one of the reading nooks, if that's all right with you."

"I certainly didn't want you hovering over my space while you fish through it." He pushed the book toward her.

Danae stepped forward and grasped the cover. Her hands came within inches of the librarian's, if only for a moment, and a tingling swarm of goosebumps swept through her body. Every fine hair on her arms stood on end. First the stranger in the church, now Hawkspur. Was there a connection? Perhaps Hawkspur *was* Greycloak. No, that was ridiculous. Their voices were entirely different, and Greycloak was tall, not stooped.

But still . . .

Hawkspur's eyes bulged. "Mind who notices that chill, Missy."

Danae furrowed her brow. "I'm sorry, what?"

An awkward moment where they both stood clasping the book ensued. The crawly sensation washed over her in wave after wave, faint and distasteful.

The librarian's cackle cut through the musty stillness. "Never you mind then. It's not my office to discuss." He released the book, and Danae backed away.

Once she put several yards' distance between herself and Hawkspur, the feeling subsided. She shook off the last remnants and hugged the book to her chest. She retreated to a seat on the far end of the room.

The book contained text in three languages, as best Danae could guess by variations in characters. She could only read one. Each left-hand page contained ornate passages penned in illuminated script, complete with intricate embellishments around the borders and at the onset of many entries. The facing pages exhibited tidy penman-ship in the Western tongue. That text admitted to providing only partial translation and paraphrase of the illuminated manuscript, for the most fluid and sweeping text eluded the translator as to origin.

Throughout her search in the text, Danae's mind continually drifted back to the haunting mark on Hawkspur's arm, and the flesh-crawling sensation his proximity seemed to induce. A maddening volley between study and worry tormented her. Danae destroyed every fingernail on her left hand, picking and peeling at them as she dredged the book for information.

Connall leaned back in a chair and dozed during the bulk of her search.

She scribbled down what snippets she found about the Elgadrim's advancements in herb lore and surgery, as well as copied a rough map of the western half of Argent, to include the approximate locations of both Dayleston and the Elgadrim capital of Bilearne, far to the south. Only when the windows of the library darkened with the threat of dusk did she relent in her furious notation.

She reached over and jostled Connall's shoulder. "We'd better go."

He sniffed, blinked, and stretched. He turned bleary eyes to the window, then sat bolt upright. "You bet we'd better. The bell's coming any minute."

Danae rose. "Will you come back with me tomorrow?"

"Uh, you better take that up with Mama and Papa. Aren't you finding anything useful?"

"I am. I've just gotten to the part that talks a little bit about the Elgadrim's areas of expertise, and I'm loath to leave off here."

Connall shrugged. "I've already shirked chores at home today, so I hope I don't catch it for that. You really think Papa will give you study time in the morning?"

"He must." Danae picked up the book and carried it back to Hawkspur's desk. She set it down and backed away a pace.

The librarian looked up from his own reading and smirked. "You'd better run along before the boogeymen come out and lock up wayward children."

Danae responded with a dark look. "You ought to see my father about that infection or whatever it is on your arm."

"Would you stop peddling your fairy-water?" Hawkspur snapped. "It's not an infection."

"But you have a wound. And the area around it looks awful."

"The scar was there long before the . . . other mark." Hawkspur hacked and gurgled.

Danae winced. "Cut yourself some time ago, perhaps?"

"You nosy brat, no. The greyfaces gave me a slice for who-knows-what reason. Now get out of here or next time you come knocking, I won't let you in."

Danae curtsied. "Good night then. Thanks for your cheerful help, as always."

She turned on her heel and marched out the door, Connall close behind. When they emerged into the street, she cast a glance over her shoulder.

Connall turned to face the library. "No wonder he doesn't like you. He's keeping mum about something."

Danae gave him a glare. "Do you think the Tebalese officer who cut him might have poisoned him? He's got a cough like Papa's, but worse. Both of them were cut by enemies. Though Papa doesn't have an awful black mark like Hawkspur's. As far as I know." Truthfully, Danae hadn't even seen the wound since it no longer needed salve or bandages,

Connall blinked. "I don't know much about this stuff. I just make deliveries."

Danae sighed.

They marched home on swift strides as the sun disappeared below the western rooftops.

~

The next morning, Danae jogged up to the library to find Connall already waiting in the street, his empty delivery bag hanging at his side. Perplexity cast his mouth in a frown.

"It's locked," he said.

"What?" Danae tried the handle. It rattled only a fraction and refused to turn. "Do you think I irked him that much?"

"I don't know, but—"

The door to the home beside the library swung open, and a pair of Tebalese soldiers jostled a stretcher through the entry. A cloth shrouded the figure they bore. The ghostly silhouette of forehead, nose, chin, and toes sent a shudder through Danae's body.

"Heaven and earth . . ." She put her hand to her mouth.

"Is that the librarian's house?" Connall whispered.

"It is." Danae cut a straight path to the soldiers, despite Connall's squawk of protest.

"Excuse me," she called in Tebalese.

The front soldier glared at her.

Danae steeled herself. "Is that Master Hawkspur?"

The soldier said, "They don't tell me names, wench. All I know is you best stand back. This one had the Hacking Doom."

"What?" She looked back to Connall. "I've never heard of such a thing."

Her brother slowly pulled a fold of his hood over his nose and mouth.

"Keep your distance, and you won't get any better acquainted with the idea. Now out of the way. This bag o' bones isn't getting any lighter."

Danae staggered back. The soldiers crossed the street, loaded the stretcher into a wagon, and drove off while she and Connall stared after them.

"Maybe it wasn't him." Connall's voice cracked in the midst of his words.

Danae shook her head. "He was a confirmed old bachelor. Always lived alone, as far as Papa knew."

"This is scary, Danae."

"I need to tell Papa."

~

*W*hen Danae returned to the shop, she found Papa nursing a cup of tea between coughs. "That was the shortest trip to the library you've ever taken."

Danae rocked back on her heels. She regarded her father from the corner of her eye. No, he did not seem as sick as Hawkspur had. Did he? "I couldn't get in, actually."

Papa's eyebrow lifted. "No?"

"You see . . ." Danae took a deep breath. "Master Hawkspur, he . . . they brought him out beneath a shroud."

Papa blinked. "You're sure it was him?"

"I didn't see him, but they came from his house." Danae looked at her lap. "He certainly coughed horribly the whole time I was in the library yesterday. They said he died of 'Hacking Doom.'"

Papa blanched. "I don't know what that is."

He shrunk. His eyes lost focus to introspection, and the longer he stayed silent, the paler he grew.

"Me neither, Papa. But somehow, I'm going to find out."

~

*T*he sun's first rays chased away the darkness outside the apothecary windows, even if they did not warm the air. Danae leaned against the counter, grinding dried roots in her mortar. Just two more tasks to finish. When Papa joined her in the shop, he would only have to check her proportions on the few batches of poultice she had cobbled together with their odd assortment of remaining supplies. Then Papa could rest and she could focus on learning what this "Hacking Doom" was.

A distant sound niggled from somewhere outside. She paused in her work, her eyes focusing far away, as if by sheer force of will she might discern what phantom whispered in her ear. After a few still moments, she realized the source of the growing disquiet.

Hooves and wagon wheels grew louder by the moment. Dropping the mortar and pestle on the counter, Danae flew to the front window, just in time to see the same old group of shaggy, stout horses plod onto her street. The morning air blew in steaming clouds from their nostrils. Following the five horsemen came four more Tebalese on foot, and a wagon drawn by two oxen. Despite the driver's position over a block away, Danae could see the leer on his face, or at least she could imagine it. Last of all, the despicable riding lizard and his broad-shouldered master trundled along.

Danae's stomach tensed. Another redistribution had arrived with the same knife twist as always. She eyed the precious flasks, jars, ingredients, and products around her, and panic began a turbulent trip from the pit of her stomach to the back of her throat.

The raiders stopped down the street at the cobbler's shop, and one of the foot soldiers marched to the door, banging upon it with the pommel of his dagger. The sharp rapping echoed through the stillness like hammer strokes.

"Submit your wares and foodstuffs to redistribution!" the soldier bellowed, in typical fashion. "All household members, present for conscription."

What? Danae clapped her hands to the sides of her head. *Conscription?*

Well before any resident could have responded, they proceeded to kick in the cobbler's door. Their work was quick, and the four plunderers soon bustled back out of the shop, arms laden with not just shoes, but gloves, aprons, and wineskins. Drex spurred his mount to the cart, where the foot soldiers loaded the goods. He sneered down his flat nose at the booty.

Danae's heart galloped in her chest. Connall. Even Anyon and

Farrell. Had they risen from bed? She'd go to her grave before seeing another brother pressed into service.

Danae opened the shop's front door and shut it behind her. She stood on the stoop, arms crossed.

Van ambled over to her. He wiped his nose on his sleeve. "Got a good mornin' kiss for me, wench?"

Danae answered only with a stony glare.

"Why don't you just call those brothers of yours down and make this easy, poppet?" Ragshir said. "We know y'ain't got nothin' worth puttin' in the cart."

Only because you're too stupid to know what's valuable and what's not. Danae clenched her teeth. "If you don't want anything we have, you might as well keep on moving."

Drex approached on his lizard mount. The beast tested the air with its slick black tongue.

"Tell me you aren't giving my men lip." He sighed at Danae.

"Oh, I'll give them a fair dose more than that if need be." Danae swallowed. *Please, please let Papa realize what's happening out here.*

Drex made a small circle above his head with two fingers.

One of the foot soldiers forced his way into a neighboring home, and then returned to the street, bearing not booty, but a fistful of lit torches. He distributed them among his comrades.

Two more soldiers grabbed armloads of dry chaff and threw them against the apothecary walls.

Danae's glance leapt back and forth before she met Drex's eyes. "What is this? You—you can't..."

"I can't?" Drex turned slowly to face her. "If there is to be order in this rat hole, there must be respect for authority."

Danae fumed. "Order? What's orderly about stealing from common folk and kidnapping their children?"

At this continued challenge, Drex's lips quivered into a livid grimace. He lunged. He grabbed Danae by her tunic, dragged her into the street, and thumped her back against the side of the cart. Panic turned her joints liquid.

"You want theft? I'll show you what sort of crime loose-lipped hussies like—" Drex's gaze locked upon her wide eyes, and his mouth froze.

Danae could sense the sudden churning of Drex's mind. His eyes narrowed and darted back and forth, as if searching for some elusive memory. A crazed smirk splashed across his face. He clenched his fist even tighter in the bunched linen of her shirt, and then flexed his arm, curling her weight as if testing it against his strength. The fabric of her sleeves cut painfully into her underarms. The flame of recognition ignited in Drex's eyes.

Slamming Danae's back against the cart so hard that her head bounced against the side wall, he cackled.

"I know you!" His face brimmed with ravenous violence. He leaned in, close enough for the heat of his breath to cloud over her cheek. "No matter daylight or darkness, your fear still smells the same."

Danae shook the stars from her vision in time to see Drex reach down to his belt with his free hand and draw out a long, curved knife, with a smooth blade of a smoky metal. She knew this weapon—the blade Drex had sunk into her father.

With a darting glance, Danae surveyed the encroaching perils. Could she escape again, with so many other soldiers nearby to re-ensnare her? The last time she had found herself in such a predicament, she and Drex were alone. This time, she was outnumbered eleven-fold. She set her jaw and lifted her hand to grab Drex's forearm.

The Tebalese captain caught her wrist with his weapon hand. "Ah, ah, ah. I've learned my lesson, little magician. Like father, like daughter, it seems."

His dagger, pinned between her wrist bone and Drex's meaty fist, loomed frighteningly close to her face. She writhed in Drex's grasp, her body shaking with cold terror.

The faint tinkling of a bell caught her ear. Her father's shop door! She craned to see over Drex's shoulder. Her father took in the scene in the street with wide eyes and a jaw that hung slack.

"Papa!" she screamed.

One of the footmen lobbed a burning flask of oil at the roof Papa's shop, which exploded in a ball of flame, instantly kindling the building. He nodded to the torch-bearers, and with crazed leers etched into their faces, they thrust flaming brands into the fodder against the apothecary walls. In mere moments, flames spread through the chaff and began to climb the building.

Drex released Danae's wrist and brandished the long knife. Danae cringed—a blade sought her and flames stalked the rest of her family.

In a clarion command, Danae's father's voice rang over the chaos. *"Pa solatis lumie is Creo attannan sen!"*

Drex's stroke slowed at its apex. He half-turned toward Danae's father.

From Papa's outstretched hand, a dazzling beam of golden light streamed toward Drex. The light split from Drex's body in a dozen brilliant shafts. The captain's body lurched, and with a roar, he dropped Danae.

"Run!" Papa called.

Papa stooped, snatched up two traveling satchels, and threw one clanking bundle to Danae.

"Through the courtyard. Now!"

The two fugitives ran. Danae followed Papa's lead as they tore through their side gate, across the courtyard, and into the alleys and side streets of the city.

"Papa!" Danae hollered between gasping breaths. "What about Mama? The boys? The fire—"

"Trust me, Danae."

"But—"

"Just keep running."

So help me, if anything happens to them, I'll never forgive myself. Still, Danae pounded onward at her father's surprisingly swift pace. Somewhere distant and behind, a horn sounded.

"Faster!" Papa cried.

They burst from an alley just across the street from the old church. Papa leapt up the stairs two in a stride and wrenched the scarred front door open. He waited with the pull in hand until Danae staggered through the entry.

Danae doubled over in the dim vestibule, her vision clouding and her stomach threatening mutiny. A prickle nipped at the edges of her mind. The thump of the closing door did not warrant her notice, but a cough from the opposite direction snapped her attention from her heaving breaths.

A crowd of people huddled at the far end of the chamber. Her brothers. Her mother. And Greycloak.

9

THE UNDERGROUND

"What in the Great Patron's name is going on here?" Danae croaked through a dry throat.

No one answered at first. A horn droned, somewhere outside, but still distant

"It appears this is not the time to explain. Follow me." Greycloak pulled out a glass-and-brass lantern, opened it, and lit the wick. He turned for a descending set of stone stairs, and Danae's family shuffled after.

Danae planted her feet. "What? We're following him?"

Papa scowled. "Didn't he just say this isn't the time for explanations? Come on, Danae."

Greycloak led the group down the stairs, once intricately inlaid with tiles, though now exhibiting more gaps in the mosaics than finished patterns. Their footfalls on the hard surface created a lamentable ruckus. That and Papa's renewed coughing.

Danae caught little more than glimpses of the hundreds of alcoves that lined the halls at the bottom of the stairs. Rectangular slabs of stone, carven with the surnames of every noteworthy family in Dayleston history, sealed the niches they passed. Intricate relief sculptures of leaves, knot-work, or heavenly beings graced the largest of the tombs, but Greycloak hurried the family past the ornamentation. Only the guttering glow of the oil lamp combated the darkness, so the group shuffled close in the pool of security it offered.

Billowing cobwebs filled the corners of the sloping passages. The farther the travelers descended, the more often Greycloak swept his hands out before him to clear curtains of sticky threads. The continual plunking of drips grew in the distance. The scent of dryness and dust fell back before a growing air of mold. Raw drafts seeped through Danae's clothes, and she shuddered.

The hall turned a sharp corner, and ahead of them, the passage walls grew rougher, though also enrobed in glistening moisture. Weylan stumbled. He reached out with a hand that skidded along the wall. After a staggering recovery of his balance, he shot a shuddering glance back at Danae.

"Slimy," he said.

The floor continued to slope downward. The capped resting places of the dead vanished, replaced by cruder alcoves chiseled from the walls. Skeletal remains reclined in the hollows, eyes sockets staring in sleepless death. Tatters of rotten burial clothes sagged in the gaps between bones. Brice whimpered, and Mama pulled him close to her side.

From the shadows echoed an occasional skitter of claws, or the faint flutter of wings that passed somewhere beyond sight. Whenever a spectral whisper passed close, Danae cringed involuntarily.

After several minutes of twisting descent, the passage came to a sudden end at a pyramid of piled skulls. The crowd of Danae's family shrunk tighter before the gruesome heap.

Greycloak turned a smile back to them. "Not as dead an end as it would seem." He reached down, sunk his thumb into the nasal cavity of one of the skulls and his first two fingers into the eye sockets.

Danae winced, her stomach taking sudden residence in her mouth.

Bones crunched and grated against stone, and the front face of the pyramid hinged aside in a cloud of dust. The triangular hole it exposed contained a downward flight of stairs. Greycloak stood to the side, the only person in the passageway who seemed unmoved. He gestured to the newly-revealed passage.

Papa squared his shoulders and led the way. The rest of the boys, roughly in age order, followed suit, the rearguard held by Mama and Danae. Once they all had begun their descent, Greycloak reached up, grabbed an iron handle, and pulled the portal shut behind them.

When they reached the bottom of the gleaming wet stairs, the lamplight reflected in shifting specks ahead of them, shimmering on the surface of slow-moving water. The ebony silhouettes of two boats bobbed perhaps twenty paces distant. Greycloak led the solemn parade directly to them. He hung his lantern on the prow of one boat, and lit another just like it on the second craft. The light swelled from their wicks to reveal faint details around them.

The hall from which they emerged opened into a cavernous expanse, taller than any building Danae had heretofore believed mortal hands could build. She shrank under the unbearable weight of its grandeur. The only hallmarks of the lofty height's extremity were evenly-spaced portals to the surface world, from which shafts of morning light lanced through gloom of the tunnel. A wide subterranean river flowed into blackness.

"It seems your 'Underground' is not just rumor after all," Greycloak said.

The countless tunnels, wrought from chiseled stone, proved this cavern had come into being at the hands of designers and architects, not by natural force. It stretched wide, a threat to swallow them, boats and all, like a whale gulps the tiny fishes of the sea.

So here was the ancient series of aqueducts and sewers, rumored to have been built by a culture that preceded their own settlement of the region some six thousand years past. Danae wished she had devoted even the scantest measure of her studies as a child to such ancient histories.

"Who built this?" she asked in a breathy gasp.

"This is no time for ancient bedtime stories." Papa's tone was both hushed and clipped.

From the braided carvings, the stone garlands that lined the walls, and the rumble of a distant current, she envisioned the marvels of a far older city, upon whose remains Dayleston perched unwitting. How could such a wonder fester, forgotten?

And amidst it all, the very air of the place sent a prickling tingle across Danae's skin. Goose bumps, separate from the type Greycloak's presence seemed to inspire, but somehow akin, rose with sudden ferocity on every inch of her flesh. She shivered and rubbed her shoulders, but it failed to allay the electrified feeling. The place seemed to defy the very nature of her home city above. For her every comfortable, familiar, memory of the surface, the Underground answered with an uncanny tug at a place in her heart she could neither fully locate nor name.

"Careful, everyone, the edge here is slick." Farrell grasped Mama's hand firmly and helped her into the first boat. Papa climbed into the second boat and took up the long pole that would steer the vessel along the course of the river. Once Danae and the younger boys boarded the boats, they untied the water crafts' tethers. The boats turned under Papa and Greycloak's guidance and drifted down the river.

Greycloak walked his pole along the riverbed. "We'll take this waterway to the Slatewash River Bridge, about a mile south of Shipman's Gate. The outlet under the bridge is concealed. If all goes as planned, the teamsters should be close at hand, ready to bear all of you away."

Danae's heart leapt. *Finally! Some freedom to solve her family's troubles.*

The boats drifted on, past columns with chipped fluting, tall, expressionless statues whose features had suffered the slow wear of countless years, and a myriad of runic carvings that Danae struggled to take in as the water swiftly bore them past. Sometimes, the lantern's scant light kindled a fleeting gleam from veins of gold, silver, rose, and violet that branched across the stonework.

Their course led straight, except for when they needed to dodge occasional streams of street drainage that spilled from spouts far overhead. One after another, the dark mouths of smaller passages slipped by, until Greycloak selected one of these arches and turned his boat toward it.

The water within the side tunnel rumbled and splashed against the confines of the narrower passage, and the pole-men abandoned propulsion for steering. The boats rocked and bumped one another. Danae's two youngest brothers hugged their knees and stifled cries at the hardest jolts, so she reached out and patted their shoulders. The walls of the tunnel closed in, and the darkness beyond the reach of the lanterns' glow oppressed with a watchful malice that grew with each passing moment. Sometimes, green-mirrored eyes peered from the crevices in the walls as the boats swept past.

After perhaps a half-hour of traveling, though Danae could scarcely tell in this place where time had no meaning, she spotted a gleam ahead. It flickered and danced. She squinted at the point of light, and for a few tense moments, feared the dark water might sweep them into the arms of whatever displeased apparition she felt had been eyeing her throughout the journey.

Greycloak said, "That's our landing. Get ready to unload, and be on your guard. There are no guarantees what you shall meet from here." They steered their boats up close and made them fast to a ramshackle wooden dock, embarrassingly crude in comparison to all around it. A single lantern hung on a post at the dock's corner. The landing led to an arch in the wall of the passage.

Greycloak climbed out of his boat last, and then made his way through the now-crowded shore to step inside the arch.

"This way," he whispered.

Single file, the family followed their guide up a twisting flight of stone stairs. One step at a time, Danae tackled the ascent, watching her footing on the uneven treads. Just as her thighs began to burn with the continual climb, Greycloak stopped.

The stairs ended at a tiny landing with an alcove set in its rear wall. Greycloak pressed his hands firmly on the dead end, and the narrow tunnel filled with the sound of stone grinding on stone. A blade of light stabbed into the darkness. As he pushed the door open a bit farther, the light of morning blazed into the stillness of the tunnel. Greycloak poked his head out the opening, and then fully leaned out. He ducked back into the passageway, the expression on his face knit into creases.

"No teamsters?" Danae's father asked.

"No," Greycloak replied. "Perhaps we were swifter than they expected."

Danae stiffened against her trembling. So help this shrouded stranger if he had led her entire family into worse danger! She sought her mind for an alternate escape for them all. But then, a flutter of sound caught her ear. Hooves outside? After a moment more, she was sure of it.

Greycloak peered back out the stone door. He flashed a smile. "Here they are. Quickly now . . ."

The group shuffled through the door single file and stepped directly from the side of a bridge support onto the stony bank of a river dusky green with silt. Danae glanced back just as the door to the passage ground shut once again, leaving not even a seam she could see. And as simple as that, Greycloak was gone.

Once the entire family had assembled on the riverbank, Papa gave Mama a tight hug. The rest of the group huddled together.

Mama peered into Papa's face for a long moment, and their expressions wended through a tangled range of emotions. Just as her eyes began to well, she dropped her gaze to the ground. She took a deep breath. "All right everyone, no dallying. Up the hill we go!"

They scrabbled up the loose stone to find a stout wagon with a canvas canopy, pulled by a pair of shaggy horses. The driver, a broad man with a bulbous nose and a crooked jaw, waved them on.

"Let's keep it moving, folks. You didn't run into any trouble getting to me, right?" the driver said.

Danae cringed.

"Most of us didn't," Papa replied. "But the one or two of us that did made quite a stir. Sit down, kids. We need to put Dayleston thoroughly behind us."

They all piled into the wagon, a cold mass of wool and leather, and the driver barked a wordless command to his team. The vehicle lurched into motion and rumbled down the Great South Road.

Danae watched Dayleston's distant walls shrink in the distance. A dark plume of smoke billowed up from within.

PART II

10

PURSUIT

It staggered Danae how her carefully-ordered life had erupted into chaos. At least her family was now clear of Drex's grasp, even if the tragic circumstances of the morning had been rather opposite of how she would have chosen to enact their departure. Their wagon lurched and bumped into the countryside, laboring along the rise and fall of the winding Great South Road, up and down the hills that huddled at the feet of the Triastead Mountains. The horses thrust their shoulders into their collars, heads down, to confront the slopes. Coarse grass and jutting slabs of slate covered the barren rises, and the region's sparse trees clustered in the crevices where one hill met the next. Here grew mostly scrub oak, with the occasional sycamore raising its mottled arms to the sky. The wind howled continually through the clefts, shaking the bare-limbed trees and pulling from them any stalwart leaf that lingered into winter. On the hillsides grazed shaggy-faced highland cattle and herds of spael sheep in their coats of long, dark wool.

Many miles to the east, the mountain range loomed, a forbidding wall, stark and charcoal gray against the blue sky. The peaks already wore a heavy shroud of snow. The memories of trips into those mountains, where she and her father had hunted minerals for the apothecary, danced at the edges of Danae's mind. The war and occupation had brought a halt to all that.

She eyed the summits. "The passes are all closed by this time of year, aren't they, Papa?"

Her father opened his eyes and leaned forward. "Oh, most certainly. They won't open again until the full force of spring clears them." He wrapped his arm around Danae's shoulder. "Don't worry. Nobody's coming through those mountains to trouble us this time of year. I suspect the mountain clans are through letting foreigners across the border."

What about letting lowlanders out? Danae dared not voice the inkling—not yet. "I don't understand how a whole army got through the highlands. Why did the clans just stand by while foreign armies marched through? They've certainly no qualms over bloodshed."

Farrell chimed in. "My understanding is that, on top of a lot of surreptitious diplomacy and a dragon's hoard of coin changing hands, the Tebalese promised the mountain clans their lives would go on unchanged. They're still free to fight in their usual clan skirmishes, and to make their own highland laws so long as they keep a grip on the border."

Danae frowned. "Why couldn't the Tebalese be ignorant brutes instead of cunning?"

Papa scratched under his hood. "They certainly proved they fight with forethought."

"I don't have much of a head for warfare and tactics." Danae sighed.

"You have such 'a head' for so much else, you have no need to brood after that." Her father gave her a firm squeeze.

The road's northward course, back the way they had come, nagged Danae despite its emptiness. "Do you think anyone will follow us from Dayleston? There's not much in the way of hiding places out here."

Mama drew a deep breath. "I'd rather we didn't talk about such things."

Papa shook his head. "Like it or not, we have to consider it. Outside the city walls isn't the first, most logical place they'd search, especially with as confident as Drex is in his level of control over our district. But we seem to have upset that today, so we had better keep a wary eye on all fronts."

Anyon stretched and yawned. "If they even care what's become of us."

"It's wishful thinking to hope they wouldn't." Papa turned to the driver. "Can the horses handle a brisker pace with these hills?"

The driver shrugged one shoulder. "If you all don't mind sore backsides. They don't make cargo wagons with a mind for comfort."

"I'm not worried about our comfort so much," Papa rubbed his forehead with tense fingers.

"Um, Papa?" Weylan reached across the wagon bed and tugged at Papa's sleeve.

"Just a minute, Weylan."

"I think it's important."

Papa sighed. "It can wait a moment until I confirm our course with the driver."

Danae reached out and squeezed Weylan's hand. "It's been a rough morning, Weylan. Just give him a minute."

"But . . ." Weylan pointed a tentative finger toward the rear of the cart. His eyes were wide and intent.

Connall leaned to Brice. "Are those horses back there?"

Danae wheeled and squinted northward along the road. They were horses indeed. A pair of them. And while the distance between them and the wagon made details indiscernible, they did seem stout of limb. "Papa!"

Papa wrenched his attention from the low conversation he had been conducting with the driver. "What now?"

Danae simply gestured with an open palm behind them.

Papa stared for a silent moment. He swallowed hard. "Farrell, take the reins. I need the driver's help."

Farrell clambered to the front seat. "Papa, you know I've only driven a team a couple of times."

"It's a couple of times more than the rest of us. Run them if you think you can manage it."

Mama grabbed Papa's arm as he worked his way to the rear of the wagon. "What's going on?"

"There isn't supposed to be any non-military traffic in and out of Dayleston," Papa said.

"I know that." Mama's voice was sharp with the crossness that clipped her words, a shortness Danae recognized as the pinch of fear.

"Someone has noticed us out here," Papa said, "and if they aren't looking for us specifically—"

A sharp hiss and then a *thunk* against the tailgate of the cart truncated Papa's explanation. A cry erupted from Danae's throat, but she clapped her hand over her mouth before it fully escaped. The haft of an arrow stuck from the wood planking of the cart.

"Where did that come from?" Brice squealed.

"They're shooting at us, can't you tell?" Anyon's face creased with livid offense.

"Farrell, now!" Papa yelled. "Whip them up."

The driver thrust the reins into Farrell's hands, bent down, and produced a crossbow from somewhere near the footrest of the front seat. He clambered into the back of the wagon and worked his way through the boys and Mama, now huddling in close pods.

After another whistle and wooden impact, a second arrow sank home in the cart frame. Papa pulled a scabbard from his pack and equipment, wrenched a long blade free of its housing, and tossed the scabbard aside.

"Deklan!" Mama rose to her knees. "What are you doing?"

"I'm a little low on choices at the moment, love."

At Farrell's sharp bark, the cart lurched forward and cast all the passengers but the driver to their sides. The tailgate caught a teetering Papa at the knees, and he pitched out the back. Two more arrows whizzed in and stuck in the canvas of the roof.

Danae fought to her feet despite the crazy way the cart tipped and jostled as the team thundered into a run. "Get everybody out of here, Farrell!"

Farrell glanced over his shoulder. "Are you nuts? I have to wheel back for Papa."

The carter's eyes flew wide. "Wait, son. You'll flip the whole thing if you try to run it in a circle on this slope."

"I'll help Papa." Danae hollered. "The best thing you can do is run everybody like mad to Aunt Moira's. I'm going to help Papa put those parasites off your trail."

Mama squawked. "You will not! Sit down."

Another arrow lanced in. It grazed the driver's arm. He bit back a yell and clapped his free hand to the tear in his sleeve.

Danae staggered through the group and reached the tailgate. Papa was already thirty yards distant, and the thugs were closing fast. "Sorry, Mama," Danae said. She hitched her pack up on her shoulders, gathered the frayed tatters of her courage, and sprang.

The road rose to meet Danae with alarming speed. Her intention to land in a run collapsed into a klutzy tumble on the frozen ground. She spat a mouthful of soil and bracken, and then shook off the ringing in her head to seek her father.

He stood near a huge boulder, sword raised, as the two horsemen thundered closer. The pursuers braced round shields, complete with gargoyle and triangle emblem. One of the riders shouldered a short bow. The other held an arrow against the string, undrawn for the moment. Their rough fur cloaks, their black tabards, and their emblazoned shields defined them as Tebalese squad members. The leader's long, pockmarked face and hooked nose clarified his full identity: Ragshir. His bulky, goatee-wearing companion, identically clad, leered with beady eyes. And where Van and Ragshir rode, Drex could not be far behind.

From his position in the lead, Ragshir pointed Danae's direction. "Keep the girl busy," he yelled over his shoulder.

The riders' courses diverged. Van galloped straight for Danae. Though still fifty yards down the hill, he would be upon her in just a few blinks. He pulled his bowstring taut.

Danae leapt to the side barely fast enough to duck the arrow that sailed in. She stumbled across the hill for a cluster of boulders, much smaller than the one her father had taken as refuge, but better than nothing.

"Go ahead and hide, missy!" Van yelled. "I can cut you down as easily as shoot you."

Dizziness swarmed over Danae's senses. Her breaths came shallow and fast. Did she have any way to retaliate or defend? Why had she not bothered to consider that before she jumped from the cart? She clapped her back against her rocky refuge and rifled her pack. A little food, her journal, a waterskin . . . all lovely when you were not looking for a weapon.

The rasp of metal against metal rang too close.

Danae's fingers closed on a leather strap. A metal ring—then the crosspiece of a dagger! She struggled to wrench the weapon free of the rest of the supplies on top of it.

The thump of hooves on the turf closed in. A cry rang out. A heavy clatter followed, and the horse's steady gait faltered and slowed.

Did she dare a peek from her cover?

Danae turned and poked her nose over the top of the boulder. Twenty paces down the hill, a horse with no rider slowed to a walk. Van sat on the ground another ten paces father away. He clutched the shaft of a crossbow bolt that protruded from his hip.

The driver's bolt? How?

Danae searched the higher ground, and indeed found the tall teamster loading another bolt into his weapon. The metallic ring of the mechanism as it clacked to an armed position sang like a heavenly choir to Danae's ears. A growing stain of red blemished the driver's shirt sleeve, and even from a distance, his stiff movements betrayed how he favored the injured limb. He ran past her and grabbed Van's horse.

The sharp knell of steel meeting steel pierced the air. Danae wheeled.

Papa deflected a cut from Ragshir's fat-bladed sword. He

backpedaled to put the boulder between himself and his opponent. Slowed but still intent, Ragshir maneuvered his mount around the obstacle and took a high swing. Papa ducked.

Danae clutched the dagger. What did she know about fighting? It did not matter. Papa could not—

"Take the horse!" a voice cried from behind her.

The driver thrust a fistful of reins at Danae, tugging the shaggy Tebalese horse along, the animal's eyes white-rimmed and nostrils flaring. She blinked at the man.

"Get on! Get out of here."

Danae swallowed—not that she had any saliva to gulp down. "I— I have to get Papa first." She wormed her pack onto her back. The dagger, she kept in hand.

"Crazy girl," the driver replied. "I'll help him. You follow your family."

An outburst down the hill sent a burst of ice through Danae's body. She spun back.

Papa held his side with his free hand and staggered left. Ragshir's extended blade caught the afternoon sun, and a crimson stain smeared its edge.

"No!" Danae screamed. She grabbed the horse's reins and leapt upon its back. No matter that she scarcely knew how to ride. How hard could it be? With a swift kick, she barreled down the hill toward Papa.

Another mechanical twang. The resulting crossbow bolt ricocheted off the stand of rock Ragshir had driven Papa back from, missing the Tebalese soldier by a hand span. He jerked his head left.

Papa swung his longsword, and it bit deep into Ragshir's mount's foreleg. The beast screamed. It crashed nose-first into the gorse.

Heaven and Earth, how did anyone ride at high speed? Danae clung to the horse's bristly mane with hands fused into fists. Even so, her seat bounced against the saddle, and every stride threatened to tip her overboard. A few jerks of the reins brought the animal around behind Papa.

"Get on!" Danae screamed.

Papa staggered, half bent, to the horse's flank, and by some surge of either self-preservation or buried experience, swung up behind Danae.

Ragshir fought his boot free of a tangled stirrup, snapped a curse, and ripped the bow from his back. He reached back and patted his shoulder blade, and then spat another oath. He spun and searched the ground around his horse.

"Go, Danae, now!" Papa wrapped an arm around her shoulder.

Danae slammed her heels into the horse's barrel just as another crossbow bolt sailed in. She did not look back. The interjection from somewhere in the vicinity of the boulders told her enough.

The Tebalese horse labored up the slope back toward the driver. He had propped his weapon on a boulder of about waist height. He took careful aim once again at Ragshir.

"What do we do?" Danae yelled over the hoofbeats. "Stop with him?"

The driver's body jerked forward, and his jaw dropped. A bloody arrowhead protruded from his ribcage.

Danae grimaced and squeezed her eyes shut.

"Where did that come from?" she managed to choke out over her sudden nausea.

"There," Papa replied.

She opened one eye to note where he pointed. Van had taken a position uphill and to the right of the driver. A trail of blood led to his spot.

"I can hold them off," the driver called. A gurgling cough mangled his words. "Run. Please run." The crossbow twanged again and Van ducked behind his cover.

Danae gasped. "But . . ."

"Do what he says." Papa said. "Heeya!"

The horse lunged forward with doubled speed.

A scream broke loose from Danae's lips.

11

PARTING WAYS

"*D*anae!" Papa called over the wind roaring in Danae's ears. "You need to grip better with your legs. You seem like you're about to fall off any moment."

"That's because I *am* going to fall off any moment."

Papa groaned. "Get your calves in contact with the horse. Force your heels down and your toes should . . ." A cough overtook his instructions. "You need to . . ." More coughing interfered. His whole body rocked with the violence of the fit, and his grip around her shoulder slackened.

Danae spared a quick check over her shoulder. Papa's face had gone pale. The coughs still came, though how he was managing to catch enough breath in the midst of them to keep hacking seemed a mystery.

"Get my water," she said.

Papa nodded. With a shaking hand he fumbled with the buckle on Danae's pack. The weaving galumph of the horse demanded her attention to the front, so she gritted her teeth and glared ahead. *Please let him find the water before he passes out.*

A sloppy sloshing and the cessation of Papa's hacking encouraged Danae that he had managed to swallow at least a little of the drink. His grasp around her shoulder remained tenuous at best. She kicked the horse. Papa's breathing whistled with each draught of air, and his weight against her back pressed in.

They galloped over the crest of the hill and down the other side, and the heartbeat in Danae's ears echoed the thunder of her mount's hooves over the hard ground. The Great South Road stretched ahead of them, and nowhere upon it did Danae spot the cart or her family. Papa's weight sagged against her.

"Papa, are you all right?"

"Not really." His weak voice bubbled through a blockage of congestion. "Coughing . . . not much help to . . . sword wound."

Danae might have slapped her forehead if she was not so busy clutching the horse's mane in self-preservation. Of course Papa would continue to deteriorate if they did not see to that wound.

"Hang on. Just hang on. I'm going to see if I can't put a little more distance between us and Drex's bloodhounds, but then we better take a look at what's going on with that cut."

They crested the next hill, and about halfway down the far side, a wagon with three wheels and a broken hitching pole lay derelict. Danae's breath caught. Where were Mama and the boys? And what happened to the team of horses? She steered her mount for the road's edge and neared the wagon at a cautious trot. With each jarring foot-fall, Papa slipped a little farther to the right. He moaned.

Once within a score of paces of the wagon, Danae caught sight of the fourth wheel, which sat apart, and lacked about a third of its rim. The hole the axle of the vehicle tipped into told the bulk of the likely tale. She guided the horse to the far side of the wagon, stopped, and dismounted. Papa pitched off the horse's back as well, but not at his own behest. A quick scurry shuffled Danae under his shoulder before he completely tumbled. Most of his tunic flared scarlet.

Danae eased Papa to the ground and tugged at his bloodied

clothes to expose the sword slash. It ran from his lowest rib to his collarbone, and several of the ribs the gash traversed peeked white through the crimson rift in his flesh. A fit of trembling swept through Danae's body.

Whether a blessing or a curse, the wound was no longer bleeding heavily. Danae bit her lip at the prospect the bleeding had slowed from what looked like a lot of blood loss. There was no time to dwell on such morbid thoughts. She pressed a wad of Papa's tunic to the lower end of the cut where the blood still seemed to flow most freely. The top end of the wound was much shallower, but as she examined it, a discoloration near Papa's collarbone, something darker than blood, caught Danae's eye.

She swabbed away as much mess as she could. Branching out from a white patch of scar tissue—a black web. It was only the size of half her palm, but unmistakable.

Papa coughed, as if to drive home her suppositions. No. This was not happening.

"Can you hear me?" Danae whispered.

Papa nodded, but he did not open his eyes.

"Did you pack anything for dressing wounds in the bags?"

He nodded again.

Danae blew out a heavy breath. She shrugged off her backpack and plunged both hands into the provisions. If there were bindings in there, they must have been on the bottom.

The crunch of dry gorse caught her ear. She grabbed the dagger once more and jumped to her feet, thrusting the blade before her at whoever approached. Just Mama and Farrell, looking disheveled and wide-eyed, but both in one blessed piece. Relief weakened her limbs.

"Plagues!" Mama cried. She dashed to Papa's side and fell to her knees.

"Where are the boys?" Danae scanned the terrain with a new surge of worry.

Farrell's pinched glance lingered on Papa. He straightened his cloak. "Uh, just a few hundred yards south—in a cluster of trees for cover. The horses too."

Mama's breath came in short gulps. "What happened?" She stroked Papa's hair away from his face.

"Those horsemen were Van and Ragshir." Danae squatted down and resumed her rummaging for the bindings. Finally, her fingers found the coarse bundle. "Papa took a sword slash, and he's pretty weak from it." She unwound a length of bandage.

Mama took them in a shaking grasp. She folded a cloth strip into several layers about the length of the cut and set them lightly over the wound. "Well, it looks awful, but it's nothing Moira can't patch up. She's seen worse bull gores."

Danae loosened more bandages. "Farrell, prop him up a little so we can wrap that packing into place."

Farrell joined the women on the ground and wormed his large hands under Papa's shoulders. He lifted with a grimace. "I don't want to make anything worse."

"You won't," Mama said.

"Danae." Farrell lowered his voice. "What's that weird bruise above the slash?"

Bruise indeed. Danae bored into Mama with a sharp stare. "That's a good question. What do you think, Mama? Does that look *new* to you?"

Farrell's cheeks blanched.

Mama met Danae's challenge with a glare of her own, though laced with welling tears. "I don't appreciate your tone, young lady. Just what are you accusing me of?"

"Maybe I'm a just a bit put out that nobody told me about this . . . bruise?" Danae clutched the bandages until her knuckles ached. "I'm convinced now this mark has something to do with Papa's cough. And if I'm right, the long-term outlook isn't good."

Farrell shifted Papa's weight. "His short-term outlook isn't good if you don't finish with the bandages. Can't you bicker about this later?"

Mama grabbed the bandages from Danae's hands and silently wrapped Papa's torso. A tear escaped her eye and rolled down her reddening cheek.

Danae drew a long breath. "I'm sorry, Mama. I'm not blaming you for anything, really. Just railing." She took the end of the bindings as Mama reached them around Papa's torso and assisted with the binding process. "I really think you and the boys had better take the three horses and get Papa to Aunt Moira's as fast as you can."

"Yes, the sooner Papa's out of the ele—wait," Mama sputtered. "You make it sound like you're not coming."

Danae's stomach twisted into knots. "Because I'm not."

Farrell gasped. "Where in the Great Patron's name do you think you'd be going instead?"

"There are only three horses, and the little one Papa and I rode this far didn't manage that well with two adult riders." Danae balled her hands into fists and stretched her fingers again. "As it is, one of the horses from the team is going to have to carry three."

Mama tied Papa's tail ends of the bindings. "You still haven't answered the question. Where would you go?"

"To find out how to cure that!" Danae jabbed a finger at the black web on Papa's chest.

Papa stirred. "Hold on just a moment." His words came barely above a whisper. He opened his eyes to slits. "What's this nonsense?"

Danae stood and squared her shoulders. "I'm heading south to go look for a cure for your cough, Papa."

"South?" Papa forced himself upright. He groaned and winced. "There's no city in Radromir that will have any better information available. Come to Moira's and we'll figure this out." He tugged his tunic, which was growing stiff in the cold breeze, to cover his chest and abdomen again.

"There's nothing to figure out," Farrell blurted. "Like Papa said, there's no place to go that would be useful. We all need to lay low at Aunt Moira's so Drex's curs don't find us and start shooting again."

"You know, I agree with you, Farrell. At least a little." Danae swallowed. She groped for her courage. Now it came to it. "You all need to get Papa to Aunt Moira's and treat that wound properly. But you're mistaken if you think I'm willing to linger someplace where there's no hope of researching that . . . other issue. So I'm going to Kelmirith."

Papa's eyes bulged. "Kelmirith? You're joking."

Danae shook her head.

Mama clapped her hand to her forehead. "Why?"

"Nobody on Argent has gathered the wealth of knowledge the Elgadrim have. No use wasting time anyplace else. Bilearne likely has the most extensive library on the continent, if not the world, and if that's not enough—"

"Do you have any idea how far it is to Bilearne?" Farrell shook his head. "And if you haven't noticed, there's a war going on."

"It's insanity," Mama added.

Danae shook her head. "Insanity would be slowing your progress to Aunt Moira's so anybody still after us catches up. All just to watch Papa . . ." Her words stuck in her throat. "I can't stand by to watch the unthinkable happen, and then wonder if there was something more I could have done."

Papa shifted on the ground and winced. "I forbid you to go."

A sick churning twisted Danae's insides. "But Papa, what I told you about Master Hawkspur."

"It's irrelevant to this discussion," Papa said. "You are my daughter, and you'll honor me with your obedience."

She breathed a troubled sigh and closed her eyes. "I have no desire to dishonor you, but I've exhausted every other resource to help you. Please let me go."

"Do you realize what you're proposing?" Mama's voice carried the sharp edge of panic. "It's not as if you're asking to go to the next town on a week-long errand. It'll take you months to get to Bilearne, if you can get there at all! And alone?"

Papa joined the charge. "I'd be out of my mind to let my only daughter walk off alone with who-knows-what in her path."

"Will anything I run into be worse than helping Mama plan an untimely funeral?"

Papa startled, as though caught off-guard Danae would dare voice such doom.

Danae continued. "We've researched this illness side by side, Papa. Can you really still insist it's not . . .?" She paused. The word *terminal* refused to form.

"There must be some other way." Farrell folded his arms

Danae chewed her lip. She flicked a glance up the hillside. "We're wasting too much time debating this. You all need to go."

Her father studied her for a long moment. "If I go one way and let you go another, I'll never be able to live with myself if something happens to you."

Danae propped a hand on her hip. "If you don't let me go, the fact is you probably won't have to worry about what you can or can't live with."

Silence crashed over the family, to leave only the sound of the wind through the grass between them.

Papa's voice softened. "I promise you, I promise all of you, I'll continue to work on a remedy at Moira's."

Danae turned a stony expression to her father. She locked gazes with him for an accusatory moment. "When did it start, Papa?"

His brows lowered. "What?"

"You know very well what. That mark around your knife scar."

"Oh, the rash." Papa's hand drifted to his collarbone.

"Rash? Are you kidding? That is *not* a rash."

"It could be completely unconnected to the cough."

"It has a sinister look to it." Danae crouched to clasp Papa's hands. "Please! I must ask the Elgadrim about the Hacking Doom and the mark. They're the last clues I've got."

"What's this about a . . . hacking doom, did you call it?" Mama asked.

A sigh trickled from Danae's lips. "Papa should tell you on the way to Aunt Moira's, since it seems he hasn't already."

Papa and Mama exchanged a nonverbal volley of expressions full of furrowed brows and tense lips. After a resigned shake of the head, he dropped his hands into his lap, though the motion came with a wince. "Danae, where do you assume you'll sleep tonight?"

"I should be able to make it to the bridge at Broanain's Run by nightfall. I'm going to ask around for a bed there."

Papa rubbed his brow, and tears sprang up in his eyes.

Mama reached into her pack. "If you insist on going, take this."

She handed Danae a bundle of traveling rations. "This should be enough to last you until you can bolster your provisions in one of the villages."

"Give her the coin pouch as well. She'll need it," Papa said. He stifled a cough behind his fist. "You're going to have to be creative with how you stretch it."

Danae took the food and money from her parents. "Papa," she said, her throat tight. "Please try to help the rest of the boys through this. They won't understand."

"The rest of them?" Farrell groaned. "*I* don't understand."

Her wide eyes begged Farrell's forgiveness.

A soft smile curled Papa's lips. "They know full well that if anyone's a lady of action in this family, you are."

Danae walked over to where the horse nosed around in the underbrush. She towed the beast back to her father's side. "Let's get you back on this horse and all of you underway."

Farrell stepped in and helped Papa up from the ground and then into the saddle. Papa moaned through his teeth throughout the process. Mama mounted up as well and took the reins.

Danae sidled in beside Mama and Papa and hugged them both around the waist at once. The hot prickle of tears stung her eyes, wet her lashes, and then left fast-cooling tracks down her cheeks. "Get them out of here, Farrell. And keep our brothers out of trouble," she whispered, though the words broke often.

"Be careful," Farrell said. A little laugh escaped him. "For a change." He squeezed her from the side.

Mama reached over and stroked wild tendrils of Danae's hair over her ear. "We love you, and we'll watch for you every day until you return."

"May the blessings of the Creator speed your journey, surround you in safety, and grant you success." Papa's voice faltered at the tail end of his words.

Could a hint of pride be glinting through his grief? Danae hung the drapery of a smile over her sadness, adjusted the shoulder straps on her pack, and took a step backward toward the Great South Road.

"Thank you, all of you. I hope I'll be back sooner than any of us can imagine."

"If there's a cure to be found in this wide world, you'll dig it up." Papa's eyelids drooped. "Now, Fiona, let's go. Not too fast, mind you."

Mama nudged the horse, and Farrell fell into step beside them.

Danae watched them for many long moments, her heart breaking with the horse's every stride. Finally, she tore her eyes from her retreating family and turned back to the empty road south. She took one step, then another, forcing herself to face the unknown.

12

S<small>LAVE</small>

*H*ow long would it take to find the cure?

The question underscored Danae's every calculation as she considered the next stage of her sketchy proposition. She hiked from one patch of gnarled trees to another, forsaking the road, but keeping a close watch trained upon it. Would more riders appear on the hunt for her family?

After a couple hours of skittish progress, a dark bank of clouds rolled in from the west, and the distant haze beneath them foretold a coming change in the weather. Danae paused long enough to pull on the fur-lined boots in her pack. While she laced them, she smiled at the provisions she found in the satchel. The presence of her journal amidst the necessities suggested Papa had been the one to pack her things—Mama would have protested the space the journal took up could have been filled with something more practical, like a hair-brush. She wound a wool scarf around her neck and resumed the journey.

Snowflakes swirled thick in the darkening murk of late afternoon and covered the terrain with alarming speed. While she hiked the snowy hills of her homeland, she mulled her options. Already, she had dismissed the possibility of taking an overland route to Bilearne. Even if the passes through the Triasteads would have been open at that time of year, the war made the roads on the eastern side of the mountains too dangerous. And the plodding pace of travel on foot could very well consume all the time Papa had left, however long that was.

A sea voyage across the bay of Verdrun to land in the neighboring country of Velon was her most likely route, though this choice presented its own set of troubles. How hard would it be to find passage on a ship bound for countries she had only ever seen on a map? Could she afford the trip? How would she proceed if the fare was beyond her means?

A stirring in the distance shattered Danae's introspection. She squinted far down the Great South Road—a single horseman headed toward her from the south. She ducked into the refuge of a swatch of scrub oak and waited.

The rider cantered past. The horse was stout, the rider fur-clad and arrayed in Tebalese military-issue leather armor, and a gargoyle shield thumped on his back. Danae held her breath. His even, triple cadence carried him past, but only after the northern distance swallowed him did she emerge from her concealment.

She resumed her route southwest, forcing speed from increasingly leaden limbs. The cloud cover and snow deadened the remaining light. It could be mid-afternoon or the brink of dusk, but Danae had no way of knowing for certain. Either way, her eyelids already hung heavy. She plodded on.

The murk deepened into the empty chill of a winter night before a distant line of split rail fencing came into view. Danae sighed. Finally, some sign she had neared Broanain's Run. She quickened her pace and reached the crest of the hill the fence line crowned. Indeed, down the slope lay a stout stone bridge over an ice-banked river, and on its opposite side, three homesteads and a barn between them. A brief rush of new energy gave her the spryness to jog down the slope.

Lights burned in the windows of two of the homes, while the third stood dark. Danae mounted the step of the first little fieldstone house and rang the bell that hung outside. She pulled her scarf down from her nose and stuffed it under her chin.

"Don't you try an' get it," a deep voice inside said. "If it's one of them grayfaces again, I mean to . . ."

The door opened, and inside stood a leather-clad Radromirian man, with a thick shock of wild red hair and a glare on his face more frigid than the weather.

Danae took a step back. "E-Evening, sir."

His eyes narrowed. He craned his neck as if searching behind her.

"Evening." His flat voice lacked the ring of hospitality.

"I'm looking for lodging on my way to Briardale, and this is as far as I could get tonight." Danae glanced behind her. "Any chance you have a spare spot anywhere? Even a shed would do."

"You alone?" the man asked.

Suddenly, Danae wished she was not. "Well, yes. Is that a problem?"

"You're sure? Didn't leave a middle-aged man behind someplace?"

"Yes, I'm sure." Danae swallowed.

The man scrutinized Danae for another moment, then shook his head. "Well, what you're doing is your business, but I'm of a mind not to make it mine. No. You can't stay here."

Danae's jaw went slack. Had there ever been a Radromirian homestead that turned one of their own away? "Beg pardon?"

"You heard me. We don't want no trouble 'round these parts. We know what it is to face the torch over nothing. Yer answer's no, lass. And it'll be the same at the Donnagain's too." He jerked his head toward the other lit house. "Take my word."

"Uh, I . . . thanks anyway." Danae backed off the step.

The man glanced back into the warm yellow glow of the lamplight of his home. "I am sorry, lass. Just 'taint worth the risk." A young woman with a burgeoning belly inched up behind him. She extended a roll of parchment around the man and toward Danae.

With a slow hand, Danae reached for the scroll. She pulled it open and glanced over the contents.

High Alert: Fugitives

The acting government of West Tebal requests you be on the watch for two dangerous fugitives who recently fled Dayleston. A malicious sorcerer and his protégé have attacked peacekeeping forces, unprovoked, with spells of deadly nature.

The sorcerer goes by the name of Baledric and is in his middle to late forties, with graying, short hair. He stands a handspan below a fathom in height, and weighs in the vicinity of twenty-five stone.

His protégé is a short female in her early twenties with strawberry blonde hair.

If you encounter these dangerous criminals, please report them to your local checkpoint. A reward of three hundred gold is offered to any person who gives information instrumental in the capture of either fugitive. Any aid lent to either individual will be considered treason and deserving of death.

Queldrik's Servant,

Drex of Cray

Every line that Danae read widened her eyes further.

"So, miss," the man at the door said. "I'd be on your guard." His glance started at her feet and climbed until it reached her head. "Wouldn't want to be mistaken for a dangerous fugitive."

He closed the door and left Danae in the purple of nightfall.

Danae backed to the roadside. She looked to the second household. The light streaming through the window winked out.

So much for the generations of tradition that dictated travelers without a bed were always to be shown kindness. The clutching fear that unfriendly eyes sought her from every dark window set her hands trembling.

She pulled a hooded lantern from her pack, along with a small bundle of her father's prized matches. She struck a match on a stone carriage stoop and lit the wick of the lantern. She rubbed her hands together in the warmth of its flame. The snowflakes that fell around her glowed when they passed through her small orb of light.

She returned to the center of the road and took up a quick pace, despite the tremble in her muscles at the continued demand. The large flakes reduced visibility to a few furlongs at best. For now, she would employ the highway, against the threat of getting lost in such conditions. Danae saw little more than her own feet, as she focused on the increasingly difficult task of executing one stride after the other. The cold deepened. Her shoulders sagged and her back ached under the weight of her pack.

She reached the summit of a formidable hill and leaned against the leprous stump of a long-dead sycamore, panting for breath. Ahead of her, the flat strip of the road wound like a ribbon stitched through the hillsides, but not a barn, house, or other refuge appeared along its length. The prospect of an all-night march sent her heart plummeting into the depths of her stomach. Sixteen hours of hiking the countryside tortured her every fiber into pleas for mercy. How would she manage weeks of this grueling travel on foot? How long could she evade soldiers and civilians alike, with so handsome a reward posed for her apprehension?

She glanced back the way she came. Her footprints in the snow zigzagged like the strides of a drunk. Oh, for even a few hours' repose. But the snow was not deep enough to build a decent shelter without hauling it from a wide radius. She trudged on.

The treacherous descent on the southward side of the hill concealed occasional patches of ice, which Danae only learned when her boot failed to sink into soft footing, but instead shot from beneath her. A wild swirl of arms could not compensate for the slick patch or her deteriorating coordination, and down the hillside she rode on one bruised hip. She clawed at the slope, but only filled the cuffs of her gloves with wet snow before she slowed to a stop at the bottom.

She flopped on her side and nestled her hooded head into the crook of her elbow. Her leaden eyelids demanded a respite. She would only close her eyes for a moment. Just enough to catch her breath. Her muscles slackened and her body slipped on another descent—toward slumber.

~

"*M*adam?"

Danae's heart leapt to a dizzying thud in an instant. Her eyes snapped open, but she could make no sense of the series of shapes, dark bars across lustrous white, before her. Her face was numb. Her body felt stiff. Where was she?

The darks bands across her field of vision focused into the long, clean legs of black horses, who stood champing their bits and blowing puffs of steam from frosty nostrils. They wore some sort of harness, but a dim halo around the edges of Danae's vision prevented her from discovering what the horses might pull.

"Madam, are you all right? Can you hear me?" It was a man's voice, speaking the Western tongue—comprehensible, but thick with an accent.

A Tebalese accent.

Danae shot upright, though her head pounded and her vision darkened further. She clapped her hands to her forehead. The prospect of running was a humorless joke.

Footfalls crunched through the snow to Danae's right. She turned. A fur-clad Tebalese man inched toward her, his hands out before him as though ready to fend off a wounded animal.

His sable cloak hung to his heels, and a wool scarf bundled thickly around his neck. Under the cloak, Danae caught the glint of a weapon hilt, a short sword perhaps, but beyond that, he did not appear more heavily armed. He stood no more than five and a half feet, his build indiscernible beneath his heavy clothes. His hair hung to his shoulders in tight curls—not in the dread locks Danae had grown to expect from one of his origin. Her hand slid to the hilt of her dagger.

"Madam, you are lost?"

Danae smacked her lips in an effort to clear her mouth of a thick layer of foul-tasting cotton. She sought her response from her Tebalese vocabulary, and then offered it in what she presumed was the man's primary tongue. "No, I'm not lost."

He cocked a black eyebrow. "Why are you lying in the snow in the middle of the night?"

How to answer? Was he hunting her, and just biding his time before he sprung whatever trap he had planned? Why had he not simply overpowered her while she lay prone and disoriented?

"I misjudged my trip today," Danae replied. Her eyes flicked to the shadowed landscape, searching out accomplices. "I'm trying to reach some decent shelter for the night."

The man blinked. "You have clearly lost the battle to exhaustion. I will bear you to the next village, if you will come with me."

Right. Into the hands of whatever enforcers manned the check-point there. Danae clambered to her feet. "No, it's all right. I'll manage." She took a few staggering steps, tripped, and sprawled in the snow. She clenched her fists. *Wake up. Get up. Run!*

"Madam, please. I mean you no harm. You'll never make it to civilization."

Danae pushed up on her arms and wiped snow from her eyes. "How far is it?"

"Four hours, by sleigh. On foot, in the snow? Well, you can imagine." The driver reached out to her with open palms. "You've nothing to fear from me. Your enemies tonight will be exposure and fatigue."

Danae stared into his black eyes, similar to Drex's in color and tilted shape, but at the same time, wholly different. They implored with human concern. She swept his attire once again. No gargoyle emblem anywhere. "Why do you want to help me?"

He sighed. "Is it so implausible I would offer such a thing freely?"

Danae eyed him sidelong. "I don't mean to seem ungrateful, but I haven't met any Tebalese who would stop short of spitting on me."

The man's features sagged. "I'm guilty by association, then. You'll have to choose whether you believe a man can be different from his countrymen. I do wish to help you. Will you accept the ride?"

Danae eyed the horses. They were tall, sleek animals with coats that reflected the sleigh's lantern light in blue-black contours —very unlike the usual Tebalese beasts. They had a polite manner, neither shifting nor shuffling even though their master had no hold on their reins, but had simply clipped them to the dashboard of a sleigh the horses drew. She chewed her lip. The sheepskins across the seat of the sleigh beckoned with a snug invitation.

The wind hissed over the surface of the snow. She needed to warm up. Her choices at this point were to die of cold on her own, or perchance, thaw a bit, and if the driver proved treacherous, at least have a fighting chance once her limbs were functioning again.

"All right." Danae rose and took a few careful steps to the sleigh. "You win."

The driver flashed a bright smile. He took Danae's hand, helped her into the passenger seat, and climbed back to his own perch.

He clicked his tongue to the team and clapped the reins on the breeching of their harness, leaving his whip in the sleeve on the edge of the dashboard. The horses picked up a brisk trot, and Danae huddled into the folds of her cloak, doing her best to seal out the wind.

"Are you warm enough?" He offered her the sheepskin. "My name is Shamir, and I'm the night patrolman of this section of the South Road."

Danae took the rug, and between it and the iron box of coals at her feet, warmth began to eat away at the cold that had seeped to her core. The swishing snow lulled her as they drifted along, but she tapped a foot to stave off her sleepiness. "Do you work as far north as Dayleston?"

Shamir shook his head. "It's too far to cover in a shift. I start and finish my route in Briardale."

Danae smirked. "Stationed in the big city, eh?"

"You must be a country girl," Shamir replied. "Briardale has the necessities."

Country girl? It sufficed for Shamir to go on believing that. "If you're the night patrolman, then there are day patrols too?"

"Don't get around much? Yes, the larger villages and cities all have perimeter patrols, though I go the farthest from my station of anyone." He turned a probing look her way. "You know, it's not encouraged for locals to wander about. Travelers arouse the suspicion of the forces maintaining control here."

A wringing tension wrapped around Danae's stomach. "But traveling isn't against the law, right?"

"No, not according to the letter of the law, for now. Unless you live in Dayleston, of course. Nobody goes in or out of Dayleston, under penalty of death." Shamir rolled his eyes.

"Really? Punishable . . . by death? I had no idea." Danae chewed her lip. Was he warning her? Did he suspect her identity? Or was the statement just that, a simple fact? She cleared her throat. "Too bad for the folks who live there."

Shamir nodded. "It really is. I'm simply thankful my role here doesn't involve enforcing any of those overbearing laws. Strategists, my people are. Diplomats?" He huffed. "But who am I to say? A slave is a slave, so I shall mind my own business, drive the fine horses with which I've been supplied, and keep young ladies like you off the road, for your own good."

"You're a slave?" The thought eclipsed her worries, at least momentarily. "How awful!"

Shamir shrugged a shoulder. "I'm better off than many free men. I have as peaceful a job a man could hope while indentured as a soldier."

"But still." Danae leaned forward. "It *is* slavery. You can't choose to do otherwise."

"No able-bodied man of Tebal may choose his destiny right now, slave or free, so really, we're all slaves of sorts. Those who are free have the added challenge of supplying their families' needs on the short pay of a soldier."

"You don't talk much like I expected a slave would."

The gleam in Shamir's glance dulled. "I wasn't born into it. I used to be a university professor, but when the theocracy wrested control of all the education in Tebal, I failed to fit the changes to my job description."

"But how does that land you in slavery, if I may ask?"

"It's too long a story to tell in detail, but the Inquisitors manipulated the note on a debt I owed, and when I couldn't pay in full, they jailed me, gave my position to one of their own, and eventually auctioned me to my current master."

Danae contemplated her lap. "I'm sorry for your losses. You say you're content, but I can't imagine how."

Shamir sighed. "I save my pity for my country more than myself. As the cult of Queldurik ensnares so many, I watch good people wither into ruthless distortions of their former selves." He fixed a furrowed countenance upon the road before them. "The cult is a poison to my people."

Danae shuddered. What little she knew about Queldurik's church involved blood sacrifices and the consulting of supernatural creatures of malevolent reputation. She had never cared to investigate further. Shamir did not fit the profile of Queldurik worshipers she had met thus far.

Danae relaxed a fraction. Either Shamir was a master thespian, or else he really was an anomaly among Tebalese. "I don't know what to make of you, Shamir. Your conduct has been . . . unexpected."

Shamir pursed his lips, the golden glow of his side lantern illuminating his smooth features. "I'm glad you find me, as you say, unexpected."

Danae shifted in her seat and wrapped the sheepskin tighter. Somehow, it felt rude to press the conversation, regardless of the legion of questions that paraded through her mind. Despite her intention to maintain vigilance, the swish of the runners over the snow, the warmth of sheepskin, and her exhaustion waged war on good sense. Her head nodded, her limbs jerked, and the moonlight, the snow, the horses faded away.

She ran up the lane to Aunt Moira's farm, but the grasses along the roadside reached out with thorny tendrils, clutched at her legs, and raked her arms. She fought free. Whether early morning or the last moments before nightfall, she could not tell, but it did not matter, only that she reached the farmhouse at the end of the lane, shrouded in failing light. Where there should have been cattle, she found empty fields. All was gray and motionless.

She shoved her way through the flimsy front door and into the parlor, but the room stood empty and covered in thick dust. A few more fumbling strides carried her into the rear bedroom, where she met a wall comprised of her siblings, their backs turned. Something smelled dreadful.

The boys parted with wooden steps to reveal her mother, her eyes puffy and her face tracked with tears. She too stepped aside. Beyond her, Papa lay on a narrow bed, his hands fixed into claws, his face pale and waxy and jaw frozen open in a dry grimace.

Danae jolted awake with a gasp. The silhouettes of snow-covered hills drifted by, the team of horses trotted on, and Shamir held the reins lightly, clicking an occasional sound of encouragement to his beasts. Her heart thumped in her chest, its pace only slackening when she reminded herself the horrific images were only dreams. Nothing more. She squinted ahead. Just maybe, a pinpoint of light winked on the horizon. She focused on it as it grew, and soon discerned there was indeed a light, among others to companion it.

"The Village of Briardale," Shamir said. "I see the gate-keeper's lamp is lit, as well as a few others. I recommend you keep a low profile."

To the east, a gray halo had begun to drive back the dark of night.

"Thank you." Danae tugged her hood lower over her forehead. A test of Shamir's intentions nestled within the nearing points of light.

13

LITTLE REFUGE

They swished up to Briardale's gate, a mere tollbooth beside an open section in the wood plank fence that surrounded the city. Danae chewed the inside of her cheek. With any luck, perhaps they would sweep right through. The sleigh neared the gatehouse, when a pike-bearing man in a thick woolen cape and hood stepped into their path. Danae slouched and lowered her chin. She folded her feet up beneath her on the seat. Did such a position obscure her height?

Shamir called a low "whoa" to his team.

The pikeman drew a plank with parchment stretched across it from beneath his cloak. "Sign in, please," he said in a monotone. His face was light and freckled, and what straggly hair poked from beneath his hood was sandy.

The jitters in Danae's limbs calmed a fraction. At least one of her own countrymen manned the gate.

Shamir took the plank and scratched a signature on the parchment. He handed the plank back to the gatekeeper.

One of the horses snorted and took a step backward. It tossed its head and laid its ears flat. Shamir's quick grab gathered the reins into his hands once more. "Steady, girl. What is it?"

A sharp bark rang out up ahead. Danae peered around Shamir and the horses. *Can we please just get through the gate?* She surveyed the street for the source of the bark, and when she found the dog, her tremulous tension returned and multiplied. A Tebalese soldier approached, straining backward against a tether on the dog's collar. The beast was enormous—at least chest height. It had black, wiry hair, and the light from the gatehouse lantern gleamed from its wild eyes in flashes of red and green. Upon its chest, a bare white triangle brand glared starkly against its dark fur.

"Ah, dependable as the sun," the soldier called. "Shamir's never late." His snide tone contradicted the complimentary words.

The closer the huge canine got, the more Shamir's horses shuffled. A burning sensation lit on Danae's goose bumpy arms and crawled across her body. She shrank into a tighter ball on the seat.

"Morning, Ghagren," Shamir said. He jumped down from the driver's seat and took a hold of the cross-reins between the horses. "If you would, stay back. Your hound seems to be a little troubling to the team." He stroked the mare's neck, as the animal craned her head high, and white rimmed her eyes.

Ghagren laughed. "Well, they better get over it, since you're taking this mongrel up to Dayleston."

Shamir frowned. "Since when is ugly pet delivery my job?"

"It's supposed to be an extremely valuable hunting hound, and one of the captains up there needs it right away."

"He'll have to wait at least a few extra hours," Shamir replied. "These horses just did a full night's work, as did I."

The dog lifted its nose into the air. Its nostrils twitched. A crazed bark burst from its maw, and teeth bared, it lunged at the sleigh. A hot, scraping wave washed over Danae, and she cringed.

Shamir's horses shied, and the horse on the left half-reared.

"Get a hold of that monster, you fool!" Shamir cried.

Danae gulped. She took quick stock of her surroundings. If she jumped from the sleigh, was there enough cover to flee the situation and lose the gatekeeper, the soldier, and the dog? The houses near Briardale's gate, upon closer inspection, were dilapidated stone structures, most of them with collapsing roofs. Every building within a block bore the black stain of past fire. Where would she go? The mongrel's long legs would likely make it terribly fast if it pursued. She hung her head, but kept the snapping, foaming creature in her peripheral vision.

Ghagren dug his heels into the slushy road and wrenched the dog's tether shorter. "Seems he doesn't much care for your uppity attitude." He narrowed his eyes. "Or maybe it's your passenger. Who's that?"

Shamir cleared his throat. A nonchalant wave swept the soldier's question away. "Uh, just a local nobody who got lost in the snow last night. The visibility was awful. I'm delivering her back where she belongs."

"You should have let her freeze." Ghagren guffawed. "One less infidel. Get rid of her and follow orders, or you might find your job around these parts gets a little less agreeable."

The dog snarled and lunged again.

Shamir shook his head. "If I have to take your cur anywhere, I'm getting fresh horses and a covered vehicle I can shut the beast into. Drag him clear. I'll be back by full dawn." He tugged the horses' cross reins and towed them forward, though they danced on skittish strides.

The sleigh ground past the soldier and hound, and only by wrapping both hands in the dog's lead did the soldier prevent the beast from leaping after the vehicle. Danae hunkered down and rubbed at her upper arms. The burning pain only abated after a furlong of travel down the road. The horses' gait returned to a steady clop over the snow, and Shamir retook the driver's seat.

He urged the team forward and craned his neck over his shoulder. "I shall leave you at the guesthouse a little further down Gate Street, but may I suggest you draw as little attention as you can?"

Danae uncurled from her protective ball and glanced back. "What makes you say that?"

A frown creased Shamir's face. He cocked his head. "Tell me you don't think that huge brute was barking at you and I'll call you a liar straight out."

A stare was the only response Danae could manage.

"And I would be concerned if any creature wearing Queldurik's brand seemed too interested in me."

They continued along the thoroughfare, and in the places where the cobbles peeked from beneath the snow, she could see they were worn with many years of service. The burned shells of houses receded and gave way to thatch-roofed homes that huddled along both the main and side streets, standing shoulder to shoulder against the sharp chill of the wind. Many of the little residences had animal pens right behind them that housed a few goats, a pig or two, or perhaps the occasional milk cow. The taller buildings along the main streets held up shingled roofs and stylish appointments like scrolling ironwork or false half-timbering.

The coming dawn cast the village around Danae in blue-gray, and one by one, lights flickered to life in many of the small windows they passed. Shamir reined the team in before a building whose many windows glowed warmly.

"This is my stop, I assume?" Danae stretched. Every muscle roared its stiffness. She gripped the frame of the sleigh and pulled herself onto wobbly legs. Her teeth chattered the moment she set the sheepskin rug aside. "I guess this is goodbye, Shamir. Thanks for your kindness."

Shamir bowed his head. "You're most welcome," he answered. "May both of our people find peace."

A gust of wind swept Danae's hood from her head.

Shamir cocked an eyebrow. "That's some hair color you have."

"Um, well, not so terribly uncommon among Radromirians as some might think." She pulled her hood back up and tucked a wayward tendril inside it.

Shamir chuckled and shook his head. "Good luck to you. I believe you will need all you can get." He clucked to the team, and they trotted out of sight.

Danae turned to the guesthouse, but when she tried the latch, she found it locked. A quick tug on the cord hanging from the doorbell clanged its clapper and sent a clear call into the morning air. Danae winced.

After a moment, a tall broomstick of a woman, her straw blonde hair gathered into a knot at the back of her head, opened the door. She wiped her hands on a spattered apron. "May I help you, miss?" Her curt tone suggested she did not relish the idea.

"Yes, please," Danae said. "I'm very weary with travel and hope to find a place to stay until I am rested."

The woman glared down her sharp nose. She pressed her lips together so tightly they disappeared. Her brow crinkled.

"I don't approve of young ladies traveling alone. Outlandish!" The woman grumbled on, as if arguing with herself. "But it won't do me any good to leave you pale and shivering on my step, either." She folded her arms. "Fine! Come in, and I'll find you a bed. But it's strange, to find you a place to sleep, when all the decent folk are just getting up."

Danae slinked past her into the guesthouse.

"So, do you want to eat first?" the lean woman asked. "If you can wait few moments, there'll be ham, eggs, and pan biscuits for all the guests."

Lady, I want to sleep. But there's no use further offending this woman if she holds the keys to the only bedroom I might find. Danae nodded and sat on the edge of a bench by the long dining table, while the older woman returned to her preparation of breakfast.

The hostess bustled about the tidy room, made homey by its family-style seating, ample fireplace and wide assortment of home-making supplies suspended from the rafters. Pulling down two bundles of dried herbs, a generous ham and a couple of skillets, the keeper of the guesthouse set to warming food for perhaps a dozen diners. As she heated one of the cast iron skillets on a rack over the fire, the smoky aroma of the seasoned pan turned the air savory.

One by one, a half dozen travelers emerged from doors in the rear of the room, some of them tousled and half awake, while others appeared fully packed and ready to head straight out the door. Danae sat mutely, listening to the sizzle of eggs as they hit the hot pan. If only someone would speak and break the awkward silence. The guests settled into meals as the hostess placed them around the table. As her plate landed before her, the rumble in Danae's stomach eclipsed her aching muscles and her worries. She shoveled food in large bites into her mouth.

"So, you folk'll be on your way south today, eh?" the hostess asked as she filled cups of tea and cider.

Many of the guests nodded while they chewed, while a short, plump man with more hair on his forearms than his head replied, "Aye, Mistress. My caravan thanks you for warm beds and hearty fare."

Danae's head snapped toward the man. "A caravan south? Do you take passengers?"

The caravan master smiled, but the expression lacked any sense of friendliness. Opportunism, more likely. "Someone you know looking to buy a ride?"

Danae adopted her steeliest business face. "Yes, sir. I have need to reach Garrabeth, and would rather ride than walk."

The man looked around the table. "How about it, gents? Anyone interested in taking a passenger if I close the deal?"

A nod from one of the less oily-looking teamsters flooded Danae with a sense of relief. "I'll take the lass. Looks like she'll add near naught to my load."

"Twenty-five silver will get you where you're goin'," the squat leader said.

I guess that's the price of safety in numbers. Danae counted out the coins and handed them slowly to the caravan master. He tossed one onto the table and turned an ear to its ring. With a nod, he scooped it up and handed a fraction of Danae's money to the teamster.

"Good enough. We'll roll out in a short while, so stay near

Donovan here, and you won't miss your ride. A pleasure doing business with you."

Barely able to stagger after the carter who agreed to drive her to port, Danae paid the hostess for her breakfast and departed the guesthouse. She flung her pack into the back of a rough wooden cart, clambered into the bed, and hugged her knees. The caravan rumbled into motion, jostling and jarring over the uneven roads, and Danae slumped heavy shoulders against whatever burlap bag of goods sat at her back. Her eyelids dragged with multiplied weight over her dry eyes. So much for rest in Briardale. But far more important than a bed and blankets was the opportunity to see the next leg of her journey safely behind her.

Not that the prospect of reaching the end of the four-day trek to the coast—with the purpose of sailing from the sole country she had ever known—gave her much in the way of comfort.

14

GARRABETH

$\mathcal{D}$anae gripped the side of the caravan wagon as yet another rut tossed her to the side. Southern Radromir certainly did not focus much on the upkeep of the highways, and Danae had days' worth of bruises on her knees and elbows to show for it. But even though the caravan moved no faster than she could walk, at least she was not footsore, nor stiff from long hours of hefting a pack.

Donovan's cart slowed to a halt. Danae peered around the low canvas canopy and found they had stopped at a wide intersection. Over the past couple of days, the other members of the caravan had turned away from the Great South Road one by one, destined for their individual terminuses. Only she and Donovan pressed on toward the coastline, where soil began to give way to sand.

"Everything all right?" Danae asked.

"Well, lass, there's a jolly tavern away to the right here that's callin' my name. I shan't head into port til the morrow, so yer welcome to come with me and finish yer ride at daybreak."

Danae glanced toward the cloudy sky. It could not have passed midday. "How much farther is it?"

Donovan scratched his cheek. "A determined type could make it by nightfall." He glanced at his shaggy team and chuckled. "Case ye'd not noticed. Buck an' Butch here . . . not quite determined."

"Then I think I'll walk from here." Danae stretched and wriggled into the shoulder straps of her pack.

"If that's what suits ye." He shrugged.

"I appreciate your help." She pointed ahead. "Just follow this road?"

Donovan nodded. "My pleasure, lass. The fortunes smile on ye." He clapped the reins on his horses' rumps, and they rattled in a wide turn to make their way west.

Danae set off at a jog along the southward road.

As midday wore into afternoon, the breeze picked up, humid, and spiked with a salty tang. The clouds broke and scattered. Climbing up a small rise, Danae reached its summit, and before her spread the great coastal plain of southern Radromir and the sprawling port city of Garrabeth. Beyond the plain, the failing sun twinkled upon the surface of the sea, a cluster of topaz in a violet setting.

Garrabeth stood beside the mouth of the river Insdrun, which served as a sheltered harbor for the Radromirians' merchant vessels. The culture prided itself on its ships, matchless for swiftness, and on its mariners, cunning in navigation and in warfare. But apparently seafarers made lousy foot soldiers, because the ports had fallen fast and hard when the armies of Tebal had descended upon them soon after they had conquered Dayleston.

Danae pressed onward, down the slope, and over the last few furlongs to the streets of Garrabeth.

As she closed the distance between herself and the city, many unwholesome smells drifted on the breeze, mingling with and eventually obliterating the pleasant saltiness of the sea. The reek of filth and burning filled Danae's nostrils. She coughed at the onslaught.

Danae gaped at the outlying shanties that surrounded the port city. Tumbledown clapboard shacks lined streets strewn with refuse.

She picked her way through the footing, sometimes closing her eyes in a squeamish grimace as she chose the least offensive muck in which to step. Not even the worst alleys of Dayleston rivaled the main thoroughfare of this slum. Here at the coast, no snow covered the grime. Indeed, if any had ever fallen, it had long since melted and joined the soupy puddles that dotted the muddy streets.

Danae rounded a corner, and a trio of ragged, underdressed children scrambled into her path. One of them looked up at her with hollow eyes that tore at her with a gut-wrenching display of destitution.

"Please," the skinny urchin whimpered, "Can you spare some food? Or a copper or two for bread for my little sister?"

"Uh . . . let me see." Danae rifled her pack to produce what food she could. Despite the quiet voice of warning in the recesses of her mind, she handed most of her bread, jerky, and fruit to the haggard flock of starving boys and girls that amassed around her. Once each child took whatever small measure of mercy she extended, they often hugged the small bit of food to their bodies or gazed at the scrap of meat or crust of bread with adoration. Her last apple passed into the outstretched hands of a boy who could not have been older than six. She turned away from the group, loath that they should see her wipe her eyes on a sleeve.

"I'm sorry. That's all I can give today." She shouldered her way through the remaining children.

Behind her, the shouts, cries, and scuffles of an argument broke out, and she turned back to seek the source of the commotion. The six-year-old, upon whom she had bestowed the apple, sprawled in the mud, and a taller sinewy boy stood over him, apple in hand. The younger boy rolled over and clawed at the bully's legs. A wrestling match ensued.

Danae ran to the punching, kicking, and tumbling boys and thrust herself between the combatants. If there was one skill her brothers had taught her, it was how to break up a fight, so she quickly had the two boys clutched by their ears.

"Listen here." She shot a glare at the fighters through the haze of tears that insisted on welling in her eyes. "There's only so much to go around. But I gave that apple to him, and I will stand here and watch him eat it if I must. No one is going to take it from him."

Danae released the boys' reddened ears and snatched the apple away from the aggressor.

"Here you go, little one," She handed the now muddy fruit back to her intended recipient. As the smaller child scrambled off into the shadows, Danae's scowl dared the bully to follow.

He sneered at her and spat on the ground. "Have it your way, rich girl. Whadda you care if I starve?"

Rich girl? Never in her life had Danae ever been accused of being a rich girl. What a difference the perspective from the gutter made. Danae took a breath to speak, unsure if she should rebut the boy, apologize for his sad circumstances, or encourage him he could be more than this, but before she could make the choice, the boy waved her off and stomped away.

Although the condition of the buildings and streets improved as Danae worked her way into the city, the inhabitants remained much the same: poor, hungry, and dejected. A cluster of young women stood beneath a street lamp, their gaudy garb and abundance of exposed skin painfully indicative of their business that evening. Their faces ranged from frightened to stony.

A group of Tebalese guardsmen hurled a few insults and laughs in the women's direction as they tromped past. None of the women met the soldiers' gazes, but neither did they react to the men's words, to which Danae could only credit a lack of comprehension. She wished she had not understood their vulgarities either.

The last embers of dusk were dying on the horizon as Danae wound her way to the docks, where crews of sailors were finishing their day's work, mending and storing nets, or moving barrels and crates aboard their vessels. Skin tones ranged from deep toffee-brown to the fair, freckle-prone complexions of her own countrymen, including every shade in-between. She suspected their garb might have varied as widely if most of their clothing had not been reduced to rags whose colors blended into a continuous palette of filth. Surely, these crews of sailors had been cobbled together from every corner of the continent. Consistently, though, the men of authority hailed from Tebal only. Tebalese taskmasters stood in the higher places, complacently overseeing the labor, chatting amongst themselves, and interjecting bellows of derision at the workers. To Danae, it seemed the overseers chose at random when to spout their displeasure, as a mere show of authority.

As one of the downcast Radromirians came close to her, Danae swallowed hard. "Sir?" Her voice came out in a squeak.

The dockworker lifted a net and examined it. He trimmed some tag ends of a tear with a short knife.

Danae cleared her throat. "Sir?"

This time, the sailor looked up, a sour expression curdling his face. "Eh? You talkin' to me? Nobody 'round these parts calls me 'sir.'"

"Sorry. My mistake." Danae trembled, but decided she had best make her query before she lost the limited patience of this grimy, sweaty net mender. "Could you tell me how I might book passage on one of these ships?"

The sailor laughed a raspy guffaw that implied a lifelong indulgence of pipe smoke. "Book passage? Ain't none that boards these ships without his feet in a set of shackles." He scratched at the ragged brown beard that ran from his ears all the way down his neck. "Now, you best git afore one o' these brutes sets his sights on ye. You'll find yerself on a trip ye never meant to take."

Danae blinked at the sailor dumbly.

"I mean it!" A hint of desperation widened his bloodshot eyes. "Don't stand around too long, or I can't vouch for what trouble ye'll run up against."

No passenger vessels? At all? She ducked behind a stack of wooden pallets and pressed the heels of her hands to her forehead.

Danae watched the business of the pier as differing classes of folk conducted their tasks. A group of men, well-dressed in waistcoats and tailored breeches, and apparently Radromirian by their light coloration and clear, recognizable speech, stood together about a dozen paces from Danae's nook. They regarded the workmen around them with unveiled disdain.

"Aye, my vessel sets out with the next tide," said one.

"That's if you can get your pack of sluggards to load it on time!" jeered another. "You must not be whipping them hard enough. Or else feeding them too much."

"Heh! My slaves have been doin' better work since I made an example of that upstart o' mine," a third said. "Nothin' like a little keel haul to boost morale!"

"Well, if the new bosses want their supplies, they'd better keep at sending us more hands. Do more capturin' and less killin' out there on the front lines."

Danae chewed her lip as she listened to the continued chatter. This cluster of Radromirians must still captain their own vessels. How could they live with the stain of not only allying themselves with Tebal, but manning their ships with slaves that included even their own countrymen? Did she dare try to find a way onto one of these watercraft, even if she could figure out where any of them would make their next port?

The docks slipped under the shadows of dusk, and one by one, the ships' crews finished their work. The Tebalese supervisors bellowed for the crewmen to line up, which they all did with plodding submission. The invaders came forward with long chains, studded with shackles, which they systematically clamped upon the ankles of each of the crewmen. Not a single sailor resisted this measure. Mottled patches of scar tissue wrapped around the ankles of some of the older, crustier slaves, and raw wounds marked the extremities of others. Danae winced for the sore, abused men as the iron bands clamped shut. The crews shuffled off, scraping and clanking along the way, and the ships' captains headed another direction. Their laughs and jibes receded.

If nothing else, the time spent waiting and watching gave Danae the time to concoct a sketchy plan. As the group of captains departed the docks, she stole through the shadows and followed them. The ample cover of towering stacks of pallets, tall pilings, heaps of nets, and other supplies of the mariner's trade offered plenty of places to hide as she tailed the group. The captains were unwary as well, but neither of these factors put Danae at ease as she crept through the shadowed places of the port.

They led her to a nearby building, long and low, built of weathered wooden planks. The group passed through a flimsy door on the end of the structure. Creeping up to one of the side windows, Danae slipped into a tall clump of stiff, prickly marsh grass. A raw bank of fog rolled in from the southwest, but she fought to ignore the chill that soaked into her bones as she huddled there.

Through the dusty glass of the window, Danae discovered the ramshackle building was a bunkhouse, sparse in its accommodations, but dry—and probably warmer than where she sat. The captains drew flagons of ale from a barrel in the corner and toasted one another heartily. Danae learned more than a few colorful phrases that referred to women of few scruples and men of ill repute as she eavesdropped on the captains' conversations, but discovered nothing about any of their destinations, since they left business out of the discussion altogether. One of the captains went so far as to demand another put a leather portfolio he perused away, claiming ale and work had no business overlapping. The reading captain shoved the documents onto a shelf over the nearest bunk.

Drowsiness hung upon Danae. Only her increasing discomfort as the fog dampened her cloak kept her awake through the endless drone of off-color banter, progressively loosened by the captains' refills of their tankards.

Still she waited. The noises of the city began to fade into sleep. Eventually, the men followed suit. When she was satisfied they all slumbered, she made her move.

Not a soul wandered the docks at this hour, besides occasional two-man patrols Danae had determined came through about twice an hour. Once the most recent patrol had receded into the distance, Danae turned her nervous focus to her open journal. "The Finding Words," she had titled the page.

Would the incantation work when she was not sure other captains would carry documents like the portfolio she had seen one of them reading? It was risky, but less risky than ransacking a room full of sleeping men, or grabbing only the known set of papers, only to find they told her nothing of use.

She began to chant, loath to speak aloud, but the words did not seem to work unless uttered. With catlike tread, she minced her way around the building to the door, which bore an iron T latch, left unlocked by the men within. She continued her murmur of the unintelligible words, pulled the door open just wide enough to slip through, and to her relief, the door did not creak on its exposure-rusted hinges. She repeated the chant a third time.

Despite the half-light of a mostly hooded lantern on a table in the center of the bunkhouse, nimbuses of faint green illumination flickered in three separate locations. A satchel beneath one of the beds. A leather portfolio on a shelf above one of the sleepers. Another bag in the very back of the room. As her words concluded, the lights failed. A sensation, something between a cold hand gripping her insides and nausea, slid through her like an eel, but she gritted her teeth against it. It would fade soon enough.

She stole through the dim building. With her heart accelerating with every step, she approached the closest bundle of captain's gear that had glowed, the satchel under the bed. She pulled at it, her muscles bound up tighter than the string of a drawn bow. The canvas of the bag sighed across the wood, quiet by any standards but the thief's. No slumbering captain seemed to hear. She slipped the bag onto one shoulder.

Now for the next target. The shelf or the back of the room? Both had their drawbacks. Danae pursed her lips. Better the quicker escape by staying closer to the door. The shelf it was.

She held her breath as she slipped onward. One step drew her closer to her next target, but not close enough. Two steps, and she could almost reach it. On the third and final step, she settled her weight onto her leading leg, and the floorboard beneath her let out a soft groan: a groan that would never have garnered any notice during waking hours, but now, to Danae's ears sounded like the yawn of a giant. She squeezed her eyes shut, her mouth like dry sand and her face burning as the screams of self-preservation rang in her mind.

The man in the bunk beside her snorted.

Danae froze, but the sleeper did not stir or open his eyes. Heavy drinking did have its benefits, if not to the drinker.

Certain her heart would burst in the meantime, Danae awaited the moment when all the captains again breathed slow and deep, with no shuffling or abrupt snores. Only then did she dare a quick grab at the portfolio on the shelf. She leaned over the slumbering man. Why did he have to be so portly? Her fingers barely reached the shelf if she avoided making contact with his round middle. She clamped her fingers on the folder. Withdrew.

Two out of three would have to be good enough. She backed away from the bunks. Her sensibilities goaded her to run, but she disciplined her twitching muscles and crept backward, a prowl in reverse.

The wet of the seaside night enveloped her again, and Danae welcomed its clammy embrace. Five strides from the captains' bunkhouse, she breathed again. Then ran.

She dashed pell-mell back to the docks, wove through stacks of pallets, and found a niche just big enough between gear and pilings for her to collapse to her knees. She felt woozy. Had she really stolen those men's belongings? The Maker permit that something she took would advance her cause. Still, the prick of guilt was sharp.

She opened the portfolio first, unwinding the string that made a figure eight around hooks to keep it closed. Several parchments threatened to spill from it as it flopped open. She juggled it, then squinted at the documents. Why did the handwriting have to be so illegible? One of the sheets listed the captain, cargo, and origination of a ship named *The Smilodon*. She continued down the page. Fees? Crew, passengers . . . no. Destination! Thelenese ports. Her shoulders sagged. The wrong part of the world.

She put the portfolio aside and grabbed the satchel. *Last chance.* Another trip into the bunkhouse tempted disaster.

She untied the pack and rifled through. It contained no portfolio, but she did find a large scroll tube.

She opened a hinged end cap on the tube. The container itself looked to be made of ivory and bronze, valuable in its own right. Hopefully the parchments within would hold the treasure she sought.

A document very similar to the one she had perused from the portfolio emerged from the stack. It seemed there was an accepted format for cargo manifests, which at least helped Danae to skip to the most pertinent information.

Destination: The port of Myslapten, Velon.

Danae flopped on the ground in relief.

She reassembled the pack. What to do with the captain's belongings? To return them risked worse luck during a second trip into the bunkhouse. To dispose of them seemed callous, and also might put the captains on alert for suspicious activities. As much as her father's frowning disapproval hung over her like a phantom, she counted suspicion the less dangerous of the two options. What a reprobate she was becoming in her desperation!

Danae slipped from behind the pallets and slunk to where the ships were moored, listening to the slap of the water on the bulkheads, but hearing no other sounds in the stillness of the night. The fog had grown so thick only the faintest outlines of the long ships loomed nearby, but she fought to pierce the gloom with her gaze. The ship headed for Velon had the name *The Sea Bear*. Which vessel was that?

She deftly worked her way along the slick boards. A carven figurehead graced the prow of each ship, as was the customary style of Radromirian vessels; one bore a fierce dragon; another, a griffin; yet another, a panther, mid pounce. Finally, as Danae came to the second-to-last ship in the row, a snarling bear of monstrous proportions reared from the front of the boat. A series of numbers, scrawled in drippy paint, labeled the hull. Danae pulled the cargo manifest one more time. The number on the ship matched an identification number on the parchment. At least here was one piece of research about which she felt fairly certain.

The remaining facets of the plan inspired minimal confidence.

Danae slunk from behind the barrels, only after a patrol of two Tebalese guardsmen passed and faded from sight, since she could now guess she had a stretch of time to proceed unobserved. She eyed the satchel and the portfolio she toted, now encumbrance without purpose. She stuffed the portfolio in the satchel, added as big a rock as she could fit, and cinched the bag tight. She closed her eyes as she stood on the edge of the bulkhead. *Hurry up!* She chided herself, but her fingers still clenched the leather. *Every moment you dally, the more chances you create to mess this up.* She let go.

The satchel hit the water with a *sploosh.* Danae winced and turned away.

*I*t was darker than she thought it would be inside the cargo hold of the *Sea Bear* at night. *Am I really trying this? It's madness, just like Mama said.* Danae drove the thought from her mind, lest it slay her resolve and end her journey there and then. If no one had seen her climb from the dock to the deck, and she had gotten so far as below deck, how could she turn back now?

The hold spread before her in a geometric sea of crates, with an island of stone-and-ore blocks stacked in its center. It smelled of salt, pitch, and stale sweat, but she could endure that for a scant handful of days. But where could she spend those days without risking discovery? There was something deeply unsettling about a dim, empty ship —the way it groaned against the bulkhead on occasion, the constant sensation of eyes on her back. She gripped her dagger as she slunk closer to the first crate she considered large enough to hold her.

Danae tried the lid, but it did not budge. Nailed shut. She sighed.

A flash of black motion tore a scream from her lips. Danae fumbled with her dagger. She wheeled toward her foe. Her wide-eyed stare locked with a pair of gleaming orbs, and she thrust her weapon in front of her in shaking hands.

"Mrrrrr-ow," mewed the owner of the reflective eyes. A shipboard cat trotted away toward the stairs that led to the deck.

Danae's shoulders sagged in a mix of relief and embarrassment. *I had* really better *hope I'm right that there's nobody up there.* Danae shimmied behind the crate and kept one eye trained around the corner of the container and upon the stairs. After the cat sprang out of sight, no other living creature made itself known. Now, to see how effective a pry bar her stout little dagger made.

After a long bout of poking and prying, Danae finally loosened the lid from a large crate enough to peer inside. Burlap sacks of dark, highland wool filled the container. At least it would be within her strength to unload. She worked the lid the rest of the way off the crate and pulled the first sack out. For each sack she removed, she found a different spot in the hold to stuff it between shipping boxes that were less-tightly packed against one another.

The last bag clunked against the edge of the crate as Danae pulled it free. She squinted at it. A quick probing of the sack produced a battered steel box about as wide as her chest. The contents rustled when she shook it.

Part of her mind cried she had no time to sacrifice to curiosity, but the inquisitive side of her nature squashed that thought. Danae lifted the hinged lid.

Inside, though the dimness of the hold made the contents hard to discern at first, Danae found dried husks of some sort of plant stalks with wrinkled bulbs at one end. She pinched one in ginger fingers and lifted it. A chattering of tiny grains rattled from a split in the bulb.

Danae gawked. Opium poppies? The box contained at least a couple dozen pods. If handled deftly, the contents of the box were worth . . .

She dismissed the thought. After dropping the stalk back inside the box and clapping the lid shut, she stuffed it back in the bag of wool. No matter what the pods' value, it would be wrong to even consider seeking a buyer for such a thing. She took greater care in hiding the drug-smuggling sack in another nearby crate.

Danae returned to the box she had emptied. After a final glance around the hold, she climbed into her newly-emptied traveling accommodations.

The crate had looked bigger from the outside.

If the hold had been dark, the interior of the crate was blind. Could she really endure days of sailing, not able to stand up unless she risked discovery, and only able to see if she dared light her small lantern? She had guided the lid back into place after she climbed in, slipping its nails back into the holes they had made in the crate frame when the sailors had hammered them in before. That would do for now. Now that the rush of fear and stealth had drained beyond the dregs, her muscles went flaccid. She curled up on the floor of her new quarters. Soon enough, she would no longer be alone, and that would offer trials all its own.

*D*anae's eyes flew open. Was it morning? Or had she dozed for just a moment? And had something fallen on her? Because the crown of her head hurt. *Thunk.* No, she had hit her head —twice at least. Her hiding place pitched and yawed, and beyond her enclosure, water roared and hissed. Perspiration beaded on her brow. Saliva pooled in her mouth as nausea clawed at her tongue.

Thudding footfalls and the clanking chains echoed somewhere above. The cries of harsh voices, bellowing curses and slurs in Tebalese, and a whip's crack also reached her ears, a discordant chorus of oppression. How glad she would be to leave it all behind! No turning back now; in the hands of unwitting slavers, she snuck her way out to an unseen sea.

15

*D*anae's sluggish muscles refused to respond. Only the sounds of her thudding heartbeat and her gulping breaths throbbed in air oddly stagnant for the outdoors. She reached. She tried to lift her feet, but they dragged along as though mired in thick mud.

Drex threw his head back in raucous laughter, his grimace revealing exaggerated points on his eyeteeth. He twisted the knife blade that found half a sheath in her father's chest. The contorted agony that ravaged Papa's features haunted her, and yet, she could still do nothing to intervene.

Black mist swirled from the wound, rather than blood.

This isn't real. That's not what happened. He bled. I know he did.

The mist stretched into knotty, charcoal vines, coiling around her Papa's wrists and ankles like shackles. Drex gave the knife another twist. The vines burst into bilious, green light.

Drex placed his foot on the chest of his kneeling victim, yanked his knife free, and kicked Papa to the cobblestones of the street. The vines exploded into dusty fragments and dissipated.

Danae's muscles were loosed. She sprang to her father's side, rolling him *off his face. She sobbed. She clutched at his shoulders and searched his ashen face for signs of his fate.*

Drex stretched tall over Danae and wiped the knife, dripping tarry ichor, on his sleeve. In a drowsy voice he said, "My, how many grains of sand have fallen through the glass. What a great many."

A thousand violent impulses born of hatred swarmed through Danae's body.

"Save me," Papa rasped. He grabbed her upper arm.

When Danae looked down, she saw no hand of warm flesh, but instead, a skeletal grip with skin breaking in dry fissures to reveal knuckles and bones.

*D*anae's eyes sprang open. The darkness all around her somehow seemed less dark. An occasional warm slit of light between slats brightened her surroundings so she could discern at least the faint outlines of the planks and cross bracing of her new home. Could her eyes be compensating for the lack of light?

Thankfully, the ship outside no longer rose and fell with such stomach-twisting variance. The distant sounds of oars splashing rhythmically, the steady beat of a drum, and the groan of the oars' wooden shafts in the oarlocks confirmed the ship still traveled onward, rather than having made port. Just as she settled into the calming monotony of the rowing, the slash of a whip cut through her peace. The taskmaster's bellow and the slave's sharp cry warned her of the peril so nearby in the waking world.

As Danae straightened her stiff back and rubbed the sleep from her eyes, her queasiness returned. Yet hunger also rumbled along with it.

Emptying her satchel, she searched its contents, mostly by feel. She gathered only enough dried meat and waybread to fill her hand. Could this be all that remained of the food she and her father had carried from home?

No. She had given all her food away in sympathy for urchins! Then she lacked the sense to replace it in port. *Idiot.* How would she manage months of travel if she could not even remember to stock her provisions?

She ate half of what she found and stowed the last few bites for later, although her upset stomach kept it clear it was far from satisfied.

The next few hours added nausea and muscle cramps to Danae's complaints, followed soon after by the nagging of an over-full bladder. Dubious as it might be, she would have to slip out of the crate for at least a moment.

She took a deep breath and inched the container's lid open. An immediate wash of tingles swept over her. She shot a startled glance around the hold.

The herd of wooden boxes looked no different than when she had snuck aboard. Rank upon rank of them receded into blinding shadow. But how could she see any of them at all? Was there a window somewhere off to the side? She leaned her head out a little farther.

An oil lamp hung from an iron hook in the overhead beam to her right and cast a wide pool of illumination into the cargo hold. What she saw beneath the lantern caused her to suck a sharp breath. A figure, deeply hooded, sat near the wall. The single light source carved his chin, lips and nose in harsh shadows. A long, clean-hafted staff leaned against the wall behind him.

Danae gaped. Though she only had a chin and a staff for evidence, no doubt lingered in her mind who sat in the shifting light. Greycloak. Again.

Why did I have to open the lid? Now there's nothing for it. He sees me, that's for sure! She gripped the lid in tight fingers. Is he smiling? Danae's astonishment robbed her of any word of greeting or excuse. The longer she looked upon the figure, the more intense the prickle in her flesh grew, like a swarm of needle-footed ants infesting her clothes. She shuddered and rubbed at her shoulders.

The man closed an oilskin case of parchments and tucked them somewhere behind him. "I was beginning to wonder when you would emerge." His voice was musical and low, and it flooded over

Danae, soothing as a hot bath. Its calming waves washed away the nigh-unbearable charge in her skin that tormented her.

"Why are you following me?" Danae whispered. She climbed from her hiding spot, but clutched the side of her crate to compensate for legs wobbly from long confinement.

"Following you?" Greycloak sat up. "Whatever gives you that impression?"

Danae folded her arms, but when the floor shifted beneath her, she shot out a steadying hand to the frame of the crate once again. "Come now. You want me to call the fact that you keep cropping up at the strangest moments of my life a coincidence?"

"I am no believer in happenstance."

"So you admit it. You *are* following me."

Greycloak chuckled. "I made no such admission. Beware leaps of logic, my dear. They tend to make for twisted paths."

"Then why are you here?"

"There are only so many ways out of Radromir in these dark times," Greycloak said.

Impossible man. Was there any question she could ask for which he would offer a direct answer? "You speak my tongue, but you don't sound like a Radromirian." Would the deep cowl reveal even a glimmer of expression? She probed the shadow with her gaze.

"Yes, I have found it is most useful to speak the languages of both your friends and your enemies."

Danae cocked her head. "Is that so? Well then, of the men on deck, which are your friends?"

The man chuckled. "You ask pointed questions of someone about whom you know nothing, young one. Why should I be so glib as you demand?"

"Because," Danae said, "if you have nothing to hide, then you could be confident in the truth of who you are, and the power of justice to protect you."

The hooded figure leaned back against the wall and laced his fingers across his abdomen. "Well, my pert friend, I am not the one traveling as cargo. Would it be wise for me to speak plainly to anyone who I can see practices at least a little deception? And your naiveté regarding the strength of what is right is becoming, but time will teach you we do not always see the triumph of righteousness in our lifetimes."

Whispers of doubt hissed in the recesses of Danae's mind, amplified by Greycloak's obliqueness and nonplussed demeanor. Her stomach protested again. "You won't tell them I'm on board, will you?"

Danae shrank as she searched for phantom eyes that now seemed to rest upon her. Just as her blood was beginning to race through her veins again, an unseen force tenderly turned her attention back to the present, pushing aside her panic.

"Do not despair." The man's voice had the smooth tone of stringed instruments, played with the long stroke of the bow. "I see no reason to expose your efforts. But you must be more careful. This voyage has yet another two days before it sees port, and rashness or impatience will betray you."

"Two days . . . and then this ship makes port in Myslapten?"

The stranger's teeth flashed in the shadows. "After a fashion, yes."

Danae narrowed her eyes. "Maybe I haven't botched that part of my journey, at least." She surveyed her cluttered surroundings. "Say, do you know if there's any food down here? I'm pretty much out, and two days will get awfully long if I don't come up with something."

The stranger looked toward the end of the deck. "I do not believe there is much. Most of the reasonably fresh food is in the galley. You could try your luck with the crates over there."

"Thanks," Danae said.

"You did not come overly prepared on this journey of yours, I daresay."

She cast a sheepish look at the enigmatic man. "I'm learning as I go."

"You will pardon me for mentioning it, but there is also a chamber pot against the wall, unless you would like to try your luck with the privy on deck."

A flush burned across Danae's cheeks. "Ahem. Uh, no. I think that will have to do."

Danae's stomach rumbled as she weaved her way over to the crates he indicated, though she barked her shins on no small number of corners as the light failed to illuminate the entire distance. She added bruises to the collection as she backtracked to retrieve her own lantern.

Never before would she have been so delighted to discover boxes of hardtack, limes, and barrels of wine. She filled her empty water skin. Making a pouch out of the front of her tunic, she shoveled a modest number of biscuits into this pocket, and then added a couple of the limes. On her way back to the little swatch of territory she had claimed, her foot bumped a small, heavy box that clinked. Danae winced. Who knew what they could hear above deck? Indeed, had anyone overheard her low discourse with the man? She glanced down at the latest noisemaker—just a box of nails. Her mind flitted two days ahead, when the sailors would unload the cargo hold. She scooped a handful of the nails and hustled to concealment.

Danae yanked the stopper from her waterskin and took a sip of the wine. It burned her throat and made her eyes water. At least it was probably free of the threats to her digestion that might have lurked in plain water. She broke off a chunk of one of the hard tack biscuits, which exploded into a powder when she chewed. Its flavor was slightly less palatable than sawdust. She choked it down, grimaced, and washed the remainder down with another small sip of the wine. In comparison, the segment of lime she ate next proved a delicacy.

Much to her surprise, with food to concentrate on, her belly relented in its persistent turning. She spent a stingy ration of lamp oil on a short study of an incantation in her journal.

Weightlessness. Danae sighed. *This has been a pointless set of words in other circumstances, but maybe, just maybe I can make it useful.*

$\mathcal{T}$he hours crept at an agonizing, unmeasurable pace, shifting only slightly from very dark to complete blackness. Danae found whenever her stomach grew too empty, her nausea reared its head again, so she nibbled a steady supply of her odd assortment of food. As the sea grew rougher, and the ship once again battled the waves, no tactic had the power to overcome her misery. Danae curled into a ball on the floor of her little quarters, feeling more horrendously ill than she could ever remember. She concentrated solely on resisting the temptation to moan in her agony, squeezing her eyes shut and hoping for the swells to relent. They rarely did.

$\mathcal{A}$ flurry of activity rumbled overhead, as footfalls clomped over the entire surface of the deck. Straining her ears for the meaning of the thumping and jostling, Danae also picked out the shrill call of sea birds.

Landfall, maybe?

She heard a voice cry, "Drop the anchor!"

She rustled through her pack for her bundle of nails. How long did it take to anchor a ship? In a scrunched contortion, Danae fought to drive a scavenged nail into the frame of the crate, and hopefully into the lid as well. Her dagger proved a distressingly poor hammer. Perhaps if she had spent some time hunting on the dock for bigger spikes . . . no, it likely would not have made a difference. With no resistance on the outside of the crate lid, her collection of nails did not bite very deep. Indeed, she could not even tell if they made it through one piece of wood to the next.

She had only partially secured two nails when a ruckus of activity clattered into the cargo hold, and the quiet Danae had endured for the past few days erupted into the scrape of crates shifting and the jingle of chains. The moment had come for her to enact the final facet of maintaining her ruse.

A surge of fear raged like wildfire through Danae's flesh, forcing every fine hair on her arms on end. *Heaven and earth, I'm drawing a blank! Why can't I remember it?* Even if she had time to fumble for her journal and locate the incantation she thought she had committed to memory, she would not be able to read it without a lit lantern. She grabbed the hair at the crown of her head and dug in with desperate fingers. *D'perineneth? No, that had something to do with . . . no matter, it wasn't the right word.* Of all the times to have studied too little!

The ruckus of scraping crates, tramping feet, and chains trundled closer. The floor vibrated beneath her, punctuated with deeper shocks when items dropped or banged against one another. She wriggled into the shoulder straps of her pack and tried to concentrate.

Ne Dillesceina u. . . . no, that definitely wasn't it. It had been short. A compound word, not a phrase.

"Keep it moving, you maggots!" a Tebalese voice snapped from a distance. "Don't waste a single grain of time."

Danae's ransacking of her memory deteriorated into morbid fantasies of what horrors befell stowaways. Would they kill her? That was probably wishful thinking. She clutched her dagger. Could she hide it somewhere, like in a boot? That was the tactic of all desperate heroes in adventure stories, right? Which made the idea seem all the more foolish. Should she just come out swinging the moment anyone pried open her lid? Surely at least some of them would be armed. What about other incantations—ones she could actually remember? She shuffled to a crouch. It seemed a more ready pose than curled up on the floor of the crate.

The floor tilted. Danae fell forward. Her splayed hands slapped on the side of the crate, and in a moment that stretched time, her horror multiplied. Her confines tipped farther.

"What the—" someone blurted.

The crate fell on its side, its lid breaking loose and smacking on the floor with a loud whack.

"Daggen, you dungheap! What's going on over there?" The Tebalese voice again.

"I dunno, sir," a man replied. "This one's not packed full."

A disgusted huff burst in the distance. "Well, look into it! Whichever of you louts put your grimy mits on any of this cargo is gonna wear stripes for it."

A pair of hairy feet in crumbling sandals appeared at the open end of the crate. Despite screams in her head to run, Danae's muscles froze. The approaching man bent down and peered into the crate. His eyes widened, and after a stunned moment, his brows knit. "Oh no," he breathed.

Tromping neared, and a pair of polished black boots joined the sandaled feet. "Well, what's the problem? The six plagues inside?" Preceded by a thick-fingered gray hand, the scarred face of an invading taskmaster lowered into Danae's field of vision.

She scrambled back, but the taskmaster caught her ankle and towed her from the crate. Her tunic bunched against the wood, and a spray of splinters lodged in her side. Her cry of pain was unrestrained.

Once he had yanked her into the relative light, the invader grasped Danae by the hood of her cloak and dragged her to her feet. He cackled. "Is this what you were afraid of, you shucked oyster?"

Danae's glance flitted over her captor's garb. The taskmaster had a cat of nine tails on his belt, in addition to a brace of especially large knives on the opposite side. His forearms and face bore enough knotty scars that Danae decided against reaching for her own weapon.

"Lose your way to market?" he asked.

That dark leer in his eyes, was it an inborn trait in Tebalese? Except Shamir. Danae shook the thought away, and searched the faces of the growing crowd around her. The shuffle of unloading had ground to a halt sometime during her discovery. Some of the slaves in the hold looked vaguely sick or worried as they watched. Many had a lean look that made her shrink. A low whistle blew from someone's lips.

"Topside with you!" the Tebalese man thrust her toward the hatch leading out of the hold. "The rest of you . . . get this load to shore. Double quick."

Danae stumbled toward the stairs that led up through the hatch and looked up just in time to see another figure coming down. Someone in a long, gray cloak, hood drawn, a staff in hand. The taskmaster shoved her from behind again, throwing her into a lurch toward the steps. She shot a glare back at him. "I'm going, you—" She bit off the word that came to mind. No use making the situation worse.

"You, Grandsire! Outta the way," Danae's aggressor hollered.

The shrouded man lingered on the stairs, but turned sideways to let Danae pass. She worked her way up the steep incline, breathing deep at the sting in her splinter-riddled side. As she reached the same step as Greycloak, he whispered in a low, gravelly voice, "Can you swim?"

Danae started. "What? Yes. But—"

The Tebalese man thumped her on the back of the head. "Shut it. Keep moving."

Danae emerged into the full light of a bright morning, blinking at the glare of sunlight from white sails. Men scuttled up and down rigging to furl them. The crash of breakers throbbed not too far in the distance, and over a stretch of crystalline sea, towering white bluffs soared above a small cove. Sea birds screeched and battled in the sky. A scow rowed toward the rightmost shore, where a few crates already sat on the sand. No other watercraft floated in sight.

How many of those scows were there? Could she row one by herself? Idiocy. As if she had any idea how to row a boat.

"Captain!" the taskmaster bellowed. He shoved Danae forward until she stumbled against a short flight of stairs.

On a raised section of the foredeck, a tall, broad man in a knee-length blue coat and high boots turned. He lowered a long spyglass he had been staring through in the direction the scow was headed. His squint furrowed his brow as his dark eyes roved the deck for the source of the salutation.

The taskmaster grabbed Danae's collar again and shook her, like a bird dog presenting a drake. "Captain, here. Your attention, if you please." The last words came from the Tebalese man's lips in a grudging tone. They may have conquered Radromir, but a different order apparently still reigned on Radromirian ships.

The captain's sun-bleached eyebrows shot up. He ran a hand through the thinning, brassy hair on the top of his head to pull the long windblown strands out of his face. He approached. Other sailors on the deck lost focus on their tasks as Danae drew their attention. Men elbowed one another. A few pointed.

"Looks like the whip-man's lucky day," one feral-glanced sailor called. Few of the men topside harbored any sympathy for her plight, if the gleam in their eyes and the curl of their smirks were reliable evidence.

The captain's icy glare lanced into his men. "Back to work, you curs."

The attention pressing into Danae from all sides diffused. Surprisingly, the captain's focus fixed upon the taskmaster next. "I don't have time for this, Kedek. Bluebacks could sail around that bluff at any moment."

"I believe she's a stowaway, sir," Kedek replied.

"Well, if it's a ride she wants, then I'll be glad to oblige her—after we've gotten the crates off. The lads who are done with the sails can do her bonds and weights now."

"Aye, sir," the taskmaster replied. He hauled Danae to the port side of the entry to the hold.

"What a waste," Danae heard one of the sailors mutter.

Bonds and weights? That can't be good.

"Up. Away." Voices called from below deck. A pallet of crates swung out of the hold, hefted by a crane midship and then lowered over the gunwales.

"Mutt, Coles!" the taskmaster hollered. "Get the ropes and the sinkers for this fool. She goes overboard as soon as we've put out again."

16

THE CHASE

*D*anae's head spun. "Overboard?"

The Tebalese taskmaster glared. "Consider it mercy."

Two men clambered down the main mast and ran for a trunk at the stern. The crane swung back from its journey overboard, empty ropes and chains dangling from the apparatus. It lowered into the hold again. How long would it take the slaves to load another crate? How would that compare to how quick Mutt and Coles were with the ropes and "sinkers?"

Danae's heart thundered. If only she had been able to study more of her father's books. Had more incantations memorized. She ran a finger under her collar, where the fabric was rubbing her skin raw from how tight as the taskmaster pulled it.

Sailors continued their work, but slowed when they passed and cast her nauseating grins. Their words to one another did not reach her ears, but their looks of disdain or sick humor were enough to set her trembling. The dark opening of the cargo hold continually drew her eye.

The gray-cloaked man emerged slowly from the depths of the ship. *Can you swim?* Was his earlier comment some sort of black-hearted reference to the fate he knew awaited her? She glared at him, but he merely tightened his pack and shuffled a few paces toward the bow without so much as a glance her way.

Ironic. She sunk the captain's manifest days ago, and now she would learn what it felt like to meet the ocean floor. Would her weightless incantation have any power over such a situation? That is, if she could manage to remember it.

Clunking and irregular footfalls thundered from the aft part of the ship. The two sailors lugged four large iron weights. *Certainly more than was really necessary for the job,* Danae thought grimly.

"Up. Away." The shout came again. Mutt and Coles parted the rearmost sailors in Danae's dallying press of hellish admirers. A partial break would have to be enough.

Danae sprang, ripping her collar from the taskmaster's unsuspecting grasp. She barreled and twisted through a scattering of men. Leapt. Reached for the pallet swinging just overhead.

She caught hold of the pallet with desperate fingers, but the whole load shifted and jerked. The corner she had weighed down bashed into the gunwale. Crates slid.

Danae let go, and once her feet hit the deck, she dove forward. Crates slid off the pallet and crashed behind her. Voices erupted from all directions.

"Grab her!"

"Can you believe . . . ?"

Cheers, gasps, and indignant shouts all collided in a chorus of disorder. Danae rolled to her feet and dashed for the rail. One of the sailors lunged, but she twisted away before he could catch hold of her. A game of two-dozen cats after one mouse was not bound to last long, though. She clawed up one of the fallen cargo containers that leaned against the scarred gunwale. Her fumbling grasp caught hold of her dagger, whipped it from its sheath, and she extended it in front of her in a grip galvanized by panic. The sailors nearest to her paused. One paled, the others smirked and chuckled. Now what? Her one idea of escape had been little more than a bungled delay of the sailors' plans. Her glance alighted on Greycloak once more. He stared directly at her from mid-deck, too far to help or hinder.

He thrust a hand forward, palm out. Danae felt an impact in the middle of her chest.

She stumbled backward. The brass rail of the gunwale caught Danae behind the knees, and over the side she plummeted. The seafoam rushed up to greet her.

~

*D*anae hauled herself onto tawny sand, cold and wet, and her trembling arms collapsed. The beach had not looked nearly so far when she first spied it from the deck of the *Sea Bear*. Another breaker crashed behind her, and its foamy reach splashed around her. The hundredth face full of water she had taken in the last few minutes slapped across her cheeks, and she sputtered. The desire simply to lie there in the shallows beckoned, but she had to know if she was safe. She rolled over, propped on her elbows and stared back at the ship. More crates lowered into a waiting scow. Slaves dragged the second boat onto the sand, at least a half-mile down the beach from her, where they would unload their crates. Nobody seemed interested in pursuit. *Thank the Maker.* She flopped down again.

The water was bitter cold as it splashed over her. Her immediate danger removed, hypothermia risked taking its place if she did not get out of the constant dousing of the sea. She hauled herself to her feet. Miraculously, she still had her pack. Her grip on her dagger, however, had apparently failed somewhere between gunwale and shore.

Why had she fallen overboard? The question nagged. Of one thing she was certain: she had not lost her balance of her own accord. The gray clad man's words and actions seemed suspect, to say the least. She mulled it while she wrung out her sodden cloak and dumped the last seawater from her satchel.

Her poor journal. Danae frowned at where it had landed with a splat on the sand. She would have to take extra pains to dry out her journal as soon as she found a civilized spot to do so.

The wind gusted along the empty beach, and Danae's teeth chattered. Where was the port? *The Sea Bear* had not moored in the traditional way, but instead, anchored off shore in this relatively secluded cove and unloaded here. *None of this makes any sense. Just what I need, more questions.* She shouldered her pack and hunted for a way off the beach.

The bluffs, comprised mostly of crumbling white sandstone, offered no simple way up from where she stood. She picked along the beach, heading closer to where the scows landed with their crates, though there was no chance she would willingly draw within bowshot of those villains again. If no way up the bluff grew apparent before then, she would backtrack and seek another way farther up the beach.

About a quarter of the way to the scow landing, Danae found a series of switchbacks that climbed the cliff face, no wider than a foot path, but serviceable. They slowly meandered along the beach, climbing with every step, and when she finally reached the summit, she stood perhaps a hundred yards from where the ox carts that struggled up from the scow landing achieved the same height. Their climb involved a steeper, wider, gravel road.

Danae pulled her hood close.

When she reached the top of the increasingly blustery heights, she discovered a disheveled collection of sandstone and plank buildings, where shady merchants peddled all manner of goods. *I assumed Myslapten would be a little nicer than this.* She glanced about the grime and squalor. It may have once been a cozy community, but any such time had faded into decay. At least she had arrived there during the full light of day. Dare she browse here in search of dry clothing?

A block down the sandy street, a cloaked man, stooped and leaning on a tall staff, made his way through the seedy market. Greycloak.

You again. It's time to make some sense of your puzzles. Clothes can wait.

She pressed closer to the cloaked stranger, keeping either crowds or merchant booths between them. Once she had closed the gap between them to less than ten yards, a tingle arose across her body—prickly as though all her skin was going numb at once but was somehow over-sensitive at the same time. If for no other reason than that, he begged pursuit. How might the Underground, the librarian, and this man share any connection?

Someone snared her wrist and slapped a glass vial into her hand.

"Love potion for you, missy?" a middle-aged woman caked in layers of white powder assaulted Danae with an ochre smile.

The vial in Danae's hand warmed uncomfortably and stung her hand as though its surface was not glass, but hundreds of minute thorns. She plucked the offending item from her palm with as little of her fingertips she could employ without dropping it.

"Only six silver to win the man of your dreams," the woman pressed. She lowered her chin and winked a black-lined eye. "No matter whom he thinks he fancies now."

"No . . . thanks." Danae held the potion out with a grimace and craned past the seller. The old man was slipping away.

"It's a bargain, miss. And guaranteed magical."

Danae shoved the vial into the woman's hand. "No doubt. But I have to go." With a spring, she slipped around the potion peddler and wormed her way through the throng to regain some ground on her target.

She avoided every glance. Her quarry commanded a singular focus if she was to keep him in sight as he wound through the crooked streets, which meandered more drunkenly than their debauched inhabitants. The staff-bearing man led her for a half mile along the bluffs, then on a downhill road into a cleft between them, to a shoreline that fit Danae's assumption of what a port city should look like—far better than the slum behind her.

A still bay jutted into the mainland between these two imposing arms of white, crumbling rock. Docks stuck out like porcupine quills all along the edge of the sparkling water, and on these quays bobbed all manner of watercraft, from small passenger vessels to towering tall ships. A forest of masts lined the shore, with a tangle of nets, ropes and other props of the seaman's trade massing like undergrowth along the waterfront. The majesty of the ships breezing into port on billowing sails stole Danae's breath.

Commerce choked the avenue Greycloak now followed. Danae dodged a two-wheeled donkey cart as the young boy who tugged on the creature's bridle shuttled foodstuffs and sundries through the street. She stretched to see around the huddles of well-dressed gentlemen who pored over cargo manifests and maps and sometimes got into heated debates. She quickened her step, loath to let their blustering sunder her tenuous view of the man she chased. The general bustle of gathering and delivering, loading and unloading threatened to frustrate her pursuit even as it had just begun.

Danae's leader skirted around the semicircular edge of the bay, and as she followed, a dreamlike sound drifted to her ears. At first, it lingered on the edge of her consciousness, mingled with the gulls' calls and the sea's distant thrum, but the louder the sound grew, the more she realized it was a sort of music. Haunting, and at once both familiar and alien. The music spoke of things too lofty for her ordinary soul, but lured her to sink into its flood and be lost. Though she could not pick out a tune, the lilt of the song embodied the ebb and flow of the tides themselves. Danae longed to stop and drown in the unearthly sound.

Such immersive appreciation would have to wait. Her quarry halted at the end of a gated dock. No crowd bustled there, but rather, a reverent halo of inactivity enrobed the area. She dared not press any closer to the gate, but instead hovered on the edge of a crowd that surrounded a clammer's wheelbarrow.

The gray-robed man spoke at length with another figure who had stepped from behind the gate. The newcomer was a tall, lean person, hooded in an ankle-length blue cape edged with elaborate silver scrollwork. The wind whipped both of their clothing like banners.

A sea bird grazed Danae's hood. She cringed and threw her hands over her head, but the bird passed by to snatch a clam that had thumped to the ground from the clammer's wheelbarrow. Danae glanced back and forth between the merchant and Greycloak.

"Sir, why is there a gate across that pier?" she asked.

The merchant, a stout man with deep creases crisscrossing his weathered face, chuckled. "Don't ye know, lass? Though by yer talk, I 'spect perhaps not. 'Tis the Delsin's dock, and they'll not abide any but their own upon it."

Danae furrowed her brow.

"Delsin?"

Again, the man laughed as he handed a sack of clams to a customer and collected the silver coins in exchange. "The Elves, missy. Don'cha know the sight of an elf ship when ye see it? None so full o' grace in amongst our boats."

Danae squinted down the dock, the dazzling glint of the westering sun making it difficult for her to discern the vessel that lay at its end. Shielding her light eyes with her hand, she spied the slender gray ship moored there. Even knowing nothing about boats and shipping, she guessed this vessel would be matchless in its speed and maneuverability. Was it the way the ship's prow tapered to a knife-like edge, keen enough to cut through even the highest seas, or maybe how the sleek lines of her hull seemed shaped by the very wind itself? With a start, Danae realized it was from this vessel that the enchanting music came. She poured herself into listening, though she could make no sense of the words that floated along. Voices interwove in blissful harmonies, chords that swelled, sweet and sublime, and Danae's heart ached to know of what they sang.

She shook herself back to reality. "Elves? Sir, you mock me. Elves are the stuff of fairy tales and bedtime stories, not sailors at the docks of the real world."

The clammer looked at Danae, a bemused grin sparkling in his dark eyes. "Ye must be quite the outlander then, me dearie. Elves are as real as these clams in me bag. Heh!" he said. "T' think there's folks in this world who ne'er heard 'em true."

Danae assembled a retort, but then abandoned the thought. The two figures who had been conversing at the gate were gone. Eyes darting to and fro, she discovered the lean figure in the scrolled cloak strode down the dock toward the ship, but he was alone. Where was Greycloak? "Foolish distractions. How could I have lost him so quickly?"

The clammer turned a quizzical glance her way, but Danae waved him off.

She searched the jostling crowd, and after a few tense moments, she caught a glimpse of gray cloak. When she also spied the walking stick in the figure's hand, she blew a sigh of relief. She dashed off to close the distance between herself and her nearly lost subject.

Danae tailed the man through countless streets and byways, as he led her into the heart of Myslapten. The sun sank lower in the sky. The buildings here leaned over the streets, casting the pavement into continual shadow, their wattle and daub walls pale like the skin of a recluse who has long forgotten the warmth of sunlight. The salt tang of the wharfs dwindled to be replaced by the homey scent of wood smoke and roasting meat. The voices of the gulls gave way to the murmur of countless families gathering for their end-of-day rituals.

The stranger took one turn after another, the hollow clack of his staff echoing off the walls of the increasingly close byways. Would the pursuit wind on endlessly? The deeper into the city she chased him, the more the streets felt like tunnels filled with the chill of dusk. The next alley he entered twisted so often that Danae lost sight of him every dozen yards.

I'm going to have to find a better vantage point if I don't want to lose him in this maze.

A nearby stack of barrels offered her just the boost she needed to begin a two-story climb to the rooftops, while crossbeams, niches in the uneven walls, and dormers aided her ascent. By clambering along the interconnected rooftops, she could still chase Greycloak, whose pace slackened. She minced her way along, careful not to slip on the steep pitch of the rooftops. Just as she closed the gap between them, the old man turned into another street.

Great. If I can't cross after him, this little game is over.

A few paces away, a narrow beam of wood stretched across the causeway, bracing the sagging walls on either side of the street and suspending a glass-paneled lantern from a rusted chain. Did she dare try to slink her way across this two-story-high, four-inch-wide bridge? She eased down the slope of the shingled roof, placing one foot on the beam, then the next. Drawing a deep breath and holding her arms to her sides, she took a few careful steps. She wobbled, but with a swift circle of her arms, her balance steadied. She stepped again, and the beam beneath her feet let out a sharp *crack* as it shifted beneath her weight.

The man she had pursued this far wheeled around, thrust an open hand out before him, and looked up at Danae's vulnerable position. His voice rang out, speaking an incomprehensible cluster of words, and an invisible shove assaulted her shoulder.

She plummeted headfirst. Again.

17

*D*isaster impending, Danae blurted a string of ancient words, whose meaning she scarcely understood, but had pieced together in secret hours of study of her father's cryptic writings. This phrase she had employed enough to offer little risk of forgetfulness.

"*Arineth da'et plumie!*"

Her two-story plummet slowed, and instead of crashing headlong to the ground, she drifted to the pavement, righting herself and landing on her feet, unharmed.

The cloaked figure stiffened and faced Danae. His gaze penetrated her very flesh and bone, reawakening the charged sensation his presence ran through her flesh. Her muscles tensed as she prepared to spring into a full run.

"You!" Greycloak called. "Come forth and tell me who you serve, if you value your life!"

What did he mean? How should she answer? His displeased attention was enough to shoot shivers through her arms and legs.

"I . . . I don't understand. I serve no man. My mission is my own."

Greycloak advanced with ponderous steps, jabbing a stern finger toward Danae. "Don't mince words with me, girl. I have shown you perhaps more mercy than you deserve, and if you are not soon forthright with your affiliations, you will find my patience and leniency have their limits. Now tell me by whose authority you spoke that incantation."

The gravity of the situation slammed into Danae harder than the frigid waves that had thrown her to shore earlier. Her muscles locked and her mouth went dry. The wrong answer at this moment boded tragic consequences.

"Truly, sir," she begged at his continued approach.

Beneath his hood, a pair of eyes glowed with white-hot light.

"I really don't know what you mean. The incantation . . . I picked it up as a child . . . sounded it out from a book of my father's. I don't serve anyone with it, or use it at anyone's command but my own." She glanced over her shoulder. The road was clear enough for a sprint.

The flaring light faded from Greycloak's eyes, and he halted a dozen paces from Danae. Half to himself, he said, "A dabbler then. Well, there is much you had better learn, young one, for you have your hand in the treasure purse of your betters."

Danae flinched as the man raised his arms, though he only lifted his hood and let it fall behind him. As she suspected from his gait and voice, he bore the heralds of dignified age: a head of graying hair and sharp, noble features surrounded by deep creases. His eyes, now devoid of their previous eerie glow, were slate gray, and Danae's glance fled his piercing attention. He wore a thin gold circlet across his brow. His face was clean-shaven, and he pursed his lips as he studied her with a look of intense appraisal.

After a few moments of squirming discomfort, Danae coiled her muscles to dash off in retreat, but the man spoke again.

"Do not bother to run. You shall not get far before I catch you, and there are further words that must pass between us. Besides, 'if you have nothing to hide, then you could be confident in the power of justice to protect you,' correct?" A wry smile lit up his face.

Danae grimaced. How foolish and haughty the words sounded. "Why should I trust you?"

The furrows in the man's brow relaxed. "Mere words rarely possess the might to win something as worthy as trust, but I am sorry if I have frightened you, young one. You may call me Praesidio."

"All right." Danae folded her arms and glanced at him sidelong to keep her escape route at least in her peripheral view. "What do you want with me, Praesidio?"

"An ironic question. Who is following who?"

"I wouldn't be following you if you hadn't created such a string of mysteries over the past month of my life."

"I may be willing to entertain some of those curiosities." Praesidio frowned at his surroundings. "If you'd be willing to discuss them in more a more civilized place. I might even tell you somewhat of myself, if you are interested in the ramblings of an old man."

Danae gulped. Could she be walking into a trap? Her wariness of the stranger warred with the deep peace that overtook her soul and smoothed away her chills. Both in the hold of the ship and during this back alley confrontation, when terror would have been natural, a foreign sense of calm had filtered into her soul. This alone drove her to entertain the old man's request.

"How is it you know my father?" Danae asked.

Praesidio lowered his eyelids and scratched his cheek. "If that is a piece of information he has chosen not to reveal to you, I don't believe it is my province to say."

Hopefully any further conversation that passed between them would consist of better than a listing of all the information Praesidio had no leave to mention.

"Where do you propose we go for this discussion?" Danae leaned back a fraction.

"There is a respectable inn several blocks from here, where I intended to stay once I had shaken you from my trail." A twinkle kindled in his eye. "Would that suit you?"

Heat swelled in Danae's cheeks. She cursed her alabaster skin that so readily heralded her emotions. Danae suspected the old man had known of her pursuit for far longer than pride in her stealth wanted to admit.

After blowing out a gust of breath, she replied, "Yes. An inn would be suitable. You'll lead the way?"

Praesidio nodded and turned down the side street, and Danae fell into step beside him, her back straight and hands clenched at her sides. They walked for a block in awkward silence, the man's staff still clacking along in the stony street. Tension, curiosity, and the resurgence of the need to get out of wet clothes all clamored for Danae's focus.

The side street opened into a wide boulevard, traveled by many pedestrians of diverse nationalities, and among this population marched a squad of foot soldiers. They each carried bright halberds on their shoulders and wore full suits of chain armor. The image of a gold rampant lion wearing a crown emblazoned their sky-blue tabards. The soldiers passed through the foot traffic, and although people deferred to them, there was no fear or distaste for them in the eyes of those around them.

"The guard of the capital city, Reidot," Praesidio said, a moment before the question had formed on Danae's lips. "The king keeps a large detachment stationed here to be sure this port doesn't fall to the enemy."

The Enemy? We'll see just who that is in this Praesidio's mind.

They walked on for another block, then came to a sprawling stone building. Its street side boasted three stories of glass-paneled windows. A lamplighter lifted his long brass pole to light the wick of the oil lamp above, which cast the entryway of the building in a warm glow. Praesidio approached the polished, oaken double doors of the place and pulled one open for Danae, bowing lightly and gesturing an invitation for her to pass. She ascended the trio of stairs that led to the doorway. Pausing for a moment on the doorstep, she noted the hanging sign that read "The North Star Inn," each letter meticulously carven and inlaid with gold leaf.

She took a step, but then hesitated again on the threshold. Her glance flicked down to her still-soaked clothes.

Praesidio turned a wry smile over his shoulder. "Do not worry. We can see to it you freshen up before dinner."

"Stop doing that," Danae said.

"Doing what?"

Voicing my thoughts, old man. Danae folded her arms and stepped through the door. She swallowed hard.

The entryway led into a towering foyer with a lectern in its center and a curving flight of stairs rising behind it. Panels of rich wood covered the walls. On either side of the foyer, doorways opened into several small dining rooms, where well-dressed clientele spoke in murmurs over meals of roasted poultry, meats, soup, and fish. The scent of these dinners drifted to Danae's cold nose, and her mouth watered for real, hot food. Dwindling travel rations and shipboard scavenging had left her with a new perception of appetite.

Her purse of silver coins felt too light on her belt.

A stately, middle-aged gentleman approached the lectern. He looked past Danae to Praesidio. "Are you expected?" the host asked in a cool tone.

Praesidio frowned. "You must be new here. I am used to being greeted with greater hospitality, at least when Oberon mans this station."

The host lifted his chin and looked at the two travelers with half-lidded eyes. "My apologies, sir."

Danae bit her tongue. If that was an apology, she could not imagine being on the receiving end of an insult.

"The North Star does not see much business from . . . wayfarers." He grimaced as though a foul taste coated his tongue. After a moment, he cleared his throat and continued, "Will it be just the two of you, then?"

Praesidio nodded. "It will. And I prefer one of the booths in the fourth room," he pressed a gold coin into the host's hand, "*if* you please." Praesidio's tone was chilling. "But before we dine, my companion would appreciate a bath drawn, and will require dry garb."

Danae's jaw slackened. Apparently Praesidio was of more significant means than his plain appearance portrayed. But in truth, her wet clothing and chill had become impossible to ignore, so she was of every mind to submit to his offer.

The host eyed the coin briefly before he tucked it into his vest pocket. "If you will give me a few moments, then." He departed through a doorway on the right-hand side of the foyer.

They waited. Just as the silence between Praesidio and Danae had begun to stretch to the point of discomfort, a short, plump maid bustled into the foyer.

"M'Lady," she said, clucking her tongue. "Now I won't be so saucy as to be askin' after how you come to such a state, but you'll be catchin' a death o'cold if we don't get you warmed. You're in luck I've just been at drawing the night's bathwater, so if you'll follow me . . . " She faced Praesidio. "And afterwards, you'll await her in the dining room?"

"That I will, madam." Praesidio performed a genteel bow.

The maid clapped her hands together. "Right then. Miss, you'll just follow me then."

Danae shuffled behind the maid through an empty dining room, past the kitchen, and into a small tiled room where a copper tub stood full of steaming water. The rosy little serving woman trundled up behind Danae and pulled her pack from her shoulders.

"Tsk. What a salty mess you are, if you don't fault a body for sayin' so mistress." She smiled. "If it's a swim you want, wait til summer. Then do it in proper bathing clothes."

A smile crept across Danae's lips, drawn by the woman's spritely air. "I'll try to keep that in mind."

"Now, you just leave those wet things aside, and we'll see about hangin' 'em proper. There's good soap there, and the water's new, lucky lass, so I'd get to it. I'll be back with a bit of a frock for you just as soon as I can turn one up."

"That sounds perfect," Danae replied. "One favor though . . . leave my journal from the pack, if you would."

Never before had Danae delighted so completely in hot water and soap, and once she was clean and warm from head to toe, she dressed in the slightly oversized frock the maid provided, braided her hair, and headed for the dining room to find Praesidio. She clutched her wet journal as she went.

She worked her way through three intimate dining rooms, and they eventually reached what Praesidio had referred to as "the fourth room." This dining area differed from the others in that high-backed booths lined the walls. Thick burgundy curtains flanked each booth, draperies the customers could draw around their table for the sake of privacy. A single pair of merchants sat along the right-hand wall of this room, and their curtains remained fixed open.

Praesidio rose from his seat in the back corner when Danae neared his table. He gestured to the seat across from him. "Feeling better?"

Danae smirked. "A little more civilized in many ways. A little frumpy in a few." She brushed at her skirt.

She perched on the upholstered cushion of the booth, setting her soggy journal down beside her and searching her memory for all the niceties of etiquette her mother had gone to great pains to teach her during her teenage years. How many forks did one person need? Praesidio reclaimed his seat across the table.

A server approached the table. "Master and mistress, today our victuals include roasted pheasant with a burgundy reduction, or boar steak tips, slow braised and served with a parsnip and potato puree. We also have a lovely trout in butter and thyme. Will you be drinking wine? Ale or mead?"

Danae's eyes widened. "Um, do you have anything . . . maybe just some bread? Yesterday's would be fine."

Praesidio smiled. "You needn't worry yourself over the meal, bath, or lodging, my lady, as I am prepared to manage these things," he whispered. "And please, don't feel beholden to me in any way because of it. I'm not in the habit of inviting a guest to the table with the expectation of recompense."

"You don't owe me any favors, Praesidio," Danae said. "I started this journey on my own, so I intend to manage."

Praesidio clucked his tongue. "Would you wittingly offend a gentleman with your desire to feel able?"

Danae's stomae's stomach fluttered. "Certainly, I meant no offense." She groped for further words of excuse, but failed to assemble a complete thought.

Praesidio turned his attention to the server. "The pheasant for both of us, if you would. And a half mead each."

"Very good, sir." The server bobbed his head and proceeded to another table of guests.

"I can understand how perhaps a girl in your position might not feel exactly herself," Praesidio said. "But, in order that we might visit with more civility, I must ask of you one thing."

Danae raised an eyebrow.

"A trifle really. Would you offer me your name?" Praesidio said.

The tense muscles across Danae shoulders loosened. "Oh, that! Of course. It's Danae."

Another man, with round, red cheeks and just a dusting of hair around the back of his head, appeared at the booth side, and filled tall wine goblets with a deep golden liquid. Its fragrance reminded Danae of highland sunshine in the height of summer.

As he set a cup before Praesidio, the server's face lit up with recognition.

"Praesidio!" he beamed. "I've not seen you in many a month! I'm glad you've returned to us. You look well."

Praesidio regarded his own worn garb. "Still a flatterer and a fibber, Rand, but good to see you. My travels have taken me far and wide in these troubled times, but I am as yet unscathed."

The two exchanged a bit more small talk, during which Danae gawked at the plush velvet curtains, the stained glass details in the windows, and the floral carvings in the wall panels around her. Rand hurried off to see to other patrons, and Praesidio returned his attention to Danae.

"It is good to see you managed well enough once outside the city walls," he began.

Danae sat up. "Not without more than my share of excitement.

What about you? Did soldiers finally drive you from the church in Dayleston?"

"I find it better to take my leave before I'm driven."

"So why come all the way here?"

"Surely I don't have to inform you about the hostility in your homeland to those who would express a belief in anything besides Queldurik."

Queldurik. Danae shuddered. "So you and Papa have that much in common. Religious background."

"Indeed." Praesidio sipped his mead, drew the cup away from his lips, and examined the contents.

"Well," Danae stalled. She twisted her napkin in her lap and searched the lined face of her tablemate. Would this man offer any wisdom about the next step of her journey? Conversely, did she risk anything by confiding in Praesidio? One glance into the old man's fathomless eyes gave her the sense he understood truths beyond any question she might think to ask.

"How is it you ended up our guide through the underground?"

"I was in your homeland conducting some research on behalf of my people, and once your father learned that I had uncovered a route out of your city, he seemed more inclined to entertain your suggestion your family make a quiet departure." He leaned forward on his elbows. "Not as quiet as Deklan would have liked, as I understand it?"

Danae examined her lap. "Things got a little out of hand." Praesidio's observation suddenly stuck in her like a barb. She turned a narrow-eyed stare to him. "How do you know about that?"

Praesidio shrugged. "Your father is a man of many gifts. We have our ways of learning things from one another." He leaned back in his chair. "But if you will pardon my saying so, your father seems, how can I put it . . . diminished of late."

An accelerating heart thumped in Danae's ears. "It's his cough. It's worse by the day, really, and we can't find a remedy that makes any difference. Although he won't admit it, I believe he suspects his condition could end in tragedy."

"Then why leave your family behind when someone clearly dear to you may be facing his waning days?"

"Because I'm convinced there's something more I can do." Danae proceeded to explain her father's persistent, growing cough, every remedy they had tried, and every disease they had ruled out along the way. As she unfolded the history, Praesidio sat back and listened, sipping his mead.

Breathless, she paused in her monologue. "But, I apologize. I'm rambling endlessly, and it must be boring you to sleep."

Praesidio laughed. "Not at all. I am quite interested. You know much about your father's trade for a young maiden like yourself. He must be very proud of your studiousness."

The food Praesidio ordered arrived, two entire halves of roasted foul on a platter set between them. A deep red sauce ran over top crisp, browned skin, puddling under the meat for tiny potatoes to steep in. An array of carrots, pearl onions, and some sort of tiny, leafy balls Danae had never seen ringed the platter. Curls of steam rose from the meal, its savory aroma invading Danae's senses and setting her stomach to audible rumbling.

After the server arrayed plates before them, Praesidio bowed his head silently. Danae froze with her utensils in hand. Once he had lifted his head once again and picked up his own knife, Danae dove into her meal with gusto. The pheasant's herbed flavor warmed Danae from lips to toes. Roasted vegetables soothed her cravings.

Praesidio finished chewing his first bite. "You have the look of a girl who has been forced to go on too little for too long. I hope you enjoy the meal."

Danae chewed, her mouth very full of food, while the heat of a flush overtook her cheeks. She swallowed after a longer pause than she feared was polite. "It's the best meal I've ever eaten. You're very kind, Praesidio." She sipped her mead. Also delectable. "Though, to my estimation, you can be dangerous as well."

Praesidio looked up from his plate and studied Danae's face. "That all comes back to whom you serve, young one."

"What does that mean?" Danae asked. "I don't know how to answer."

Praesidio drained his cup and leaned back in the booth. "Your father has taught you nothing?"

A spike of defensive anger lanced into Danae's chest and further sped her heart. "Now that's not fair." She took a deep breath. "He's taught me plenty of herbalism. But no, he's never been willing to discuss his . . . *other* abilities with me."

"What about yours?"

"Mine?" Danae shook her head. "Papa doesn't know I have any such thing. I think he hasn't wanted to see, for some reason."

"Then you do not know by whose authority you spoke those words of incantation, the words that prevented you from crashing to the street?"

"No, I guess I don't." She shifted in her seat.

"Incantations like that are no trifling matter." Praesidio rubbed his forehead. "The power they invoke comes from forces far greater than ourselves, and if you don't learn the truth of this, you will find yourself in much peril."

Danae bit her lip. "What harm could I have possibly done? I memorized words and discovered what they did when I called them. I only know a few sequences, but they've come in handy here and there."

Praesidio shook his head. "You are at a deficit then, Danae. The power to enact such results comes from either Creo or from the Impenetrable Darkness, and I think you will be displeased to learn by whose leave you have used the abilities in the past."

Creo again? Religion must be one of this relic's favorite impolite subjects.

"A deficit? To whom?" Danae shivered.

The clinging sense of soiling, or phantom disapproval that always haunted Danae after she used words from her journal prodded at the back of her mind. *Is the magic evil, then?*

Praesidio sighed. "Listen and hear what I have to say, young one, for you need this teaching more than you know. It is not the magic in and of itself that is evil, but the source from which you choose to draw it that begins the trouble. When the abilities come from Creo, we call them 'Virtusen', and the words to enact them we refer to as 'Utterances.' The process of incantation in which you have been embroiled comes from, well . . . elsewhere. We call those 'curses.'"

Danae peered sidelong at the old man. Surely she had never intended to work anything anyone else might call a curse. While tempted to protest, she held her tongue and continued to listen.

"What you have been doing, utilizing incantations you do not understand, is what many do." Praesidio said. "And to their chagrin, one day discover they owe payment to the grantor of power. For such people, ignorance is their only mistake, but that does not lower its cost."

Danae leaned forward in her seat, as if too much distance between herself and the old man might dilute her understanding of his words.

Praesidio lifted his cup, frowned at it, and placed it back on the table. "Now Creo, he does not grant powers to any but those who have sworn their lives in service to him, and he enables his servants the blessing of Thaumaturgy so they may do good in his name. Have you, Danae, done such a thing as to swear fealty to Creo?"

Danae's response came haltingly. "Well . . . we've always acknowledged the Creator in our home. I believe there's, well, a divine force behind the universe, if that's what you mean."

"No. That is not what I mean," Praesidio pursed his lips. "Agreeing to the idea that Creo is out there somewhere is not the same as committing your life to his service." He fixed his eyes upon Danae's, and his gaze held hers, as though she were transfixed.

A queasy flutter rose in Danae's stomach.

"Try to digest this, Danae. You have been working the curses of the Darkness every time you have uttered one of these 'spells.' Evil grants these powers, seemingly for free, at first, and when it is most inconvenient, when it will cost you the most, evil will come to you and demand payment for your 'spending.'"

"P-P-Payment? What kind of payment?"

"Do you know anything about the practices of the cult of Queldurik?" Praesidio asked.

Danae shuddered. "Not much. I don't like to linger on the types of things I've heard."

"The Impenetrable Darkness delights in pain, in suffering, and in chaos. Queldurik and his followers are but thralls to the appetites of that Greater Evil, and in this age, they serve as the Darkness's primary emissaries. You will find yourself owing it a debt of atrocities, brought about by your own hands, if you continue to use your 'powers.' There is no earthly escape from this obligation."

Danae looked down at her plate, the appeal of her previously tantalizing food diminished. Her mind tumbled from one thought to the next.

"Do not panic, Danae."

Once again, a soothing warmth overtook her soul. It was growing familiar.

Praesidio reached across the table and took her hand in his calloused fingers. "My intuition tells me you are not yet deeply indebted. But you need time to consider the words I have spoken. Then you can decide if you would like me to teach you more."

Danae opened her mouth to let loose the flood of questions that raced through her mind, but Praesidio released her hand and stayed her words with his palm. "However, now is not the time for further teaching. You must contemplate what I have told you so far, and decide how earnestly you want to learn from me. The road of wisdom is long and fraught with trials."

"Can't I just ask one question?"

Praesidio chuckled, and his laugh was like a fresh breeze through her spirit. "How will you choose which one? No, no, young learner. Save your questions until the morning. You will be more ready for answers then."

Danae blew a long breath from her mouth, fluttering the tendrils of hair that hung over her forehead. *All right. I'll do this your way, for now.* "I guess that means we're through here, at least for tonight?"

"Only if you plan on taking your leave of me before dessert."

Danae brightened, spirits lifted in the face of the sobering news. "That, I can wait for."

18

THE CURSE

*P*raesidio seemed content to allow silence to settle over their table, with his fingers steepled in front of him and eyes distant, but the quiet's sharp edge made Danae squirm. She sipped her mead and observed as patrons filtered in and filled every table in the dining room around them. Rand's pace from table to table picked up speed until he all but ran from one set of customers to the next, filling goblets, clearing plates, and answering demands.

"Praesidio," Danae said, "since you apparently knew I was following you from the docks, could you tell me about the gated pier where you stopped and spoke with someone? I asked a merchant about it, but I think he was mocking me."

The old sage cocked his head. "Why would he do that?"

Danae rolled her eyes with a slight shake of her head. "As if there are Elves who sail in and out of Myslapten, and the slender gray ship I saw actually belonged to them. I would have laughed the whole thing off, were it not for the strange music coming from the pier."

Praesidio cocked an eyebrow. "A millennium of no contact between your peoples seems to have bred forgetfulness in Radromir."

Danae clenched her teeth. The farther from home she traveled, the more she suspected she knew distressingly little about the real world. She forced a laugh.

"Next you'll tell me their princesses ride around on unicorns, and the woods they inhabit are dripping with fairies and flowers that grant wishes."

Praesidio leaned back. "No, no, my dear. Unicorns are not beasts of burden and will only bear a rider if the need is dire. And not all Elves live in forests, though many do."

Danae sat back in her seat, crossing her arms. Would the old sage break into a roguish smile, admitting to a jest? His expression stayed constant, with neither a grin nor frown upon his lips.

Rand appeared back at the tableside to deliver a scrumptiously sticky cinnamon and honey cake. Despite Danae's earlier loss of appetite, such a confection set her mouth watering. She breathed the aroma of the dessert deep, reminiscing about family holidays that only rarely presented such luxuries as sweets. After her first slow, appreciative bite, Danae said, "If there really are *Elves* in this wide world, why don't they have dealings with my people?"

Praesidio served himself a portion of dessert. "It is a strand of history that few teach in Radromir, I fear. Do you know the tale of the colonization of your homeland?"

"You mean the arrival of the Velonese explorers, the seafarers?"

"Yes."

"What does this have to do with the Elves?"

"My, but you are a pert one!" Praesidio sat up. "Where do you suppose the Velonese learned to sail? From whom did they glean the skills of the shipwright?"

Danae stared blankly at her tablemate.

"The Elves! The Elves bore the settlers north in their masterfully crafted ships and trained your people to build your own. Today, your people, the descendants of these early pioneers, still build the greatest ships among human sailors."

Danae sat a little taller.

"Though their skill is somewhat diminished from what it was in the beginning."

"Oh, really?" Her moment of pride deflated.

"Diminished, too, is the nobility of your people, for what began as a talent plied in shipping and exploration deteriorated into piracy. Radromirian buccaneers attacked even Elven ships, and this insolence stoked the Elves' anger to flame. They sent their navy to ferret out the raiders.

"Thus began the long blockade of Radromir, and the decimation of her fleet of proud ships, ships of such master craftsmanship that many of them passed from father to son through many generations. It saddened all the watching world to see the necessary conflict and the resulting hardship that fell upon the Radromirians. Only when the Elves were content that the corrupt suffered utter defeat did they relent."

Danae frowned as Praesidio unfolded his tale. "I've never heard about this blockade."

"I expect not. Your people are a very isolated sort, at least those who are not among the sailors. It is easy for such a culture to repeat only the details that reflect well on the tellers. Few who live today recall the truth of those times, and so what was once enmity between two cultures has metamorphosed into a general distrust of the uncanny."

Another reason for Papa's tight lips on it all, perhaps. Danae nodded. "First you school me on the underlying aspects of magic, and now you unfold the finer details of the history of elves and the founding of Radromir." Danae studied Praesidio's carven features. "Where do you learn all these things?"

Praesidio bowed his head. "My people pride themselves on the life-long pursuit of knowledge."

"You're one of the Elgadrim, aren't you? I wouldn't know one of your people by feature or accent, but even we in heathen Radromir have heard of your wisdom." Danae smirked.

"Don't take my recounting of your culture's failings as anything but observation, my dear. But you are correct, Elgadrim I am."

A tender shoot of hope sprouted in the back of Danae's mind. She leaned in. "Then perhaps you or someone you know can help me unravel the mystery with my father's illness! I hoped to make my way to Bilearne to see if your people might be able to offer me something my father and I have not yet tried."

"A bold choice." Praesidio placed a bite of cake in his own mouth, having eaten little while he spoke.

"More likely crazy and half-meditated," Danae replied. "But all the sane options haven't gotten us very far. Praesidio, have you ever heard of something called the Hacking Doom—something that could possibly be brought on by a stabbing with something like a poisoned knife?"

Praesidio's countenance clouded over, and he descended into a sudden silence. He chewed for a long, thoughtful moment, swallowed his bite, and leveled his gaze at Danae.

"Stabbing? You're saying Deklan has been stabbed recently?"

Danae nodded. "Over the summer."

"Tell me, Danae, has your father ever spoken arcane words in the presence of enemy soldiers or priests?"

"Well, yes. As a matter of fact, he has done a few much more powerful incantations than I've been able to discern from his materials. At least the few times I've seen him," she said. "I guess he didn't tell you about the incantation he used to attack a soldier on our way out of Dayleston."

"He *attacked* a soldier? No, he did not mention it. But before that —before the summer? Any Utterances?"

"The day Drex stabbed him, actually."

"It all starts to make increasing sense as I piece things together." Praesidio narrowed his eyes. "Danae, you must think back. Can you remember anything more specific about the knife the captain used?"

"Oh, yes. I got a closer look at it than I ever care to repeat. I'm lucky Papa intervened before Drex used the awful thing on me too. It was a long, curved-bladed knife, and the blade itself was crafted from a smoky-colored metal. The weapon had no cross-piece, and the pommel was set with a sculpted iron gargoyle head with small ruby eyes."

"What of Deklan's wound? Did it scar?"

"Not much," Danae replied. "Although there is this other mark..."

Praesidio gripped the table's edge. "A spreading black web of streaks?"

The confirmation of what Danae had seen punched her in the gut.

"Young one, I believe the trouble your father has is not medical, but spiritual. The knife you described to me sounds like a 'Marking Knife,' and that would also explain Deklan's failing health."

Danae's heart skipped multiple beats. "What do you mean, his problem is 'spiritual?'"

Praesidio pressed on. "You said Drex intended to stab you as well. Had he seen *you* use incantations?"

Danae smoothed trembling hands over her braid. "Yes, I'm afraid I did use one of the powers on him, when he caught me out one night after curfew," Danae said. "I managed to escape then, only because I know a sequence that shocks like a little charge of lightning."

"But you put yourself in greater danger by using the power than if you had just taken the punishment for your law-breaking," Praesidio said.

"I don't understand."

"Of course not. I will try to be clear on this . . ." Praesidio tapped a forefinger on closed lips. "Hm. This may be too hard to hear just yet."

Danae sucked a sip of mead into her throat. She graveled through the half-choke. "Not hearing some clue you have would be far worse!"

Praesidio's gaze lingered on the ceiling—or beyond—for a moment. "Then you are warned, what I say will be hard to hear."

Danae leaned in, holding her breath.

"I believe the knife Drex wounded your father with has cursed him."

Danae balked. "But why would they want to curse Papa? He's the most law-abiding Radromirian the Tebalese ever saw, I'm sure. Well, besides that little issue of attacking soldiers."

"You touch precisely on the heart of the matter." Praesidio said. "A physical attack would have meant little to them. But when Queldurik's followers find a subject who has an affinity for 'magic,' so to speak, it is a different matter entirely."

"And this is what Drex was going to do to me, too." Cold seeped into Danae's core. "But what kind of curse? To grow ill and die?"

"If only it were that mundane," Praesidio said. "The victim falls into poor health, over the course of perhaps a year, or eighteen months if the victim is a hardy one. He will appear to die, although the illusion of death masks the fact that the victim has actually fallen into a sort of stasis. The followers of Queldurik will then retrieve the body, their typical excuse being the corpse must be isolated because it is contaminated."

Danae gasped. "The Hacking Doom! Just like the librarian."

"So you have witnessed more of this phenomenon?"

Danae wrung her hands. "Yes, but the librarian's cough was much worse. And his black mark looked like it covered most of his arm."

"So perhaps Deklan has time," Praesidio said. "But when that time runs out, a powerful Curse-Bearer will then bind your father with a powerful incantation."

Horror flooded over Danae. "What? Why?"

"The incantation will enable the emissary of Queldurik to use the subject as a magical slave, drawing power from the victim to augment his own." The old man shook his head. "Some magical intentions require much more of the user than their own frailty can abide, you see. This power channeling wears the victim down with alarming speed, as it is very hard on both the body and soul. I have never heard of a bound slave surviving even a year in this arrangement."

Words fled Danae's tongue. What horrors might descend upon her father, and how near she had come to sharing this fate. She locked her eyes upon Praesidio's. "How can I stop this? I'll do anything."

"You cannot do anything by your own power. Such a curse can only be undone by Creo's will."

"What?" Danae erupted, pounding her fist on the table and rattling the empty dishes. "There must be something I can do!"

The dining room fell quiet as other patrons stared at Danae.

She curled into herself and waited until the shocked silence abated. With a hard glance fixed on Praesidio, she whispered, "I'm not one to hope some far-off creator of the universe, who plunked everything here and probably hasn't given us a passing glance since, might suddenly decide to bestow his mercy on my father. I'll die before I let him become some kind of magical fuel for the fires of the enemy!"

She gasped for air.

Praesidio leaned back in his seat and folded his hands across his abdomen. "You are unfamiliar with Creo's ways, I am afraid, to assume he sits far off, regarding not his creation, the children of his thought."

"Don't talk theology with me right now, Praesidio!" Danae fumed. She blew out a deep breath and smoothed her hair. "There must some way I might earn Creo's favor and mercy on the behalf of my father. I can't have come all this way to go back to my family and say there is nothing we can do other than hope."

Praesidio bowed his head into his hand and rubbed his brow. "Danae, I must take some time to think upon this matter. You see? Did I not say we should have concluded serious discussions before dessert?" He smiled sympathetically. "We each should get some rest. Both of our heads will be clearer in the morning."

She folded her arms and slumped in her seat. Five months ago, Drex had cursed her father. Could she possibly find a way to save Papa in time? She dug her fingers into her hair and held her aching head in her hands. Praesidio was correct. Her mind was beginning to swim with shock and fatigue, and this was the worst moment for a rash decision that would shoot wide of her target.

Danae drifted in a fog through the conclusion of the evening, and when she settled into her luxuriously appointed room, she gave small heed to the tasteful decor, the scent of lavender in the sheets, or the play of the moonlight through her window. She sat down with her journal and feverishly scribbled down all she could remember Praesidio had told her, despite the way its damp pages made writing that much more difficult.

Only when her deep fatigue left her nodding at the little desk in the corner of her room did she surrender to exhaustion, flopping onto the feather mattress and allowing her eyelids to shroud her burning eyes. Whatever the obstacles, she would learn the secret to casting off Papa's curse.

THE ANNEX

*D*anae marched through a once-again crowded dining room, straight for the booth where Praesidio sat with a steaming cup to his lips. "Now, about this 'curse' business—"

"All in good time, young one." The old man offered a warm smile. "I trust you have been comfortable and well-tended?"

Danae slid into the booth and poised herself on the edge of the leather-upholstered seat. "Oh yes! More so than ever in my life." Funny, how a proper bed had so much power to help her feel rested after a week of sleeping in harder places.

"Excellent. Then are you prepared to listen to my opinion on how you might proceed?"

Danae bobbed her head in an earnest nod.

"Tea?" Praesidio poured hot water from a ceramic pot into a cup on the table.

"Tea? Danae said. "Oh, no, I assure you, we've tried every tea that could be made from herb or ore—"

Praesidio chuckled and held up the tea pot. "Would you like some this morning?"

Danae slouched. "Oh, yes, please." She pinched a cluster of dried leaves from a bowl on the table into a little muslin pouch. After giving the drawstrings a firm tug, she dropped it into her cup.

The same stout woman who had conducted Danae to her bath appeared at the table, laden with a tray containing baskets and platters of fruits, breads, and sausages, which she set before them.

Praesidio dished out a variety of the offerings, first to Danae, and then to himself, as he spoke. "I propose you join me as I report to the local annex of the Knighthood of the Elgadrim here in Myslapten. If we have luck, I may find a member of my order there with whom I may confer about your dilemma."

"Your 'order?'" Danae blew gently over the surface of her drink. Even after she stopped, the chestnut surface of the liquid trembled, despite her efforts to hold her hands steady.

"My order is known as the Knights of the Phoenix," he said, "And we are charged with overseeing the divine powers mortals use in this world. We are the enemies of Curse-Bearers and trainers of Thaumaturgists throughout the lands."

"So your people would know something about countering curses."

Praesidio shrugged, but the curl of his lip rumored a different response.

She steeled herself and held his gaze. "Yes, I think I had better go with you today. Though I'm warning you, I have lots of questions."

Praesidio chuckled. "I am resigned to that fact." He plunged into his meal.

After they had each finished as much as their hunger demanded, Praesidio led Danae from the inn. A steady patter of raindrops filled every puddle with round ripples. Danae frowned at the leaden sky and pulled her hood up. So much for her trousers and tunic, clean and dry from the chambermaid's care.

City life in Dayleston failed to prepare Danae for the seeming chaos in streets of Myslapten, streets she had widely ignored the previous day in her dogged pursuit of Praesidio. The city proper, now that they had left the quays, towered over them, with block-paved streets that climbed the rugged terrain of the Velonese coast in every direction, whether left, right, up, or down. Danae swept along behind Praesidio at a near jog. Who knew a man who employed a staff could move with such long, swift strides?

Gargantuan structures reared up around her, solid walls of building upon building with no breaks between them. Most every-thing gleamed a creamy golden white, constructed from slabs of sandstone. So much glass. So many windows in the faces of every building reflected even the weak light of a rainy morning back in flashes of brilliance.

The morning's drizzle thickened to a steady, soaking shower, but this did little to clear the streets of the throngs that clogged them.

"Does everybody always rush like this?" Danae called to Praesidio over the din of feet, voices, wheels, and general bustle. "Or is it the rain?"

Praesidio turned a confused glance back to her. "Rush? Oh, no, this is typical. You should see it as the Midwinter Festival draws nigh."

Huge carts of goods rolled in from side streets, coming to a halt beside bright canopies that jutted from the faces of many of the buildings. Burlap-clad laborers hurried to unload sacks, barrels, and crates, and shouldered past anyone who came within range. No pleasantry lilted from any lip to ear, unless it overlaid an exchange of coin between merchant and customer, and even these words had a perfunctory sound. As far as Danae could see up the wide boulevard, more awnings, further crowds, and an ever-widening array of goods filled the thoroughfare. Such a variety of supplies she could send to her father's shop, had she the time to search them out and the funds to purchase them...

Praesidio leaned over to her. "The Avenue of Commerce, or Hagglesborough as the locals call it, is generally safe, but not all of Myslapten is a place for the unwary to tread."

"I think I saw a bit of that when I got off the *Sea Bear*." Danae shuddered.

"Ah, yes, Cliffsborough. Be glad you did not lose your way there. Even so, mind where you are headed, and do not wander from my side, or you may find yourself in trouble more quickly than you expect."

The two travelers worked their way through the crowds to cover blocks and blocks, passing one oversized stone building after the next. They dodged hurrying residents, carts, carriages, and soldiers as well as an occasional cascade of the contents of a washbasin dumping from somewhere up above. After her initial awe of the city sunk in, the rhythm of the place took her captive and swept her along in its steady current.

The shower falling from a leaden sky intensified into a drenching deluge that made Danae wish they would reach Praesidio's annex very soon. The funk of warm bodies steaming inside wet wool dominated even the salt of the sea, for the rain fell through a windless calm. After another quarter-hour of dodging, shouldering progress through the city, the avenue they followed opened up before them into a wide plaza, surrounded on three sides by buildings with thick walls, deep windows and a cumbersome heaviness to their architecture. These employed a darker stone, carven in blocks.

On the northeastern side of the plaza, however, stood a broad and elaborate gate. As if to defy the lumbering look of the structures nearby, this gate exhibited intricate scrollwork and delicate detail, alien to its surroundings. It soared at least twenty feet in height. While reflective like metal, the gate shone a whiter-than-silver hue that all at once recalled summer sun, crisp winter wind, and rushing water. Danae stared at the metalwork, mesmerized. Attending this portal stood two tall, lean guards who had greatcloaks pulled about their bodies and hoods drawn against the increasingly heavy rain. They both held pole arms, their curved blades etched in an ornate fashion akin to the gate.

Danae strained to glimpse whatever lay beyond the guards, locked away behind graceful metalcraft, but the thickening fog and

Praesidio's swift pace prevented her. She did notice the silhouettes of buildings with elegant, soft contours, as well as many trees, bare-limbed in their winter slumber. Only now did she realize that nowhere else in Myslapten had she seen plants of any type, except for perhaps the occasional weed poking from between the stone blocks of the street.

The old man made not for the gate, but for a daunting silver stone construct at the opposite end of the plaza, seemingly comprised of nothing but arches, buttresses, and towering spires rising triumphantly above the city. The building had the feel of a church in many respects, but its regal majesty commanded more solemnity than any structure Danae had ever approached.

They ducked within the doorway of this building and shook the rain from their cloaks before Praesidio lifted the pitted iron handle and stepped inside. The spicy scent of incense drifted through the air within the entry. As they shut the door, the catching of the latch clattered throughout the cavernous interior with irreverent clamor.

Lancet-arched windows lined the walls. The rainy morning's poor light filtered through and illuminated great marble pillars, carven in the likeness of toga-clad warriors and ladies. Two lines of the stone guardians stood like sentinels down the length of the room to support the ceiling that rose fifty feet above. Glass lanterns suspended from polished silver chains hung from the lofty height. One in three of these lamps glowed with a warm, golden light, steadier than flame.

Clacking footfalls rang through the silence, and Danae searched her surroundings for whoever approached. A splendidly arrayed warrior marched toward them. The man's bright plate mail gleamed with meticulous care, and his plum cape swept the floor at his heels. Under his arm, he carried a tome so thick and broad that it looked like it would take a warrior's strength to heft it.

His baritone echoed off every corner of the room around them, rich and grandiose, but the words that came from his mouth meant nothing to Danae. She stared. Would she be forced to trail after Prae-sidio, beholden to his willingness to navigate her over the language barrier? She put her hands on her hips and blew a puff of air through her nose.

Praesidio's attention on the warrior faltered. He lifted a palm to the soldier.

"Danae, I assure you I will suggest we all use the Western Speech as we proceed," Praesidio said. "But I must ask you to hold your tongue unless one of my people addresses you, and when you do speak, be plain. The men of the knighthood are busy and beleaguered people, with little time for sorting through the private affairs of outsiders."

Danae shifted her weight from foot to foot. "But you're willing to take the time to involve yourself in my affairs."

A soft smile curved the sage's lips. "Yes. I believe there is a worthwhile investment to make in you, young Danae, but it may take some convincing to bring others to my stance." He led her up to the knight.

"Knight of the Amethyst," Praesidio said, using the Western Speech, much to Danae's relief.

The knight raised a quizzical eyebrow.

Praesidio extended an arm toward Danae. "My guest does not speak the tongue of the Elgadrim. I believe it would only be hospitable to speak words she might understand."

"But who are you, brother?" the knight asked. "Archadion bids I locate you in the annals."

"Archadion?" A barely discernible sag weighed upon Praesidio's shoulders. "Very well." He stepped forward and produced a bright silver amulet from beneath his cloak, showing it to the knight. The amulet pictured a phoenix, its wings spread and curling flames licking the edges of its tail feathers, as well as wrapping around it to form a circle of fire.

The soldier's eyes widened. "Forgive me, Lord Protector!" the knight bowed deeply at the waist. "I had no idea."

"Nor could you have. Take us to Archadion, if he is the only Elder Knight within these walls." Praesidio tucked his amulet back inside his unassuming gray robes.

The knight's glance flicked to Danae.

"She is my guest and under my keeping," Praesidio said. "I shall assume accountability for her actions."

"Very well." The knight turned. "This way, please."

Danae and Praesidio followed silently after their escort down a long hall that ended in a set of oaken doors, carven with images of men as well as mythical beasts. The knight raised his gauntleted fist and rapped smartly on the wood. After an answer of foreign words drifted from behind the door, the knight opened the portal just wide enough to poke his head inside.

"A Lord Protector to see you, sir. And his guest . . ." His glance darted to Danae, and hesitation slowed his words. ". . . a speaker of only the Western Tongue."

Danae turned to Praesidio. "That's not entirely true, you know. I also speak—"

The door swung open, and a broad man stood in the gap. An invisible assault like a strafing hailstorm rushed over Danae, and she quailed.

The man's blue-eyed glare darted between the two visitors. His gaze was sharp, and decidedly unfriendly, though he nodded to Praesidio and stepped aside for him and Danae to enter. He shut the tall door with a resounding boom. He turned to his guests and regarded Praesidio through narrowed eyes.

"Archadion," Praesidio said, giving a short bow in greeting.

"Hail, Praesidio," Archadion replied with a stiff nod. His tight-lipped frown settled upon Danae. "And who is this? Not a Radromirian! And a craven one at that."

Despite her thudding heart, Danae puffed up her chest. Just as she took a breath, Praesidio raised a palm in warning.

"Oh, right. Sorry," she whispered. Would Praesidio come to her defense, here among his own people?

"I introduce to you Danae Baledric, alchemist's apprentice and Curse-Bearer," Praesidio said.

A strangled cry fought to escape Danae's throat. Archadion already had a sour enough disposition regarding her presence. Was this the most fitting introduction Praesidio could devise under the circumstances?

Archadion's eyes widened for a brief moment, then settled back to their previous squint. "You had better present an excellent reason for bringing a servant of the enemy into Creo's hallowed place of worship."

"Peace, brother," Praesidio replied, maintaining an air of calm. "She serves not the Darkness wittingly, but through a lack of understanding."

"Even power bought through ignorance has its price," Archadion said. "But again, why come here? The care of souls is not my calling."

Praesidio's jaw tightened. "I had hoped to find Leanterras today. He might have shown more interest in the girl's plight."

Archadion muttered under his breath as he moved to sit behind the desk that stood in the rear of the small room. "I fear I shall prove a disappointment to you, then."

Perhaps coming to the Church of Creo was not going to bear much fruit.

Praesidio shook his head. "Let us not start on such poor footing. I've come to take council with you, a respected member of the Knighthood, as the statutes decree."

"Very well, Praesidio. About what do you seek my council? Please say it is a subject in which I am knowledgeable. I have little time to banter about matters outside my interest or expertise."

Danae traced the grout of the floor tiles with her toe.

"I shall come to the heart of it, then, since you value time more highly than the souls." Praesidio folded his arms across his chest. "Mistress Baledric has brought a disheartening dilemma to my attention. She is the daughter of a cursed man, and she seeks the wisdom of our people on the reversal of her father's unfortunate circumstances."

"So you come to me to acquire the necessary witness and remain within protocol for another of your mercy missions. You are correct that Leanterras would have served your purposes more aptly. What is it you propose to do?"

"Danae has left her home and family in Dayleston, driven by determination and love, and her tenacity has touched my heart. I believe we should give her what aid is in our power to grant."

Archadion scratched at his clean-shaven cheek, and a contemplative frown twisted his lips. He sighed.

In the agonizing silence that ensued, Danae squirmed. Sweat dewed her lip. Her glance flitted to Praesidio, who echoed Archadion's quiet. Desperation thrust its way from its enclosure in the recesses of her soul.

"Please! I don't understand what Praesidio has to get from you so that he can help me, but I beg of you!" She opened entreating hands to Archadion. "Praesidio said Papa needs Creo's mercy, and if there's some deed I can do to earn that, I'll tackle it with all the strength I have."

The first shift in expression that could possibly be construed as a smile crossed Archadion's features.

"What use would Creo have for a waif like you?" he asked. "You believe you have something you can offer the Creator of the Universe that he does not already possess?"

Danae took an involuntary step backward. Tears sprang to her eyes. "What?" She wheeled toward Praesidio. "Why did you bring me here, if not to barter some deal for the Elgadrim's help in this?"

Praesidio scowled at his contemporary. "Perhaps I was wrong. I thought perhaps some shred of human kindness might still linger in Archadion's heart, that he would see your plight as I do."

"And why should I? Pity and tenderheartedness do not win wars, Praesidio. I have weightier matters on my hands." Archadion turned a sneer to Danae. "One misguided Curse-Bearer has little value from where I am forced to stand in these perilous times."

"And what does?" Praesidio thundered, truly terrible in his sudden fury. The measure of danger under Praesidio's plain exterior lanced from between chinks in his façade. "Value? Does it reside in such things you cannot seem to lay your hands on? The Sword of the Patron, for instance? Perhaps if we invested more in *people* to champion our cause..."

Danae's head swam. She backed from both terrible men.

"Is that your parting shot then, Praesidio?" Archadion asked, a bitter grin twisting his features. "Alas, the Sword remains unrecovered, for the war demands all those Elgadrim who might have the wiles to hunt it."

Praesidio scoffed. "Only because people like you, who have lost all ability to appraise wiles, say there is no one."

"Who would you send?" Archadion asked. "Who can we spare from commanding an increasingly beleaguered army who fights a growing host of the damned?"

Perhaps they might not be able to spare anyone, but what if...?

Danae latched onto Praesidio's arm. "I don't know what this Sword of the whatever-you-called-it is, but maybe I could go look for it, if you'll tell me where to start. If I could find it for your people, then would that earn the help I need?"

Archadion laughed aloud. "You? Seek the Sword? It is not something one shops for in the market!"

Danae pivoted back to face Archadion's scorn. "You! I would never believe you and Praesidio come from the same forefathers, with the insufferable brute you are! You don't know a thing about me. Maybe I *do* have the mettle to find this thing. What do you lose by letting me try?"

Praesidio grasped Danae's shoulders and turned her back to face him. When Danae looked upon his expression, she sought to unravel it. On the surface, he showed a countenance of concern, but the sparkle in his eye spoke another motive. "Now, Danae, you must not speak rashly." He then looked past Danae to his kinsman. "But she has a point, Archadion. Why not let her seek the Sword in exchange for a favor from us?"

"You have lost your mind!" Archadion jabbed an open hand toward Danae. "Look at her! A scrawny daughter of lesser men after the one artifact that could sway so much?"

"Sometimes the most valuable treasure can only be found through a careful sifting of that which lies beneath the surface."

Danae stamped her foot. "Would you two stop talking about me like I'm not here?"

Archadion sprang to his feet and slammed his palms on the desk. "Our discussion is not to your liking? Very well! I shall have you conveyed to another place, so that Praesidio and I can talk about you without enduring your interruptions."

"Conveyed?" Danae said. "I'm not just a piece of luggage that you and your—"

Praesidio raised a hand, the tempest of his anger stowed once again. "Perhaps it would be best, Danae, if Archadion and I discussed this at more length, one-on-one."

"You're taking his side?" Danae's jaw dropped.

"Fear not, Danae. I side with you, but I understand the needs of my people as well. Can you not await our informed decision?"

She slouched. Warring disappointment, fear, and offense churned in her chest. "If I must wait while you two bicker, I guess that's all I have in my power to do. But since I won't be able to speak on my own behalf, know that I'll endure any trial this task brings, if it will make a difference for my father."

"Your point is made, girl," Archadion clapped his hands, and the door swung open again. A slender young woman stood in the entry. She smoothed her long, burgundy robe, and her hand drifted to an amulet upon her chest. The amulet, made of gold and mother of pearl, pictured a spreading tree with thick roots.

Archadion pointed at Danae. "Galletta, take this girl to the Guest Hall."

Galletta curtsied. "If you will follow me, then, maiden."

Danae hesitated. At Praesidio's simple nod and smile, she drew a gulp of air and followed the woman from the chamber. Once Archadion's door clicked shut, the continual assault on her senses dwindled to almost nothing. *Finally.* Danae rubbed the last phantom needling from her upper arms.

Galleta led Danae to a long corridor filled with a dozen doors. Opening one of them, she revealed a sitting room, furnished only with a small table, a chair, and a chaise. A square window, small but set deep in a thick wall, allowed grey daylight into the room.

"Please, make yourself comfortable while you wait." Galetta said. "Have you any other need than this?"

Danae shed her wet cloak and hung it on a wall peg, then settled down on the chaise. Rain thrummed on the thick glass window. She laughed. "Physically, I suppose I don't need anything. But I find more and more there are a great many intangible things I never knew I needed."

"'Tis true," Galleta said. "The Protectors will probably converse for some time, so please, feel free to rest for now. I will peek in on you again later, if you like. When they are through, Master Praesidio will return to you."

"Thank you then," Danae said.

Galletta slipped from the room. Danae reclined on the chaise and allowed the drone of raindrops to lull her. Perhaps if she did sleep, the agonizing wait for Praesidio would seem shorter.

20

A Deepening Stain

*D*anae tripped over roots and rocks, fumbling through a dimly lit wood. Some malevolent vine snagged her toe, and the hands she braced before her met with tearing thorns. Brambles clawed at her clothes. Her breath came in labored gasps as she fumbled along, sweat pouring down her back. Most notable, however, was the heart-gripping fear that squeezed inside her chest and drove her to continue to run. From what?

Part of Danae's consciousness knew her struggle was but a nightmare, owing to the familiar inability to pump her legs up and down. The dusky light of the forest revealed only hazy silhouettes of nature's huddled obstacles. She stumbled down the embankment of a winding stream and fell with a jolting splash into the black water, whose spray stole what little breath she had.

A low howl rose in the distance, joined by others, and her heart thumped faster at the sound. She must get up; she must keep running. She clawed her way up the far bank and hauled herself upright.

Too late.

A crash raged through the underbrush not far behind her. The green glint of many eyes flashed, and from their midst, a monstrous black hound leapt. Its mouth bristled with foam. It bared its yellow teeth for the attack.

The scream would not come, even when the beast's teeth clamped upon her throat.

a firm grip upon her arm wrenched her from the twilight.

The forest vanished, and so did the horde of hounds. Hounds all too familiar as she recalled them. Danae again beheld the little parlor, and Praesidio's pinched expression hovered over her as he held her arm.

"Are you all right, Danae?"

She reached to her throat, and found it smooth and unscathed. "Yes." She swallowed. "I'm fine. Just a bad dream, that's all."

Praesidio cocked his head, pressing his lips together.

"My business here is concluded for the day, but Archadion bids we should return in the morning, that he may consider your plight and offer his advice after he has sought Creo's will in the matter. We shall return to the North Star to rest and seek Archadion's council at daybreak."

Danae sat up. "All right. I hope Creo is better disposed to me than Archadion."

T he weather conditions had shifted dramatically by the time Danae followed Praesidio back outside into the plaza. A stiff wind had swept the rain away, and what remained of the clouds drifted to the east in tattered ribbons. The bright sun peered between scattering clouds and reflected with a cold, garish light off the wet pavement. As Danae and her companion crossed the square, Danae's eyes again drifted to the high gate on the opposite side of the plaza, where two attendants still stood. She leaned over to Praesidio.

"At the risk of sounding ignorant ..." Danae bit her lip.

Praesidio laughed. "The Elves again. Like their dock on the

wharfs, they keep a quarter of this city unto themselves, standing as sentinels to protect elven interests in this part of the world."

"Can we talk to them?"

"I don't recommend it," Praesidio replied. "While your people may have forgotten the reasons behind the blockade of old, these port-dwelling, seafaring elves have not. They rarely permit humans of any type in their quarter, and a Radromirian? Never."

As she and Praesidio continued on their way, Danae's gaze remained fixed upon the interweaving metal vines and flowers of the gate and the shrouded figures before it. What did the guards look like? Why did Praesidio need to march onward with such focus? Her strides slowed.

"Mistress Baledric, if you please!" Praesidio called, surprisingly far away.

Danae turned toward his call and found him at the edge of the plaza, some fifteen yards ahead. She jogged to his side. After a final glance back toward the guards and gate, she quickened her steps to maintain Praesidio's pace.

They made their way back toward the North Star Inn, and all along the trip, Danae kept a close eye on the surrounding landmarks, whether a noteworthy shop, a building that towered above the rest or a cart merchant who peddled his wares from a corner. When they reached the steps of the inn, Danae slowed to a stop and glanced back.

"Praesidio? I think I'm going to use some of this afternoon to have a look around Myslapten."

Praesidio rubbed his chin. "Do you think that wise? I have other business I must conduct within the city today, in which I regret to report I cannot involve you. I worry after your intentions to wander on your own."

Danae batted winsome lashes. "No need to worry about me. You manage your errands, and I'll see you back here in the evening, perhaps?"

"You'll forgive me for exhorting you to take utmost care, then?" Praesidio said.

"You have nothing to be concerned about. I grew up in a city, and know my way around a questionable street, should I fumble into one. Which I probably won't."

Praesidio glanced at her sidelong with a quirked brow, but Danae dismissed his skepticism with a bright smile and a wave. "I'll see you back here tonight."

With a light hop in her stride, she turned away from the inn and joined the flow of foot-traffic along the busy Avenue of Commerce.

There could be no harm in wending her way back to the Annex Square to get a closer look at the elven quarter of the city. She might not gain passage through the gates, but she would not pass by a chance to see a living, breathing elf. If she kept her hood up, maybe they would not notice she was Radromirian—at least not right away.

She backtracked along the route she had noted on the return trip to the inn, but before she emerged into the square, she turned right and slipped into a crooked easement. A few dead ends and retraced steps later, she spied the outer wall of the elven quarter, silver as moonlight, just a narrow block away. A quick glance over her shoulder revealed no onlookers, so she minced her way to the wall.

With every step she drew closer, the deeper a sense of foreboding grew in the recesses of her mind. The uncanny sheen of the wall drew her, and yet the warning in her heart first whispered, then announced, then finally screamed her foolhardiness. The inner war slowed her steps until she pressed on as though she battled a stiff headwind. The wall loomed within arm's length.

The obstruction was not particularly tall, perhaps only a story-and-a-half. A short block to her left, enough ivy encrusted the wall to mitigate the sheerness of the stonework. She would not actually go in . . . just scuttle up, take a quick peek over, and be on her way. No harm in that.

She skulked along the wall toward the ivy. Still, no watching eyes. She paused before the plants that offered her a ladder up. Her heart thudded. She thrust the admonition bubbling to the surface under thick layers of curiosity and justification. Then reached for the wall.

When her fingers touched the surface of the stone, a sharp jolt rocked her arm with bone-searing pain. A yelp leapt from Danae's throat, and she jumped back. Her arm fell numb to her side, limp and useless.

"*Caerdeth!*" a voice commanded from above.

Danae clapped her good hand onto her dead arm. Motion upon the summit of the wall shifted at the edge of her vision. A cloaked figure, silhouetted against a bright sky, bent a bow at her.

She sprang around the closest building, stumbled over her own feet, and scattered milk pails and bushel baskets before she broke into a pell-mell run as far from the wall as she could manage.

She ducked and dodged and tried to retrace the route she had followed from the main street to the wall of the elven quarter, but after only a handful of turns, the buildings around her jogged no recollection. After another couple blocks, Danae's stomach filled with fluttering concern. A flicker of motion caught her eye. Had the bowman followed her? She glanced about the street, but could not catch sight of the disturbance just outside her peripheral vision. She turned and continued along the street, her senses on sudden edge.

Don't gawk. Pretend you belong exactly here. Danae gulped but kept walking, slower than she wanted. There was no denying it. She had lost her way.

She spun on her heel. The best choice would be to backtrack until she recognized something. Anything. Once she performed her determined about-face, her line of vision met with a disquieting stranger who shuffled up the center of the road. The swart man's bulging eyes peered from beneath the sagging brim of a battered hat. Not the elven bowman, but trouble enough, if his seedy appearance held any significance. Danae focused upon the roadside instead of the man as she marched forward, but somehow his hawkish glance repeatedly caught her own.

Please don't let him try to talk to me.

As she came within a half-dozen paces of the man, his soft, sibilant voice hissed from behind a predatory grin. "A newcomer to the Big City, dearie?"

Danae rubbed her arm, which had regained a little of its sensation. At least she could wiggle her fingers. "What does it matter to you?"

"My, my, my," the man said with a click of his tongue. "We mustn't be so rude! Perhaps you've not been welcomed so nicely by the locals."

Danae kept walking, working her fingers and wrist to accelerate the return of sensation. The stranger steepled his fingers and fell into step beside her. The look in his dark-circled eyes was shrewd. Piercing. Hungry. "Maybe my dearie is hunting work here in town? You have the look of one who seeks good fortune in bad times."

The man slithered too close, and Danae curled her lip. He stank of clove-laden smoke marinated in a lifetime of heavy drinking.

"There are a great many services a fresh young flower like yourself might provide a city full of disheartened folk, folk who pay handsomely for pleasant distractions."

Danae gasped. "Do you really mean what . . .?" She stopped and would have folded her arms if her numb limb would have assented. "I may be a little disheveled from traveling, but I'm certainly not desperate!"

"Oh, a shame. Are you hurt? That's no way to go about." The man reached toward her.

Danae shrank away from him. "I'm fine. Really. Don't touch me."

Unruffled, the man rubbed his stubbly chin and drooped thin, bluish eyelids. "Don't get so bothered in such a hurry, missy. Perhaps there are other trades I might offer you. I've many choice products that need selling, if they're more to your taste."

Unfamiliar territory or not, Danae refused to fall prey to a back-alley mongrel. "I assure you, if I were looking for work, I have respectable skills I might ply. Good day to you, sir!" She took another long stride forward, but the man slipped in front of her.

"Let me give you another chance, flower." His earlier grin slipped away to leave only a dark, venomous stare. "Volunteers always land the better work."

Danae's eyes darted around the narrow street. Of course, they were alone.

"No thanks," Danae said. Her earlier astonishment was beginning to crumble to pronounced unease. "Now if you'll excuse me . . ."

The man placed a tiny silver whistle in his mouth and blew a short peep. Out of an alley a few paces ahead, two burly, fur-clad men emerged. Despite the cold, their arms, banded in muscle, lay bare. One of them cracked his knuckles. A nasty leer creased his cheeks.

Danae froze in a half crouch.

Both of the barbarians lunged in a grab for Danae's arms, clamping upon them with steely force. Danae squawked, but could find no breath for a proper scream.

"Don't make this a scrap, flower," the hissing voice warned from behind her, "or I'll let my heavies here break you in a bit."

Danae writhed in the dual grasp of her enemies. *The words, the words! What are they?*

Just as the three men turned for the alley dragging Danae with them, she finally discovered the elusive incantation. A moment's hesitation wedged in her throat. *What about Praesidio's warnings about using the powers?* Surely, in an emergency, she wronged no one by calling upon such knowledge. She blurted the string of words she had called upon to assault Drex, adding a tiny twist at the final moment.

A burst of lavender electricity snaked from her heart and down her arms, flashing with blinding intensity as it met the flesh of her captors. Both men hollered, releasing her, muscles twitching involuntarily. Danae scrambled between them, back down the alley. She skidded around the corner on the wet cobblestones.

"Don't bother," the sibilant man griped, though the sound receded as Danae ran. "There's money of a different sort to be made on that one."

Danae fled all the faster for any place where more people populated the streets, heedless of what strange meaning lurked under the villain's words.

If only she could outrun the stain that deepened within.

21

EARNING FAVOR

*A*rchadion shut his chamber door with a solid boom, spun, and fired his piercing gaze into Danae. She clenched her teeth against the assault of his scrutiny.

"When Praesidio brought you to me yesterday," Archadion said, "I was inclined to dismiss whatever troubles you had without a second thought. After all, why should I spend my resources on a meritless waif who belongs to a people that is divided, overrun, and given to violence and theft?"

Danae clenched her fists but made no retort. The more she learned from Praesidio about history according to cultures other than her own, the more she wondered if many of Radromir's leaders had indeed forfeited the mercy of others. No wonder they stood alone, with no help from neighboring nations against the Tebalese invasion.

Praesidio thumped his staff on the thick carpet. "No need to berate the girl, brother."

Archadion's brows lowered. "I have not finished." He sighed. "I have discovered, however, it does not much matter what I think, because Creo makes it abundantly clear I should aid you with your request. But you will *earn* the help of the Elgadrim, for our wisdom is bought with much toil."

Danae leaned forward, her pulse quickening. "I don't fear hard work. Please tell me what to do."

"You heard Praesidio mention the Sword of the Patron yesterday, did you not?"

Danae nodded, though a sickening wave rocked within her belly. What was this thing, and how could she learn all she needed to know without appearing incompetent?

"Tell me what you know about the weapon," Archadion continued.

Could he have chosen a more humiliating question? Danae stretched her fingers against the urge to break her nails as she stared at the floor. "I'm afraid I know naught of it, my Lord."

Archadion huffed and shook his head. "Clearly they teach nothing of history, theology, *or* arcana in Radromir, so I suppose I shall have to cram a little of all that into your thick skull right now." He folded his arms. "Do you at least know what a Patron is?"

Danae lifted her head. "Yes, that I can answer. A sort of mythological being said to do the will of God, correct?"

Archadion snorted. "Mythological? You shall discover soon enough that the spiritual battle Creo's Patrons do on his behalf is as real as the four walls around us. While we do not always see them, their role in the swing of world events is undeniable."

"Try to be civil," Praesidio said. "It is not reasonable to expect Danae to know more."

Archadion continued to sear Danae. "Now, tell me, do you know anything about the Rise of Queldurik?"

"Only through folk songs," Danae answered. "I recall the Patrons and hordes of fiends figuring prominently in those ballads, but it's been years since anyone in Radromir dared sing them."

"Perhaps you will also recall the lay of the Patron Mystrin,

personal protector of High Philosopher Aromen. It was this particular Warrior Patron who the fiend Ba-al Drelix slew."

Danae's brow furrowed. Sweat rose on her lip. "The names are
familiar . . . I suppose. I'm sorry for my spotty knowledge."

"No matter. Just listen closely. I will not repeat myself." Archadion
paced as he went on. "The fiend, after striking Mystrin down in
combat conducted here on the mortal plane, kept Mystrin's weapon
unto himself. For what creature would not covet such a marvelous
thing, a Sword with a will and a mind, as well as the capability to slay
spiritual beings? He bent the Sword's will to his own over many years,
as he hid beneath the ruins of the Elgadrim Fortress of Ven Draugos."

Archadion's eyes sparkled with a feral light as he told the tale. "In
recent years, an elven hero rebuilt this stronghold, and in the process,
discovered Ba-al Drelix and the Sword there. This elf won the Sword
from the fiend, but held it only a short time, for Queldurik's minions
stealthily gained entrance to Ven Draugos and stole the Sword.

"We believe the weapon is now in the Temple of Queldurik in the
Tebalese capital of Garash, so that is where you must go. Recover it,
and you shall have your wish of the means to release your father
from his curse."

Danae stared. Her shoulders coiled. Go to Garash itself? Find the
sword of a spiritual being, and take it from whatever evil person had
it? The prospect seemed impossible. Yet, if this quest held the answer
to saving her father from the doom before him, then she must find a
way to see it done.

She clenched her teeth. "I'll do my best."

Praesidio placed his hand upon her shoulder. "Do not worry,
young one. You will have my help, and I will find us a guide, that we
will not wander in the wilderness between this place and Tebal."

Gratitude washed over Danae in a flood, but every sentiment she
conjured to express her thanks seemed too frail. But what if, in the
end, Praesidio recovered the Sword, and not she herself? Would the
Elgadrim still consider her part of the bargain fulfilled? A growing
list of "what ifs" began to assemble like ranks of enemy troops.

"You will provision yourself and be ready to leave at sunrise tomorrow. Now that your needs are intertwined with mine, I will set at least this much of the timeline. Since Protector Praesidio has volunteered to oversee this task, I place it in his hands, and bid you good morning." Archadion sat at his heavy oak desk and began writing on a long scroll of parchment.

I guess that's it, then.

Praesidio made a slight bow to his contemporary, then ushered Danae from the chamber.

As the two of them passed through the emptiness of the sanctuary, Danae struggled to choose which of her mounting concerns to air, but Praesidio spoke first.

"You must see to it that you procure some armor, leather, I think, as well as whatever weapons with which you feel proficient. See also to your traveling clothes, for our journey will march us right into the heart of a Tebalese winter. Were your father's need not urgent, my counsel would be to wait on the Sword's recovery until spring. But alas, that option is not among those we should choose, so heavy traveling gear it shall be."

Armor? Weapons? Clothing? The worry over the cost of provisions settled into Danae's stomach like a lump of iron.

"Oh, and of course, you shall need to purchase a horse," Praesidio added.

The lump of iron turned to a burning coal. Though she had not formally counted the money her father had given her, she had a feeling she would be stretching it very thin to cover so many expenses.

"Will you be shopping today as well?" Danae asked, sure to conceal the note of hopefulness in her voice.

"No, young student, I must spend my day in making arrangements for our guide. There are a few in Myslapten who I know and trust, and I must see if any of them are currently within the city and able to commit to our journey," Praesidio said. "You should be able to find all you need in Hagglesborough." He swung his cloak over his shoulders and headed off.

Danae watched his departure. *Don't panic,* she told herself, with little success in slowing her fluttering heartbeat. She had the crushing feeling the first step she took toward The Avenue of Commerce would start an avalanche of circumstances she had little hope of controlling.

Taking a deep breath, she squared her shoulders, held her chin high, and headed toward the merchants of Hagglesborough with forced purpose. Confident posture would convince any she dealt with that they should take her seriously. She hoped she could convince herself.

*T*he leatherworker's shop distinguished itself amidst the many stores and businesses in the marketplace with a nauseating collision of stenches. As she rounded the building to seek the entrance, ammonia, salt and an array of other gag-inducing aromas assailed her. Life as an apothecary's apprentice had subjected her to many awful fragrances, but the prospect of whatever horrifying muck cured the hides sent a shudder through Danae's body. But no business mishap that might occur within the walls of the leatherworker's shop could be worse than the smell outside, so Danae rushed through the door of the shop.

Danae wended her way around other customers who perused the leatherworker's wares, awaiting a moment when the merchant might be free to deal with her requests. She scanned the satchels, shoes, aprons and many other household goods that hung all about the room.

No armor.

The shopkeeper stepped up to his counter and leaned on it. His forearms were as thick as tree trunks, and his middle as broad as an ale barrel. He had a plain, honest face, creased with years.

"What can I get fer ye, maid?"

Danae jumped. Of course he was going to ask her business. She cleared her throat, glanced about the room, and replied, "A few things, actually. I need some heavy gloves, which I see you have, but I'm also searching for leather armor."

The man cocked a graying eyebrow. "Gloves I understand. But what's a maid like yerself needin' armor for? Last I heerd, the army's not in the way of callin' up womenfolk!"

A few other customers in the shop snickered, while the oldest shopper among them, a rickety old woman, sneered outright.

The urge to slip into a dark crevice in the floorboards crumpled Danae's posture. "I have some traveling to do, and the countryside is full of dangers in these hard times. It's only prudent of me to be prepared. Let's start with the gloves, then?"

The merchant shrugged and handed her a sheepskin-lined pair. "Warmest you'll find in Myslapten, I guarantee it."

Danae slipped them on. They fit her hands well, and her fingers immediately began to sweat, though whether owing to quality of the gloves or the way her shopping trip had become a bit of a sideshow to the other customers was difficult to determine. The gloves' stitching was tight and the leather supple. A good sign.

"And about the other items I'm seeking . . ."

Somewhere behind Danae, a grating voice spoke. "What business does a young lady have in hunting after armor?"

Enough was enough. Danae turned a narrow-eyed glare on the old woman in the shop, who leaned close to the man beside her as though to share in a conspiratorial murmur. "I already explained myself once. If you weren't listening, too bad."

The woman gaped. "I suppose armor's a good match for your lack of decorum and those mannish clothes you're wearing." She shook her head. "No shame. You and all those other women who don't know your place. Tainting society . . ."

"Bag it, Isolde," the tanner cut in. "If you did as much spendin' as you did watchin' and whinin', you'd have the favor of many a merchant 'round these parts. Now stop drivin' off actual customers." He met Danae's eyes. "Armor is it?"

Danae stifled a chuckle behind her hand and nodded.

"Well, I think I've something that'll fit ye, though I sized it for a page-boy whose stomach turned out too weak for the job," he said. "You're lucky you're not buxom."

Danae barked an insulted cry as the man trundled off to a large closet at the opposite end of the shop. He rummaged through its contents and produced a breastplate of worked leather, stained a deep liver brown. The shoulders bore hooks for a cape, but otherwise, the armor was unadorned and spartanly functional.

Danae tried the breastplate over her tunic, buckling and shifting it, and found the tanner did know his business. It fit her well.

"Thirty silver," he said.

Danae's shoulders sagged.

"I canna' ask less, lass."

"Throw in the gloves?"

The tanner folded his arms, but a smirk curled one side of his mouth. "You'll take the armor at thirty?"

It was worth the asking price, judging by what little she knew about weapons, armor, and shields.

"I will." Danae thrust out a hand.

The tanner clasped it and gave a firm shake. "Deal."

With a grimace, Danae counted out the silver, mourning each coin that passed from her hand to the tanner's.

He hefted the silver, and his face broke into a crooked-toothed grin.

Well, as long as I've got his favor, maybe I should squeeze as much information from it as I can. She twisted and strained to look down her own back, then smoothed her hands over the fine surface of the breastplate. "You're right, it's worth every copper chip. This will do just perfectly. Now, where would a sensible man like you shop for traveling provisions, should you find yourself in need?"

The tanner ducked his head and rubbed the back of his neck for a moment. Apparently compliments, even from a girl in mannish clothes, carried some weight. "Ah, lass, well that shouldn't be so difficult. Abelard's General Store is just a step down the lane here, an' he should have most anythin' ye hope to buy for travlin'. Though why a lass would think of such a thing right here at the front end o' winter is somethin' I canna' guess. But say Abelard's is outta somesuch item ye need, well then Maugis's Dry Goods'd be yer next best bet. That's just up the Avenue, oh, I'd say . . . what is it now, three blocks?"

A smattering of nods from other men in the room confirmed the tanner's opinion, though Isolde stood aside with her arms folded and her lips pinched together.

"Excellent." Danae curtsied, thanked the tanner, and turned for the door.

*H*eavy laden with a pack brimming with traveling rations, bandages, rope, a change of warm clothes, extra water-skins, and a smaller oilskin tent than she had wanted, Danae stood at a split rail fence on the western outskirts of Myslapten. She hitched her pack up on her shoulders for the twentieth time, and took another sweeping look at the dozen horses penned on the opposite side of the fence. The animals closest to her stood tall and bright-eyed. The farther down the line the horse, the scrawnier and more dejected it became.

Beside the nearest steed, a young ostler spoke to a gentleman clad in a fine woolen greatcloak. "I guarantee you'll find no better horse for fifteen gold outside of Da-Shir itself."

Danae choked. Fifteen gold? She doubted all the money she had carried in her pouch before she started shopping for provisions had totaled as much. How far down the row would she need to shop before six gold would buy her a mount? The last horse on the line coughed and drooped its bony head. Danae chewed her lip. She slipped through the gate, clasped her hands behind her back, and strolled toward the animals.

The horse the ostler was currently touting stood so tall Danae could not even see over the creature's back. The horse next to it was only a hand or two shorter. Skipping over the next three prospects,

Danae slowed near a small gray mount that dozed with a hind foot cocked. That one at least seemed less than terrifying.

"Surely a more elegant palfrey would be better suited to the lady's needs," a voice said behind her.

Danae spun to meet the ostler's gaze. He held a hand out toward a lovely, trim horse with a meticulously-combed tail that hung in gossamer strands to the ground.

She pursed her lips. "Something a little sturdier, I think. I've got a long way to go."

The ostler took a step back and patted the neck of the horse one closer to the head of the lineup. "Then here's what you need, miss. Solid as stone, this one."

"Is it as expensive as that first horse?"

"Nah." The ostler laughed. "I could part with this one for ten."

Ten. It might as well have been a hundred—the price was no more attainable.

Danae shrunk back. "Um—what have you got for half that?"

The ostler's smile came across more like a grimace than warmth. "I really wouldn't recommend skimping on the horse if you're planning a large trip."

"It's not by choice."

After heaving a sigh, the horseman led Danae down the line to the second-to-last animal. It was a little bay mare with more nettles in her mane than hair, but at least the creature pricked her ears toward the ostler when they approached.

"She's a little shaggy now, but she'll clean up plenty respectable," the ostler said. "I'd just start out slow with her once you get on the road, for safety's sake."

What did that mean? Danae might have asked, if she did not suspect the horseman's explanation would present her with more questions than answers.

She purchased the horse and her tack for the painful six gold she could commit to the need. In the white light of mid-afternoon, she led the animal back to the North Star. The groom at the stables behind the inn raised his eyebrows when Danae handed over the reins.

"I'll need this horse ready in the morning," she said.

The groom nodded. "I'll do my best by her, m'lady."

Just inside the front door of the North Star, a small sign on the lectern in the foyer read, "Luncheon in the Tavern." An arrow under the words pointed her through a right-hand doorway.

There's a tavern? Well thank goodness. I doubt I have enough left for yesterday's bread in the dining rooms.

The common room of the tavern held nary an empty chair Danae could see. Men and women alike sipped a hearty soup, or tore at bread and smoked poultry, drank flagons of ale and mead, and on occasion, a glass of garnet red wine. Conversations mingled with the sounds of clanking tableware.

As Danae sought a place to sit, a barmaid shouldering a huge tray of foam-crowned tankards swept past her.

"No seats around the floor, miss, but a stool at the bar if you want it."

Danae squeezed her way through the bustle to the stool, and plunked down with a relieved sigh.

A broad-chested man with long, mahogany hair and a close-cropped beard hustled to and fro behind the bar, joking with his customers, filling drinks, taking silver, and cleaning the counter all at once. His smile was genuine and his customers mirrored his affable mirth as he worked.

Before Danae had given half a thought to what she wanted, the barkeep approached her spot and asked, "Something drink, eat, or both today, miss?"

"Um . . ." She glanced around the tables nearby. "Barley pottage and mead?"

The barkeep nodded. He reached his hand up, making a few brisk signals with his fingers as he looked across the room. He filled a brown earthenware cup with mead and set it before her. "Two silver, then."

Just as Danae was reaching into her pouch, another man at the opposite end of the bar called, "Lucas!"

"Right back with you miss." The barkeep turned to the beckoning customer.

Another barmaid placed the pottage before Danae not an instant later. Lucas took Danae's silver in one hand while both holding a mug and operating a tap with the other.

She spent her mealtime watching the dynamics of the busy inn, while she jotted the details about the Sword of the Patron and her subsequent quest to find it, lest she forget all that Archadion had told her that morning. Customers began trickling from the dining room, having finished their meals. Some lingered on, however, and these appeared mostly to be travelers, who, much like Danae, carried large packs of provisions, and many of them weaponry as well. None of *their* gear looked quite so new as her own. Their armor did not squeak, and they did not fuss with their weapon belts. Could she become one of these seasoned travelers?

After Danae had finished a quiet, exceptionally modest meal, she glimpsed Praesidio stepping through the street side door of the establishment. She rose from her seat.

"I trust all of your affairs are in order?" he asked, with a brief glance at her pack and armor.

"I think so. Were you able to . . ." Her words trailed off as she caught sight of the person several paces behind the old sage.

His attire was not so outlandish, as he wore scuffed, high boots, a rough tunic and breeches, thick gloves, gauntlets, and a wide belt. Even though he looked like an armory on legs, with his countless sheaths and scabbards, and his bow and two quivers of arrows across his back, Danae could cope with this. But his sky-blue skin, his bald head, his large, curious eyes, and his less than three-foot stature, these widened her eyes. She averted her stare, but then worried that she appeared to be trying to avoid his gaze. He had a tight-jawed look on his face, and Danae got the instant impression that crossing this diminutive warrior would be about as smart as cornering a wolverine. A wolverine who could wield knives.

Praesidio sat in the chair beside Danae and gestured to the creature behind him. "Danae, this is Mizzletorp. He has agreed to serve as our guide on the long road to Garash. I have traveled with him before, and he has continually proven a skilled woodsman and warrior."

She smiled in greeting. "It's nice to meet you, Miz . . . Mizzle-torp," she said, careful to sort out the syllables of his alien name.

"I'm just-a bustin' with the pleasure o' meetin' ya!" Mizzletorp sprang up to Danae, and vigorously shook her hand, until she felt as though her shoulder might slip out of joint. His enormously long, pointed ears waggled with his earnestness.

"Uh . . . I . . . well . . . it's a pleasure to meet you too." Danae remained in the captivity of his handshake for another few moments before he finally released her, stepping back and placing his fists upon his hips.

"So, you're just crazy enough to make a trip to Garash, eh?" the creature asked. "And with this old troublemaker?" He looked up at Praesidio with a broad grin. "Well, if that don't just put the pepper in my pot-pie!"

"Yes," Danae answered. "It's only out of necessity, I assure you. We depart in the morning, then, as Archadion bid?"

Mizzletorp rubbed his chin, furrowing his brow and nodding. "Yes, yes. Best to get a jump on trouble! Strike out at dawn and meet the nasties in the broad light of day!"

Praesidio shook his head. "Now, my earnest friend, no use piling premature fear on the girl. It is my hope we will avoid most of the dangers of the road. At least, that is much of your job in the endeavor."

The sparkle in Mizzletorp's eye fizzled. "Ah, yes, always the safest ways with you tall fellows! Good enough. I'll find you here at first light?"

"Yes, that is my intention. Now, if you will excuse me, I wish to retire early." The older man headed toward the door near the foyer. Mizzletorp made a slight bow to Danae.

"Just you wait. This'll be a trip worth rememberin'. You just watch ol' Mizzletorp here—he'll see ya through." He whipped around and sprang across the room, beating Praesidio to the door.

Danae stared after them long past the time they exited the room. That was a lot of energy in a small parcel. What would the long hours in the wilderness hold, with the strangely intense Mizzletorp as a guide? With every moment that passed, the burden of the journey weighed more heavily upon her heart. Even so, she suspected she had only the slightest inkling how difficult the task ahead of her might become.

22

THE HOUND

In the predawn hours of the next morning, Danae sat with rigid posture at a table in the Common Room of the North Star Inn. Butterflies fluttered in her middle. She pushed her oatmeal around with a spoon, having only forced down a couple of bites. Curse the way her anxieties filled her stomach, especially at a time when a solid meal was so important. Her gaze drifted from her lumpy, unappetizing mush to the gear that waited in a tight bundle on the floor beside her. Had she remembered to buy everything she needed? How could she know? She had never traveled for more than a few days at a time; how could she possibly anticipate all she would need for a journey whose length she had not even calculated?

As the dark of night gave way to the cold, harsh light of a winter morning, Praesidio entered the common room, fully arrayed in a thick cloak, tall, fleece-lined boots, and his customary woolen robes. Loops of brassy rings meshed together into mail peeked from beneath the garb. He smiled at Danae. "You seem prepared to set out."

"More than ready." Danae pushed her bowl away.

"Our guide will join us at the stables shortly."

Danae tugged at a loose tendril of hair. "Praesidio? About the guide. I know this is going to sound foolish, but—well . . . what is he?"

The old sage smiled. "Forgive me, Danae. Sometimes I forget the only creatures on two legs you have probably seen are humans and birds. He is a forest gnome. Few surpass their stealth and cunning."

"Are all forest gnomes so, well . . . how can I put it? Boisterous?"

Praesidio's smile grew into a full-bellied laugh. "No, I suppose none so much as Mizzletorp. They all tend to be dramatic, and his mood does often turn from light to dark faster than you can snuff out a candle. But then, he sparks to life again just as fast."

That should keep things interesting. As if they needed to be any fuller of the unexpected. Danae rose from her seat, took a deep breath, and squared her shoulders. Praesidio paid the bill for their stay, then they both walked out to the stables. Just as they entered the courtyard, Mizzletorp rode up on a light-boned gray pony. The pony tossed his head continually, ears pricked and head high.

"Don't you worry lad," the gnome said softly to his mount. "We go, we go, we go!"

A towering chestnut courser marched from the stables, his neck arched with a proud bearing. The horse led the stablehand holding his reins more than the stablehand led the horse. His oiled hooves rang over the pavement as he approached Praesidio, and his tack gleamed with meticulous cleaning and polishing. Not a rivet or a buckle had a grain of grime beneath it.

Praesidio reached out and clapped the horse on the neck. "I see you have been in good hands, Chancellor, my friend. We had best make a quick start to this trip, before you grow fat and flat as a tabletop with all of this comfortable living."

The horse whickered and nudged Praesidio's shoulder.

Not far behind Chancellor, the groom led Danae's little mare, who had received a thorough grooming. Where there were once knots and nettles, the bay mare now had a smooth, flowing mane and tail. Her coat, dull so few hours before, gleamed like polished wood.

The groom handed the reins to Danae. "She cleaned up pretty well, I daresay. Seems you didn't make so terrible a purchase. But I'd watch her feet. Especially the front right."

Watch them for what? Danae took the reins in hand. "Of course. You've done a wonderful job in getting her ready."

The groom ducked his head. "'Taint a job worth doin' if you don't do it well."

Praesidio slipped his foot into his stirrup and swung his body onto his tall stallion with lithe ease. As he settled into the saddle, Danae blinked. Here was a man more at home on the back of a horse than on his own two legs. Somehow, man and beast seemed an extension of one another, wearing the same look of wisdom, pride, and patience on their faces.

It took Danae three hops before she gathered enough momentum to haul herself astride her own horse. Her palms sweated inside her gloves. She watched carefully as Praesidio and Mizzletorp nudged their mounts with their heels and did her best to mimic their technique. With all the travelers mounted, they set off, the sun hovering above the tree-covered hills of the horizon.

Once they passed from the outskirts of the city, the wide road dove beneath the cover of light forest, with bare-limbed trees of maple, elm, and sycamore. The traffic of commerce flowed both directions on the highway.

As they rode, Praesidio explained their course. "We will head east upon this road for about a week's journey until we reach the southwestern arm of the Triastead Mountains. To a Radromirian's view, they will seem little more than craggy hills. On the eastern side of the range, we may find the roads in that region no longer even exist." He turned to Mizzletorp. "You are comfortable with forging across the wild in that region?"

"Comfortable?" Mizzletorp laughed. "That's when things'll just start beggin' some attention."

Praesidio looked to the heavens and shook his head. "The march from there will carry us through my ancestral homeland of Kelmirith, and if we make good time, we could cross the Tebalese border after a score of days."

"It's not as far to Tebal as I thought," Danae said.

Mizzletorp shook his head. "Old Praesidio's only given you the short end of the story. Garash is as far from anywhere civilized as a city could be. If we're gonna to keep all this as secrety as he wants, we'll be tramping across a lot of nothing nigh on two moon cycles."

Danae wheeled an aghast stare to Praesidio.

His face remained placid, his tone matter-of-fact. "All told, it is my hope we may complete the journey to Tebal and then south to Bilearne in five month's time, allowing for delays."

Danae sat up. "Five months? It's really that far? I'll be hard pressed to make it back to Radromir inside of a year since my father's 'marking.'"

"'Tis the most direct route, so it's as fast as we may go," Mizzletorp chimed in. "That is, by land!" He turned to Praesidio. "I don't suppose you've patched things up with old Grumbauer?"

Praesidio frowned at Mizzletorp. "He did not see fit to make amends before he went into hibernation. We shall see if he wakes up again in my lifetime." The old sage shook his head and finished, "But even if dragon-riding were an option, I do not think that would be the best way to make an inconspicuous entrance into Garash."

Danae might have laughed as though Praesidio was joking, were it not for the many astonishing events that had piled into her life of late. Dragon-riding? Horseback riding, while at least familiar, seemed difficult enough.

"Well, let's pick up the pace while the road is safe, then." The gnome raised scraggly azure brows. He nudged the flanks of his steed, who instantly picked up a swift trot, and the other horses followed his lead.

As Danae bounced along behind Mizzletorp, her tack and gear jingling and jostling, the gnome turned a pained expression back to her.

"Now, missy, no use wearing that little mare out with all your workin' against her! Just you mind me, and we'll set you right. Make you a rider instead of a holey bag of turnips on her back!"

Danae wanted to shrink down until she disappeared.

Mizzletorp dropped his reins in order to gesticulate with wide arms as he talked, apparently guiding his pony with his knees and seat instead. "Now first, let's get you sitting that trot, and if you pick that up, maybe we'll work you into a post." He shook his head at the mare. "Tiresome, tiresome work, you poor beast!"

Danae shifted on her already-sore seat. *Poor beast, indeed!*

Five days of riding, camping, watching, and worrying passed, with weather that remained fair but cold. The road worked its way from a hilly, lightly forested landscape into a craggy stretch strewn with tumbled rocks. The infrequent trees here grew stunted and gnarled. They clutched with roots that probed into fissures in the rocky terrain, searching for a foothold against the gnawing wind.

The only sounds to drift through the stony silence were noises the travelers brought with them. The horse's iron-shod feet squeaked and scraped over the footing. The group's voices fell dead in the open air. It did not seem to bother Mizzletorp, however, for he filled long stretches with endless chatter, whether he fumbled through bits of half-remembered poetry, or regaled them on all the opulence of the Gnomish Midwinter Feast, which he would miss this year because of this little jaunt. Clearly, he had no intention of allowing Praesidio to forget that particular intrusion, though he delivered his admonishments with a laugh.

In the next moment, however, he grumbled about the disrepair of the road, casting a scathing glance at the highway as if he might expect it to rearrange itself and relieve his displeasure. Listening to the guide was more like having a conversation with three or four different people at once, none of whom was in the least bit concerned with speaking about the same subject.

*A*s dusk fell on the sixth day, Danae slid from her horse and landed with a weak-kneed thump on the ground. She pulled her bedding from the bundle on the mare's rump, then cast a weary gaze up the wall of rock that would provide only a semblance of shelter for the night. At least it broke the numbing westerly gusts that froze her nose, ears, and fingers. The rocky ground made it impossible to pitch any tents. Tiny as the oilskin shelter she had purchased was, she would have gladly used it if it were possible. The sky had turned ashen, though it only released intermittent squalls of swirling flakes that filled crevices but failed to coat any flat surfaces.

Danae sat with her back to the rock face, her mount nosing around in the cracks to find some sprig of last year's grasses to tear up and chew. Mizzletorp examined each horse's legs in turn, feeling up and down their cannons and lifting their hooves.

"Shards and slides!" Mizzletorp said. "These rocks show less mercy than a pack of ten dogs after one bone. The sooner we can get out of this hill country and onto some decent grass, the better."

"The horses aren't doing well?" Danae asked.

He let the mare drop her foot back to the ground. "Your beast is the closest to going lame of all of them, but that's the fault of the farrier who shod her. I'm of a mind to pull her shoes off once we hit friendlier terrain."

"You'd know better than I would." Danae sighed. She, too, would be glad to be out of the twisting rock of the foothills, if for no other reason but to be able to ride with less jolting, jarring, and picking their way.

Darkness deepened around them, and the flat cloud cover left the campsite in starless blackness that reduced their vision to just a few feet. Danae snuggled into her nest of bedding. No matter how tight a ball she curled into, the cold constantly found ways to worm its icy fingers to her flesh, and she squeezed her eyes closed tight against the realization this would be the state of affairs for the foreseeable future.

A sharp cry somewhere nearby jolted Danae from a tenuous slumber. Mizzletorp's bow creaked as he bent it and let an arrow whiz from the string. From the sound of it, his bolt skittered off the rocks, finding no mark in the darkness. Springing from her bedroll, she drew a dagger and scuttled to the archer, who stood within the faint patch of illumination provided by the coals of the fire.

"What is it?" she whispered.

"Don't know. Something's coming. Hit it once, but I've lost it in the rocks and dark." His large, golden eyes flitted left and right.

In an eruption of scraping claws and snarls, a hulking beast no smaller than Mizzletorp's pony sprang from a cleft in the rocks. The gnome's poised arrow shot wild. The creature lunged at him, raking his chest with gleaming teeth.

When the enemy rushed past, a gust of air fluttered Danae's hair, and in its wake, a wave of needles swept over her.

Oh, no . . .

"Praesidio!" she shouted.

The beast snapped again at Mizzletorp, who fended the blow off with a punch to the animal's snout. He groped for a hilt at his belt and tossed his bow aside.

Was it a bear? No, the muzzle was too long, its legs too gangly. Unsure of what else to do, Danae lunged forward at the four-legged foe. She thrust her dagger. The blade skittered across the beast's wiry-haired hide, but left only a shallow scratch.

The creature snarled and turned a venomous glare upon Danae. It bored into her with a gaze full of unnerving comprehension, and the intensity of its stare stabbed blades of terror into her heart. The prickling assault on her skin swelled to a flesh-crawling intensity. The enemy, a freakishly oversized hunting hound, growled with quivering lips. A white triangle brand on its shoulder gleamed pale in the firelight.

It leapt.

Danae threw her arm across her face. She stumbled back from the toothy offensive.

The whistle of a blade rent the air, just before Mizzletorp's short sword landed a blow upon the hound's shoulder that tore a deep gash. Something hot spattered on Danae's cheek, and she winced. She swiped at her face with her free hand, and found her glove streaked with blood. Her revulsion thrust her back a staggering step. She forced herself to lunge again, but her attack fell clumsily to the hound's side.

Mizzletorp brought his sword around again in a great arc and hacked into the ribcage of his opponent, sending it tumbling. The animal regained its feet.

The gnome's eyes widened and his jaw dropped. "Stay down, ye mongrel!"

The hound's flaming glance flitted back and forth between its combatants, then it lunged at Danae again. It caught her shoulder in clenched jaws. Her dagger jolted from her hand and tumbled out of the firelight. A nightmarish wrestling match began, with Danae tumbling and wriggling, but the enemy clutched her tighter the more she struggled.

Mizzletorp drew a long knife in his off hand and erupted into a whirlwind of attacks. Blades screamed past Danae's body, head, and limbs. Many cuts fell upon the enemy. The majority of the strokes glanced off the sinewy hide of the beast, but a lucky few bit deep. The more relentless Mizzletorp's assault, the tighter the hound clenched his jaw. Danae cried out, kicking and scratching for her freedom.

A beacon of light flared somewhere to the left, a pillar of blue fire that dazzled Danae's eyes. The hideous creature yelped, finally releasing its grip on her, and she scrabbled away from it and the approaching shaft of flame. Danae rolled until she bumped a rocky wall. She clamped a palm on her throbbing shoulder and patted her bandoliers with her opposite hand in search of a hilt.

As the light advanced upon the cringing hound, Danae found its source. Praesidio bore aloft a sword of flame, and the hound cowered before it with widening eyes. It backed away. Mizzletorp held the beast at sword and dagger point from one side, the cliff face rose up on the other.

With the crazed look, the hound sprang at Praesidio, who blocked the attack with his crackling blade. Brilliant sparks flew in all directions. The old man plunged the flame toward his opponent, opening a deep wound across the beast's haunches. Soon, Mizzletorp added his sword strokes to Praesidio's. The hellish cur twisted to dodge their attacks, its eyes wild and white-rimmed. In a feint, it lunged at Mizzletorp, but the attack melted into a retreat through a cleft in the rocks.

The crackling discomfort across Danae's skin faded to a tingle, then abated entirely. She heaved a sigh and slumped on the ground. *How is this possible?* It could not have been the same beast she saw in Briardale.

Could it?

Praesidio lowered his weapon and muttered something in his own language, which could not have been at all couth, judging by the tone of his words. He turned his gaze to Mizzletorp, who shook his head and began pressing a fold of binding rags to his chest. Praesidio's sword dimmed to a slim beam of fire. The old man hurried to Danae.

He knelt beside her. "Are you hurt?"

Danae propped up on an elbow and looked at her hand, which bore none of her own blood. "No, I'm all right. The fangs didn't break through my armor." She squinted at the rift the hound had used as an escape route. "What in the world was that horror?"

Praesidio set his jaw, his eyes flinty. "A servant of Queldurik, no doubt."

Mizzletorp scowled. "Tougher than hacking at an anvil! I better not have dulled my weapons on the blasted brute, or I'll chase him down and use his eyeteeth as a whetstone."

"Any chance it was actually just a big dog?" Danae asked. "One we surprised in its wanderings? Whose territory we encroached on?"

Praesidio's eyes softened. "You have much to unlearn, Danae, about the world and what is true. All your life, you have depended upon what you can see and touch, about what you can reason out and order into logical sense. You shall find we finite beings understand precious little of that which goes on around us, and even less of the events within realms beyond our own."

Danae cocked her head. Realms? Did he mean countries? Or something more fantastic than that?

"Wherever Creo's work is being done, there our enemy will pursue us and attempt to undo it." Praesidio's focus shifted beyond Danae and into the unseen distance. "It is a war that has raged for millennia past, and will continue to rage, so long as there are servants on both sides to make battle. Our enemies are cunning enough to know that many small deeds done in Creo's favor can build a fortress of might."

Danae rubbed her temples. Not very long in her past, she would have laughed off the very idea that a big dog could be the servant of a malevolent supernatural being, but the persistence of the hound's attack, coupled with those confounded pins-and-needles, nagged her to heed the old sage's words. No ordinary predator would have continued to attack in the face of the assault Mizzletorp had waged upon it. The memory of the hound's searching eyes made her muscles coil.

But what of Creo's work? How could she understand that? Did she really need to? After all, had she not spent much of her young life chanting incantations and expecting results, despite having no empirical evidence as to why they should? No scientific knowledge could explain these powers. This wide world full of oddities that she had only begun to glimpse fell into the same category. Rising from the stony ground, she brushed herself off and hugged her arms around her trembling body.

Mizzletorp cleaned his blades and returned them to their scabbards. He paced the perimeter of the camp. His vigilance, full of darting glances and jumping at shadows, compelled Danae to keep a dagger loose in its sheath. She shuddered and hopped in place a few times to shake the tremors from her limbs.

Praesidio still held his uncanny weapon, whose blade of fire bathed his features in cool, undulating light.

A small step drew Danae a little closer to him. "How do you do that?"

"Oh, the Sword of the Sacred Fire, you mean?" Praesidio swept the blade in a tight figure-eight. "It is a Virtus granted at need to the members of my order, and a much more impactful weapon against the summoned servants of Darkness than an ordinary blade or arrow."

True, her own dagger barely nicked the hound's hide, but was the keenness of her blade or the bluntness of her inexperience to blame?

"I know it will not be easy, but we must try to get back to sleep," Praesidio said. "An exhausted traveler does not make a trustworthy watchman." His weapon dissipated, leaving his hand empty once again, and he headed back to his bedroll.

Danae, too, curled back up in her camping spot, but lay awake for some time, imagining unseen enemies. In the end however, sleep did come. Thankfully it was dreamless.

From a high bluff, Danae surveyed the landscape below. The rising sun fought a losing battle against a flat blanket of cloud cover. A winding path cut its way down the craggy slope ahead. Far off, a silver ribbon of sparkling water meandered its way in and out of clustered glens.

Praesidio led them down the switchbacks. The lower they descended, the thicker the vegetation became, though all of it bare of leaves. The horses ambled down the rocky path, their quickening footfalls painting them eager to bid farewell to the bite of stones beneath their feet. The wind died down, though the weather maintained a steady chill, and the lowering clouds darkened the advancing day.

When they stopped to take their customary mid-day rest, Danae plunked down beside Praesidio. "I would like to know more about the Sacred Fire."

"Would you now?" Praesidio beamed. "We do face many miles ahead, so perhaps there will be time to do it justice. But where to begin?" He leaned back on his elbow and tipped his chin to the heavens. "My order, the Knights of the Phoenix, is a division of the knights of the Elgadrim, direct warrior servants of the High Philosopher of our people. Our calling is to oversee the use of Virtusen and curses in this world, and see to it Curse-Bearers are enlightened, or at least, kept from harming others with their corrupt powers. For always it is their goal to conquer and subdue others to their desires."

The difficult nuances of the strange powers Danae always knew existed but almost feared to grow better acquainted with weighed on her mind. "I'm still unclear on how there can be different kinds of magic."

"The curses are a perversion of something created for good. We seek to educate those who do not realize what casting curses will mean to their futures, and to turn them from this destructive path. So our lives are ever filled with confronting evil, and cultivating within ourselves a teacher's heart to help the unknowing."

"Like me." A smirk tugged at Danae's lips. "An unknowing 'Curse-Bearer,' right?"

Praesidio lowered his eyelids. "Yes. When I discovered you were wandering through the powers granted by darkness, it was my sworn duty to rescue you."

Danae laughed. "And I thought perhaps you were helping me out of sympathy for my story. Now you tell me you're just doing your job."

Praesidio, too, laughed, but then his smile dissolved, and he regarded Danae from beneath his brows. "Just because I am doing the work I have been called to does not mean I do so only out of obligation. I care about you personally, Danae, and about every gifted soul I meet who could do great things with only a little guidance."

Great things. Danae wrapped her arms around her middle. The smaller pursuit of sorting out her apparent spiritual issues seemed daunting enough.

Mizzletorp's voice cut through her thought. "Enough chit-chat.

This stretch of road has some unsettling tracks in it, and I'm of a mind not to meet with the makers."

Praesidio narrowed his eyes, but the gnome merely shook his head. Whatever non-verbal exchange passed between them seemed to satisfy the old man. He rose and swung onto his horse. "It seems the rest of my story will have to wait."

23

DURIK'S LEGEND

*B*y late afternoon, they had reached the foot of the rocky mountain path. Miles of rolling countryside stretched before them to the east, north and south.

"Welcome to the northern reaches of Kelmirith," Praesidio said. "As my people are much diminished in number, I think we will find these lands mostly empty. We must make for the Ford of Jovanov of the Great River Nuruhain, which crosses our path between here and the border of Tebal. There once was a road that led to the place, but over the many years of disuse, I am not sure how clear that path will still be. Do you know the road, Mizzletorp?"

The blue-skinned guide nodded. "Yep. We shall see if we can come to it without adventures of the hack and bleed sort. With the way you Elgadrim all huddle together to the south and can't fuss with matters so far from Bilearne, this region's grown pretty tangled with bandits, brigands, and worse over the past score of years."

Worse?

"Is there some other course you'd recommend?" Danae's voice shook.

Mizzletorp let out an explosive laugh. "Another course, she says! Sure, there's always another way, but do you really feel like waging a three-man offensive on one of the bridges the Tebalese hold? They've got 'em all, ya know."

"But not the ford?"

"Nope. Too close to elf-territory. Not even the Tebalese are bold enough to tramp in the Delsin's backyard. Not yet."

Praesidio frowned. "There is no debate here. The ford of Jovanov is the logical path. I am not concerned about brigands."

The easier terrain of Kelmirith allowed for faster travel, and once the sun had retreated far enough to transform the gloom of the day to the deepening murk of night, Mizzletorp chose a sheltered spot for them to make camp within a tight glen of oak and maple. He picked about the floor of the campsite and loaded dry wood into his arms. He dumped a large load the ground at camp's center, and pulled a small spade from his gear to dig the fire pit. Danae edged close to him as he stacked the wood. He considered each log with tight-lipped scrutiny before he chose its spot in the pyramid of fuel. Such perfectionism. But then, his fires always burned bright, long, and practically smokeless.

"Well, lass!" Mizzletorp sang as he leaned the last log into stack. "What do you think? Will it do the job in keeping the chill out of our bones tonight?"

"To be honest . . . I guess I don't know." Danae shuffled a foot in the leaf litter. "That's why I'm watching you. I've got a long way to go on this journey, and I figure I had better learn something along the way, and not just clutch your coattails the whole time."

"Now if that don't just butter my bread on both sides! I like a lass who's ready to take on somethin' new." His gaze turned piercing. "Big things in store for this one, I think!"

Did he mean her? It was so hard to interpret what he spoke of, especially when he drifted away halfway through his sentence. Did any word pass through his mind that he failed to speak aloud? Much of the day he chattered, and less than half of his words were directed at anyone in particular.

Mizzletorp snapped back to her. "C'mon, Peach. Let's get this blaze a-cracklin'!"

Peach? So he's given me a nickname. That's a sign of acceptance, right? It seems like a fond sort of name . . .

He proceeded to give Danae a short lesson in wood stacking, tinder arrangement, and some of the finer points of fire building. By the end, she found herself laughing alongside the quirky little wilderness guide.

Praesidio pressed closer to the edge of the merry bonfire, and flashed a bright grin to Danae. "Well, if that's not a blaze to drive back the Impenetrable Darkness himself!" He popped the last bite of his waybread into his mouth.

"I hear you sometimes speak the name Queldurik, and other times, you say the Impenetrable Darkness. Aren't they one and the same?" she asked.

Mizzletorp scowled.

What had she said? Hopefully, whatever it was had not put too large a dent in their new camaraderie.

Praesidio shook his head. "In broad daylight, you ask me about my order, and the things that are good and just in the world, and in a time of shadow, you begin questions about the evils that plague us. You have strange timing, young one!"

"Strange timing or not," Danae said, "if we're headed directly into the homeland of Queldurik's staunchest worshipers, I think knowing something about them would be prudent, don't you?"

Praesidio sighed and brushed the last crumbs of his meal from his robe. "All right then, to answer your question, no, the Impenetrable Darkness and Queldurik are not one and the same. Queldurik is merely a servant of the Darkness. Unlike Creo, the Darkness is not omnipresent, and must have emissaries to gather information and to do his bidding."

Danae frowned. "So does Queldurik have any real power of his own?"

"Hmph." Mizzletorp picked up his bow and quiver and stomped away from the fireside.

"What did I say?"

Praesidio pressed his lips together and gave a small shake of his head. He waited until Mizzletorp had vanished beyond the firelight.

"Don't doubt the reality of Queldurik's influence on our world, though how he came to his place of false godhood is a strange tale, for certain." Praesidio sat against the trunk of a stout maple, stretched out his long legs, and laced his fingers behind his head.

"This looks like it's going to be a long one." A hunger for knowledge drew her close to the old sage, and she sat cross-legged at his feet.

Praesidio nodded. A smile creased the skin around his eyes. "Long, long ago, when my people's civilization was in its flower, we were able to help a great many in the far reaches of this continent, and even others, all in Creo's name. But always, there are those who doubt, those who cannot accept that one man would trouble himself for the benefit of another, and in their disbelief, scorn those who do a good work. Such was a young merchant by the name of Durik, a man of the Vareinor of old."

"Vareinor?" Danae asked. "Who are they?"

Praesidio sighed. "Let it suffice to say, in a bygone age when my people were greater, we called ourselves the Vareinor. Perhaps the time will present itself for me to explain the events that led to our current namesake."

Danae laughed and folded her arms across her chest. "I'll hold you to that. All right, so what of Durik's scorn for the Vareinor?"

"Durik argued the Thaumaturgists of Creo merely dazzled the people with tricks, and the knights and the Council ran an elaborate ruse to keep the ordinary people in their place. He denied Creo's existence, loudly at that, and boasted that all our Virtusen could be explained with careful study; that enough sleight of hand and alchemy in combination could affect the same events we called the power of Creo."

"That's absurd." Danae scoffed. "You can do a great many wonderful things with alchemy, but match a ... Virtus, is it?"

"Do not so quickly discount Durik's claim, Danae. You would be surprised at the breadth of this world—your father has only introduced you to its safest edges." Praesidio pulled his cloak tighter around his body. "But Durik set out to prove his theory, and indeed, grew into quite possibly the greatest alchemist ever to walk the earth. He produced monumental, and often destructive, chemical events."

"I can't imagine the Elgadrim—Vareinor—just stood by and let him destroy things." Danae leaned in, elbows on her knees.

"Not at all. The Council grew concerned about the arsenal that Durik was amassing in his laboratory, and called him to a meeting to discuss the responsible management of his resources, for the general safety of our people. Being already quite mad from years of relentless study and a complete absorption in proving the nonexistence of Creo, Durik lashed out at the very idea of discussing his laboratory and its contents with the Council. He assumed they hoped to destroy his hard work, out of fear of his growing power.

"When the nine Council Members arrived on Durik's property to try to force the discussion, which, if I may interject my opinion, was their great mistake in all of this business, he lobbed a ball of some explosive material in their midst, killing five of them outright, and irreparably maiming three of the four who survived the attack. The knights of the Sapphire, an order of peacekeepers, fell upon Durik. Although they took heavy losses, they managed to bring him before the High Philosopher of that time, Aromen. The High Philosopher decreed Durik's formulas confiscated and that he should be banished to the northern wastes, lands that were largely uninhabited, save for a few packs of primitive nomadic tribes that lived there."

Danae lowered her chin. "Banished him? Why didn't they keep a madman like him locked away?"

"My people have always valued freedom highly, and perhaps Aromen did so to a fault. He assumed Durik could do little harm in a place so short on resources, but determination often proves to be the most valuable raw material of all. Durik's heart burned with deep hatred, and in his years of exile, his bitter anger gnawed him from within.

"One day, an emissary of the Impenetrable Darkness came to Durik in his lonely place to strike a deal. The Darkness, you see, has ever been at war with Creo, and now wished to work this war upon the mortal plane, to destroy Creo's most powerful servants, the Vareinor. In my people, Durik found a common enemy with this fiend emissary, and he began to reconsider his disbelief in the supernatural, given the unearthly horror of the creature sent to speak with him. In exchange for great increases in knowledge and power, Durik was to lend his destructive discoveries to the armies of the Darkness.

"So, into the far reaches of what is now northern Tebal, this fiend led Durik to a fortress of ice, where many followers of Darkness gathered and planned their assault on the Vareinor. Their strength, however, was lacking, and their army green. They spent many years there, so far to the north that none thought to even look for a people group in that place. But in their privacy, they grew. When they felt the time had come to test their strength, they struck out and swept into northern Kelmirith, visiting much destruction on the peaceable farmers and herdsmen who lived there."

Danae frowned. "Very brave of them. I see not much has changed about Tebal's armies in the past few thousand years."

Praesidio shrugged. "Bilearne sent her knights, but the repelling of the Host of Darkness proved to be a more bitter fight than any imagined it might be. Durik's destructive expertise, amplified by the dark powers wielded by the followers of the evil deity, drew the battle out for many months, though the Vareinor eventually pushed the enemy out of Kelmirith.

"Durik had certainly proven himself cunning and greatly useful to his new master. In little time, he attained the role of not just chief alchemist, but High Commander of the Dark Army. Many of their victories they owed to his craft, as they continually struck out over the next few decades, harassing the borderlands of their newly declared territory of Tebal, and even forging into the countries of North Deklia and Da-Shir to gain allies or capture slaves.

"But Durik, though blessed with the long life of my people, saw the count of his years was waning, and could not abide the idea of going to his grave before he saw the Vareinor cast down. Thus, he petitioned the highest fiendish servant of the Darkness he knew, Ba-al Zechmaat, to strike this deal with his master on Durik's behalf. Durik demanded the Impenetrable Darkness grant to him unending mortality, in exchange for his service in seeing the Vareinor destroyed." Praesidio paused to take a long drink from his water skin.

Danae took this moment to interject a question. "Unending mortality? You mean to never die?"

"Yes, but this is not to be confused with the immortality of Creo or the Darkness." Praesidio prodded the coals under the fire, and the flames leapt. "Durik was granted his request. In his pride over his new longevity, he changed his name to Queldurik, as 'quel' has the root meaning 'eternal' in our tongue. However, there is one caveat in the arrangement he has made with the Darkness, who will suffer no rival. Only if Queldurik can maintain a steady flow of sacrifices from his followers, will he remain in this undying state. If the sacrifices stop, then he will wane and die.

"His followers, however, are numerous and zealous, and more than glad to perform sacrifices to this creature who they elevate to the status of god, under the false assumption Queldurik grants them great power in exchange. Indeed, any power they might wield comes from Queldurik's liege, the Darkness himself. So, as you can see, by drawing a following, Queldurik further builds an empire for the Impenetrable Darkness."

After a moment of digesting the details of Praesidio's story, Danae opened her mouth to add another question, but motion in her peripheral vision cut her thought short.

Mizzletorp emerged from the darkness and returned to the fireside. "Are you two finished?"

Danae wrinkled her brow. "I suppose we can be. Have I done something wrong?"

The gnome plunked down. "Good Master Praesidio does too well by the vermin who serve Queldurik. You want to know why so many people, not just you, Peach, have never seen a forest gnome? The devils from up north see us as pests, sending their rat catchers of soldiers out to kill us off . . . all of us, ne'er sparing even wives or young'uns. Not unless it's to drag 'em off as slaves. I once had a wife and a little lad by her. Those brutes, best as I can tell, dragged them off when they mowed over our little village. As I lay, hewn and left for dead, I could hear them screamin', cryin' for mercy."

Mizzletorp swallowed hard. "And that's my last memory of those I loved. Not for a lack of tryin', I've never been able to find them again." He stood up, and kicked a loose stone off into the darkness beyond the firelight. "The only talk I can abide about Queldurik's swine is talk of how to bring their ruin."

Danae stared at Mizzletorp's haggard face. She managed to stammer a weak, "I'm so sorry to hear . . ."

Mizzletorp waved it off. "Don't be. If you wanna make a difference about what happened to me—leastaways help keep it from happenin' to others less able to brook it—get the Sword. The sooner we can get it into the hands of someone who could use it to cut down that dung heap Queldurik, the better."

Danae glanced back and forth between the gnome and Praesidio. "Does someone intend to try to wield it? That is, if we can even find it."

Praesidio shook his head and turned a dark scowl to Mizzletorp. "The fate of the Sword is as yet undetermined. The members of my order are divided over our next course of action, should we succeed in the Sword's recovery."

"If you ask me," Mizzletorp said, "It's pretty clear what the Council should decide. That is, unless they have a mind to go on fightin' war after war 'til Queldurik whittles you down to nothing."

Praesidio sighed and stared into the fire. Danae clamped her lips together, silenced by the depressing turn the conversation had taken. Long after she retired, she lay awake, troubled over how important her recovery of the Sword might be, not just to her own situation, but to the swing of history. It was a burden that had a way of slowing sleep's approach.

24

___

The Ford of Jovanov

The hiss of whispering voices caught Danae's ear as she lay in the dark security of her tent. She strained after the sound.

"Did you catch sight of the blighters tonight?" Mizzletorp said.

"No," Praesidio replied. "They seem to have grown more cautious."

"Any chance they've given up?"

"Little to none."

"Slippery devils, for sure," Mizzletorp said. The characteristic *whoosh* his blades made as he spun them into their sheaths reached her ears. "There'd be less bile in my gullet over it if we knew what was back there. Or if it's just happenstance we've noticed 'em more than once."

"I have a few guesses, given other events of this journey."

"They wouldn't be bolder than to just trail us through the countryside for days in and out?"

"No. Not without a tactical advantage." Praesidio's voice lowered further. "See to it we don't hand them one."

Danae propped on her elbow and leaned closer to the canvas wall of her tent, but either her comrades had stopped speaking or had found whispers below her range of hearing.

Her tent flap flung aside. Danae scrambled back and clamped her hand onto a dagger.

Mizzletorp stood in the opening. "It's just me, Peach. Your turn to look out."

He shuffled to his camping spot, though it seemed to Danae his gaze lingered over his shoulder and burned into her with a smoldering edge. Praesidio was nowhere in sight.

Danae crept from her tent and perched on a pile of mossy stone at the edge of their small circle of firelight. The mound comprised the tallest portion of a ring of tumbled quarry blocks, likely the ancient remnants of a watchtower or highway patrol booth from the forgotten days when Praesidio's people still occupied these northern marches of Kelmirith. Now only ruins and weed-choked highways lingered to hint at waning tales.

The late-rising moon cast its stark blue light over the lands around them. A nearby dell of birch trees gleamed in the moonlight, as if the trees' white bark emitted a glow of their own. Beyond them stood the dozing silhouettes of their horses, picketed for grazing. Tatters of clouds drifted across the night sky. A few settled over the moon, blotting out its light, when something rustled in the underbrush.

She wheeled around, her pulse quickening as she pulled a dagger from its sheath. Near the edge of the dell, a glint flashed between tree trunks. Perhaps the green mirror of eyes? The darkness concealed who or what lurked beyond sight. Loath to awaken her comrades over what was probably no more than a raccoon or opossum, she waited. Another rustle and swish. Had she heard a low growl?

"Probably just a few night hunters drawn by the—"

Out of the shadows crept three monstrous hounds, as black as the night sky. The leader she knew by its glance. And its scars. She did not wish to find out if its new companions matched its proven tenacity. The prickling wave that enveloped her preceded the hounds like a cloud of heat emerging from the opening of a masonry stove door.

"Back off, you monsters!" She thrust her hands out. "*Cauternnen . . . uh . . . ballinire!*"

A flash of purple light burst among the hounds, sending out sparks that singed their hides.

The beasts stalked, unflinching, toward Danae with the slow, menacing prowl of predators.

Ugh. This was not the time to stammer. What else do I know? She pressed her heel of her hand into her forehead. *Think!*

With a searing crack, the embers that had drifted to the floor of the glen erupted into a secondary explosion. The hounds yelped, and all three fled into the darkness. Danae straightened and brushed her hands together.

A strong hand grasped her by the scruff of the neck and hauled her from the rocks upon which she stood. She twisted around to collide with Praesidio's infuriated glare.

"What in the world are you doing? Just how many curses would you like to pile upon the load you already bear? I thought you understood the implications!"

A film of sweat broke upon her brow. "The sparks drove the brutes off, didn't they? Better to avoid potential wounding out here in the wild, don't you think?" Danae stepped back. She brushed at her cloak and straightened her tunic, despite the roiling turmoil in her stomach.

"Driven them off, have you? Do you really believe *your* small spray of sparks was all it took to send them into retreat? You accrue a costly debt over a few fireworks."

Danae sucked her teeth. So, the secondary explosion had not been her doing, but rather a more effective attack delivered from Praesidio's hand. "I'm sure I'll be able to work out this 'debt' you assess me to be in later. For now, I wasn't interested in letting those beasts come a step closer. Don't you trust my judgment to use what spells I know, when the situation is dire?"

"No, Danae, at this point in your journey, I do *not* trust your judgment. In your return to these incantations you know, you are much like the drunkard, who daily returns to the bottom of his cup, seeking forgetfulness. Although he may find what he seeks, the search itself is poison to his soul." He clasped her shoulders. "Hearken to me! In the Darkness, your drafts on the evil power are tallied, and this is a debt you cannot afford to pay when the collector comes to demand it."

Surely the last five years of practice in studying these incantations had taught her their proper use. She readied a glare for the old sage, but the potency of his words seeped through her façade. As she looked into his wisdom-lined face, the smolder in her heart faltered.

She took a few short paces away from Praesidio. "The longer I travel with you, the more foolish I feel."

Praesidio pursued her with a long stride. "You recognize foolishness when you see it, so that is a start. But I must admonish you. Please, do not utter another word from your father's books. All you have accomplished tonight was to confirm in our hunters' minds you are surely the target they seek."

"You're holding back on me." Danae folded her arms. "You know about troubles I don't."

"I saw no need to trouble you with speculations. But now that I have seen them more than once, I am convinced the Hounds of Queldurik are hunting you, Danae."

"Hounds . . . of Queldurik?" Danae swallowed. "That doesn't sound promising."

"No, I'm afraid not. They will return to their master and lead him to you."

"This has something to do with this debt you keep talking about, doesn't it?" Danae twisted the fabric of her cloak.

"It has everything to do with your debt. But now we are sure of our enemy, and he of his quarry." Praesidio circled the fire, rubbing his temples. "We will have to ride hard for the ford over the next week or so and pray we can lose them in the crossing."

∿

*D*anae pushed sweaty hair out of her eyes with one hand as she gripped her mare's mane with the stiff knuckles of the other. She patted the mare's damp neck. "Good job, girl. I know it's been a lot of running today, but I'm afraid it can't be helped. I owe you something tasty when we're done today, if I've got anything."

The dales that opened in rolling golden stretches between forested hillsides made for easy galloping. But even that pace left Danae fretting over the continual suspicion they could not ride fast enough to outrun the trouble somewhere behind, always worrisome, but never in sight. At least Praesidio and Mizzletorp had they ceased correcting her riding technique.

By midday, Danae's breath no longer came in frosty clouds from her mouth. Indeed, her cloak felt over-warm, and the air clung to her, humid and laden with the smell of rain. A faint tingle ran across Danae's scalp. The catacombs, the librarian, Praesidio, Archadion . . . she could see how perhaps all these might inspire a similar sensation. But here, in the open? With nothing but grass and trees and an ever-thickening bank of lead-colored clouds rolling in, why now?

As soon as the first rank of ominous clouds had assembled, they dumped torrents of rain that started in a sheet and fell with blinding steadiness from then on. Danae's tingle turned to a constant needling she had to grit her teeth to endure. Thunder rumbled and lightning flashed. The horses startled often in the foul weather, especially Chancellor, who bared his teeth and struck with his forelegs at the empty air. His ears remained flat against his skull, and his wild eyes kept the other horses at a distance. Praesidio often patted his mount's neck and spoke fluid words in the tongue of the Elgadrim, which settled the horse for a few moments, but with the next flash of lightning, Chancellor returned to his erratic dance.

"Heaven and earth, I'd give just about anything to get out of this rain," Danae said as the day wore toward evening, with no end to the downpour in sight. "I hope my horse can see better than I can, because I've given up trying to wipe the water out of my eyes." At least the chill of her sodden clothes had finally overridden the other, unnamable source of goose bumps.

"We cannot expect to press on to nightfall in this tempest," Praesidio said. "We should camp as soon as we come upon a decent spot."

Mizzletorp, the muddiest and most bedraggled of the group, jumped from his pony with a sloppy splat. "Hold it right there, mates." He handed his reins to Danae and slipped through the underbrush.

After a minute or two of sullen waiting, the shrubs beside Danae rustled, and she jumped. Mizzletorp materialized right out of the foliage. Rather than his usual blue, however, his skin had taken on a blotched green and gray tone. Between that and his soiled garb that blended seamlessly into his surroundings, it was no wonder he had surprised her.

"We're in luck!" He beamed. "Looks like ol' Creo saw fit to offer us accommodations tonight."

"What do you mean?" she asked.

"There's a snug little cave not a hundred paces off thataway. Follow me." As he spoke, his face slowly shifted back to the blue Danae expected.

They followed the gnome to his choice of campsite. After tethering the horses in the semi-shelter of the thicket that obscured the cave, they bustled inside the cramped quarters. Each traveler brought with them all the equipment they had room to spread out for drying. Nowhere was there even a twig of dry wood to use for a fire, so they ate their meal huddled around Danae's lantern.

"I would never have expected rain like this, not at this time of year," Praesidio said as the thrum of the torrential downpour rose even higher. "This storm should be snow, especially this far to the north."

Danae shuffled to the mouth of the cave. "Does the weather always come out of the north here in Kelmirith?" She squinted at the sky and then turned her back to it.

Mizzletorp shook his head. "No. Not rain, leastaways. Blasts of deathly cold, yep, those come from the north. But rain? South or west is where she finds her strength and tumbles on over." He sprang over to his bedroll and flopped down into it. Turning to Praesidio, he added, "Sure doesn't add up, does it old man?"

"No. I daresay not." Praesidio sat cross-legged on the floor.

"Is it possible . . ." Danae rubbed her arms. "Can people affect the weather with magic?"

Praesidio's spine straightened. "What makes you ask such a question?"

She shrank into herself. "Um. I can't really say. It just seems like... I don't know."

Praesidio rose and approached her with slow, definitive strides. With every step of ground he covered between the two of them, an uncanny flesh twitter skittered across her front in increasingly intense waves, while the continual, lesser irritation drummed on her back.

"What are you doing?" She stared at Praesidio, wide-eyed.

"I am no longer shielding you. I was not entirely certain I needed to, but now I suspect you are very uncomfortable as I move into your vicinity. Is that not so?"

Danae swallowed. "Why?"

A rush of warmth smoothed over her skin, and the crawling torture abated.

"That is better, correct?"

"How do you know this?" Danae's heart thumped in her ears.

"I cannot know anything unless you tell me," Praesidio replied. "But I have long suspected. I restrained my curiosity about your shudder in the moment we spotted one another in the cargo hold. But the way you quailed when you first met Archadion, who would have taken no pains to shield an inexperienced sensor from his particularly intense signature—I could not ignore that."

"Sensor?" Danae narrowed her eyes.

"Yes, Danae. Some of those gifted with otherworldly talents also possess the ability to sense those who also have the gifting. I understand it usually presents as a prickling or tingling in the flesh."

A single laugh burst from Danae's lips. "Is this a good thing?"

Praesidio shrugged. "What is good about something that simply is? It is how we use what we have been given that makes such gifts either good or bad."

Danae folded her arms. "Well, if I'm one of these 'sensors,' why have I never felt any kind of tingle around my father? I've seen him work incantations."

"You probably did feel his signature when you were very little. But you can grow immune to signatures you experience on a daily basis. By the time you were old enough to have memories, you had probably long grown used to him."

"Interesting," Danae rubbed her brow, sorting through her earliest childhood recollections of her father, but no encounter of any 'signature' from him emerged. One instance of the tingling did surface, however . . . the day her baby brother was born. *Weylan!*

"You all right, Peach?" Mizzletorp asked.

She cleared her throat of the tightness that had arisen within it. "I'm fine. This is just a lot to come to grips with." Was it not enough that this 'gifting' of magic had already endangered two members of her family?

Praesidio placed a hand on her shoulder. "It is a bulky burden, young learner, and you can inform me as to whether you would like to endure my signature for a few weeks so you can get over it, or if you would like me to continue to shield it. For now, you confirm my suspicions about the nature of this unlikely storm, though the motive behind it both eludes and concerns me."

~

The rain hammered down for the next week, never slackening, and only the precious items stowed in oilskin satchels managed to escape saturation. During those days of travel across the Kelmiri wilderness, the countryside transformed from rolling foothills dotted with stands of trees to a region thickly blanketed in coniferous forest. The rain blew through the saturated woodlands. Large, slapping droplets that shook from the limbs of the firs repeatedly smacked Danae in the face. Her mare shook her mane every few moments.

Danae sweated as she leaned as far back as she could in the saddle, her wet hands raw with the constant pull of the coarse leather of her reins, her warm gloves long stashed in her pack. Even at a careful pace, the horses often struggled with the footing. In some spots, the deep mud sucked at the beasts' legs. In others, a thick blanket of fallen pine needles presented the constant risk of slipping and tumbling. The travelers' progress slowed to a crawl.

"Should have the ford in view tomorrow," Mizzletorp called to his companions as they trundled down a slope.

"I hope you're right," Danae replied. "The sooner we're off these hillsides, the better."

"With all this steepin' in the wet, I'm thinkin' our poor beasts'll be rife with thrush if this weather doesn't let up," Mizzletorp grumbled. "It's got nerve to be rainin' at all this time o' year, let alone to insist on it, day after day."

"I am more concerned about how easy we are to track," Praesidio said. "Our three mounts are cutting quite a swath through the mud as we go."

Danae twisted around in her saddle. The churned earth left no question about their passage. She drew a tremulous breath and urged her mare as fast as she dared in the miserable conditions.

*D*anae awoke before dawn on the eighth day, teeth chattering. Curling into the tightest ball she could muster made little difference against the damp that had penetrated her clothes. All seemed strangely silent.

The constant pattering on her tent had stopped.

Danae thrust her tent flap aside. The rain had finally moved on. All it left behind was a sky of bright stars and puddles that already wore a layer of white, crystalline ice. Maybe they could finally make some reasonable progress toward the ford when they set out that morning.

Once the sun rose, they resumed their ride, but only the topmost layer of the ground had firmed up from the cold, so the horses' hooves cracked through the frozen crust on the ground and squished into saturated soil. At about mid-morning, somewhere beyond the constant hoof beat, creak of leather, and jingle of buckle her group created, Danae sensed a distant sound. It was barely audible at first, but grew in intensity as they rode. It began as only a whispering undercurrent to their travels, but the more distance they put behind them, the more the whisper swelled, until the unbroken reverberation nagged at the back of Danae's mind. Was it the wind picking up in the distant trees? She strained her ears to listen. It was not wind she heard, but water.

"Praesidio, Mizzletorp." Danae tugged her reins and brought the mare to a halt. "Do either of you hear that rushing sound?"

The men reined their horses in, and they both cocked their heads. Mizzletorp's brows scrunched.

Given time to listen only to the distant murmur, Danae had an epiphany. The far-off roar came from a tumbling current.

Praesidio's eyes went wide, and he and Mizzletorp locked gazes.

The gnome's face contorted. "Confound it all, of course! All that rain has run down here to end up in the Nuruhain. I'm guessin' the ford'll be no kind o' crossing at all."

Praesidio gritted his teeth. "We had better go on and have a look at the river and decide what to do from there."

The riders nudged their horse's flanks, and they crested a small rise, beyond which Mizzletorp's dismal prophecy took shape. In a torrent of yellow foam, the Nuruhain careened through the valley below, its usual banks long overrun, and the water rushing with deadly depth and speed. They rode thirty yards further down the embankment and came to a halt. The horses tossed their heads.

"We'll have to try to head—" Praesidio began, but his horse bolted.

As if taking a cue from the old sage's stallion, the other horses shied as well, and Danae grabbed with clumsy haste at her reins to shorten them and regain control. She searched their surroundings for what could be causing the animals' sudden skittishness. The truth sunk into her chest like a blade.

Three black hounds strode forward from the cover of the trees with ponderous steps, their teeth bared, and greenish foam dripping from their maws. Mizzletorp wrenched his bow from his back in a fraction of a moment. He let an arrow fly toward the beasts. The shaft stuck fast in the lead hound's chest, and yet, the murderous creature continued forward, growling and snarling.

Danae again drew a dagger from her sheath.

"No incantations," she whispered.

Out of the cover of the trees came more figures. A half dozen, no, eight or nine twisted people, if they could be called such, lurched with crooked gaits up behind the Hounds of Queldurik, brandishing fearsome, stout bladed swords and heavy shields, their bodies covered in piecemeal armor. Quite obviously, the shambling wretches had plundered their gauntlets, breastplates, greaves, and helms from many different victims, and had taken no care to maintain the rusting and rent plates over time. They all had mottled skin of a sickly palette of white and green, and some of them allowed bluish-gray tongues to loll from their mouths.

The blade of fear in Danae's chest turned to ice. Her grasp tightened on her hilt. She drew a dagger in her left hand as well.

"*Kherak-tul!*" Mizzletorp cried, pointing to the approaching warriors.

Danae glanced back and forth between Praesidio and the gnome.

"River goblins," Praesidio said.

He glared at the creatures and nodded grimly, summoning his sword and sweeping it in a circle around his head. His steady posture dared the enemies to advance.

Danae trembled. How could she and her companions survive an attack by so many? The hounds had proven tenacious enough on their own.

As the goblins closed the distance between the travelers and themselves, another figure, more horrific than the hounds and the goblins put together, crashed from the dense forest. It towered over a story high, and the ground trembled under its footfalls. Clad in only a ragged garment of hide, the creature likely never gave a thought to armor, for its skin looked as thick and rugged as the bark of an ancient redwood. Its powerful arms hung so long from hunched shoulders that its knuckles brushed the needles on the forest floor. The creature's breath steamed from between its rotting, yellow teeth. If ever a creature from bedtime stories of old fit the description of ogre, this was it.

It lumbered toward Danae and her companions, drew a massive, stone-headed hammer from its back, and bellowed a thunderous roar. The mob of horrors broke into a run, charging down the hillside, weapons high.

With a squeal, Danae's little mare shied sharply, tossing Danae from her back. Danae found the presence of mind to tuck into a roll and landed on her feet, but she had no time to celebrate the move.

The hounds barreled toward Danae, and the whooping goblins darted forward, outpacing their lumbering commander to engage Praesidio and Mizzletorp. Mizzletorp's bow twanged in swift repetition. Out of the corner of her eye, Danae saw Praesidio's blade of flame cut across the body of the first goblin to attack him.

Ducking and dodging, Danae avoided the first assault of snapping jaws, and even managed to land two blows upon the beasts with the daggers in her hands. She wheeled, kicked, and stabbed. Her frantic tactics at least seemed to give the creatures momentary pause.

With a mighty spring, the lead hound leapt and caught the hood of Danae's cloak in his teeth and slammed her onto her back. Another mongrel dove in. Just before the second mauler crashed down, Danae bent her legs up in front of her. She caught the beast against her feet. Thrust her legs up. The hound emitted a high-pitched bark as it catapulted over and behind her.

Danae rolled and slashed, catching the lead hound across the face, and with a yelp, it released her cloak. She sprang to her feet, barely in time to dodge a lunge from the third hound. One of her enemies snapped, ripped a gash in her pant leg, and scored her flesh with a searing sting. Everywhere she turned, teeth flashed. Hackles bristled. Claws gouged.

A tree branch above offered a slim chance of refuge. After a final slash, Danae sheathed one of her daggers and sprang. She caught the branch firmly in the free hand, but her other fingers groped to retain a weapon and grasp the limb. A screaming pain stabbed through her foot.

One of the beasts had clamped onto her boot. She kicked with the other leg and planted her heel in its eye. The dagger-toothed jaw slackened just enough that she could swing her legs up. Hauling upward with all the strength she could muster, she clambered into the embrace of the tree. The hounds leapt at her, but their jaws caught only air.

Danae wrenched herself higher and settled in the crotch of a thick branch. She heaved for breath. The spot commanded a view of the battle, and she surveyed the mayhem unfolding below.

The goblins exchanged blows with both Praesidio and Mizzle-torp, who both bled from enemy sword slashes. The great ogre advanced upon the melee, and behind him, yet another adversary emerged from behind a dense cluster of holly. He stayed back, unengaged, and yet his presence raked icy claws of terror over every inch of her body. After his fell aura had frozen her flesh, its chill seeped into her marrow.

He wore a deeply hooded robe of ebony black, trimmed in red, and he observed the battle, his arms folded across his chest. Though he was no bigger than an ordinary man, how was it he struck Danae as the most dangerous of all the combatants? Was it merely from the unsettling signature he emitted?

Praesidio wheeled about and cut down his foes with deadly precision, for two already lay motionless at his feet, though three more opponents surrounded him. Mizzletorp's plight was similar. The huge ogre's lumbering strides bore him straight toward Praesidio. Was Praesidio aware of the villain's approach? Even if he was, he could only counter so many opponents at once, and no doubt, the ogre increased the enemies to a number beyond even a knight's limit.

She needed to help.

Danae grabbed a length of rope and grappling hook from her equipment. She cast a stomach-twisting glance down the bole of her tree to the leaping and slavering hounds clawing at its trunk and laying the wood bare. Hounds aside, she clenched her teeth and wound up the grapple for a throw. Her fingers sprang open and the grapple sailed into the tree closest to the knight of the Elgadrim. A forceful tug confirmed it had caught firmly in the branches. She groped for the nerve to actually employ the rope but found such courage just out of reach.

"Praesidio!" Danae screamed, but the din of the battle and the thrum of the rushing water devoured her voice. The stench of blood filled her nostrils, and her chest tightened. The ogre closed in. Just as the towering monstrosity loomed within a few strides of Praesidio's unguarded back, Danae squeezed her eyes shut. She crushed hemp in quaking hands.

She swung.

Would the force of her insignificant weight serve as enough distraction to belay the force of the ogre's hammer, otherwise destined for the swamped knight? The monster prepared a blow. Danae's trajectory was not quite—

The hammer came screaming in. Straight for Danae. Her ribcage exploded in blinding pain. The force of the ogre's blow sent her hurtling toward the torrent of the river. Somewhere in the distance, a guttural voice burst with a series of what must have been curses and admonishments. Churning brown river foam raced up to meet her.

Another collision. Shocking cold.

Darkness.

PART III

25

UNLIKELY DISCOVERY

*T*he coppery tinge of blood tainted the breeze. Culduin breathed the all-too-familiar scent and yanked his hand ax from the trunk of the tree before him. He squinted off to the north, between the slender trunks of the young white ash around him, his pointed ears pricked for even the tiniest sound or disturbance. Whatever the kill or wound, it must be distant, for the wind bore no audible rumor.

He swung the ax to hew at the notch in the sapling before him. The trunk of the tree cracked, and with a creak and a groan, it descended to earth and landed with a bare-limbed rattle.

His glance lingered upon the felled sapling. Such was the fate of a good tree in the wrong place, a grove already in want of thinning before this tree had taken root. But its wood would fashion a fine bow in due season.

The wind stirred the branches of the remaining trees around him, and brought the blood scent to him at greater intensity. His muscles tightened. He belted his ax and pulled instead his sword, a long, slender blade. Too much went on in these lands so near Nuruhain that necessitated a sword at the hip, at the very least.

The distant churn of the swollen river, the silence of bird and beast, the sigh of the winter wind all filled his ears. A groan pierced through it all. He dropped to a half crouch and stole toward the river, still beyond his line of vision, but near enough.

The land fell in a rock-strewn slope toward the overrun bank of the river. Culduin's steps over sodden leaves made nary a sound as he rolled his soft-soled boots with each step, just as his brother had instructed. His every sense stood on edge.

Coughing shattered his focus. And again the groan—a feminine sound to be sure. He surveyed the landscape and the river's edge until he finally spied a young woman who lay wedged within a cluster of boulders. Shallow, churning, foaming water swirled between them and rocked the girl's body amidst the stones.

Creo's mercy, how had she come to this spot?

Dark blood stained the young woman's nose and trickled from the corner of her mouth. A tangle of mud and leaves mired most of her hair, though an occasional strawberry-blonde gleam fought through the mess. Water sloshed over her face. She sprawled unflinching, her eyes closed.

Culduin bounded down the remainder of the slope. He slogged right into the water, sucked a deep breath against the shock of its cold, and pressed through the current to arrive at the maiden's side. She was perhaps just over twenty years old, arrayed in simple but well-crafted leather armor and outdoor traveling clothes, with a pack strapped to her back. Her blue lips set in an alabaster face warned Culduin of her mounting peril. Whatever her other injuries, exposure would prove her worst enemy if he did not pull her from the frigid waters. Her breaths were shallow, irregular, and labored.

A Radromirian, by her complexion. Culduin exhaled. That should spur some spirited conversation back at the cottage.

With a quick stoop, a firm grasp, and a heave, he swung the maiden up to perch her waist upon his shoulder. Muddy water ran in torrents over Culduin's torso, compounding the aching chill already numbing his legs. He shuddered and sloshed back to shore.

Once upon the bank, he laid the maiden upon drier ground. Still, she made no move or sign of life. Culduin reached out, but his hand paused near her wan face. He swallowed. His tentative touch parted the eyelids of her left eye, where a fully dilated pupil nearly engulfed the green iris around it. The right eye yielded a wider rim of green.

Culduin set his lips into a line. He pushed the maiden's flaccid arms out of his way and grasped the lowest buckle on the side of her breastplate. The cold and the water had stiffened the leather so much that Culduin had to throw his gloves aside to dig his bare fingertips into the fastener and pry it loose. Beneath the breastplate, her olive tunic clung to a petite torso in wet folds. But when the maiden breathed in, half her rib cage sucked in, while the rest expanded. When she breathed out, the area that should have normally contracted bulged.

This was no wound to treat in the field. He prayed he had not already worsened her injuries beyond repair by hauling her from the river. Culduin brushed the woman's matted hair away from her fine features. She was especially delicate in appearance—for a human.

From afar intruded the rank odor of sweat and the constellation of stenches that heralded death. He must get this poor victim as far as possible from whatever befell her.

～

*T*he warm glow of sunlight caressed Danae's eyelids as she slowly rolled her head to the side, though despite having awakened, her body felt like lead, and her eyes would not assent to opening. Something was very wrong, for her torso felt wooden. Her every motion was clumsy and sluggish. She tried to place her hand on her pounding forehead, but ended up jabbing herself in the side of the head instead.

Heaven and earth! What's the matter with me?

Opening her eyes demanded a disproportionate strength of will, but finally, she forced her eyelids to part. The room around her blurred as though she peered at it through foggy glass. Where was she?

A soft mattress cradled her, and a silken cream coverlet warmed her from chin to toes. The texture of the bedclothes surpassed any material she had ever felt against her skin, spun of some fiber suppler than even angora. Overhead, beams of wood carved with knotwork and vining of exquisite detail boggled her with their intricacy. She had seen such artistry before, though where? Designs in stone played at the back of her memory like the tatters of a fragmented dream.

The white sunlight of a bright afternoon streamed through a window above her bed, and a merry fire crackled in a tiled fireplace across the room. Perhaps the tiles comprised some sort of mosaic, but the colors shimmered and danced in the blurry distance. Homey smells of fresh bread and maybe even soup wafted from somewhere nearby.

Danae attempted to sit upright, but her sluggish muscles resisted, and a sharp pain spread across her side.

What's wrong with my ribs?

Just as she began to lift the coverlet, a door opened with a *whoosh*. Danae snapped her glance toward the sound. The room spun, and she choked back the burn of a protesting stomach.

In the doorway stood a tall figure, and while clearly masculine, this was no man. She squinted at the new arrival. His lean, graceful features, his large, crystalline blue eyes, his wavy copper hair, almost metallic in its sheen, and his unmistakably pointed ears all set him apart from humankind. The keenness of his gaze added to the turmoil already clenching her beleaguered stomach. He leaned against the doorframe and waited.

"Where am I?" Danae asked. Her voice was raspy and dry; the words slurred together.

He smiled gently, then turned his head over his shoulder and called something into the room behind him in a flowing and musical language. After turning his attention back to Danae, he said in an accented western tongue, "You are safe, but in no place you could name by town, for our cottage is remote. I am Culduin. Am I correct you are called Danae Baledric?"

Danae flushed. Her mind swam. "Um . . . yes?" Why would she even hesitate to recognize her own name? The unnerving sensation of confusion made her queasy. Or was it the blinding headache? "Do I know you?"

Culduin ducked his head. "Nay, madam, for this is the first we have ever spoken. Forgive me for searching your equipment, but that is where I discovered the name."

Danae crinkled her brow, probing a patchwork memory. "Equipment? What kind of equipment?"

"Traveling gear, by the look of it." Culduin turned his head to regard a cloak and satchel that hung neatly on pegs on the wall beside the open door.

Traveling gear? Where am I going? From where? But first . . .

"Why do I feel so, well . . . drugged?" She shrank back and regarded him from the corner of her eye.

"Please, Mistress, the medications are only in your best interest. Your ribs look like you stood between a battering ram and the gates of Bilearne, if you will pardon my saying so."

Danae sucked in a sharp breath, though it brought tears to her eyes and set stars dancing throughout her field of vision. "Bilearne." She rubbed her brow. "Bilearne . . . the city, right?"

"You know it?" Culduin arched an eyebrow.

"To be honest, I'm not sure. It's significant, somehow." The elusive memories that flitted just beyond reach compounded the throbbing behind her eyes.

Another male and one female appeared in the doorway, peering around Culduin. The male, though shorter than Culduin, and of sandy hair rather than copper, bore a striking resemblance to him in features. They must have been close kin.

The female of the group, long of limb and golden of hair, was of such striking grace Danae felt rustic and plain in her presence. Even though this tall maiden dressed much like Culduin in a long cream tunic edged with gold embroidery and fawn-colored breeches and boots, she still exuded an air of elegance and dignity. The maiden smiled and spoke, but again, the words were only a pleasant sound, so foreign was the language.

Culduin nodded, but then added, "Mistress Baledric speaks the western tongue. Out of regard for our guest, so should we." He gestured to the newcomers beside him. "Mistress, these are my brother and sister, Thalius and Luidriana Caranedhel. We have all watched over you with much concern and are glad to see you have finally awakened."

"Finally?" Danae frowned. "How long have I been . . . well, I'm assuming . . . unconscious?"

"Four days, since I found you."

A gasp escaped Danae's lips. She gritted her teeth against the lancing pain as she thrust her arms into the mattress in a clumsy, hampered effort to sit up.

Culduin's eyes widened and he rushed to her side. He gripped her arm. "Please, Mistress, do not try to rise. Perhaps you misunderstand. The ribs on your right side have undergone significant trauma, broken loose from your ribcage altogether. You must lie still and give them time to heal."

Danae's pulse quickened at Culduin's proximity and grasp. A waft of cinnamon, cloves, perhaps eucalyptus, hung about him.

This is no time to be girlish.

Her quick heartbeat pounded inside her skull with increasing intensity. Her eyes crossed, and she placed her hand on top of her head.

"Oh, and I neglected to mention, you also have a significant head injury."

"It looks as though I have little choice but to do as you say. But please, how did I end up here?" Danae shook her head.

The sandy-haired brother, Thalius, spoke up. "Culduin found you on the River Nuruhain's edge." His voice was deeper than Culduin's, with a jolly lilt even in the delivering of sober news. "The fact that you did not drown in the high water was a miracle in itself. We shall see if he has managed to work miracles of medicine in the tending of your broken bones."

Danae pressed on her side, and a haze of black crept in from the edges of her vision. She yelped in her self-inflicted pain.

"I can see you are a stubborn patient, Mistress Baledric," Culduin said. A hint of reproach underpinned his words. "I trust you will consult my expertise before you probe your injuries again?"

Danae squeezed her eyes shut while the pain subsided. Once the torrent of agony had ebbed to merely a fiery ache, she said, "I'm in your debt for saving me from . . . I don't even know what. I'm so confused, though. I have the sense I'm on an urgent errand, but to where? Why?"

Thalius smiled crookedly. "Well, nothing lifts a burden like the inability to recall it!"

"So typical of you, to laugh in the face of misfortune," Culduin said with a scowl. "Please try to find in your heart some sympathy for this maiden's plight, being away from home, badly injured, and lost even in her own head."

"You have grown so dour, little brother. The years ahead will stretch long, should you continue squelching their every joy," Thalius replied.

Luidriana shot them both a scathing glance. "Come now, do not overwhelm our guest with your endless banter. Take your arguing elsewhere, and I will help Mistress Baledric to get re-settled." Luidriana stepped to Danae's bedside and propped up several thick pillows. "Perhaps you could bring her a cup of broth and some of the bread."

Culduin beat Thalius to the door.

"Culduin is a bit of a worrywart, my dear," she whispered to Danae. "I shall help you sit up, though I apologize for any pain it causes. I can see no harm in your being upright, as long as you do not shift too much more than that."

Despite her slender physique, Luidriana lifted Danae without so much as a grunt and propped her back against a fluffy bolster. Danae fixed a stoic mask over her pain.

Culduin's brisk strides swept him back into the room, and the scents of food intensified as he approached. He approached the bedside, though upon surveying Danae's upright posture, his jaw tightened. After he set a tray arrayed with a modest cup of broth and a slice of bread over Danae's lap, he folded his arms and shot a reproachful frown to his sister.

"Did I not say she ought not rise?"

Luidriana shook her head. "She certainly cannot eat lying prone."

Culduin sucked his teeth for a moment. He turned back to Danae. "I had hoped to ask of you the details of your misfortune." A sympathetic smile spread across his face. "But it seems you do not have this information at hand."

"Sorry about that," Danae replied.

"Oh, no apologies necessary. For now, rest and mend, and no matter whether you remember your errand or not, you must not leave that bed. The strain may undo all of my handiwork," Culduin said. "Are you uncomfortable, or in any other need?"

"I'm reasonably comfortable, given the circumstances." She sipped the broth.

"Then we shall allow you some peace and quiet." Luidriana took her brothers by the sleeves and ushered them to the door.

Danae bit her lip. "One more question, if you please."

Culduin paused in the doorway.

"I shall hold you to one," he replied. "An overburdened mind is no help to physical frailty."

Danae took a deep breath. More sharp pains ripped through her torso. "You promise not to laugh?"

"Why would I do that? Please, say on."

"Are the three of you, indeed . . ." Danae swallowed hard. Sudden heat dewed the small of her back. "Elves? I don't recall ever having seen anyone like you, but to call you elves is my best guess."

Culduin's grin revealed a row of straight, white teeth. "Yes, mistress, elves we are. Our race is known as the Delsin, as we are elves of the west of Argent. However, our history and lineage, if it is unknown to you, must wait. For now, try to eat and to regain your strength." With that, Culduin excused himself and stepped from Danae's small quarters.

Danae shook her head. How had she come to this place, bedridden among a trio of elves, in a nameless wilderness with no idea if it was home or a distant country? Not weariness, nor pain, nor confusion would stand between her and the truth.

26

FLASHES OF THE PAST

A sharp yelp jolted Danae from her slumber. She bolted upright. Waves of agony tore across her ribs, stealing her breath. The darkness around her whirled like a ride on a wild horse, and Danae covered her mouth as she strained to keep her dinner in her stomach. What had awoken her with such jarring insistence?

As her pain and queasiness ebbed, the sounds of snarling, growling, and the scrabbling of many feet amidst undergrowth grew clear. A buzzing sensation rippled across her body. The metallic slide of a blade slipping from its scabbard cut through the ruckus. Its cold note added goosebumps to the strange shiver she already suffered.

"*Thalius, vi vetirre! Et canir is ugrath!*"

Danae hauled herself around to kneel upon the bed and peer out the window, despite the protestations of her injuries. She squinted into the starlit night to find a tall, lean silhouette engaged in the dance of combat with something . . . a small horse? No, it was some sort of giant dog. The tingle in her skin rose in malicious waves, and brought with it an urgent desire to flee. She dropped from the window and huddled beneath her quilt.

More footfalls, these running, joined the tumult outside. The hound howled and whined, while swords whistled through the air and landed with repeated, wet-sounding thuds. Again, Danae's stomach threatened to perform an evacuation.

The heralds of conflict outside stilled, to leave behind only heavy panting. The buzzing that prickled at her drained away.

"*Gratiserra, ve philenni,*" someone said. Perhaps Culduin? It was hard to tell between his deep breaths.

"*Na. Ve halemente . . .*" The voices trailed beyond Danae's hearing.

After a few moments, Culduin poked his head through Danae's partially ajar door, and Danae met his gaze. He started. "You are awake? I am sorry if the disturbance outside interrupted your rest."

"It's all right." Danae hugged her middle with trembling arms.

Culduin's features softened. He approached Danae's bedside and knelt. "Rest assured, Mistress Baledric, you are safe here."

"That . . . thing you fought. It seemed terrifyingly familiar." Danae squeezed her eyes shut against the inexplicable horror. "How do you sort memories from wild imaginings?"

Culduin pursed his lips. "I must admit, the beast was wholly unlike any I have met in battle. Well, no matter." He stood. "Thalius and I have dispatched the creature, as we will if any other like it approaches this dwelling, Mistress Baledric."

"Please, 'Mistress Baledric' seems far too formal to last through what I'm assuming might be a long convalescence."

"I did not want to risk offending your sensibilities, Mistr . . . Danae." Culduin shrugged. "If such an address of familiarity does not trouble you, than I shall be happy to refer to you thusly."

"Excellent." After a moment, Danae added, "You're very kind to tend to a total stranger."

"It is my pleasure. When I came upon you and found you still clung to the breath of life, how could I do otherwise but see to your mending? Some blessing must have been upon you, to bring you this far. Hopefully, as time passes, both body and mind will enjoy a full recovery. But now that tonight's little skirmish is over, try to sleep."

Danae settled back into her bolster as Culduin rose and headed for the door.

"May your repose be sweet from here." He stepped out and pulled the door shut.

~

*D*anae rubbed her nose at the itchy scent of mildew that emanated from the thick, tattered book with yellow pages that lay across her lap. She flipped a few leaves in the tome, then ran her finger down a column of meticulously penned calligraphy and stopped on a word with an embellished first letter. A few words in the following sentence, she had managed to glean from study, but far too many more remained beyond her grasp.

In the room just beyond her doorway, Culduin sat, pen in hand, singing a soft tune as he wrote.

"There must be a better way to learn Elvish than the way I'm going about it," Danae said.

Culduin perked up and approached. "Daily exposure, of course is best, but given the nuances of the accent, singing is often the way we teach outsiders."

Danae folded her arms across her chest.

"Ahem. Humans." Culduin blushed. "Friends."

"Singing?" Danae quirked a brow. "I'm sure that would only make matters worse. I'm no singer."

Culduin raised his voice in a tune, the complicated Elvish words flowing from his lips. The song, both alien and hypnotic, had a haunting quality that gripped Danae's soul, and somehow reminded her of a song she had heard . . . somewhere before. She closed her eyes and drank in the syllables.

When Culduin reached the end of a phrase, Danae said, "It's so lovely. What is *sadehvir*, though, the word you keep saying?"

Culduin tilted his head. "Sadeh . . . oh! *Sarevir!* Of course. The middle sound is an r." He leaned to her bedside table and scribbled the word upon a parchment, though his handwriting hardly clarified the situation.

Danae smiled. "Ah. *Sarevir*. What does it mean?"

"All things considered, you are picking up the nuances of the accent quite well." He winked. "For a Radromirian."

Danae huffed, folded her arms, and flopped back on her bolster, although doing so made her grimace.

"To answer your question, the western tongue renders it 'ship' or 'vessel,' in the seagoing sense."

"*Sarevir*," Danae repeated.

Culduin returned to his melody, his warm tenor filling the air with a soothing resonance. He sang through a verse and what Danae judged to be the refrain, when Culduin stopped again.

"Is that the end?" she asked. A hint of disappointment laced her words that she had not expected.

"There is one more refrain—it's simple. Sing it with me."

Danae stammered over a handful of half formed words before blurting, "I couldn't. I'll just ruin your song."

He nudged her shoulder with his. "I shall only teach you the translation of the words you sing with me."

"That's a dirty tactic," Danae said.

"Do you want your Elvish to have a Radromirian accent? Not to mention, singing will encourage the deep breathing I keep nagging you to do for the sake of your lungs."

Danae scowled. "Fine. Just this once."

Culduin broke into a bright laugh. "*Well, then, my friend, uvenna se musineri e pa umne!*"

Danae rubbed her temples. "Raise ... something ... to the—"

Culduin threw his hands into the air. "Raise your voice to the heavens!"

His voice rang with a clarion sound in the stillness cottage, though at first, Danae's own voice quavered and was lost beneath his strength. With time, repetition, and gentle coaxing from her elven teacher, however, Danae's confidence grew. Culduin beamed as they intertwined their voices, and she could not deny the warm sense of satisfaction she got in pleasing him. The transforming quality of singing together stirred Danae's heart with both cheer and longing.

As they wound down the refrain, singing of the gentle roll of the sea that bore a faithful ship home, Danae's mind's eye thrust her into the dark and musty hold of a cargo vessel, pitching and yawing upon high seas. Nausea clawed at her.

Her voice faltered. She pressed her fingertips to her forehead. So many snippets of half-remembered images subjected her to more confusion than clarity. She clenched her teeth against the disorientation and uncomfortable sense memories—what place in her darkened mind had Culduin's song unlocked?

Amidst the crates, the walls smeared with pitch, and the glow of an oil lamp, a sharp-featured face with a smile full of wisdom emerged. She groped for his connection to the events on the ship. The full sense remained just beyond her grasp, obscured by a nebulous veil of confusion. Underscoring it all came the refrain of some half-memory—a sense of profound sadness and pressing urgency—but its lack of meaning made the spotty recollection little more than a nuisance.

"Danae?"

Culduin's voice snapped her back to the little bedroom, the soft coverlet and the white light of a snowy afternoon streaming through the window. The fire in the fireplace crackled with all its little might against cold gusts that rattled the roof shingles and whistled down the chimney to make the flames gutter.

"Just another useless smattering of images," Danae grumbled. "I'm back now."

Culduin placed his hand upon her shoulder. "The memories will connect eventually, I am confident. Now, *sarevir*. Do you have it?"

"Yes. *Sarevir*. Ship."

"Very well, then perhaps we can talk a bit about the subtleties of pronunciation. The Elvish r is much softer than Westerners typically use ... thus your confusion over your 'd' instead of 'r.'"

"Actually, most of the sounds have a familiar ring to them. Somewhere in my life, I think I had a book, filled with . . . what were they?" Danae rubbed her brow. "Incantations. That's what they were. Anyway, they used words similar to many in your Elvish vocabulary."

Culduin straightened. He swallowed and shifted on his seat. "A book of incantations? You have used them in the past?"

The question smacked into Danae like a hammer.

"Driven them off, have you? Do you really believe your small spray of sparks was all it took to send them into retreat? You accrue a costly debt over a few fireworks." The wise shipmate of previous memories scowled at her with knee-buckling fury. As she recalled the fire in his sea gray eyes, his image flared out in the brightness of a pillar of blue flame.

The column of light drove back the ebony veil of a starless night, a blade of fire in the hand of a masterful wielder.

The darkness closed in again, then slowly retreated from just a pinprick of gold. From just a dancing flicker, this swelled to a small orb of candlelight on a dining table in an inn. The gentle illumination revealed the old sage's face once more. He served a chunk of gooey cake, and Danae's mouth watered at the scents of honey and cinnamon.

The table scene rippled away as though it were a mere reflection in water, and a stone had been cast into its center.

"Now tell me by whose authority you spoke that incantation." The strange-yet-familiar man stalked toward her in a wet cobblestone street. In the next moment, the same man bowed to introduce himself.

"Praesidio," Danae whispered, her gaze distant.

Culduin waited a moment, his glance fixed upon her. "Pardon me?"

"The man on the ship's name was Praesidio." Danae's voice sounded thin. "He was very concerned about the fact that I've used incantations, and somehow that's intertwined with my journey." She closed her eyes. Her forehead threatened to rupture at any moment.

Culduin closed the book they had been perusing. "You have grown deathly pale. I think we have pressed beyond your means."

"It's not the lesson, Culduin." Danae rubbed her brow. "A lot of information seems to be flooding in today. I take it that's a good sign, however unnerving."

"Indeed, it is. I know this will not help your frustration, but every disjointed image brings you a step closer to full recollection." Culduin closed her book and lifted it from her lap. "It will suffice to say today's lesson in Elvish is concluded. I will leave you to rest. Perhaps when you feel refreshed, you can sort through what new memories you have discovered." He turned to depart.

"Wait! That book I mentioned. Is there a book in all of that equipment you said I had?"

A doubtful frown overtook Culduin's features. "I do not know if it would be wise to tax your strength, Danae."

"Please tell me. Is there a book . . . a journal, with only some of the pages written?"

Culduin blew a sigh through his nose. "Yes, there is. I went to great pains to see it dried."

A tremor ran from Danae's scalp to her fingertips. What might Culduin know about her that she herself could not even remember? "Did you read it?"

"Only the inside cover, where I found your name. On my honor, I read no more." Culduin chewed his lip.

"Please, Culduin, bring the book to me. The words to my incantations are all copied there, and I think I also wrote about my journey here as well."

"I insist you get some rest first, and then I will see about bringing you the book."

"I won't be able to rest until I have it." Danae thumped her fist on the mattress. "Maybe I can piece together these fragments of the past if I see it."

Her caregiver hesitated at the bedside.

"Can't you find some sympathy for my need to sort all this out?"

Culduin sighed. "If there is one thing I have never been called, it is unsympathetic." He stepped through the doorway. "But you must pace yourself. Do not wear yourself down."

The elf retrieved Danae's tattered book. He placed the journal at the bedside and departed.

Danae's glance lingered in long hesitation upon this collection of parchments of which she expected so much. The binding strained against rippled pages that refused to lay flat against one another. She reached for the journal. She closed her fingers around it. A clammy slick of sweat dampened her palms. *It's the only way to really know.*

Eyes squeezed shut, she opened to the first page.

*T*he firelight burned low, and Danae's room succumbed to the march of dusk. Danae turned a page well beyond the midpoint of the journal. Its blankness stared at her in stark contrast to the pages and pages of her own script she had lost several hours in reading. It had been a strange transition, from wondering what might be behind the journal's cover, to submerging into a growing sense of recollection and familiarity with the words. This familiarity grew to an ability to predict what she would find on the next page, at least where her more distant past was concerned. The more recent events, especially those since her father's stabbing, read more like a story that had befallen someone else, where Danae acted as simply a reader of a fantastic tale. She rubbed the insistent throb in her temples.

So, here it is. The whole reason I've left home and kin. But I can barely breathe without wincing, and if I move too fast, I reel. How long will my broken body bind me here? And the book, of course, says nothing about how I've come to such a state.

As Danae lit the oil lamp within reach of the bed, Luidriana stepped into Danae's room, bearing a tray of steaming dinner, which brought with it the savory aromas of meat and roasted grain. Danae's stomach rumbled. When had she last eaten? She glanced at another tray on her bedside table, which contained a chunk of bread with only one bite out of it and a cup of soup, still full. Somehow, she had forgotten all about the meal as she instead devoured words earlier that day.

Luidriana cast a slight frown at the largely untouched lunch.

"I'm sorry." The heat of a flush warmed Danae's cheeks. "I didn't mean to waste your food. That was very insensitive of me."

"That does not worry so much as the effect skipping a meal might have on your comfort and your recovery, my dear. Though your incisions are nearly healed, your deeper wounds are working hard to mend, and you cannot neglect them in the name of studiousness." Luidriana set the dinner tray over Danae's lap and picked up the other.

Danae shoveled a bite of what appeared to be some sort of pottage mixed with a little game. Unfortunately, like every other meal she had eaten in the elves' care, this one was more a study of textures than flavors. She gulped the lump of pottage. The tray left just enough room for her to set her journal beside the bowl, and she opened it once again to a section of her past that she needed to teach herself, since she could not truly recall it.

Luidriana clicked her tongue. "You have much time of recovery before you might act on what you learn, so I beg you, do not overindulge your appetite for truth and thus fill your plate with troubles."

Danae smacked her palm onto the open pages of the book. "Now I know what I've set out to do. I also see, with every day I'm forced to wait upon my mending bones, my father drifts closer to an unimaginable fate. I'm too tired tonight to explain it all, but I must set out again, as soon as I'm reasonably well."

Luidriana met Danae's assertion with a steady gaze. "The better you rest, the sooner you will mend. Eat. Sleep for now. A night of contemplation and rejuvenation will give you clarity. Remember, lean not overmuch on either head or heart—neither is made to toil alone."

*D*anae set her jaw. *It's not going to hurt this time. I'm nearly healed, I'm sure.*

Culduin bent over her as he stood at the bedside, and he placed two fingers on one of Danae's healing ribs. Steadily, he increased the pressure.

Danae held her breath through the mounting, fiery pain, until finally she blurted, "All right, all right—it's too much!"

A frown creased Culduin's forehead. "Then my order stands. My pins are holding, but the bones still need time. In this bed you shall remain."

"Really? It's been what? Three weeks?" Danae threw up her hands. "I promise I'll avoid laughing or coughing. I don't see how walking around such a small place would be a hindrance. If I'm going to be ready to make the journey to Garash, wouldn't it be better if all my muscles hadn't turned to mush?"

Culduin's eyebrow shot up. "Avoid coughing? I wish you luck. And with my brother around, laughter is inevitable. Yes, you shall need to regain some strength, and that time will come. That time is not now."

"But how long?"

"I will not risk giving you any number of days to count. Not at this stage. It will suffice to say you have a long way to go. Are you really so eager to be quit of us?"

Danae shook her head. "That's far from my reasoning, Culduin, and you know it. You've all been so kind, and I couldn't ask for a better place to rest and mend. The trouble is, I won't rest until I have this Sword in hand. Especially with what it means for my father."

"Do you know how it is the servants of Queldurik in Garash came to possess this particular Sword?"

Danae plopped her journal into her lap. "I did once, I think. Let me see if I can find it again." She flipped back and forth through the last dozen pages of her writing. "Aha, here it is. Praesidio—or was it Archadion—told me it was stolen from a keep called . . .Ven Draugos."

Culduin sat up straight. "Ven Draugos?" He turned to call over his shoulder. "Thalius, was Formenos originally called Ven Draugos?"

Thalius strolled in the door, chewing on a strip of dried meat. "Why yes, yes it was. Lord Kaylonos renamed it when the Elgadrim gifted it to him." He paused for a thoughtful moment.

Culduin measured his words. "And so the Sword that Lord Kaylonos kept in his trophy room re-emerges in your life, even with you far from the keep."

"What are you driving at?" Thalius said.

"Is there any doubt the weapon Danae seeks is the very blade we both laid eyes on while at Formenos?" Culduin said. "The hubbub that ensued upon its disappearance, coupled with its striking appearance . . . add those to the significance the Elgadrim have placed upon Danae's errand."

Thalius's usual grin froze into an icy glare, and a long moment of silence hung between him and Culduin.

Culduin stared at a wall away from Thalius. "What griefs might never have been, had you realized the intent of those who took it before you admitted them to the keep."

Thalius clenched his fists and closed his eyes. "If I have answered your questions, then I shall return to my cartography." He marched from the room and shut the door with more force than necessary.

Danae twiddled the fraying ribbon bookmark on her journal while she pretended to read in the awkward silence that lingered after Thalius's departure.

Luidriana poked her head through the doorway. "Is there a fist-fight brewing for which I ought to keep a sharp eye? At least there's enough snow on the ground to make plenty of ice packs, if that is the case."

Danae closed her journal. "I think the little conflict is subsiding. At least I hope." A twinge of heartsickness welled up within her. Funny, how something that once stuck in her like a burr as much as her brothers' constant bickering could become the very memory she longed for. "Anyway, I was just touching on some of the finer points of my need to hurry up and head to Garash."

"Danae, you cannot intend to find your way on your own." Luidriana came in and sat at the foot of the bed. "At least spring will be on its way once you are able to depart, but the road is long and dangerous. I do not believe your Elgadrim companion would have ever intended you try the journey by yourself."

"But in the absence of his help, I still must find a way. Perhaps the task is impossible, but I'll give my life in the attempt, if that's what it comes to."

Culduin sighed. "Your fierce commitment to your family is admirable, but you must have some planning in place before you stride out our door. We could not release you to battle such overwhelming odds in good conscience."

Danae regarded the tight bindings around her midsection. "Given your earlier decree, I still have some time to think on how I might begin. A bodice of bindings makes poor traveling attire, I'd imagine."

"Very true." Culduin smirked. "That gives us some time to help you prepare, if you are unswerving in your determination to go."

27

MEMORY AND LOSS

"*D*o you think it's possible to learn the entire geography of everything between Bilearne and the northern reaches of Tebal with three maps and a few weeks to study them?" Danae pored over the yellowed vellum spread across her coverlet.

Culduin sat back on his stool until his shoulders met the wall, and he laced his fingers behind his head. "Thalius's maps, though few, have always proven accurate at any scale. You stand a good chance of gaining a cursory knowledge of the route you've traveled, in addition to the one you intend to plot."

Danae traced her finger over a long river that cut close to the place marked as the location of the cottage. Along the river's length, the word *Jovanov* stood out among the many Elvish labels on the document.

"Is that the Ford of Jovanov?" She pointed to the spot on the map.

"Yes, it is. Why do you ask?"

Danae furrowed her brow. "Something about that name murmurs

in the back of my mind, but the reason keeps slipping from my grasp."

"Hmmm. If Praesidio and Mizzletorp intended to convey you to Garash, it is my guess they must have chosen the Ford of Jovanov as your point of crossing the Nuruhain. None of the other fords would have been practical. The Tebalese hold the western bridges, and the battle rages there, and the next ford to the east would have drawn you far out of your way. But, if a journey to Tebal is your aim, the Nuruhain you must cross."

Danae's face brightened. "You're right! We did intend to cross at the Ford of Jovanov, but did we accomplish it? No, we couldn't have, because you said the river was flooded beyond anything you had ever seen. But why did I end up on this side?" Danae drummed her fingers on her leg.

As she felt the tickle in her throat that always announced a coming cough, she tensed her body in anticipation of the customary lance of pain it would bring. She cleared her throat, but it was insufficient to stifle the irritation, and finally, the air burst from her lungs.

The sharp sensation took her back to the river's edge, to the tumult of battle ringing in her ears. Danae placed her hand upon her sore ribs and relived the crushing agony of the ogre's hammer smashing into her side as she swung to save Praesidio. The clang of the weapons and the guttural cursing from an unknown source echoed in her ears. The smell of blood filled the air. Mizzletorp and Praesidio held their ground against many foes. So many. How had they learned to fight like it was an art? Lastly, the churning yellow foam of the swollen Nuruhain rushed up to meet her.

Danae blurted, "Culduin! I finally know what happened! I know how I lost Mizzletorp and Praesidio!"

Spilling words in an endless stream, she recounted the events of that day, and Culduin listened, leaning forward, eyes locked onto hers. Breathless, she came to the end of her story and brushed a loose tendril of hair from her eyes. "As horrible as those events were, you can't imagine what a relief it is to now remember them, rather than having them lurking somewhere in the back of my mind, waiting to be retrieved."

"It is an amazing story! Though the hounds concern me. I do not doubt they will seek you still, once you are outside our walls." Culduin rubbed his chin and pursed his lips. "Your tale also reminds me of something Luidriana and Thalius told me some time ago, though I did not mark it as important until now." He hesitated.

"Culduin," she whispered, laying her hand upon his forearm. "If you think it will impact my journey, you must tell me."

The elf tightened his jaw.

"Even you yourself have said I'm made of sterner stuff than one might expect." Danae spread beseeching palms. "Please, what is it?"

Culduin reached to clasp Danae's hands. "Thalius and Luidriana found a new grave near the Ford of Jovanov two weeks ago. They also saw signs of a pyre, though the burning was so thorough that there was not much to tell from it. Goblin weapons they could see, but not much else."

Danae gasped and tightened her grip on Culduin's fingers. Somehow, the connection between the two of them helped to steady her in the flood of emotions that threatened to sweep her away.

She lowered her gaze to her lap. "So one of them didn't survive the attack," she thought aloud. "And yet, one of them did, to do the burning and the burying." She blinked hard. "I can't see how Praesidio could've been the survivor, with all the enemies that surrounded him."

Culduin rose from his seat at the bedside and wrapped Danae in a gentle embrace. He whispered in her ear, "Do not despair. Praesidio was of the Elgadrim, and a Thaumaturgist. Do not assume that his was the grave."

The comfort of Culduin's embrace mixed with a nervousness and thrill that fluttered her insides and warmed her cheeks. Within his clasp dwelt both danger and allure. One part of her wanted to melt heavily into his arms, while the other bade her curl up in a cocoon of grief. A timeless stretch of tantalizing, terrifying moments passed as he held her.

The cottage door creaked, and they both jumped. Culduin cleared his throat. He sat back upon his stool and scooted it from the bedside with a noisy scrape across the wood floor.

Thalius sauntered to the doorway of Danae's room, looking at his brother with a crooked smile. He glanced back at Luidriana, who stood, arms folded, in the living area.

"Well, Culduin, should Luidriana and I find something else to patrol for a bit?" Thalius said. "It would be insensitive of us to interrupt your . . . study."

Culduin shook his head. "No, not at all, my misinterpreting brother. Please, go make sure the door is fully shut. Either it stands ajar, or you have brought a draft with you."

Thalius chuckled. Both he and Luidriana turned away, and a solid thump of the front door confirmed one of them had seen it closed.

Danae picked up one of the larger maps and made a show of studying it, though hiding behind it was her chief aim. Praesidio, dead and buried? Nothing seemed more wrong. Unjust. In contrast, the brief warmth and security she had just found in Culduin's arms, while unsettling, had a compelling rightness to it.

She slapped the map down upon her lap again. "Heaven and earth, how awful of me! I didn't even express a hint of regret about the possibility the grave at the ford may have been Mizzletorp's resting place!"

"Do not fret about that, Danae." Culduin took a few steps toward the door. "In this brief time we have spoken about him, I can see you have grown close to Praesidio, despite your short acquaintance. Your souls, in some small way, are kindred. You admire him, and he has extended you both mercy and wisdom. You are quite justified in worrying about him first, and I know you did not mean it as a slight to Mizzletorp."

We are kindred. I admire him. Danae smiled. Not words spoken about a man assumed dead, but a quiet optimism in his survival. But even if Praesidio was not dead, that did not solve her problem of still needing to pursue the Sword without him. She sat back, her limbs suddenly heavy. How much strength it would take to regain confidence to strike out alone again.

28

CULDUIN'S COMMAND

*D*anae sat with her open journal upon her lap. She flipped to the empty page that followed her last penned words, lifted a quill from an inkwell, and hovered the tip over the parchment. She chewed her lip. Sighing, she dropped the pen back into the bottle. The bare walls around her stared with oppressive plainness.

She listened to the activity and conversation of the three elves in the other room, but most of their fluid tongue still escaped her, due to the speed with which they spoke.

"*Naneme, Luidriana.*"

This she understood. Culduin and Thalius bade their sister farewell, doubtless heading out for another patrol. Hinges creaked, the latch clicked shut. Near silence hung over the small dwelling.

After enough time had elapsed that Thalius and Culduin must be well on their way, Danae called out, "Luidriana?"

The elf maiden appeared in the doorway. "Are you well?"

"Quite. Help me get out of this bed, won't you?"

Luidriana cast Danae a sideways glance. "Do not assume I have failed to hear all the wheedling and cajoling you have directed toward Culduin about this cause."

Danae dropped her journal on the bedside table with a leathery slap. "Oh, have a heart. I'm stir-crazy in this bed, and I really do feel strong enough to at least walk around a bit. Besides, it will prevent me from getting bedsores."

"I still do not know—"

"I promise, I'll take every grain of the blame should I injure myself—which I won't, if you just help me stand up."

A bright smile broke across Luidriana's features. "Very well. You have a determined soul, Danae."

Danae swung her legs to the bedside and placed her bare feet on the smooth planking of the wooden floor. Its chill sent a swarm of goosebumps up her legs. She clasped hands with Luidriana and shifted her weight forward. Her legs trembled, and clenching her stomach muscles awoke the pain in her ribs anew. Thoughts of freedom eclipsed her discomfort.

Once upright, she blew a huge sigh. "There, see? Not so bad. I'll just have a little walk around."

The next couple of weeks afforded Danae many opportunities to stroll the cottage as Thalius and Culduin patrolled. At first, her legs trembled and faltered, but each walk rebuilt a little of what she had lost.

One snowy afternoon, sweat dewed her lip and brow as she forced herself on yet another lap of the dwelling. Danae leaned against the wall with one hand and clutched her ribs with another.

Luidriana emerged from the storage room and clasped Danae by the elbow. She guided Danae toward bed.

Danae locked her knees. "Please, can't I at least sit at the table? It's like getting back into a cage."

Luidriana rolled her eyes. "I never knew humans had such a flair for the dramatic." The elf maiden released Danae's arm and pulled a chair out. "The tea water is already hot, so what will it be? Chamomile or passionflower?"

Danae eased into the chair. "Passionflower, please."

Luidriana returned with the tea and scooped a scant spoonful of the elves' precious store of sugar into her own cup. "I shall allow the full brunt of Culduin's ire to fall upon you, should he and Thalius return from patrol and find you up."

"What is it you patrol out here anyway?"

"Thalius and I have been assigned this post by Lord Kaylonos, in order to ensure the keep Formenos, which we mentioned before, does not suffer the approach of enemies from the east." Luidriana sipped her tea. "The keep guards a pass through the southernmost arm of the Triastead mountains, and a swift runner from here could give the keep and its little town of Formenar a life-saving warning should people of malevolent intent approach."

"What about Culduin? Is he under Lord Kaylonos's command as well?"

"No, not anymore." Luidriana waved her hand. "Culduin has only come to us for a short time and of his own accord, that he may learn some additional woodcraft from his older brother. He is a quick study, and I suspect he would have already been on his way had your treatment not forestalled him."

"Where will he go once he's finished here?" A twinge of tightness bound the muscles in Danae's shoulders. She bit back a series of further questions about how soon he might move on and what would draw him to another place.

"That, I do not know. He is a talented medic and skilled wilderness traveler, but has not yet forged his own link in the great chain of elven society. He still searches for his greater purpose."

"I find this Delsin belief in the 'Chain of Society' very interesting. Few people in my home country seem to look out for anyone but themselves." Danae's chin drooped.

"Yes, as an elf matures, he is expected to apply himself in whichever way he might be of the most benefit to his brethren. Otherwise, it is our view the gifts and talents bestowed upon each of us are much wasted." Luidriana took a long draught of her tea. "An elf has a long life in which to wander into pursuits that rot the soul, if he does not make a concerted effort to better the world around him, and hence, himself. When the individual members of our people cease to bear the load of improving our great society, then we will surely wane."

"Well, let me learn from this wisdom. I'd like to contribute to the little society we've got here. Tell me how I can be useful. I know my way around both a kitchen and a chemistry lab." Danae said. Finally, some hope of expelling the stretches of boredom remaining bedridden cultivated.

Luidriana shook her head. "I will assign you no duties without first consulting Culduin."

"You don't have to assign me anything. Just tell me what you don't like to do and I'll take up a share of it." Danae drained the last drops in her cup and rose from her seat. "I'm feeling rested again, so while Culduin isn't here to coddle, I'm going to help straighten up. Then I'll get something together for dinner."

"Now, Danae, I must caution you—"

"Don't." Danae laughed. "Really, I feel stronger every day. I'm up to it."

"Very well. Mind your symptoms, and rest if they flare." Luidriana smiled and sat back in her chair. "And by the way, I loathe cooking."

~

"*T*halius, come here," Culduin called over his shoulder. "It appears our friend the owlbear is back in the area."

Thalius's footsteps neared, and he leaned over Culduin's shoulder. His breath steamed from his nostrils as he blew a sigh. "We've seen those tracks before, sure enough, little brother. How old do you deem them to be?"

Culduin crouched to squint at the deep prints with claw gouges that splayed in an arc in the snowy riverbank. "They are fresh. The wetness in the bowl of the pad has not yet refrozen."

"Good." Thalius clapped him on the shoulder. "Not that it pleases me to wander the same path as a beast as touchy as this one has been."

At first Culduin merely shrugged, but the more he thought about it, the more his brow furrowed. "I would rather a surly creature not wander afield in the lands of our keeping. Passage within a reasonable distance from our post ought to be safe."

"You fret not for Luidriana's safety. Nor mine." Thalius thumped his brother's bicep with a lazy fist.

Culduin tilted his head, though he could only pray the slight overheated feeling in the small of his back would not creep up and flush his cheeks.

Thalius locked onto Culduin's gaze. "She is leaving soon. We all know it must be thus, and she shall have it no other way."

"What I would pay for a few darts loaded with sleeping tonic to send this beast into a little hibernation."

"I would wager your sweetheart could teach you how to brew some."

Culduin aimed a hard punch at Thalius's arm. A late block turned the blow. The brothers tussled through the snow and along the frozen banks of the Nuruhain, though neither gained a distinct advantage in the conflict.

Winded and flushed, Culduin raised his conciliatory hand as he paused to catch his breath. His groundward glance caught upon another set of tracks, however, neither boot print nor the heavy pad of an owlbear. He looked to Thalius, whose gaze fixed upon the prints as well.

"Canine, for certain, by the pads and claws." Thalius rubbed his chin. "But far too immense and heavy for even a wolf."

Culduin felt the blood drain from his features. "They are not overly fresh. But I think we can guess their makers."

"We can?"

"Were you swinging a sword in your sleep that night I called upon you for help in dispatching those black monsters that prowled the perimeter of the cottage?"

Thalius stared down at the tracks for a long moment. He raised his eyes to meet Culduin's.

Culduin tightened his pack. "Patrol concluded for today."

Thalius nodded. "Home it is."

~

*T*he cottage door swung open, and the knife Danae dried with a scrap of towel nearly clattered from her hand. She surveyed the table, set with wooden dishes, the steaming mugs of cider, the ample pot of venison and root vegetables ready to serve. As Thalius stepped into sight, followed by Culduin, a lump lodged in her throat.

Thalius tossed his snowy boots into the corner, and raised his eyebrows at the table setting. "My, it looks as though a little civilization has cropped up in our midst. And whatever bubbles over the fire smells delicious, so I know it could not be my gentle sister's handiwork!" He winked at Luidriana.

The elf maiden waved a dismissive hand at her older brother. "The culinary arts have never been among my gifts."

Culduin stepped inside as well and took a deep sniff of the savory air. "Do I smell sage? Whatever awaits us, I am famished." He scanned the room until his glance reached Danae. Fire kindled in his eyes. "How is it you are not where I left you?"

A surge of prickling heat swept through Danae's body. "I couldn't bear another moment in bed, Culduin." Why did her voice have to squeak now? She cleared her throat. "You would have had a mental patient on your hands in addition to an injured one if I didn't get up and do something."

Culduin shot a glare across the room that drove into Luidriana. "I am not pleased Danae has been out of bed long enough to prepare a meal." He clenched his fists, but his voice lowered to almost a whisper.

"Don't blame Luidriana," Danae slunk over to Culduin. "Your sister warned me more than once about wearing myself out, and I stubbornly ignored her." She adopted a coy pout. If the expression could soften her rules-driven Papa, it would work on anyone.

Culduin folded his arms. "Luidriana spoke words of wisdom." He passed several moments in silence, and rubbed his forehead with his fingertips, eyes closed. "If you cannot abide by my instructions, I will not be able to unbind your ribs as soon as I have been planning."

As soon as he had been planning? How soon was that going to be?

The tall elf moved so close she could feel the cold of the day's patrol still radiating from his skin and clothes. Her thoughts crumbled away. He took her chin in his hand, and his clear blue eyes pierced her to the marrow. Her stomach fluttered. Her mouth grew dry. Apparently, tactics for use on a father had little potency when applied to a young male elf.

Reaching around Danae, Culduin pulled a chair up behind her, and Danae could not help but sit, her eyes wide and locked onto his, as though his will held them in place.

His nose brushed hers, and he implored in a throaty whisper, "Trust me in my craft, Danae. Your body still needs time."

Danae's heart raced. She nodded, unable to even blink, and the furious heat of her flushing cheeks flared. Just as the tension had boiled to a level that threatened to escape Danae in a squeal or something even less dignified, Culduin broke his hold on her and walked to the fireplace.

Was that just the slightest smirk I just saw on his lips? Danae propped her fists on her hips as she stared after her healer. No, this elf would not be so easily manipulated as the men of her past, for here was a personality more daunting than any she had met, save perhaps Praesidio.

The snap and crackle of the fire held a solo performance in the stillness.

"The meal's ready whenever you want it." Danae hung her head. "I'll just . . . take a bowl back to bed."

Culduin turned a smile to her, and her heart leapt. He pulled a chair out. "No, that will not be necessary. Since you are already up, it is more sensible for you to join us at the table." He dipped his chin and raised his brows at Luidriana. "If my sister will do the serving."

*T*he elves all ate enthusiastically, which released at least some of the knots from Danae's stomach and shoulders.

"You have provided us with a hearty, delicious meal to warm us after a long day of cold work," Culduin pushed his empty bowl toward the center of the table and propped his elbows upon the tabletop. "For that, I am grateful. But please, if you intend to cook in the future, do so in reasonable spurts, for my sake. For I know you will not do so for your own."

"I promise, Culduin," Danae said. One power struggle with him for the day had been more than enough.

Luidriana set down her spoon. "Enough of Danae's chastisement for now. I believe you said something about the removal of her bindings?"

"For such a traumatic offense to the ribcage, the most conservative course of action would be to keep it wrapped for eight weeks—"

Danae choked on her cider, and she blurted an interruption between coughs. "Eight weeks! I'll never complete the task and return to Radromir in time."

Culduin raised his hand and waited for the end of Danae's outburst. "Even if my surgery has been successful, you most likely also had bruising to your lungs. You will need both healing and endurance before I could dismiss you to the wild."

Danae sighed and leaned back in her chair, but winced at the pressure of the wooden back upon her own. She counted the time in her mind. It would be at least another fortnight before Culduin would even consider checking her ribs, and then there was no guarantee her healing would be complete. Spring crept ever nearer, and with every passing day, the task before her hung upon her soul with multiplied weight, especially now without Praesidio's help and guidance. The next two weeks would be the longest of her life.

"And what of your patrol, my brothers?" Luidriana asked.

Thalius and Culduin exchanged a beleaguered glance before both of their gazes fell upon Danae. Their concern was palpable.

Thalius blew a sigh out the corner of his mouth. "On this side of the Nuruhain, we saw quite a few large tracks, the paw prints of heavy hounds, I fear. They paced the muddy bank for some time, or else their numbers were great."

Danae twisted her napkin at the news.

"My one solace," Culduin added, "was they searched the bank at least a mile north of where I found Danae. And of course, I would be greatly surprised if they were to find any scent after all this time, even if they did come to the place where she washed ashore."

Luidriana shook her head. "I do not think the hounds hunt by ordinary scent. Thaumaturgists and Curse Bearers leave behind a trail of another sort, so I am told. I do not know how long such a trail takes to fade."

If it ever does. More than ever, Danae longed for Praesidio's wisdom.

29

DARTS AND DARKNESS

Cooking and cleaning did little to pass the time with anything better than agonizing slowness, and the study of geography and Elvish vocabulary even lost their luster despite their pertinence. The days crept by, unhurried in their progression despite Danae's mounting urgency.

Danae lingered just outside the doorway of her room. She forced a fake yawn. "Goodnight everyone. I think I'm going to get a little extra rest."

"Truly?" Culduin looked out the window, where the blush of sunset still painted the western horizon.

Danae nodded. "Big day tomorrow, you know."

"Ah, yes," Thalius said. "The bandages come off in the morning, correct?"

"All I have promised is to check Danae's progress. Nothing more." Culduin returned to a parchment he was penning.

Luidriana returned dishes to their shelves. "Then Thalius and I will be sure to return before dawn from our overnight patrol. No sense missing the news."

If there is any. Danae slipped into her room, picking at and breaking her last intact fingernail as she went. Her glance lingered on the cracked map draped over the stool at her bedside. The space between the cottage and Garash, even on a small map, was very wide.

After a few minutes of pacing her little room, she flopped onto her bed. Perhaps sleep might bury her worries, at least for a little while. Full-fledged fear, its fidgets, hammering pulse, and resulting dizziness, chased sleep beyond finding. Danae huddled under her feather quilts and trembled.

She tossed and turned while endless catastrophes that might befall her on the way to finding the Sword paraded through her mind. The Hounds of Queldurik still prowled somewhere beyond the cottage's perimeter. Even if she managed to avoid them, so many dangers she knew nothing about could intercept her on her journey —alone. She gripped the sheets with straining knuckles.

"Dear Creo." Danae winced. "Ugh. How stupid. I'm not writing a letter. It's been so long, I don't even really know how to pray." She cleared her throat and looked to the ceiling. "I hope you are listening, even so."

She drew a long breath. "All my life, I've had a passing acquaintance with you, and accepted you as the one who brought all things into being. But now . . . I need you to be something more than the creator if the universe."

What would she dare ask of the God of All? She wrung the blanket in sweating hands. "I beg of you, show me some way to fill in the gaps where I don't have the knowledge to succeed on this journey I'm facing. And please . . . please, when Culduin checks my ribs tomorrow, let my bones be mended enough, so I won't lose any more time."

She rose from her bed and stared at the few bright stars she could see from her bedroom window. The world beyond her little room seemed crushingly vast. "I don't know you as well as I should, Creo, but from what I've learned from Praesidio in such a short time, I know you can do these things. Help me, and I'll repay you. Somehow. Show me how to serve you like Praesidio did."

She crawled back into bed and bowed her head to her knees. Tears trickled down her cheeks, but an inexplicable loosening of her muscles smoothed away her panic. Her flitting, haphazard thoughts quieted. Could this be the mark of Creo's presence? The calm in her spirit certainly did not come from her own sense of control. She stretched out on her mattress. Her eyelids drooped.

A guttural voice jarred Danae awake.

In the same moment she bolted upright, blackness enveloped her. It stole all sense of up, down, left, or right.

"Culduin!" Though her lips formed the words, an oppressive silence swallowed the sound. She screamed again, with the same result.

Was just her room subject to this darkness? Perhaps she could blunder out. Just as she swung a leg over the side of the bed, an iron grasp wrenched her from the mattress, drove her to her knees on the wood floor, and twisted her arm behind her. The impact sent shards of pain up her legs. She struggled, but merciless, muscled arms overpowered her in the crushing darkness and silence. The hand that held her wrists enveloped half her forearms in thick fingers. The stenches of rotting teeth and filthy garments clouded over her, and Danae's stomach heaved, though she still twisted against the attacker's grasp. Even with all the scuffling, her surroundings remained as soundless as if she had been stricken deaf as well.

Someone dug fingers with long, sharp nails into her hair and wrenched her head back. Danae's cry of pain again made no sound, but even if it had, the coarse cloth jammed into her mouth would have muffled it at once. If she writhed, searing pain tore across her scalp. She stilled as the gag tightened. Hot tears tracked down her cheeks. The attacker that held her arms wound rope around her wrists.

Panic crashed through Danae in an avalanche. *I need to get to my feet. I've got to run.* She wrenched her left leg from beneath her and planted her foot, but before she could regain both her feet, a heavy shove drove into her middle. Her ribs reminded her that no matter how healed, they were still tender. She tipped forward. Her waist propped on a lumpy, precarious perch that lurched into motion. Footfalls clomping over a wooden floor changed to tromping in leaf litter and soil. The warmth of her chamber turned to brisk wind. For many minutes, she jostled along. Her captor twisted and maneuvered with awkward dips and turns along the way. No amount of strain or struggle broke the hold of the thick fingers that clamped around her knees, and her lower legs began to crackle with a lack of circulation.

Her black prison dissolved, and the sudden starlight seemed bright by comparison. The world swept by in a blur as she hurtled through the air and crashed to a wooden floor. Bars clanged shut behind her. Wooden walls surrounded her on three sides, except for a small barred window at the top of the wall opposite the door. She shook her scrambled head and focused beyond the barred door--the cottage was nowhere in sight. Nothing but empty woodlands under the shadow of a moonless night.

Was Culduin safe?

Danae's worry submerged under a hail of needling pain across her skin. Her heart thundered. She had felt such intensity before.

A monstrous ogre lumbered away from the bars, and a black-robed figure strode forward to set a rusted lock through the latch. The uncanny pain washed over her in waves.

Danae stood and shrieked as loud as her lungs could manage.

"Scream yourself hoarse." The robed figure scoffed in a guttural voice. "There's no one to hear you."

Danae's shouts faltered. The huntsman had finally outsmarted her.

"You have caused me much grief, little Curse Bearer!" the villain continued. "Cost me some of my best hounds in addition to several of my slaves, but don't worry, you shall have the chance to repay me."

The huntsman marched out of sight. Danae's prison rocked slightly, and her captor barked in a rough, unknown language. The chamber around Danae tipped backward slightly, then rattled forward. It was not just a cage but a cart.

The jolt of the cart threw Danae to her knees. Thudding footfalls sounded, and the cart bounced in rhythm, tossing Danae about mercilessly. The rough wood of the cage floor bit into her joints. She collapsed and clenched the gag between her molars, but no force of will could restrain the angry sob that erupted from her soul. With such dread malevolence pitted against her, what hope of escape remained?

~

Culduin rolled onto his back, and the unwelcome pelt of a cold water droplet upon his forehead jarred him awake. His eyes fluttered open. Gray daylight filtered through a gap in the planked ceiling above, and a steady patter of rain chattered on the roof. He blinked haze from his vision—this was not his and Thalius's bedroom, and the hour was surely past his usual waking. He rolled his head to the side and scanned his surroundings. A few axes, a shovel, coils of rope hung upon a wall of wood. The shed. Why is the Great Patron's name was he sprawled in the shed?

He stood. A sharp pain pricked his thigh, and his knee on that side buckled. Culduin grabbed one of the wall studs to steady himself and glanced down—a fletched dart stuck out of his leg just above the joint. One firm, painful tug plucked the offending item from his flesh.

At first, the slim steel point, the hollow black shaft, and the green feathers shifted and doubled before his eyes. He shook his head to clear the fog, with only partial success.

"Danae?" Culduin called. Only pattering rain over the forest floor replied. He stumbled from the shed toward the cottage.

"There you are!" Thalius burst from the cottage door with Luidriana close behind.

"Culduin, what has happened?" Luidriana said.

Culduin panted for breath, and his exhalations steamed in the cold rain. He held up the dart.

Thalius took it. A bewildered look widened his eyes and lowered his brow.

"Maker's mercy," Luidriana said. "Danae . . ."

Culduin broke into a staggering run for the cottage.

Inside the elves' home, he found their dining table and chairs overturned in the main room. Culduin's longsword lay on the floor near the entry. His stomach dropped. He charged toward Danae's room, grabbing hold of the door jamb to keep from falling as he swung around it.

Her sheet and coverlets were wrenched askew, the stool he had occupied so many times at her bedside sat jammed into a corner. Culduin's foot crunched on a thin object. He looked down and found her nib pen under his foot, her journal half under the bed, and her ink spilled in a dry puddle on the floorboards.

Thalius and Luidriana approached the doorway.

"What happened?" Culduin clapped his palms to his head. A surge of panic tightened his throat.

"So much for hoping you would know," Thalius replied.

Culduin squeezed his eyes shut. Danae had gone to bed early. He had been working on a record of her treatment. Thalius and Luidriana left on patrol. He stepped outside for a breath of air to clear his mind . . . and then he woke up in the shed.

"How could I have let this happen?" Culduin said. "Clearly some kind of struggle went on, and I did not even notice?"

"The whole point of the dart, I would expect," Luidriana said.

Thalius turned once again for the front door. "I believe we will find more rumors outside."

Culduin followed his brother outside once again, although waves of nausea threatened to overtake him. Near the cottage entrance, Thalius crouched to examine churned leaves.

Culduin swallowed the lump in his throat and fought to focus on Thalius's point of attention. The leaf litter in this spot must have borne the weight of a creature with shoes the length of his arm. Culduin wheeled to seek further prints from this monstrosity, and indeed, they led in long strides into the woodlands.

"What behemoth could this have been?" Thalius said.

"Nothing native, of that I am sure," Culduin replied. "Are there any other tracks that you have seen?"

"Not yet," Thalius said. "Follow these huge prints with me. Luidriana, keep watch."

Culduin bounded after the clear tramping the heavy-footed creature had made. After a few furlongs of hunting from track to track, he came upon ruts left by wagon wheels. Their parallel gouges in the wet soil gave him a clear direction for pursuit.

"I must gather supplies, but clearly, this is my path," Culduin said.

Thalius balked. "What? Go . . . after her? Granted, this is all regrettable, but—",

"What would you have me do otherwise, brother?" Culduin cried. "I am not assigned, as you are, and therefore, I am free to choose. I cannot leave her to whatever fate this abductor has planned, and every moment of debate propels her toward that."

"Getting embroiled in the affairs of men has a historic precedent of leading to woe," Thalius said. "The affairs of *women* even more so."

"Can you not see? Somehow, it is all connected!" Culduin paced. "You cannot dismiss as coincidence the turn of events that brought us a girl seeking the sword you . . . *we* Delsin lost."

Thalius's expression darkened. "You have always seen things from a more cosmic vantage point than I have. You also discount the chance that Danae will escape without you riding in to play the white knight."

"Until I know she is free, Danae's peril is my problem, Thalius." Culduin thumped a fist on the cottage doorjamb. "And even if she needs no 'white knight,' the retrieval of the Sword of Creo's Patron will prove challenging enough, without the added trouble of finding her way to Garash. Studying maps does not make one a seasoned traveler."

Luidriana eased toward Thalius and Culduin. She bent in a low crouch and lifted a palm. "Have a care, brothers, you miss details in your haste."

Culduin eased closer to Luidriana, drawing slow breaths against his hammering heart. Thalius squatted and ran his fingers over an odd impression by Luidrana's boot. A three-toed foot with curved claws? Bipedal, as best Culduin could determine. They all exchanged knowing glances, and an oath escaped Culduin's lips. This meant one creature in his experience.

"Provision well, Culduin," Luidriana said.

Culduin nodded. "Creo forbid I should be too slow in pursuit."

30

TRAILS

Culduin loped across the forests that had been in his keeping, lands he had labored in making safe, led onward by the wagon ruts and the deep impressions of the behemoth. The trail mocked his efforts. His breath came in steaming clouds as the chill rainwater ran off the tip of his nose. His stomach churned, though whether from his mounting concern over Danae's welfare, or some lingering effect from whatever poison the dart had injected into his system, he could not tell. While the dart wound still stung, at least his leg muscles now responded predictably.

The trail led on through the raw night. As the temperature dropped, the precipitation shifted from numbing rain to stinging needles of ice. Clear though the trail remained, he would be of little use to Danae should he arrive at her side too impaired by exposure to do anything besides suffer capture or death himself. The seeping cold of his partially frozen clothes leeched the strength from his bones and the clarity from his mind. Several hours after midnight, as best Culduin could judge, he conceded victory to the weather's endless battering and set up shelter. After swapping dry garb from his oilskin pack for his sodden array, he dropped into a tentative reverie.

After a few hours of restlessness, Culduin rose again to find the world around him wearing a thick coat of glimmering ice. Only after delivering a few solid kicks to his tent was he able to loosen the frozen sheets from it well enough to collapse it and roll it again. Running proved to be a slapstick performance at best. A few teeth-rattling falls convinced Culduin he would have to pursue the wagon trail at a steady, though much slower walk than the previous day.

The wheel ruts wove and wandered, mimicking Culduin's own difficulty in negotiating the frozen terrain. Deep gouges in the earth revealed where the creature he tracked had landed hard on elbows or knees in the slick undergrowth and litter. Regardless, the signs offered no evidence of a break in their journey. No camp, no fire pit. He had lost precious hours to the captors' continued flight.

A long day of slippery pursuit dragged on. A windless night had fallen and deepened when Culduin reached the edge of a beaten track, the first road to intercept his path since he left the lane outside his brother and sister's cottage. The more groomed the terrain, the more guesswork Culduin would have to employ in tracking, but for now, the territory was still familiar enough for logic to assist as guide. The road led through the pass Thalius and Luidriana monitored for the protection of Formenar. To try another way would only take Danae's captors to impassible mountains or the banks of the Nuruhain, far from any ford. Culduin tightened his pack and followed the easterly course into the mountains.

~

*C*reo certainly has a strange way of answering prayers.

The pre-dawn sun cast the eastern horizon in a pale glow, and Danae watched the light slowly overtake the lowest stars. She lay on her side on the warped floorboards of the cage where her captors had tossed her three nights ago. The ratty pelt the huntsman had provided her offered the scarcest comfort against the raw chill that left everything around her feeling damp. Over her time of suffering as a passenger, she pieced together that the ogre who had originally overpowered her now served as a beast of burden, pulling the cart. He lumbered on, day and night, with only occasional moments of rest. Why, just when she was preparing to set out on the mission to serve Creo's chosen people, did the Maker allow this complete disruption of her plans? Perhaps Luidriana had been right —that Creo could not intend for her to pursue the Sword alone. But to fall into the hands of a huntsman seemed a drastic act of course adjustment.

She groaned. *Probably over-spiritualizing this whole thing. Bad luck simply caught up with me. And why not, since I waited around for it for weeks on end? Maybe I should have snuck away one of the times Culduin was on patrol.*

Danae scoffed at the notion. The elves were right. She was ill-equipped to embark on any kind of hero's quest. Given days upon days with no other distractions, she could not even find her way out of a cage, let alone find her way to a foreign city and liberate one of probably a million swords within its walls. No wonder Culduin had been so hesitant to release her.

Culduin. Danae's chest tightened. Had the huntsman killed him to ensure Danae's capture? And what about Luidriana and Thalius? What course did they choose when they returned home and found Danae gone?

A thought jabbed Danae with sudden possibility. With all the trouble the elves had gone to in caring for her and insisting she not put herself in danger, it was not outside reason to imagine they would seek her. She sat up. Her head swam. Although her stomach had given up growling a day ago, hunger's deeper impacts now plagued her. Her limbs felt leaden and her breath was short. After her balance returned, she fought through the weakness and scooted to the rear of her cage.

The dirt road they traveled had left the mountain pass behind and now traversed a wide wilderness of rocky hills and increasingly sparse trees. Intermittent rain and snowfall kept the landscape gray and sodden, and to Danae's thankful observation, also left the road soft. Wagon tracks and huge footprints stretched behind them into the unseen distance, visible even in the predawn light.

If she dared hope members of the Caranedhel family sought her, at least the trail remained clear.

The cart slowed to a stop.

Danae wheeled around. She peered through the high window at the front of her enclosure. Ahead of the ogre who pulled them along, a gated arch stretched over the road. The left side of the arch connected to an embankment of rock that bordered the road. A field-stone gatehouse, whose door swung open, sat beneath the arch. Out stepped a broad-built man, clad in banded mail and a skullcap helm. He raised a lantern to eye level. A fresh slash ran down the middle of the gatekeeper's nose, far too precise for a battle wound. No, this cut would heal to build another other knotty scar on the man's ashen face.

"*Ypred du Cray, ket oved'kle?*" the gatekeeper said.

Danae sorted the Tebalese words. *Onward to Cray, as usual?*

The huntsman grunted, reached into his robe, and produced coins. "Nowhere else to go out here," he replied in the gatekeeper's tongue, though his accent mangled the vowel sounds.

Cray. Just perfect. Danae slumped against the bars. *Out of Drex's clutches and dragged into his home town.*

The huntsman turned around in his seat at the front of the cage-wagon to peer through the barred window at Danae. "Thirsty, Curse Bearer?"

Danae glared. "Hungry too." She wrinkled her nose. The hunts-man's proximity brought with it an acrid odor. Though his painful aura clawed at Danae continually, she had learned to endure it. The stink, however, still offended her senses.

He barked a single laugh, then unstoppered a waterskin with gloved fingers. "Take what you're offered or you'll get a whole lot you never wished for."

Danae ground her teeth. Truth be told, she needed the drink.

The huntsman tipped the waterskin through the bars, and Danae scrambled to position herself beneath the stream of water he poured. She caught much of it in the face, but at least some in her dry mouth. Still, however, she got no glimpse of the huntsman's features, always obscured in a deep hood, and she had a feeling he was additionally masked beyond that.

Before she had quenched her thirst, the huntsman withdrew the waterskin and urged the ogre onward. Through the gate they drove, and best as Danae could guess, over the Tebalese border.

All the jostling, jarring, and awkward maneuvering had worked Danae's rib bindings loose, and she found they hung around her hips in loops. She drew a breath. Then another, deeper draught. Only the longest gulp of air drew protest from her injuries. At least she would not need to figure out how to re-wrap her middle despite bound wrists. The irony of being well enough to reengage her mission but still being caged against it burned like a smoldering coal.

The sun peeked over the horizon, and with its arrival, the huntsman stretched out on his wide seat, as he did each morning of their journey. Apparently a nocturnal lifestyle suited him.

Danae settled back to the floor of the cart and constructed Thalius's map of Southern Tebal in her mind's eye. Cray was not very far over the border—perhaps two days' travel, if she recalled correctly. The farther into Tebal they drove, the more arid the climate would become. If any of the elves were tracking the cart, the footprints and wagon wheels would not leave such telling impressions on dry, cold roads.

I wonder if they think I'm dead.

A sign.

I should leave behind some kind of sign. Danae inventoried her options. *But it's too cold to sacrifice any clothing. The pelt would tell them nothing.*

Danae searched her foggy mind for options. What about the bindings? The elves might recognize the stretchy weave if they saw it along the trail. She wriggled her way out of the loose coils of bandages, but then stared at the pile on the floor.

It's too big. Even that dull ogre would probably notice if I tried to toss that whole thing out the back.

Danae's new mission to leave a trail filled her weak limbs with new purpose, despite her hunger and frustration. By lifting the bandages in her teeth, she eventually managed to snag a section of them on a protruding nail in one of the floorboards. She ripped at the long strip of fabric until she had a smaller piece torn away. Her evaluation of the piece, however, deemed it too nondescript to serve her purposes.

She glanced to the huntsman and found him still in a posture of repose.

Danae drew a deep breath, squeezed her eyes shut, and bit her lower lip so hard floaters appeared in her vision. The metallic taste of blood tainted her saliva. After awkward repetition of touching her lip to the scrap of bandage, Danae managed to roughly dab in red "Cray-DB."

I must look like some kind of demented chicken pecking at the floor.

She dismissed the ridiculousness of the process and picked up the bandage-note in her teeth. She eased her way to the rear bars of the cart. With a quick puff of air through her lips, she sent her note, daubed in blood, into the road behind them.

~

*I*n the growing light of dawn, the countryside around Culduin gave way to tight clusters of building upon building, cast in the pinkish orange glow of the sun's inevitable appearance over the horizon. A carven sign swinging from chain links hung from a frame over the highway. In burned letters, it read *City of Cray*. Culduin clutched the collection of tattered bandages in his fist, each of them inscribed with their message of blood. Doubt gnawed him. What if he had missed or confused the signs somewhere along the way? The short message on the rags was far from clear, and the hope could easily have skewed his interpretation.

"Your problem isn't your skill set." Thalius's voice echoed in his memory. *"It's your perception of it."*

Leagues ago, the wagon tracks and footprints he followed had arced to merge onto this northeasterly highway—and from there, only the intermittent rags along the road served as evidence for him to press on. At least the captors, whoever they were, had not chosen to drag Danae to the war's front lines. Culduin chuckled darkly at his thoughts. Dire times were upon them indeed when an elf was relieved to see a prisoner carried into Tebal.

He blinked against the half-light of early morning, but found his vision no clearer. A flutter of unease flitted through his chest. He quickened his pace. Even with his vision compromised by the limbo between darkvision and daysight, better to avoid the waking population of Cray as best he might.

Culduin passed into the outskirts of Cray on brisk strides, his hood drawn down and his cloak wrapped tight. Lights sprang up behind many-paned glass windows as he went. Women leaned out from upper stories to shake out blankets or rugs. The streets he passed through suffered none of the roadside sludge he had seen in so many other human settlements—not a single chamber pot tipped out any window he saw. And yet, so many flew Queldurik's banner. A strange mix of sterility and barbarism found its symbiosis in the people of Cray.

The architecture, while cleanly crafted, lacked variety. The accuracy of every square corner and plumb doorframe showcased the skill of Tebalese craftsmen, but in comparison to the lithe, nature-inspired design of Culduin's own people, Cray felt alien. Sterile—even hostile. The weather was not the only element that made Cray cold.

Culduin shuddered. He stifled a yawn. Where to begin?

31

THE HUNTSMAN'S ULTIMATUM

*T*he cart groaned to a halt in front of a black stone building that frowned down at the street below. A collection of thorny spires rimmed the structure's central gilded dome like teeth around the mouth of a leech. Danae peered through her bars and the secondary cage of icicles that hung from the roof of her confinement. Upon the ledges and outcroppings of the architecture perched sculptures of sneering gargoyles. A cold fear gripped Danae's throat. Crimson triangle banners flapped in the breeze, emblazoned with a monstrous but familiar face, the heraldry she had seen on so many of the soldiers' gear back home in Dayleston.

Danae's shrouded captor appeared at the door of her cage and fitted a thick iron key to the lock. His ogre servant followed. When the jailor swung the door wide, the ogre grabbed Danae by the collar and dragged her from within the little prison. Any fight against his grasp only rewarded Danae with sharp knocks against the ground, a flight of ebony stairs, and the doorframe of the building's towering entry. The doors shut behind them with a sharp clang.

The vestibule was full of deep shadows cast by braziers of red fire that studded the walls. Arches crisscrossed the vaulted ceiling like whip wheals marking the charcoal backdrop. Far off, deep, monotone chanting throbbed from an unseen chamber, and the smells of charring and smoke stung Danae's nose. She squeezed her eyes shut. This place could be nothing but a temple dedicated to Queldurik's macabre worship.

The ogre hauled her down a curving flight of stairs, and he bent low to duck through yet another doorway, fashioned to resemble the jaws of a massive serpent with ram's horns. This opened to a dank corridor lined with iron-bound doors, each with a small, barred window. The ogre cast Danae through one of these doors and onto the floor.

She staggered to her feet despite the protest of fresh bruises.

The cloaked figure strode into the cell and placed a burning torch in a wall sconce. He turned and jerked the gag from Danae's mouth. "Now, Curse Bearer, the time has come for us to have words." He reached up and pulled back his black hood, which revealed the gruesome head of a lizard, with bright red eyes, greenish gold scales, a long snout, and twisting horns slanting back from his head.

A gasp escaped Danae's lips. She took an involuntary step back.

He smiled, if the face he made could be called such. "You expected a mere human as your pursuer? My kind is far more skilled in the hunt."

Despite a swirl of faintness, Danae gathered her wits and snarled at the creature. "I'm unimpressed by your skills. Does it always take you so many tries to capture a single girl?"

"You keep difficult company, Curse Bearer. But now that we have severed you from your protectors, I deem you will be much simpler to bend."

"You can stop calling me Curse Bearer. I'm a servant of Creo now!" Danae cleared her throat. In the strongest voice she could muster, she spoke the Utterance that would summon a hail of sparks.

And waited.

A rush of cold swept through Danae's body. Had she said all the words? Had she mispronounced something?

The creature met her outburst with a low chuckle that slowly grew into a scoffing laugh.

"Pfah! That name will not save you today, oh mistaken one. You do not have the mark of his servant, despite whatever lip service you have paid him in the desperate hours of the night."

Danae's posture sagged. The mark of his servant? What more must she do to sunder her ties to the curses of darkness? Tears threatened to betray the new chink in her resolve.

The reptilian beast sneered. "Now that we are clear, Curse Bearer, I have come to see your debt to the Almighty Queldurik is paid. It is really quite simple, and once you have sacrificed the number he requires, you may go forth in life as you wish."

"I won't . . ." Danae swallowed the quaver in her voice. "I'll never add to your abominable idol's pool of sacrifices!"

The creature folded his arms. "It seems you are not yet as malleable as I would like. You will change your mind before I am through. You have no choice, indebted one." He then spun on his heel to leave, but hesitated. "No, I am mistaken. You do have one choice. You can resist your duty and choose to become a sacrifice yourself."

He swept from the cell and stopped by the pair of Tebalese guardsmen that stood on hand. "Since hunger has not driven her to listen to wisdom, no water for this prisoner either."

The door at the end of the cellblock boomed shut. One of the guards pulled the torch from its sconce and turned with businesslike impassivity to depart. The door shut with a dull thud and enveloped Danae in darkness, her only light that which streamed through her little window. She stared dejectedly at the bands of illumination on the floor. From one set of bars to another. Silence crashed over her.

Danae sunk to her knees, and the tears she had withheld since her capture broke loose. *What's the use? Maybe I should just get it over with. Face the final horror. One way or another, I only have a few days before I'll be dead.*

The events of her captivity drifted through her mind. How much worse would they treat Papa when they came for him? She swiped her running nose on her shoulder. She would not let that monster starve her into mumbling whatever he wanted her to say. No, for Papa's sake, there would be no quick surrender. For him, she would find a way to go on.

*D*anae hung her heavy head back on her weak neck and scanned the rough ceiling of her cell. The chiseled rock above had a sheen of clamminess. If she could reach the ceiling, somehow, would the stones wet her thickened tongue and sticky mouth? Hunger was only a memory now, driven off by the endless monotony of what must have been days of unchanging darkness.

The world around Danae tilted. Her legs trembled. She slumped back to the unforgiving floor. In a desperate hope of staving off defeat, Danae ransacked her mind for even the tiniest shred of hope. No one was coming for her. Perhaps the huntsman had even given up, decided she was too insignificant to even bother splaying open on an altar.

Danae shrank against the wall, stricken by the mental image of human sacrifice—her own body feeding Queldurik's flames. While her heart still beat, she must find courage enough to resist any aid to the enemy's designs. Courage. *Adhennet*, in Elvish.

Adhennet. A song lilted to mind, as misplaced as it seemed. A song Culduin had taught her while she healed at his side. Had any time or place in her life been as beautiful? Even the memory of that warmth suddenly felt stronger than the gloom around her.

What bizarre memories to fixate on under such dismal circumstances. She felt neither daring nor heroic. Still, the melodies worked their way past her lips in a low hum. In a faltering, cracked voice, Danae mumbled the phrases of Culduin's elf song.

Before long, her voice swelled to full, albeit hoarse, singing.

From the hall came a disgruntled snort, the scrape of a chair, and the shuffle of approaching footfalls. Lantern light swelled through her little window, and a face appeared just outside the bars—a guardsman. "You! Quit your squeaking, sewer rat!"

A crazed giddiness tickled the back of Danae's mind. She shrugged and sang louder. The elf song in her heart urged her on. Goaded her. Brought unbidden laughter to her lips.

"Gah! Looney. Thirst must be addling your wits." The guard tromped back down the cell block. "Wake up, you sluggard. I'm going to refill my tankard."

The latch on the door rasped and hinges creaked. Someone at the end of the cell block yelped, and then came the unmistakable *thunk* of a skull hitting the stone floor. Danae staggered to her door and pressed her face to the window bars.

The other guard, bleary and wild-eyed, dashed toward the door, where the first guard lay flat on his back, the shaft of an arrow piercing his forehead. The second guard fumbled to draw his weapon. Within the window of the guardsman's hesitation, a black-robed man charged in. He brandished a slender blade. The slashes came in a furious blur. The guard caught the first cut in a parry, but the attacker's speed defied his next effort. In a matter of seconds, guard number two lay dead beside his comrade.

"Danae?" A soft voice called in the hallway. "Danae, are you down here?"

She swallowed a squeal. "Culduin? Is it really you?"

As she strained on tiptoe to see out the window, her friend lowered his black hood and met her gaze. He knelt by the dead guards and searched their bodies. A rapid string of words tumbled through his gritted teeth, though Danae only recognized one phrase: *no keys.*

Culduin sprang to Danae's cell door.

"I understood your Elvish about the keys," Danae said. "But you haven't taught me the other words you used."

"Nor shall I. They would be most unbecoming!" Culduin offered a dark smile. "We have to get you out of here, but with no way to open the door . . ."

Danae eyed the satchels hanging from Culduin's shoulders. "Is that my pack? I have some tools in it that may be useful in picking the lock." Danae wavered on her feet. She leaned against the door as the room swung around her.

"What is it?" Culduin peered at her with crystalline eyes. "Are you wounded?"

"No."

Culduin clicked his tongue. "By the look of your skin and lips, they have not been overly hospitable. First things first, then." He unstoppered his waterskin and held it up to the bars. "Take this and drink."

"Um, my hands are tied."

Culduin rolled his eyes and shook his head. "Of course they are. Here." He pushed the skin partway through the bars and tipped it.

The water dribbled over Danae's lips and tongue in a cascade of absolute delight. Never had water seemed such an elixir of divinity.

"All right, we have to hurry," Culduin said. He withdrew the skin and rummaged through his pack. He produced a serving of waybread as well as a small flask of honey. "Eat a little of these while I look for your tools."

He drizzled some honey on a bite of waybread and popped it into Danae's mouth.

She gagged, but forced a swallow. "It's far from comforting."

"I know. I am sorry. One more bite. You can do it."

Danae obliged his request. "More water, please?"

While Culduin served her another drink, his brow furrowed. "We need to see about freeing your hands."

"True, and finding my tools."

Culduin tilted his head. "I do not know what use your tools will be to us."

"For picking the lock."

"I know nothing of the craft."

"But I do."

"Danae, you are not thinking clearly. The lock is on my side."

Danae huffed. He was right. Her mind was cloudy at best.

"Let me find something to cut your bonds, though you will have to manage the task yourself, since I do not imagine you can lift your wrists high enough for me to do it."

Danae smirked. "I may be many things, but a contortionist isn't one of them."

"See? You regain some of your spunk already." Culduin dashed to the bodies of the felled guards and yanked a knife from one of their sheaths. He dropped it through Danae's window. "See what you can manage while I hide these bodies."

Danae fixed her glance on the cellblock entrance. "Hide the bodies, sure, but there's an awful lot of blood on the floor."

Culduin heaved the first body into the cell opposite Danae's. "I see a couple buckets near the door. We can hope they are water." He dragged the second body to join the first. He retrieved the buckets with a grimace and an exhale. Nonetheless, he poured their contents over the puddled blood the second guardsman had left behind. The noisome vapors stung Danae's eyes.

She bent to pick up the knife. With an awkward juggle, she positioned the blade's edge against her ropes, but would she be able to saw enough to actually cut them?

The latch on the hallway door scraped. Danae stashed the knife in the fodder that served as her bed. She leapt back to the bars. Culduin was out of sight. She could only assume he had ducked inside the cell-turned-morgue and pulled the door mostly shut.

Into the cellblock strode the reptilian huntsman, followed by a burly creature, half the huntsman's height, who carried an iron clamp of some sort. The huntsman scowled. His eyes locked upon the puddle in the aisle. "Where precisely are my guardsmen? And why is this post the most unreliably manned in all of Queldurik's dominion?" He visually followed the trail of the liquid on the floor toward Culduin's cell.

Danae's heart thundered. "Hey, you. Back so soon?"

Please don't look too closely at that other cell.

The huntsman narrowed his eyes at Danae, produced a ring of keys from his belt, and unlocked her door. He swung it wide.

Danae backed to the center of the cell. She braced herself. If only she and Culduin had enjoyed the luxury of a moment to plan what to do next.

"On your feet, Curse Bearer?" The huntsman tilted a quizzical head. "Perhaps you have eaten my guards for the strength to hold yourself up." He laughed mirthlessly. He glanced back to his companion and jerked his head toward Danae's doorway.

Perspiration beaded on Danae's brow, though she glared at the pair of dreadful creatures in spite of it.

The dragon-faced servant of Queldurik paused. "You are more trouble than you are worth, you scrawny alley cat!" He spat. "I ought to sacrifice you now and save myself some pains. This is your final chance to embrace wisdom. I suggest you listen closely." The huntsman paced the length of the cell, brought his feet together, then bored into Danae with mottled eyes. "Go from this place and sacrifice, in Queldurik's name, either eight innocents, or four enemies of Queldurik over the next week. If you can do so, I will consider your debt paid. If you fail, then the binding curse I place upon you will lead my hounds to you, and I will carve your life from you in a most drawn out and unimaginable way."

"And if I simply refuse?" Danae forced a swallow.

"You won't. Grolik and his thumbscrews are very convincing, should you find my logic resistible."

The pock-marked Grolik leered and licked his lips with a pointed tongue.

Danae dropped back a step from the huntsman. Over Grolik's shoulder, she could barely make out Culduin's face in the cell window across the hall. An arrow sat upon the nock.

Danae straightened. "You wasted a lot of breath on all that."

Culduin's bowstring twanged. Dark blood spouted from Grolik's throat where the arrowhead emerged. He lurched and fell forward.

The huntsman whipped around to the collapsing servant. Danae sprang at her captor. Though she barreled shoulder-first into his chest, the huntsman merely squawked, clutched her with scaly claws, and tossed her aside.

Culduin burst from his hiding place, sword in hand.

Whirling toward the elf, the huntsman thrust out a claw. A green bolt of lightning shot forth and caught Culduin full in the chest. Culduin launched backward into the wall. The beast gestured again.

Bereft of any weapon beyond her feet and wits, Danae righted her stance and swept her leg in a wide arc. She caught the lizard at the knees. His legs buckled, and he hit the floor. The rippling energy that had been coalescing around the huntsman's hand vanished in a white flash.

Danae cheered.

Culduin thrust his weight away from the wall. He brought his sword down to cleave a bone-grating gash into the huntsman's arm.

Semi-prone but undaunted, the beast snapped its alligator jaws, his teeth snagging Culduin's pant leg. As Culduin twisted beyond reach, his opponent rose. Rage boiled in his eyes. The huntsman drew a flanged mace from his belt.

Danae had to help. The knife. She was useless until the confounded bonds were off her wrists. She ducked back into her cell, but kept the melee in partial sight. She kicked fodder around until her toe bumped the blade she sought.

Again, Culduin thrust at the huntsman, and his blade found its mark in the beast's abdomen. The huntsman roared. He brought his mace around with murderous force. The sharp flanges connected with Culduin's free arm, and the elf's eyes flew wide. He bared his teeth and wrenched his blade free.

Danae juggled the knife grip. She worked the blade between the cords and her skin. The blade snicked her wrists. At least it was sharp.

With tiny strokes, she sawed the blade back and forth. The metal rasped against hemp.

Culduin spun and cleft his enemy's leg, then pivoted back. He speared the creature's chest near the shoulder. The reptile answered by slamming his mace into the ribs Culduin left open. The smash threw Culduin to the side.

Danae's wrists burned. Her fingers cramped from the awkward motion. She gritted her teeth against the ache and persevered.

For every collision of mace and elf flesh, the huntsman suffered multiple sword cuts, until the villain's robes hung in tatters and his deep garnet blood spattered the floor. In a clumsy upswing, the huntsman caught Culduin's hand. The elf's sword hurtled down the cellblock.

Culduin tumbled beneath a wide swing of the mace and pursued his weapon.

The huntsman staggered. His mace slipped from his grasp.

Danae started. *What's he doing?* Her bonds were finally loosening enough to allow freer motion in her hands. A few more scratching strokes, and the ropes slipped away.

In a drunken shuffle, the huntsman planted his feet shoulder width apart. He traced patterns in the air with writhing claws. Unwholesome words snaked from his maw, while trails of yellow light formed into sigils that floated before him.

Oh, no you don't! Danae scuttled up behind the huntsman. She stabbed. The guard's long knife sank deep.

The huntsman's body jerked. Shuddered. Went limp. He collapsed in a heap.

Danae recoiled. She gaped at her empty hands for a moment before all the strength drained from her arms, and a wave of nausea swept over her. A hazy curtain of black closed in.

Culduin, though battered, caught her. "Very nice. Right between the second and third vertebrae, it looks to me. How did you know where to strike?"

"I didn't." Danae panted.

Culduin's lips parted in an incredulous smile. "We had better run before someone notices our mess."

32

ANOTHER TRAVELER

*D*anae scanned the cellblock. "How much hope do we have of making it out of here?" Her words slurred as multicolored lights danced in the haze that deepened before her.

"It is the middle of the night, and the temple above is nearly empty. If we disguise ourselves, I think we might have a chance of success. But first . . ." Culduin fumbled for the water skin on his belt. He lowered Danae to the ground and gave her a long drink of the water. "We shall never get so much as up the stairs with you so unsteady on your feet. Put your head down for a moment while I grab some robes."

Culduin dashed from the cellblock, and Danae shivered. Alone. Again. He returned in mere seconds, carrying with him a bundle of black fabric. On his shoulder, he once again carried both of their packs.

Culduin helped her sit up and handed her a robe. "Here. Put this on. Do you feel any better?"

Danae accepted the robe in weak fingers, but managed to fumble her way into the sleeves and clasp the front. "Yes. I think I can follow you now."

They stole into the hallway. It was so dark Danae could hardly make out Culduin's form beside her. His firm grasp closed upon her forearm.

"Once we ascend the stairs, there will be more light."

A curved flight of stairs led them up and away from the dungeon. They emerged from the stairwell in a long corridor, lit sparingly in the deep red glow of a single brazier. The temple was indeed empty, and their flight to the doors progressed unhindered, even if the passage through the halls did send tremors down Danae's spine. Once outside, the open air and the starlit sky smoothed away her jitters.

After they fled a reasonable distance from the temple, Danae ventured to whisper to her companion. "Why do you suppose the huntsman came to speak with me at such a late hour?"

"The dragon-kin are nocturnal. Perhaps he felt if he made his requests of you at a time when you were disoriented from being woken, you would be more pliable." The elf shrugged. "But I am guessing. Most of my experience with the creatures was to either dispatch them in battle or to patch up the rents they made in my comrades."

As they walked through the quiet streets, they kept to the most shadowed places and avoided the few residents who stirred so late. Those they did see staggered under influence of hard drink so that Culduin and Danae easily eluded their notice. The buildings thinned and the city limits drew near.

"I'm glad there's no gate to negotiate," Danae said.

Culduin nodded. "Good fortune smiled upon us in this turn of events. Between the rain that made the wagon so easy to track, the accessibility of the city, and the timing of my finding you, circumstances did give us the best advantage possible."

Culduin rummaged inside his cloak and held out a crumpled bundle of small rags. "Sharp thinking on the notes you left, by the way."

Danae ducked her chin. "At least I had one moment of clarity. But how did you know to come to the temple?"

"I did waste some time hunting for you in the slave market. But when I stumbled upon the temple of Queldurik, it made sense that was the place they would take you, given your . . . abilities."

"And you simply knew to head downstairs to the dungeon?"

Culduin laughed. "Once within the twisting hallways of that place, I do not know if I would have found you had I not heard your singing. An odd thing—I have to goad you into a few notes in pleasant times where we are in warmth and safety, and yet, you sing of your own volition when you are imprisoned and half-starved!"

Danae offered a sheepish smile. They continued in silence for a while longer into the outskirts of Cray, but despite Danae's will to flee onward, her breath deteriorated from labored to gasping. Her steps faltered.

Culduin smiled wearily. "It looks as though we could both use a respite."

They sank to the ground to huddle in a shadowed nook behind a shed. Danae dragged a leaden arm around Culduin's shoulder and squeezed.

The elf's eyebrows arched.

"That's a thank you for coming after me," Danae bit her lip. Heat crept into her cheeks.

Culduin propped his hand upon her shoulder. "I would do so again. But let us hope the occasion does not arise."

The warmth of Culduin's arm around Danae lulled her, and her head drooped.

A rub on her shoulder dragged her back from the edge of sleep. "It would be best if we put many miles between ourselves and Cray before daybreak," Culduin whispered. His voice was gentle but urgent.

Bleary eyed, Danae struggled to her feet. "You're right. Lead on. I'll just have to do my best to keep up."

Less than a mile beyond the city limits, Danae slumped to her knees. Hunger and dehydration would not relinquish their hold in so few mouthfuls.

"I'm sorry, Culduin." Her words slurred.

"No apologies." Culduin stooped, wedged his shoulder under her arm, slipped a forearm under her knees, and lifted her as if she were no heavier than a child. "You have suffered much."

She rested her head upon the taut muscle of his neck. The battle she waged with exhaustion turned in weariness's favor, and she slid into a surprisingly blissful oblivion.

The next thing she knew, the sun hovered over the western horizon. She bolted up, struggling against a thorough wrapping in blankets and oilskin. Culduin crouched a dozen paces off.

"Culduin, you really shouldn't let me snore on and on."

"You do not snore."

"Be serious." She propped a hand on her hip. "You deserve rest, too. I can shoulder some of the load."

"You would be surprised how little sleep I need. Keeping watch while you regain your strength is no trouble."

Danae shrugged. "I'll accept that—this time. I'm intending on giving up my full-time role of damsel in distress, though."

Culduin chuckled. "You are correct—it does not suit you." He waved her over to his position. "Look. I believe this place served as a camping site as recently as last night. I see indicators of two horses, though I can only find the tracks of one rider." Culduin pointed to an area of trampled grass and the remnants of a small fire pit.

Danae ran her hand over a boot print in the earth.

"We should keep a watchful eye before of us." Culduin said. "Who knows what sorts of wayfarers might traverse these reaches?"

Danae swallowed. "Enemies ahead and behind?"

"Possibly. I shall rest but briefly, and then let us march again under the night sky."

Culduin had no need to assert the urgency that they reach Garash swiftly. Though the lands around them still wore the bleak mantle of winter, other places on the continent—even Radromir, with its extensive winter—edged toward spring. With spring's arrival came the pressure of summer's inevitable descent. Midsummer's day would mark the anniversary of her father's receipt of the curse, her memory of it now all too vivid.

～

They pressed for days to the northeast, leaving the rocky terrain of Cray behind. The dry weather surrendered to humid, overcast nights that left dew-laden grass come morning. Seemingly overnight, the light kiss of spring transformed the wide plains ahead of them from gray to green, and the rolling meads erupted into a multicolored palette of wildflowers. Danae marveled at the sudden change.

While the weather never exactly became warm, the air lost its frosty bite. Culduin plucked an array of flowers while they walked and nimbly worked them together into a small garland of delicate intricacy. Once he had adjusted every stem and blossom to absolute perfection, he turned to Danae and extended the woven flowers to her.

"A crown of springtime to grace your golden locks, maiden?"

Danae blinked. "It's lovely, but I . . . oh, heavens."

Culduin crumpled. "But . . . but you what?" He stammered and flushed. "Have I misread your speech and that which has transpired between us, unsaid?"

Danae fixated on the flowers in Culduin's hand. "Uh . . . I—well, I certainly take the flowers as a compliment, and I don't want to slight you. But I'm not sure I'd be saying the right thing by taking them."

"What exactly would you be saying?"

A rush of heat overtook Danae's cheeks and ears. Was she inferring too much? "Flowers carry a certain meaning in my culture. At least when a man gives them to a woman."

"Would you rather I expressed no such sentiment?" Culduin squared his shoulders and lifted his chin.

Danae clasped her hands behind her neck and stared skyward. Never had she felt such a wash of exhilaration as she had experienced when Culduin drew close. Surely she was simply fascinated—real relationships were more practical than this. But should there not be at least a little fascination in the realm of romance?

"I . . . you . . . Culduin Caranedhel! What a corner you've backed me into." Danae raised her index finger. "Now, I'm only speaking in theory. In the hypothetical. But I've been thinking. An elf must consider any kind of involvement, friendship or otherwise, with a human to be largely futile."

Culduin tilted his head. "Futile?"

"Aren't the brief vapors of a human life little more than a season to you? That is, compared to the centuries you'll live on, long after any human you know now has withered, died, and gone to dust." She splayed her hands before her.

Culduin smiled gently and clasped Danae's hands. "Of course, as with all of my kindred, I have pondered such things in my heart. But you must understand, we elves are accustomed to the ebb and flow of all things we see and enjoy in our lifetimes." He took a step closer to her and leaned to her ear. His voice took on a husky tone. "Should we not pause to delight in the beauty of the morning glory, merely because we know its tender blossoms will fade in the heat of the day?"

The warmth of his breath fluttered the loose strands of hair tucked behind Danae's ear, and she shivered. She glanced across the wild expanse of blooms around them. Her palms began to sweat. She took a faltering step back. "I'm not sure what's going to happen once I finish this journey on my father's behalf. *If* I finish it. A lot could happen between now and then."

Culduin waited a moment. He held the garland out to her again.

Tightening her lips proved useless. A smile broke across Danae's face. "All right. For now, I'll take your flowers, since you worked so hard on them."

He met Danae's smile with a wide grin and set the garland upon the crown of her head. He surveyed his handiwork. "Now this suits you."

After a nonchalant wave, he continued northward.

Danae followed, a few paces behind her guide. Wisdom warned her to avoid leaning on her heart alone. But in her head, she knew an unfamiliar part of her heart had quickened the day she locked gazes with Culduin Caranedhel.

Thankfully, Culduin did not press her. In fact, he talked much less than at any point since they met, leaving Danae to long stretches of uninterrupted contemplation. He led them on to cut a narrow channel through the flowering grasslands, though he plucked not a single bloom.

*D*anae walked backward, surveying the horizon, and found it empty of all but a roving herd of caribou. She stepped back, bumped into something, and staggered to the side.

Culduin rose from a crouch. "No use fretting over what is not behind, Danae." He furrowed his brow at the grass at his feet and rubbed his chin. He circled a patch of crushed greenery.

Danae blurted, "You tell me not to fret. What about you? This has to be the dozenth time today you've stopped to pick at the grass, and never mind how many times you've done the same thing over the past ten days. What are you looking at? Please don't wave it off this time. You can't hide there's something nagging you."

Culduin crouched again and brushed his hand over the bracken. "Hoof prints. Less than a day ahead of us, though they do not push their mounts beyond an easy walk. I wonder, should we increase our pace to see if we might overtake these travelers, or shall we leave them to their business and hope they stay out of ours?"

"If the travelers are Tebalese, I think it's unlikely we'd meet with a friendly reception."

"Very true. Though if we continue at our usual pace, I doubt we shall overtake horsemen, even if they walk and we jog."

"I suppose we'd better keep our course. What else can we do?"

Culduin shrugged. "It seems very little. But let this serve as a reminder to be on our guard. Empty as these steppes may seem, we are fools to hope we are alone in them."

*T*he next day presented no encounter with any makers of tracks, but still, setting up camp in the nakedness of the landscape gave Danae the jitters. She lay in her tent and peered through the gap between the flaps. Sleep eluded her, though whether that was due to her temper or the recent descent of the sun, she could not tell. She crawled from her tent and sought Culduin, who she found pacing the camp's western edge.

"Still no one follows from Cray, I guess?" Danae said.

Culduin jumped. He straightened his sword belt. "No, it seems not, thankfully." His words came through the tight jaw of a poorly-concealed yawn.

"What about ahead?" She pointed to the northeast, where a pinprick of light winked along the purple horizon. "Is that a low star, or some other light I see?"

Culduin squinted in the direction Danae indicated. "I cannot see much in any direction. It must get darker before I am of good use."

"I'm inclined to think it's a fire." Danae began to pace. "What should we do?"

Culduin glanced at Danae sidelong. "Keep watch, as we always have?"

"I'm feeling unsettled. What if that fire builder has noticed us, too?"

"Well, though I am loath to separate, I could—"

"No, please, Culduin. Let me figure this out. I need to decide."

"*You* need to decide?" His brow furrowed.

Danae thrust her arms out to her sides. "All I've done since I've left home is clapped myself onto other people's expertise. Huddled under some protector's wings. I'm weary of needing continual rescue and everyone else's help. I've got to do this for myself."

Culduin placed a hand on her shoulder. "Do you? Is it such a terrible thing to utilize the resources in your path?"

"Maybe it is. I'll never learn to tackle things on my own if I always look around me and say 'You'd know better, tell me what to do.'"

"Perhaps it is a cultural disparity that I do not understand. To whom must you prove anything?"

Danae walked a small circle, picking at a fingernail. She stopped, her glance dodging Culduin's. "In the most immediate sense, Creo, I suppose."

"What could you possibly have to prove to him?"

She rolled her eyes to corral a mist of tears. "I've got to earn his mercy on my father's behalf. If Creo is the only 'person' who can really help Papa, that's why I'm out here, isn't it?" The pitch of her voice rose with every word. "If I'm so helpless and useless, why should Creo even begin to consider what I want?"

"What an odd question." Culduin tilted his head to the side. "Why do you believe you owe Creo some intangible debt?"

"I guess it ties into something Archadion said. About how I couldn't possibly offer Creo anything he doesn't already possess. If that's true, why am I even doing this?" Danae looked full into Culduin's face. "How can I possibly be smart enough, good enough, competent enough to earn the favor of a god?"

"Forgive me for saying so, Danae, but what you say sounds errant to me. Granted, I am minimally schooled in Creo's statutes,"

"So where does that leave me?" Danae huffed. "What if I just sit here, and another of Queldurik's servants captures me again?"

Culduin winced.

Danae gulped. A prickle of guilt skittered up her neck. "I mean, really, don't feel like I'm blaming you. I'm blaming me. Apparently talking about this is only making matters worse."

"What would you have me do?" Culduin asked, his voice tentative.

Danae covered her face with her hands. "I don't know that either! I should have the answers, because this is my quest. And I don't! Maybe I should just take some time alone."

After meeting Danae's gaze, Culduin took gentle hold of her chin.

"If it is as you say, and only Creo can affect the ultimate outcome of your quest, then I believe you put too much on your own shoulders, Danae. Seek your solitude. Probe your soul. In the meantime, I am going to watch more closely on this side of camp." He took a few steps to the northeast. "At least it will grow fully dark while you think. Then I shall be more comfortable with whatever you propose."

Danae ducked into the isolation of her tent. Flight seemed as doubtful and dangerous as investigation of the not-too-distant situation.

Almighty Creator, how can I show my worth? Is this situation concerning the fire part of that? Is this a chance to show I can mind my own business? An opportunity to prove my bravery and willingness to combat your enemies? May I make the right decision and find favor in your sight.

She spent as long as she could bear in silence, but her unabated anxiety twisted her shoulders into knots. Had she prayed the wrong prayer? This business of discerning divine will when she knew so little about Creo, his Patrons, or anything else, left her wringing her hands. Once it grew clear that huddling in her tent would provide no further wisdom than pacing outside, Danae returned to Culduin. Full dark had fallen.

"Any change?"

"None that I can see. How have you fared?"

Danae exhaled. "No change for me either. My restless spirit tells me to investigate, simply to escape this sense of running in place."

"I shall follow in whatever choice you make. If it's any comfort to you, I hear Creo can work even through our mistakes."

A smirk tugged at Danae's tense lips. "Very reassuring. Let's gather our weapons."

33

CONVERGING PATHS

*D*anae and Culduin stole forward, silent of stride, the little firelight growing ever closer. Once within a hundred yards of the campfire, Danae could faintly discern the shadows of two horses, who stood with their heads low and relaxed. As for the travelers who used the horses? Nowhere.

"We shall need to press closer," Culduin whispered, leaning just inches from Danae's ear. Despite his efforts, his voice was jarringly loud in the empty air. "Do you agree?"

Danae wriggled her damp fingers that clutched her dagger. She nodded.

Yard by yard, they crept toward the campsite, bent low enough for the tall grasses to offer concealment, but spotted only a tent and a pack within the circle of firelight. They stopped about twenty-five yards from the horses.

"Not a soul," Culduin said.

"Where would they go?"

Culduin shrugged.

"Let's hunker down and watch for a little." Danae lowered her belly to the ground. At least in watching, she could pretend her indecision had not emerged master of the moment.

The larger of the two horses threw its head into the air and wheeled to face them. The proud beast bugled a shrill whinny that cut through the hiss of the breeze in the bracken.

Danae's heart nearly stopped. She clutched Culduin's arm. The elf placed his hand upon hers as he turned his head a fraction and narrowed his eyes to slits.

The slightest crunch of dry grass reached Danae's ears. "What was that?" A growing skitter of pinpricks up the backs of her arms sank a lump of dread into her core.

Culduin whirled around to face back the way they came, his sword blade ringing free of the scabbard.

Danae, too, wheeled on the threat. A tall, cloaked figure had somehow skulked up behind them. Culduin leveled his sword at the gray-clad traveler, whose hood shadowed all but his clean-shaven chin.

The stranger raised his hands. "*Restrir se ferrutus, amman Delsin. Vi gera na humeaat is Tebal.*"

Danae gasped and clapped her hand over her mouth, as if that would keep her squeal of elation contained. Despite the accent of the complicated Elvish words he spoke, she could not deny the familiarity of the voice.

"Praesidio? It can't be!" She threw back her hood.

This mysterious figure reached up and removed his hood as well, and indeed, Danae beheld the unmistakable face, the straight gray hair, the fathomless eyes of the old sage.

"Danae?" Praesidio gaped. "How is this possible? How on earth did you survive being swatted into the river like a—" He shook his head. "Forgive me, this is no way to learn of your journey over the past months." He bowed, his fist clenched over his heart, facing Culduin. "Warmest greetings, elf of Delsinon. I am Praesidio of the Knights of the Phoenix. Perhaps Mistress Baledric has spoken of me?"

Culduin sheathed his sword and returned Praesidio's genteel bow.

"Yes, Master Praesidio. I have heard tales of your wisdom and prowess. I am Culduin Caranedhel, scout and medic of the Delsin. Well met, indeed!"

"Will you join me in my camp?" Praesidio extended an arm toward the fire. "I have many questions to ask of young Danae, if she can abide them."

Finally, a chance to riddle Praesidio with the questions that nagged Danae from every direction. "Gladly."

They all bustled to the fireside, where Praesidio's tall stallion stamped, and the little mare Danae had ridden tossed her head and fidgeted at the larger horse's excitement. Praesidio stroked the stallion's neck and murmured to him.

"You caught my horse," Danae said. "Of all the troubles that day at the ford, you managed not to lose her?"

"Chancellor here saw she did not tear off into the woods when she completely lost her head that day." Praesidio gave his chestnut horse a last firm pat. "He has been much absorbed in seeing to her well-being ever since. I am endlessly thankful for this wise beast, for it was he who caught a scent the other day and gave me some warning I was being followed."

Danae narrowed her eyes. "How did you know he caught our scent?" She folded her arms. "We weren't following you, by the way."

Praesidio grinned. "Still the same skeptic I lost months ago, I see. While the horse cannot speak with me in plain words, we have a sort of language between us. He is no ordinary beast of burden."

Culduin stared at Chancellor, the sparkle of reverent appreciation in his eyes, "I should think not, being the bearer of a knight of the Elgadrim. Looking at this Chancellor of yours, I am inclined to believe he is the pinnacle of his bloodline."

"I am sure he thanks you for your compliment, Master Caranedhel." Praesidio sat beside the fire. "But please, I must know the story of how you came to intercept me."

Danae joined Praesidio. "If I didn't know better, I'd say it was luck that brought us up behind you. I can't say I've been a very skilled pilot on these seas of chance."

"But let us not begin at the end of the tale, young one." Praesidio leaned in. "Please, if you can, return to the day of the attack at the ford and tell me where you have been. What you have been doing."

The old sage listened without interruption, lacing his fingers together as Danae and Culduin unraveled all they had endured and triumphed over together in such a short time. He nodded, a smile playing at his lips. "Well done, young travelers. It sounds to me, Danae, you have learned much in my absence, and I hear in your words a growing trust in the Maker."

"Do you? I feel like I only have more questions." Danae's head hung.

"Clearly something has shaken your young faith."

She drew a shuddering breath. "The huntsman sneered at my insistence Creo would help me. He didn't even blink in hesitation."

Praesidio lowered his eyelids, then gazed into Danae's face. "You have taken but the first few strides in a lifelong journey beside the Creator. Patience will reward you with understanding."

"Time is the one thing I have in dwindling quantities." Danae thumped a fist into her lap.

Praesidio placed a strong but wrinkled hand on her shoulder. "You stand in the hardest place of all in a journey into Creo's service, but I cannot speed this section of the road for you. I can give you this, however." He reached into his pack, produced a small leather book of many thin pages, and handed it to Danae. "In these pages you will find all of the wisdom Creo has bestowed unto his servants. Do not worry if it makes little sense to you at first. As you grow, Creo will illuminate the truths you need."

Danae gingerly lifted the tome from Praesidio's hands and examined its dark leather cover in the firelight. Debossed into the face of the book was a spreading tree.

"What's the significance of the tree image on the cover?"

Praesidio tipped his face skyward. "The servants of Creo see themselves as deeply rooted in Creo's wisdom, so they might grow strong and weather the storms of the Darkness. Only by drinking his statutes will we grow and flourish."

Danae traced over the image with her finger. "Thank you. I'm guessing I don't know half the value of what I've been given, but I assure you I'll squeeze every drop of understanding I can from its pages. But right now, I want to hear your side of the story—how you escaped destruction at the ford, and what you've been doing since then. I suffered a long delay, and yet here we are. On the same path."

"Ah, how to relay it best?" Praesidio rubbed his chin. "If only you were one of Culduin's immortal brethren with the gift of reading rumors, then all you would need to do is take my hand, and you could see the day as I saw it. But let me think." He rose, stepped over to his gear by his tent, and lifted a round bronze shield and a water-skin from the pile. "Yes, there is another way."

Danae quirked an eyebrow. "I've never seen you use a shield."

"I rarely do. Still, it seemed foolhardy to set out bereft of one." He returned to the fireside and laid the shield on the ground. Once he had worked the stopper from the mouth of the skin, he poured the water into the concave face of the shield. Firelight danced on the water's surface. "Gaze into the water, Danae, and let Creo illuminate what you missed."

Danae knelt beside the shield, but cast her mentor a sideways glance.

The amber glow on the water shimmered and swirled at first, but then shifted into a hypnotic undulation. Danae's eyes blurred, and her lids felt thick. The patterns melted into the churning, foaming yellow waters of a river. The perspective widened, and the soggy banks of the Nuruhain came into view. Praesidio stood beside Mizzle-torp, their feet in wide stances, Praesidio holding the sword of the Sacred Fire in a lateral grip above his head, and Mizzletorp with shortsword and dagger at the ready. Both their lips moved in silent discourse. Indeed, no rush of river roared in the background, no wind rustled through the pine boughs around them.

The horde of goblins crashed into view, and Danae's two friends whirled in a complicated dance of thrusts and parries. Mizzletorp spun his dagger and sent the pitted blade of an opponent hurtling into the brush. Praesidio held one goblin in a bind. He kicked his opponent with a thrust that sent him sprawling. Goblins lost weapons, limbs, and lives at a rapid succession that widened Danae's transfixed eyes. Praesidio endured several cuts to the torso, but bore them with continued ageless speed and vigor.

A tremor shivered the surface of the water. Both knight and gnome fought on, beset on all sides with foes, encircled by those already fallen. The water in the shield vibrated again.

The towering figure of the knotty-skinned ogre emerged from the edge of Danae's window into the battle, and he drew his fell hammer with a stroke sure to land in the center of Praesidio's back.

Danae's own likeness swung into view from the opposite side of the field. How jarring to see herself in something other than a looking glass. Every motion slowed as the hammer careened toward Praesidio, but then on a path for her interposing body. The ogre's yellowing eyes flew wide. His mouth twisted in a snarl. He threw all his weight back against the momentum of his blow, but too late. The hammer slammed into Danae's ribs.

The memory of old pain flashed across Danae's flesh as she witnessed the bone-rending stroke. Her figure within the vision launched beyond the scope of the window.

Praesidio and Mizzletorp wheeled back and forth between Danae's trajectory and their new enemy, but Praesidio's focus soon locked beyond the ogre. More soundless words spilled from his lips. He cut down the last goblin in his path. A few leaping strides carried him past the behemoth while Mizzletorp assumed Praesidio's place as the ogre's toe-to-toe opponent.

The water shifted and shimmered—had Danae reached the end of the vision granted? The image coalesced again. Praesidio barreled for a black-hooded figure.

Danae shuddered. She had liked it better when she did not know what hid under that hood.

The huntsman wove his gloved hands before him, and a pulse of fire shot forth from his gesture. Praesidio threw his divine weapon up in a parry, and the huntsman's assault shattered into an array of sparks that kindled the pine litter on the ground to smoldering.

Praesidio skidded to a stop, pointed his sword at the huntsman, and a burst of blue light swelled around the fiery blade. It exploded into a conical shower of icy shards. The huntsman threw his hands up to shield his head.

More volleys passed between them, Praesidio breaking an invisible stranglehold, the huntsman collapsing momentarily in craven trembling.

Seizing the huntsman's disarmed moment, Praesidio closed upon him. He leveled his sword at his foe. The creature raised one hand. Praesidio's stance relaxed, if only a fraction.

The huntsman rose to one knee, and he pulled a little flask from his belt and uncorked it in a fluid motion faster than any warrior might draw a weapon. He thrust the vial into his hood and tipped it back.

Praesidio's lips parted in first a slack-jawed gasp, then some percussive word. Brows lowered and teeth clenched, he lunged for the huntsman, but his sword passed through a mere vapor that dissipated on the wind. The old sage threw his hand down, and the Sacred Fire vanished.

Praesidio spun, and the perspective of the whole vision with him, a motion that plagued Danae with a sudden dizziness. She shook free of the vertigo and blinked the vision back into focus in time to witness Mizzletorp's engagement against the ogre. He wobbled off balance, and down the ogre's hammer came in an overhand blow. Danae squeezed her eyes shut before the stroke fell.

At sniffle off to her side, she opened her eyes and glanced at Praesidio. The wet tracks of tears shone down his cheeks, but he swiped them away with the back of his sleeve.

When Danae turned back to the shield, only ordinary water and firelight remained within. "Mizzletorp fought bravely. It's a horrible shame..."

Praesidio cleared his throat. "Indeed. I feared I would need to dig two graves that day, but despite my searching, I found no trace of you."

"But this was all months ago. How is it you're here now?"

"Having lost a friend and a dear student, my sense of purpose foundered, so I decided to return to Bilearne for a time of reflection and the seeking of Creo's will." Praesidio sat back. "In time, the Maker revealed to me that I should resume the journey for the Sword's recovery, though why I should attempt such a task on my own seemed very unclear. But long ago, I learned that even blind obedience has its rewards."

Danae crinkled her brow. Sometimes Praesidio peppered the strangest riddles into his stories.

"During the time I spent in Bilearne," Praesidio continued, "the offensive line of the allied armies splintered under redoubled attacks by the enemy, and the allies, routed and in a panic, scrambled to reassemble in the countryside of Kelmirith. We learned the enemy had more than doubled his force by bolstering it with monsters of all shapes and sizes, from the evil gnomes of the forests of North Deklia, to the dragon-kin whom Radromirian pirates shuttled in secret from their exile on the Isle of Desolation."

"And I suppose that's part of why the Tebalese were so determined to hold the western shipping lanes," Danae said.

Praesidio nodded. "You begin to perceive the wider view."

Culduin clucked his tongue. "We in Delsinon feared Queldurik would make increasing use of the dragon-kin. While their numbers were few in the skirmishes my people have endured in the early part of the war, it appears they have proven their usefulness to Queldurik and thus purchased their rescue from exile."

"Useful indeed," Praesidio said. "The dragon-kin's companies of fiends, so resistant to the weapons of all but the knights of the Elgadrim, swamped the Servants of Creo. They rained their curses down upon our forces without restraint. Soldiers quailed, regiments foundered, and all the ground gained by our armies fell to the enemy, and then some. Alas, our numbers are too few to combat this host."

"So, if things are so dire, why are you so many miles from the front lines?" Danae asked.

Praesidio winced, and a sickening twinge of regret rattled in

Danae's stomach. Could she not sift her words before she let them spill off her lips?

"I took long counsel with my order and with our Philosopher King, and we determined that if the incomparably mad and deathless Queldurik was to be stopped, we must place the Sword of the Patron in the hands of the greatest warrior alive today, for only its power may slay Queldurik in his arrangement with the Darkness."

"So, your people have decided upon the fate of the Sword, that is, if we can recover it."

"Yes, it appears this weapon may have an important role in the ending of this destructive conflict that threatens to overrun us all. Our numbers wane, and the enemies' grow. Unless we can strike the serpent at the head, we will eventually all be destroyed." The solemnity in Praesidio's voice grew with every word.

"But what does this have to do with my original mission to help my father?"

"You will discover the ways in which this journey intertwines with your father's plight. It is not mine to reveal such intricacies of the Maker's plan."

Could his answer have been more frustrating? Danae lowered her eyelids and took a long breath.

Praesidio resumed his tale. "After many weeks of meeting and meditation in Bilearne, I found the prompting of Creo unmistakable, and the order of my King indisputable, so in the end, I set out for Garash. I rode for many weeks, made a wide circle around the fighting in central Kelmirith, and crossed the Tebalese border. Shortly after, Chancellor caught your scent, and I feared who might pursue me.

"As misfortune would have it, your little mare, whom I have taken to calling Ariandne, began to show signs of lameness, even serving as a pack horse bearing a light load. Though I was loath to, I tried to set her free so she would not slow my progress, but she limped after us, whickering and pleading. For the first time in our long partnership, Chancellor acted more the mule than the warhorse, and would not go on without her. I had to stop, rest her, and hope I would prove a match for whoever dogged my steps."

"And so, as fate would have it, we pursue the Sword together. That is, if the Elgadrim's offer to me still stands." Doubt gnawed at Danae's gut.

"Fear not, young learner, we still walk the same path."

For a moment, only the crackle of Praesidio's little fire filled the air.

Culduin asked, "Protector, you spoke of placing the Sword of the Patron in the hands of the greatest known living warrior. I wonder, does your council have such a warrior in mind?"

Praesidio turned to Culduin. "Funny you should ask this, Master Caranedhel. We do have a person in mind, yes, but the choice is problematic."

"In what way?"

"Though the Delsin have not yet committed to coming to the aid of men, the warrior we would charge with the task of wielding the Sword is one of your own. High Commander of the Windriders, Vinyanel Ecleriast."

Culduin nodded. "The choice is not a surprise, for Lord Vinyanel's reputation is legendary. Should he agree to undertake this dread role on the behalf of men, I don't suppose the Elgadrim have a plan on how to persuade our brethren in Sarn Celevon to resist sundering ties with the Delsin?" He heaved a deep sigh. "Alas, if only those who ought to stand on the same side of the conflict could be of one mind."

Praesidio rose and eased to the edge of the firelight. "It has been a battle against the current, to be sure, but much diplomacy transpires between the Elgadrim and all the peoples of the Elves. It is my hope great progress will have been made by the time we see Bilearne."

Culduin smiled. "You are an optimist, I see. That is good, for the darling realist we companion will do the worrying for all three of us." He gripped Danae's shoulder and gave it a firm squeeze.

Danae pressed her lips together against the temptation to stick her tongue out at the elf's taunts. "Praesidio? With so many dragon-kin in Queldurik's service, do you think another huntsman will come after me?"

Praesidio shrugged. "Who can say, Danae? Until Creo assumes your debt, there is always the risk Queldurik's servants may come to demand payment."

Danae's face fell. She wished she knew for sure how the whole business of serving Creo worked. It was far less concrete than she liked.

"Despair not, young one," Praesidio offered. "My instinct says the enemy may bide his time and not send a huntsman traipsing all over creation after a single Curse Bearer. There is much greater devastation for the dragon-kin to enact on the front lines." After a breath, he added, "But do not think that gives you any license to start throwing around incantations again."

Danae pulled her cloak tighter around her shoulders. "I understand, Praesidio." But it was a lie. The more she listened, the clearer it became what a wealth of truth still remained beyond her grasp.

34

THE CANYON OF QUEL-MAHAAR

A brilliant red sunrise cast the contours of Ariandne's coat in flaming copper. Danae slung her pack over her shoulder and approached the mare, where Culduin and Praesidio crouched at the horse's shoulder, examining her foreleg.

Culduin stood and stroked the horse's neck. "Your day of rest has drawn all the heat out of this leg, Praesidio. Her gait looks good, but I think we would be wise to keep her work as light as possible."

"Excellent. Danae, Ariandne is fit to be your mount once again. Culduin and I can ride double on Chancellor," Praesidio said.

Danae tied her gear behind her saddle. "Do you think you could lead me on my horse so I don't have to rein?"

Praesidio raised an eyebrow. "You are perfectly capable in the saddle. Has your last fall spooked you so much?"

"No, it's not that. I was hoping to read the book you gave me while we ride. I won't be able to do much of that in the dark of camp, and there's so much I need to learn. I discovered that from the few pages I browsed before bed last night."

A warm chuckle overtook Praesidio. "Very well. I can never resist a student's hunger for truth. Tether her to my cantle."

Danae lifted a brow. "Your what?"

"The back of his saddle," Culduin said. "There's a ring upon it."

Thus arranged, they set out across the open steppes. Danae juggled her copy of what Praesidio had called *The Tree*, squinting in an attempt to focus on the words even through the mare's jostling gait. Danae loosened her spine and joints, which served to absorb some of the motion. By mid-morning, she had finessed the art of steadying her book, and she drank in at least two hundred pages. What a volume of puzzles it turned out to be.

From the pages within, however, she distilled one important truth: the great servants of Creo selflessly put their duty to God above all else and asked nothing in return for their deeds of obedience. Would enough time and patience teach Danae to find peace in such surrender? It all seemed so contrary to her every instinct. Still, she read on, inexplicably compelled by the foreign behavior of the characters that populated the pages.

"Praesidio," Danae called up to him as they rode single-file. "Am I supposed to interpret the events in this book as true? Historical? Or are they metaphors?"

The old sage looked back, a bemused grin in his eyes. "What do you think?"

She huffed. "You're impossible. I mean, really. Whole cities turning to ice? Battles between legions of Patrons and fiends? People literally flying from the jaws of death?"

"I would be a poor teacher indeed if I made it so easy to decide what you should believe. It is not something one does with one's head alone."

"Do *you* believe it's literal?"

"When you are ready for that answer, I will give it to you." He turned forward once again.

Danae sighed. She weighed the book in her hand. Even if Culduin's estimates on how long it would take to get to Garash were accurate, that long stretch of days would prove insufficient to sort through the convoluted pages of *The Tree*.

*D*ays of travel swelled into weeks. The flatness of the steppes grew rockier but remained treeless, and the ground stretched before them in what seemed an endless, low-grade slope. The long grass the horses grazed upon in the southern reaches of Tebal disappeared, giving way to moss, lichen, and short bushes whose roots spread mostly above the soil's surface. The gentle caress of spring they had begun to enjoy in the southern marches of the country withdrew its touch from these bleak stretches of tundra, for the air was dry and chill. The rare, solitary plant would bravely put forth tiny white blooms, as if to defy the endless cold of the place, but their frequency dwindled the farther north they pressed.

After so many days of continual riding that Danae began to lose count, the tundra landscape finally changed. A wide gash cut across the northeastern distance.

"What's that we seem to be headed right for?" Danae pointed toward the cleft.

"The canyon of Quel-Mahaar," Culduin answered. "The last major obstacle that stands between us and Garash itself."

Praesidio reined in Chancellor. "The horses will not be able to manage the crossing of the canyon. I fear I must trust in Chancellor's wisdom to lead little Ariandne to safety."

Danae's jaw slackened. "You mean you're just going to turn the horses loose and hope they don't fall prey to wolves, or worse?"

"Chancellor has many years of experience in finding his way home without me," Praesidio said. "I am much less worried about his eventual arrival in Bilearne than our own. Besides, the grain I've packed won't last in this barren landscape. The horses must return to lands where they will enjoy decent forage."

Danae glanced at Praesidio's proud stallion, the arch of his neck, his powerful stance, and most of all, the spark in his eye, and abandoned any further argument about Praesidio's suggestion. She dismounted, unbuckled what gear they had lashed to the beasts, and helped with the task of setting them free. Her breath came in uncharacteristic gasps for so light a task. She pressed a palm to her chest.

"It is the elevation that steals your breath." Culduin cast her a sympathetic smile.

"I've been away from Radromir too long." Danae swallowed.

Chancellor nudged Praesidio's shoulder, tossed his head, and trumpeted a great cry, which Ariandne answered with her own shrill whinny. The two beasts sprang to the south, their manes and tails streaming behind them in the morning sun. Praesidio, Danae, and Culduin watched them as they disappeared over the horizon.

"Creo preserve you," Praesidio whispered as the horses vanished from sight.

*D*anae stood on the wind-whipped edge of the canyon and surveyed the long descent to the gorge's floor. They faced a couple of days of strenuous work ahead. She tightened the wrist straps on her gloves.

"So, Danae, how are your climbing skills?" Culduin asked.

"Actually," Danae replied, "pretty good, if I may say so without the risk of boasting. Before the occupation, Papa and I made quite a few trips into the mountains, hunting minerals."

"Well then, perhaps you now have something you might teach me." Culduin peered over the edge. "My experience is minimal."

Danae crouched and rooted through her pack. "I see we have ropes and grapples, but no climbing harness, right?"

Culduin's weak grin provided the answer.

"Are you sure the distance is too great to circle around either to the east or west?"

"Yes. To circle to the west would add a week to our journey, and to travel east would lead us into a quagmire of miserable fens, inhabited by disease-ridden insects as well as fell creatures that are half frog, half men, who hold their kingdom there. I would rather risk two days of climbing than confront those villains in their unmanageable terrain."

Praesidio's emphatic nod confirmed the dubiousness of such a course.

Danae rose and looped some of the length of the rope under the wide leather belt around her waist. "While not ideal, I suppose the ropes and our belts will have to suffice. Evening will come early to the floor of the canyon, so we had best get to it."

Under Danae's instruction, Culduin and Praesidio mimicked her assembly of makeshift rappelling apparatus from the rope they had, and they began the slow descent over the southern lip of the canyon. Danae led the way in choosing winding paths to hike, or occasional short stretches that demanded more careful climbing. After only a dozen fathoms of descent, however, the face of the stone grew too sheer for anything besides hooking their grapples and lowering themselves over another edge.

"I'll go first," Danae said. "Watch how I let the rope slip through my belt, and mind your grip. The length I've set the rope will keep you from hitting the next ledge if you slip, but . . . I recommend not slipping."

Danae walked backward down the crumbling shale wall. The burn in her arms and shoulders reminded her just how long it had been since she had done any meaningful climbing. A lot of canyon depth still awaited conquest.

Praesidio made his way down next, and his slow, deliberate handling of the ropes, his surefootedness on the rocks, and his unruffled expression convinced Danae there was little the knight had not tackled in his long service to Creo. When the old sage reached the bottom, Culduin released Praesidio's grapple to allow it to tumble down.

Culduin climbed over the edge.

"Less raw muscle, more bracing and balancing, you show-off!" Danae yelled up to him. "Don't worry, we can see your biceps from here, and I promise, we're very impressed. But you'll never reach the bottom if you don't save your strength."

Culduin turned his torso away from the rock face and smirked at Danae, when the shale under his boots crumbled. His eyes went wide. He slid.

"Grab, grab, grab!" Danae screamed. "Get your feet on the wall!"

Though he scrambled with his feet and snatched at the rope, the loose stone broke free in a shower of fragments. The rope whined against his belt the elf sped down its length. With a sharp jerk, Culduin came to an abrupt halt about six feet above where she and Praesidio stood. He had reached the end of his length of rope. The force of the fall hitched his belt up to his ribs. He mouthed a word that looked something like "ouch."

After the surge of terror that had gripped Danae abated, she winced. "I'm sorry, Culduin. I shouldn't be joking around at a time we all need to concentrate. Are you hurt?"

"Not permanently, but I do not want to repeat that mistake," Culduin said from between his teeth.

A frown creased Praesidio's brow. "But now we have a lingering grapple at the top."

"That's all right. Now that I've done the climb, I can go back up and get it, and then use a short tether to work my way back down. But we can't afford to leave any rope again." Danae threw her hook. "There are no guarantees I'll be able to fetch them in other spots."

*T*he sun slipped below the lip of Quel-Mahaar as the climbers touched their feet to the floor of the gorge, and its depths donned the blues and purples of twilight. Danae's hands ached from the long hours of clutching the ropes. Despite her leather gloves, her palms felt raw. She tugged the gloves off, dropped them on the pebble-strewn ground, and bathed her hands in the cold current of the stream that wended through the bottom of the canyon. Even in the cold dryness of the tundra, Danae's tunic clung to her sweating back. A shiver ran through her body.

In weary silence, Danae helped Praesidio and Culduin set up camp. She cast herself onto the uneven ground, glad to catch whatever rest she might before her watch came along. The echoes of the chattering stream off the towering wall to the north spoke a mocking promise—the coming ascent out of the canyon would be grueling.

*D*anae scratched her head with a dusty glove. She squinted up the wall of the canyon from the narrow ledge she and her companions had gained in a several-hour climb, while the morning sun bathed the canyon in white winter light. A jutting sandstone outcropping overhead hung too far out for even the best-thrown grapple to catch.

"I don't want to suggest we should climb back down and seek out another way." Danae rolled a sore shoulder.

"Then do not," Culduin said. "This last leg was arduous, to say the least." He reached back and rubbed his neck.

There must be some other way. Danae chewed her lip and surveyed the cliff face one more time. A gnarled stump clung to the rocks to the east. *Maybe . . .*

"If we could get a rope set off in that direction, I might be able to first climb laterally." Danae pointed to the stump. "That would put me at a better angle to throw a line to the top of the overhang."

"I do not see much in the way of hand or footholds, Danae," Culduin said. Stress, fatigue, and grime lined his features.

"It may look sheer, but I think I can jam my hands and feet in enough of those fissures to make it. We'll never get a rope to the top of the overhang from here. Our landing is too shallow compared to the overhang."

Praesidio exhaled, and a smile creased his dirt-smeared cheeks. "Today, we defer to you, climber."

Eyes narrowed and teeth clenched, Danae wound up her throw and let the grapple fly toward the stump. And then she tried again. On the third release of the iron hook, it hit its mark and stuck, and Danae flashed her friends a grin.

Danae crept sideways along the stone wall, her body pressed close to the surface, and her fingers and toes seeking the minute chinks in her path. She forced her glance from one fissure to the next, since the sight of Culduin's hand-wringing only compounded the stress of the climb. The closer she got to her goal, the shorter she cinched the rope through her belt, even though it served as more of a security measure than a boon to climbing. Finally, she wrapped the crook of her elbow around the snarled oak stump. She had only ascended a couple of fathoms from where her companions waited, but had struck out along the wall twice that distance.

From her perch, supported only by her grip on the stump and one toe she had wedged into the rock face, she could see the top of a shelf much deeper than the one where Praesidio and Culduin waited, and its surface boasted enough crags to make for an easy grapple catch. At the back of the shelf stood a dark cleft in the rock, which Danae hoped would provide good terrain for the next stage. She heaved a grapple, and it caught on one of the shelf's boulders. A firm tug confirmed the grapple's stability.

Danae crept over to the ledge, as deftly as a spider skittering across the cliff-face. Once she stood with both feet upon the shelf, both Praesidio and Culduin heaved sighs. She found a crag near the shelf's edge that could support both grapples, hooked them, and let the ropes fall to her friends.

Praesidio grabbed his rope and threaded it through his belt. He stepped close to the foot of the overhang, pulled the rope taut, and began his climb, walking his feet up the sloping rock.

Danae chewed her lip. It would not take much for Praesidio to lose traction on the rock face and end up in a bind.

Culduin grabbed the second line and made a swift ascent, hauling himself straight up the rope rather than utilizing the wall.

Danae chuckled. *There he goes again, hand-over-handing it. Oh, well, he'll get here, so I'd best keep my critique to myself.*

Culduin and Praesidio climbed within ten feet of the ledge. Praesidio's arms quivered under the strain. He stepped to brace his foot against a scant foothold, but the sandstone cracked and crumbled away. Praesidio grunted as he swung out from the rock face.

Culduin shot out one of his hands to snatch at Praesidio, but his fingers only brushed a fold of Praesidio's tunic. They both spun.

"Get up here, Culduin! You're no help to him down there," Danae yelled over the edge.

Amidst the grating of the shifting grapples on the rock and the constant undertone of the wind, a scraping clatter caught Danae's ear. She furrowed her brow but pushed the sound from her mind as she sought a solution to Praesidio's predicament. A chill raised the hairs on the back of her neck. The glare of sunlight on the rock around her dimmed in a growing shadow.

Danae snuck a reluctant glance over her shoulder. A black, chitinous monstrosity closed upon her, its long, segmented tail curled over its back. A scream froze in her throat. The sun gleamed off a single drop of venom that hung from the tip of the tail's stinger. Danae's only options, a retreat over the shelf's edge, or perhaps . . .

The scorpion snatched at Danae with front pincers large enough to catch her around the waist, narrowly missing her as she dove into a somersault under its body. It took a second roll to clear the creature's length. She regained her feet behind the monster and wrenched two daggers from the bandoliers across her chest.

A galloping pulse throbbed in her temples. The creature rotated left and right, but never entirely wheeled to her. Time to strategize. She slunk behind a boulder near the dark crevice at the rear of the shelf. The stone eclipsed the monster beyond.

The clatter of its armored legs continued, but remained at a distance. Danae swiped a sleeve across her sweaty brow and dared to peer around the boulder's side. The scorpion snapped with ridged pincers at the cliff's edge, the very place where Praesidio rolled and dodged, his body only halfway onto level ground.

Nothing like an emergency to abort planning. Danae leapt to the apex of her hiding place and flung one dagger after the next at the monster. One stuck between plates of its carapace. The creature flinched, but then lunged at Praesidio. Danae's second dagger glanced off the scorpion's back and tumbled to the ground beneath its legs.

"*Ayet!*" Culduin's voice echoed from beyond the shelf's edge in a grunt.

Up? Danae translated. She narrowed her eyes.

A thrust heaved the rest of Praesidio's body onto the shelf. Culduin must have found some way to give the old sage an extra boost. Praesidio rolled to the side, and the Sword of the Sacred Fire erupted from his hand.

The scorpion recoiled from the Sword's brightness. Praesidio staggered to his feet. He hammered the creature with a flurry of sudden strokes. The first three blows made only moderate rents in the creature's armor, but one bit deep and opened a smoking gash. A screeching hiss ripped from the creature's mandibles.

Still it came on, with the frenzied speed of desperation. It snapped with pincers, it plunged its deadly tail. Praesidio ducked and twisted with all the nimbleness of a man half his age. His sword sent a chunk of the enemy's black armor flying. The creature side-scuttled with an erratic gait to the lip of the rocky ledge, and the four legs on its far side slipped over. It clutched the shelf's surface with the four nearer, shuddering limbs.

Praesidio raised his weapon for an overhand stroke, when the scorpion flicked its tail like a bullwhip. The sideswipe caught Praesidio behind the knees. The old sage's legs buckled, and he knocked the back of his head on the stony ground with an ugly thump.

Gravity stole the victory from the beast. However it clacked and gripped with its four land-bound legs, the pointed members scraped through the sandstone. Its body ground over the edge of the precipice and out of sight.

Danae scrambled to Praesidio's side. She hauled his flaccid body farther from the precipice, though it was cumbersome work. His eyes rolled in their sockets to reveal mostly whites. He made no response to her touch or cries.

What about Culduin? A stabbing sensation of dread wrenched Danae's gut.

She dashed toward the edge. Both Culduin and the scorpion dangled fifteen feet below, like marionettes engaged in a gruesome performance of war. The scorpion thrashed against Praesidio's rope, which had looped and knotted amidst its many legs. Every glancing blow of Culduin's sword sent him into an out-of-control spin. How had he lost so much of his ascent? It did not matter. The only question that did—how could Danae help him?

With a chilling screech, the scorpion snatched the elf with its crushing pincers. It drew its prey closer. Culduin hacked furiously at the appendage, but his sword stuck between two plates of armor and would not wrench free no matter how he writhed.

As the monster raised its dread tail. Danae wound up for another dagger throw. Dare she risk hitting Culduin as he and the enemy twisted on tangled tethers? She stayed her throw in search of the lowest-risk moment.

The scorpion thrust its stinger at Culduin with deadly accuracy. The sharp barb plunged deep into Culduin's chest. His muscles seized. He thrashed. Foam bubbled to his lips.

The scrape of metal and the crack of crumbling rock sliced through the air. The stones that held the grapples split. Before Danae could lunge for the grapples, the rock that supported them splintered into dust. Both scorpion and elf plummeted. Culduin's gurgling scream came to an abrupt end as they landed in a bone-crunching pile some fifty feet below.

35

THE PATRON

*D*anae hooked the last grapple and launched her body over the lip of the cliff. When her feet touched the ledge where Culduin and the scorpion had come to a stop, the beast wheeled to her and slashed at her with both claws. She dove aside. Wide wounds opened smoking rents in the creature's hard crust, but clearly she would have to inflict deeper damage to stem the assault.

Danae crab-walked to avoid the snapping pincers, and her hand landed on something that grated with a metallic shriek against the stone. Culduin's sword! She snatched it from the ground only an instant before another murderous plunge of the creature's tail drove toward her. With a clumsy swing, she fended off the attack, sweat and grime pouring down her forehead and stinging her eyes. She swiped at the pain, only to win the reward of greater agony when the scorpion raked her leg with a sharp claw. Her upward cut knocked the claw back.

The crunch of rock and running footfalls announced Praesidio's arrival at the foot of the cliff. The breath gushed from Danae's lungs at the prospect of his help.

The Sword of the Sacred Fire blazed once again. The knight charged in to hammer great retribution upon the monster. Before Danae had taken another swing, Praesidio deprived it of one great claw.

The creature spun and scrabbled. It screeched. It trembled. With its remaining claw, it scored a glancing snap on Danae's arm. Praesidio plunged in and sunk his sword into the beast's compound eyes, giving Danae an opening to slash at the creature's tail. The stroke took all her might, but Culduin's lithe blade severed the deadly member.

The armored villain shuddered, stumbled, collapsed.

Still gulping for breath, Danae charged to where Culduin lay and skidded to a halt when she reached his prone body. The reality of the matter was quite clear. Neither man nor elf should ever turn his head to such a gruesome angle. Danae fell to her knees, searching beyond hope for a pulse or breath of life.

"Culduin! Culduin, answer me!" Her voice rose shrilly as she screamed his name so many times she stopped hearing herself. In time, her voice faltered, and she stared numbly at her fallen friend. "You're not—" She buried her face in her hands. "Oh, please say you're not . . ."

The wind whistled through the rocks as Danae abandoned words. Slowly, mechanically, she straightened the tall elf's body. For a bleak moment, she stared at his blood streaked, ashen face and his closed eyes, until she could do nothing but sink down and rest her head upon his chest. A deep blackness settled upon her soul. A silence of utter despair. She too closed her eyes, and though her heart begged to weep, her body would not comply.

She remained there for an uncounted time. *I should be the one lying dead on this crag of rock. Not him. I did nothing. I hesitated when I should have struck. And now . . .*

Her thoughts collapsed under the weight of unutterable remorse. Perhaps she might never rise again.

With silent stealth, into the deep recesses of her heart crept a faint light, a small ripple on the edge of the black waters of a still pool. She thrust aside this tapping upon the door of her soul, but the compulsion to sit up grew within her. But no, she would not remove her head from Culduin's cooling chest, not yet. So she merely opened her eyes. Sandaled feet stood nearby.

Danae bolted upright. At Culduin's feet towered a great being, at least seven feet in height, clad in a robe whiter than the light of the winter sun. White eyes blazed from a chiseled face like burnished copper. Upon his back spread two immense wings, more gloriously arrayed than the plumage of any great hawk. He held a gleaming scepter in his right hand.

A tremor ran through Danae's body until her limbs shook. She buried her face in Culduin's tunic again, and in her mind's eye arose legends he had taught her about great warriors, who upon spending their lives in great deeds, were borne into glory. As she cowered before the terrifying presence, she groped for her last tatters of courage.

"Please," she whispered, her voice barely crackling from her throat. "Intercede on our behalf, that Culduin might live beyond this awful day. Don't sweep him off to Creo's halls. I already have the blood of Mizzletorp on my hands. And perhaps my father's. I would die myself before adding Culduin's to my guilt."

A voice echoed in Danae's mind. *Young wanderer, I come not to gather in the soul of this elf, but to work through you on behalf of the Maker. Your words are but a reflection of his omnipotent will, and so you will trust his supremacy, he sends me to this place. May you learn the unmatched power of Creo, as you serve as the earthly channel of his might.*

Danae sniffed, tears beginning to stir in her eyes. "I don't understand what you mean, but if you help me know Creo's will, I'll do whatever that is." As the reality struck, a strange sensation coursed through her. Was it revelation? Fear? Resignation? "I have no strength of my own. I will do as you say, for Culduin's sake."

That is good. You have wandered far afield, but you draw nigh the true path. Kneel beside this elf you call Culduin. Be a vessel of Creo's incomparable power as he sheds from you the last clinging garments of darkness.

Danae's head lifted from Culduin's chest, her muscles pulling irresistibly against her racing mind until she had risen to a kneeling posture. She focused on the rocky ground, careful to avert her gaze from the glory beside her.

Place your hands upon him.

Creo's messenger touched the scepter to Danae's forehead, and a wave more potent than any power she had sensed before rushed through her flesh. Her hands throbbed as though they would burst. A bright nimbus of light enveloped Culduin's still form.

As this elf has sown mercy and healing in his lifetime, so shall he reap it from Creo's hand.

The light flared to blinding intensity, then vanished with jarring suddenness. Danae blinked in the muted sunlight of a cloudy morning.

Culduin's chest heaved upward. His eyes shot open, wild and confused.

Danae jumped to her feet and took several strides back, her stare fixed upon her spread hands, which still glowed with faint golden light. Tears streamed down her face. Her head swam. Once the light around her hands faded, she turned her eyes to the elf.

He sat upright on the rocks, taking in the scene around him. Could his eyes be brighter than ever before, and his hair richer in its copper luster? His every wound had disappeared—even the damage to his clothes and armor from the longs weeks of travel. He stood.

"I walked in a hall," Culduin said, his voice vague and dreamlike. "But I was not alone. A winged Adonis walked beside me. We stopped at a tall set of doors, and how I longed to pass beyond them. My whole heart yearned for the other side, though I knew not what drew me.

But my companion placed a hand upon my shoulder and told me the day for my grand entrance had not yet arrived. Everything vanished. I felt as though I rushed to the surface of deep water."

Culduin surveyed the rocky landscape. "Only now do snippets of the events that brought this scorpion's ruin return to me."

Praesidio strode forward and clasped Culduin's hand until the tendons in his wrist bulged, He clapped the elf on the shoulder with his other palm. "Virtusen take form in your flesh today, Culduin Caranedhel!"

Danae sank to a rock behind her. Her eyes refused to behold anything but Culduin's vigor. Her whole body felt numb.

Culduin stepped closer to her and knelt. "Danae, let me help you. The scorpion has done you much harm, and we had best see to those gashes."

Danae shook her head, as if to drive off the last vestiges of sleep. What wounds? Nothing hurt. But yes, blood soaked her sleeve and pant leg.

Culduin lifted her chin to turn her eyes to his own. "Danae?"

"Wounds. Yes, we'd better bind up the wounds." She drew a tremulous breath. "Then we can get back on task, or we'll never reach the rim today."

A bright, musical laugh escaped Culduin's lips, which echoed through the canyon like the chiming of bronze bells. "Endlessly driven, you humans have always been, but none so much as you!"

He pulled bindings and other tools of the medic's trade from his pack and dabbed at the gash on Danae's upper arm. As the cold water touched the wound, the torn flesh burst into fiery pain. Danae yelped.

"I am sorry," Culduin smiled gently. "These are the first open wounds you have needed tended on this journey, are they not?"

Danae managed a grimacing nod. "I think I liked it better when you patched me up while I was unconscious."

Culduin took on a gentler hand in the dressing of the wound. After cleaning, stitching and wrapping her gashes for some time, the elf cleared his throat. He maintained steady focus on his work. "I was dead, was I not?"

"Yes," Danae replied. "I think your neck snapped when you and the scorpion hit the ground."

"But somehow I am alive again, with no trace of any wounds from the fight. How do you explain this?"

Praesidio moved over to the rock where Danae sat.

She fished for the right words. "Some sort of servant of Creo came to me and told me I was to be a vessel of Creo's power. I'm still a little hazy on what exactly happened, really."

Praesidio laughed. "Some sort of servant? Have they no artwork portraying Creo's Patrons in Radromir?"

"A Patron?" Danae shook her head.

"Were it that I could have heard his voice! What did he say? Will you not enlighten an old servant?"

"Aside from the directions on how to restore Culduin, he said I'm closer to the correct path. Does that mean I'm Creo's servant now?" Why did such a thing still seem so unsettling?

Praesidio tilted his head and sat silent for a moment. "I believe that means you are now cleansed of the darkness, but only you and the Creator himself can know your level of devotion."

Danae pressed her lips together. Surely a life serving God would have its mortal price.

Culduin finished dressing her wounds. "You are still troubled," he whispered. "I am certain all will grow clearer with the passage of time." He stroked a few wild tendrils of her hair away from her face.

Danae's stomach fluttered. "Thanks, Culduin." Heat crawled up her neck and into her cheeks, which she concealed behind a sudden bustle to gather her things. "They certainly couldn't get much muddier."

Praesidio approached Danae and patted her back. "At least the fall seems to have brought us the advantage of a better path up." He pointed to a winding ridge of rock, easy climbing with no forbidding overhangs like they had faced before.

"It does look better," Danae replied. "So long as we avoid anything remotely like a scorpion den on this route."

*W*hen the ridge path ran out, Danae and her companions found only ropes and grapples could defeat the remaining ascent from the canyon. Before the end, Danae's wounds mounted a fiery protest even her strength of will could not defy.

"You will hold onto my back, Danae, and I shall finish the climb for us both," Culduin said.

"How are you—"

Culduin scowled. "There is no need for you to endanger yourself. You have nothing to prove, especially not to me."

Danae wheeled to Praesidio.

"Listen to the elf." Praesidio took Culduin's pack and climbed his rope.

Danae sighed, but stepped behind Culduin and wrapped her arms about his neck. She could feel the shuddering tension in his every muscle, but still, he ascended the rope at nearly the pace he had climbed on his own.

He hauled them both over the lip of the cliff. They collapsed on the flatness of the ground, staring into the periwinkle sky as the sun sank below the distant horizon.

*D*anae marched after Culduin, her muscles already tight from trying not to limp, even though they had only put a couple of hours' morning travel behind them. "How many more days until we reach Garash?" Ugh. No matter what she said, the ache in her wounds transformed her words into a whine.

"Two," Culduin answered.

"How will we ever get through the city without being noticed? I don't think the Tebalese here are going to leave us to our business while we search out the temple."

"No, I do not imagine we would have much luck getting even beyond the walls without a framework of a plan," Praesidio replied. "Though a skeletal framework it will need to be, for we must be ready to survive by our wits at any moment. My initial thought is this: I shall disguise myself as a man of Tebal, and claim the two of you as my slaves."

Culduin shrugged. "I imagine such a position would be one of the few that might gain me entry into such a city with my life still in my possession."

Danae frowned. "Couldn't I masquerade as a Radromirian who has turned on her own people? I wish such a thing wasn't so commonplace as to be plausible. I could be a pirate, or even a mountain clanswoman."

Praesidio shook his head. "It is too complicated, Danae. The more details you add to the lie, the more unstable your façade."

Danae blew a long breath through her nose. "I suppose slaves we are, then. What should we do to look the part?"

Culduin laughed. "Well, with all this travel and tribulation, *you* certainly look worn and tattered enough to pass as the grossly underprivileged. I suppose we will need to surrender any visible weapons to Praesidio. I hope that, coupled with his disguise, convinces Garash's gatekeeper."

By nightfall, the evidence of human settlement appeared on the horizon, as well as a straight, wide road cutting across the land. Ahead of them were still only scattered villages and other homesteads of Tebalese natives, for another day of travel lay between them and the city gates of Garash.

Danae spent her watch huddled on the north side of camp, scrutinizing the occasional clusters of torch-bearing figures that traversed the road. By their formation, they were probably patrols. Likely armed. She shivered despite the warmth of her cloak. The handful of memorized statutes from *The Tree* seemed a small shield against the enormity of the encroaching unknown. Yet even a small buckler could block blade or dart, if positioned properly. Danae drew the book from her pack, sat on the ground, and sought fortitude by the scant illumination of the setting moon.

36

GARASH

*F*or the first time on the entire journey, Culduin awoke to the jostle of a hand gripping his shoulder. How strange his dreams had been during his few hours of sleep while Danae stood watch. But then, perhaps dying and coming back to life again might do that to an elf's mind. Only in a short, incalculable time before dawn had his sleep-tinted thoughts ceased churning and left him to a little placid repose. Many times that night, he had relived the surge of desire to see what lay beyond the lofty doors in his death vision, what it was beyond them that lured him to pass through their alabaster loveliness.

His eyes fluttered open, and a wholly different alabaster beauty filled his waking vision—Danae's flawless northern complexion smiling down at him. Ah yes, a stirring reminder what tethered him to mortality, at least in part. She knelt in the opening to his tent, the gentle light of morning casting her in a halo.

Danae said, "Praesidio withdrew a ways to pray, but he said it's time for you to get up, sleepy." Her smile faded. "Do you feel all right?"

Culduin rolled to his stomach and propped his chin in his hands. "Never better. But what about you? How are the wounds?"

Danae shrugged the shoulder opposite her damaged arm. "As good as can be expected."

"You still have pain." Culduin eyed the hasty mends in her sleeve and pant leg. "We ought to re-dress them before we set out."

"I suppose. If we have plenty of bindings. I don't want to waste even a thread."

If I have anything to do with it, you shall need not a further scrap of the stuff. Culduin laid a light hand on her knee. The warmth in the connection tingled in his fingers. "I shall gather the supplies."

Danae glanced at the spot on her mid-thigh where the worst of her two wounds lay. "No need. I'm all set to leave, so you go ahead and eat and pack up. I can see to the dressings." She backed out of his sleeping area. A twinge of disappointment pulled a quick sigh from Culduin's breast.

He sat up and spent a moment rolling his stiff neck and shoulders.

"Halt!" Danae blurted just outside the tent, not in her own tongue, but the fluid language of Tebal. "Not a step closer."

Culduin sprang from his bedroll's warmth into the morning's brisk wind in a single leap. Danae pointed a dagger at a stocky, cross-gartered, beady-eyed Tebalese footman, though fifteen paces separated them. The man held up his gray-skinned hands.

"You two really must stop pointing weapons at me," the Tebalese man said. He laughed, and the laugh belonged to Praesidio.

Danae cast a sideways glance at the man, but only relaxed her guard a fraction. "What's going on here?"

"When I said I was going to disguise myself as a Tebalese native," the man continued, still in Praesidio's voice, "you did not think I was simply going to steal some poor unsuspecting rustic's clothes, did you?"

"With your usual height and complexion, no." Culduin settled his weight back on one leg. "We would convince few in that manner. Though you might need to work on your accent."

Praesidio's eyebrow shot up and one side of his mouth curled. "Is that so? I shall have to use our last day of travel to tidy that up. Are the two of you prepared to set out?"

"Nearly," Danae rustled through one of the food satchels and produced a bundle of the usual: hard tack, dried fruit, and nuts. She handed the pack to Culduin. "There's not a lot in here beyond this, you know."

Culduin shrugged. "Not much else keeps on such a long journey."

"No, that's not what I mean. The food's getting short."

Culduin unwrapped the parcel and took a bite of the hard tack. He waved his other hand. "The hunting will be better as we make our way to Bilearne with the Sword."

A little smile smoothed away the tense creases around Danae's mouth. Culduin's heart warmed. He needed to be sure he kept a steady flow of assurance washing over Danae the closer they got to Garash. Only Creo knew what they would confront there, but having her in the best possible spirits was a necessity.

While Danae rewrapped her wounds, Culduin's muscles bunched in restraint. Why had he agreed to let her handle the task on her own? *Ah, right—the Maker forbid I should close in upon her emotional boundaries too swiftly again.* But neither would he withdraw entirely. Every time their eyes met and she briskly thrust her notice elsewhere, Culduin smirked. Her haste only confirmed his suspicion an ember of affection for him smoldered in some concealed part of her soul. However, mission and follow-through led the way. For now, it was better not to challenge that.

Praesidio moved to Culduin's side as the elf tied the last thong on his rolled tent. He knelt to Culduin's eye level. In a murmur, he said in Elvish, "Be wary, friend elf. I suspect the hammer of what lies ahead will fall hardest upon Danae. You best not allow the heart's tempest to cloud what Creo intends for both of you in the coming days."

Culduin flicked a quick peek at Danae, who had her nose buried in *The Tree*. She would overhear little in such a state. "Is it so apparent?"

Praesidio smiled. "You may be Elfkind, but I have still walked a longer road than you, and those years have not yet made me blind. Seal up your heart, Culduin, though you already feel it nigh upon bursting. By Creo's word, the time will come where you shall want to shelter your little dove, and you must not."

Perhaps future events would clarify Praesidio's admonition. For the time being, Culduin nodded and packed the warning away for later reflection.

"It is also time for you to hand over your weapons." Praesidio put out an open palm. "No use risking the appearance of ambiguity."

Culduin unloaded a bow, his quiver, a brace of knives, and a sword into Praesidio's keeping. "Regret asking, old sage?" He chuckled.

Praesidio faced Danae. "So long as Danae is not hiding the remainder of a king's armory on her person, I shall survive."

She looked up from *The Tree* and scrunched her eyebrows together.

"Your daggers, Danae." Praesidio held out a hand.

The next forty-eight hours of travel saw them onto the main highway leading through an increasingly populous countryside that continued to rise in elevation. Homesteads and villages proliferated and eventually collided into a collage of full-blown urban sprawl. The clamor of other travelers' voices and bustle along the highway rang in Culduin's ears, gratingly loud in comparison to so many weeks of traveling in small numbers.

The land before them rose steeply, and all three travelers labored for sufficient gulps of air to reach the many-spired city that perched upon the plateau. Halfway up the slope, Danae began to favor her injured leg. How could she not, when the climb made Culduin's own thighs burn? He pulled her arm around him so she could clasp his shoulder for support.

The black wall that surrounded Garash reared up from the dark earth beneath. A line of evenly-spaced windows flashed sunlight like beacons of warning to any who approached. A busy road switched back and forth up mounded earth that made the ascent to the city gate at least plausible, though the horses that pulled finely appointed carriages up the slopes leaned heavily into the collars of their harnesses. Praesidio led the party as far to the side of the thorough-fare as he could, and Culduin maneuvered Danae to the outer edge of the group. More than once, a rushing carriage or horseman clipped Culduin's roadside shoulder. He gritted his teeth and pulled his hood farther down over his nose.

The only people on foot beside themselves were plain-clad slaves who bore sedan chairs with drawn curtains, or others who labored with loads or the task of sweeping away the evidence of animal traffic. Yet even these servants barked at others on the road to make way. Frustration and disgust hung in the air like a fume.

The sun touched the horizon when they made the last turn to the gate. Several men piled with leather plates and metal studs stood at the outer edge of the gate tunnel, waved their hands, and bellowed. "Gate's closing for the day. Get within or without, or else you'll wait 'til morning."

A herd of boys ranging from plump-faced childhood to lanky, coltish adolescence jostled and elbowed their way through the crowd while cuffing and wrestling one another in the process. The smallest of the group squirmed his way out of the tight grip of his dirty comrade, stumbled toward Praesidio, and tripped over the old man's foot.

"Watch where yer goin' ya merc!" the boy snapped as he stood, brushing his hands together to shake off the gravel from the street. "Isn't there a war you should be getting stabbed in?"

The smell of the boy's filthy body assaulted Culduin's nose, and he coughed. His clothes were fine silks, elaborately embroidered and fashionable of cut, but smudged and grungy.

Praesidio only grunted.

The other boys laughed and jeered. "He's got some nerve trippin' up somebody beyond his caste," one said

One of his companions added, "Maybe we ought to call for one of the Inquisitors to take a bite out of him. Then maybe he'll remember his place."

Danae leaned toward Culduin's ear. "Do I want to know what an Inquisitor is?"

Culduin replied, "The law enforcement agents of the Tebalese theocracy. I have never heard any reports of leniency in their meting out of justice."

Praesidio's eyes widened. He talked from the corner of his mouth. "Not to mention, they are all priests. Scrutiny from an Inquisitor is the last thing we need. If any mortal man might see through my disguise, it would be one of their numbers."

"Oh, look," another boy jeered. "There's one of the scourgers coming up the bend now. Inquisitor!" he yelled. "We need ya!"

Culduin glanced back. A red-cloaked individual carrying a cat-o-nine-tails snapped his head their direction.

"Time to get through that gate," Danae said.

"Agreed," Praesidio thrust his weight through the crowd of boys and dragged his slaves between the waves in a perilous sea of vehicles jockeying for a space to pass under the portcullis. Already, one of the mailed guards stood by the winch.

"Inquisitor!" a boy hollered. "I want that uppity merc's hide!"

More curled-lip and narrow-eyed attention from the finely-clad Garasheans began to settle upon Praesidio, Danae, and Culduin. They needed to make it to the gate before word of the unrest reached the gatekeepers through the crowd.

Whether prompted by rumors or merely by the slip of the sun below the horizon, Culduin could not tell, but the grind and screech of chains set the portcullis into a slow descent. A final flurry of whips and clattering wheels swept the crowd into a frenzied motion. Drivers barked horses into canters or faster as they fought to squeeze past the barricade in the last moments.

Culduin grabbed Danae's arm and tugged her along, though when she grimaced, he shot her a wordless apology with tight lips and a pinched brow.

"Culduin, look out!" Danae cried.

He barely spun fast enough to dodge an oncoming troika of thundering horses. He hauled Danae against his chest to shield her from the animals and their vehicle. They dodged the opposite way as a chariot fought to pass.

Despite the churning current of vehicles and slaves, Culduin managed to lead Danae under the gate right on Praesidio's heels. The gridlock of thick iron clanged into its deep fittings in the street a handful of seconds after they cleared it. An uproar from those who had not made the gate passage in time erupted behind them. Culduin forged through the dark of the city entrance.

Once they emerged from the gatehouse tunnel, the crowds of vehicles and residents thinned. Pristine buildings with plumb corners and clean glass windows frowned at them, and their sterile haughtiness made Culduin's flesh crawl. Nonetheless, he clenched his fists and shuffled onward in the slumped posture of the prisoner he was supposed to be.

The city of Garash warred with itself. Ostentatious colonnades, gilding, balustrades of intricate ironwork, bright mosaics, and meticulously maintained landscaping squared off in riotous competition. A quiet moment in his brother and sister's tree-bound cottage seemed a priceless luxury.

Praesidio beckoned them onward.

After another dozen blocks, the monotony of towering buildings opened into a wide plaza, encircled by a dozen or more inns and taverns bustling with customers. Many pedestrians meandered from one business to the next. Men and women alike laughed louder than typical inhibitions allowed, and many of them weaved or hung upon one another for balance. Outside the taverns sat the same variety of vehicles that had clogged the gate, along with appropriate numbers of slaves to attend them. Some of these slaves slouched sullenly, while others chatted together or played simple games of chance in the street.

Danae glanced around the square. "Praesidio, you're not thinking of stopping for a bite to eat?"

Praesidio frowned. "Of course not, but if we are ever to find the temple, we need some direction. Do you have any idea how large Garash is?"

"Bigger than Dayleston, that's for sure." Danae shrank as she cast a gaze up to the skyline.

"But do you know what we shall do when we find the temple?" Culduin asked.

"It is my intent to imply I bring the two of you as sacrifices." Praesidio laid a hand on each of their shoulders. "It is my hope that this story will gain us entrance to the temple itself."

"But what then?" Sweat beaded on Danae's brow.

"If memory serves, there should be a presiding priest in the sacrifice chamber," Praesidio said. "We may have to capture this individual and coerce the location of the Sword from him."

"Capture and interrogate?" Culduin folded his arms. "That plan has more than a few risks."

Praesidio set his jaw. "I realize this. Being within a hundred miles of this place has inherent risks. My idea is a mere framework. We cannot afford to become rigidly adherent to any plan. Who knows what we shall confront? For now, our task is to find the temple."

Praesidio marched to a polished coach and four. "Driver! Tell me where I will find the Temple of Queldurik."

The driver shifted a bland gaze down to Praesidio. "Six blocks to the north, to the Avenue of Remembrance, and then turn west for five more. You'll see it." He jerked a thumb toward the far side of the square.

Praesidio nodded and marched off in the direction the slave had pointed.

Danae's gaze crept slowly over one set of slaves to the next. She studied each of them for so long Culduin's stomach tensed. He put his hand upon her back, his pressure gentle but insistent. "You cannot save everyone today."

The stricken look in Danae's eyes smote Culduin's heart. Still, enough hurdles waited within the temple walls, so he would need to dredge up whatever strength he could find for both of them. He steeled himself, took her hand, and led her forward, despite her reluctant steps.

37

THE TEMPLE

*T*he double width of the Avenue of Remembrance distinguished it from the surrounding streets, making it easy to discover. Danae shuffled behind the more experienced, more confident warriors who led the way. The prattle of crowds, debauched jollity, and bustling entertainment faded. A stiff breeze hissed over the cobblestones of the cold and empty avenue.

Too soon, the High Temple of Queldurik glowered ahead of them, eternally displeased with all that surrounded it. Its countless spires stabbed into the cobalt sky; the glare of every lamp's light reflected from the central dome's garish gilding. Gargoyles leered from every outcropping, sinister and forbidding. If the temple in Cray had been intimidating, Garash's shrine was terrifying.

Praesidio marched toward the place, though Danae quailed in the building's shadow. A palpable sense of unbridled evil slithered along her flesh.

As they ascended the long flight of stairs that led to the front door, Danae gripped the balustrade, but the rail pressed a curious, irregular shape back against her palm. She glanced at it. Rather than a handrail of iron or wood, an immense collection of bones and skulls flanked the stairway, cunningly crafted together. Empty eye sockets bored into her. Grins of death mocked her revulsion. Danae recoiled, and despite the weakness in her knees, refused any further support from the gruesome railing. She staggered up the stairs after Praesidio.

At the pinnacle of the stairs, an intricate relief sculpture of hundreds of small figures, human, bestial, and demonic swarmed over the arched doorway of the temple. The artwork depicted acts of the most unimaginable cruelty and violence.

So this is how Queldurik's worshipers choose to glorify him. She shuddered.

Culduin's countenance was a hard mask of stone, his shoulders squared and jaw set, though all Danae could manage was to shrink under the oppressive vulgarity around them. Oh, to be so hardened by the battlefields of war. Would her friends extend to her some word of encouragement?

The temple door swung wide. A guard glared at them from behind a steel mask wrought to resemble a death's head.

"Is the hour too late for the devoted to offer sacrifice?" Praesidio cast his glance to the floor and bowed slightly.

"That depends." The guard's voice echoed from behind his mask. "What do you bring the almighty Queldurik?" His folded arms spoke what his inscrutable face could not from behind the mask.

"This Radromirian dabbler and Delsin warrior," Praesidio replied.

A shiver ran through Danae's members, and the hair on her arms stood on end. Her glance darted about the shadowy halls beyond the doorway. A shuffle, a sigh, or some other half noise drifted from the dark recesses beyond her sight.

She tugged at Culduin's sleeve.

He lowered his brows and pursed his lips in a silent effort to hush her as he turned back to Praesidio and the guard. Her hands grew clammy as she squinted into the darkness, but all stood silent.

The guard nodded. "I suppose the elf's value makes the inconvenience to the high priest justifiable." He stepped aside to admit them. After shutting the door behind them with a reverberating clang, he shuffled back to his post beside the entry. In the dim light of the narthex, Danae could barely see down the several hallways around them. It did not matter. A corridor much wider than the others, lined with smoking copper braziers, clearly heralded the way to the main sacrifice chamber. A hostile stillness filled the passageways, with only an occasional hushed conversation drifting to Danae's ears.

They followed the lit corridor to the heart of the temple, and it ended in a pair of imposing doors of smoke-colored metal, emblazoned with the hallmark gargoyle within the triangle—Queldurik's mark. Praesidio paused before the doors. He closed his eyes, raised his chin, and clutched his chest to grip his phoenix talisman through his clothing. Just as the creeping sense they had lingered at the doors too long had filled Danae's arms and legs with fidgets, the old teacher broke his reverie, took a deep breath, and pushed on the doors.

The entryway opened into an expansive circular room, with so lofty a ceiling that the arches of its dome were lost in murky shadows. Danae choked on the smoky air and stifling heat as they stepped within. The inhalation of smoke left a greasy, bitter film on the back of her tongue. In the center of the cavernous space, a circular moat cleft from the stone floor surrounded an altar platform that dominated the room with its malevolent presence. The ominous red glow that played on the moat's walls insinuated what filled its depths. A continual hiss of flame throbbed in the air.

Praesidio stepped behind Danae and Culduin, and the point of a knife pressed lightly into to her back. She whipped her head around.

"Go on!" Praesidio said with a growl. He then added in the lowest whisper, "I cannot allow you to look too willing."

"Oh . . . right." Danae took a few tentative steps deeper into the chamber.

Her gaze fixed upon the obsidian altar that rose from the island of rock in the middle of the moat. Colossal statues of winged devils loomed over all, both drawing and repelling Danae's glance. While sculpted with a master's skill, the grotesqueness of their features personified raw hatred.

All around the inner rim of the moat stood a long rank of man-sized sculptures. Featureless and identical, each statue held its arms out before it, as if to bear a load. From the wrists of each figure hung chains and shackles. Blackened scorch marks scarred the iron figures. Through the haze of smoke, Danae discerned the lowering mechanisms, gears, and tracks that served to plunge the figurines over the lip of the moat and into the flames that crackled and smoked at the unseen bottom.

"Idols of sacrifice," she whispered, her voice breaking as she spoke.

"Indeed," Culduin whispered back. "Try not to linger on the thought. May our victory today lessen the number of innocents brought to such a horrible end."

He clasped her shoulder, and his grip conveyed a measure of his strength into Danae's muscles.

"No dallying!" Praesidio snapped. "Where's the priest? I'm anxious to be rid of your infidel hides!"

Danae gulped, but the lump in her throat did not budge. *So now it comes to it. What am I supposed to do? Please let me make choices that will please both Praesidio and Creo.*

She squinted toward the altar platform, where a figure emerged from behind the altar. Danae's breath caught. This was no human servant of the foul god. Back and forth strode a heavily muscled, ebony-skinned creature, who easily stood head and shoulders taller than Culduin. His draconic wings lay folded against his back. His face, only mannish enough to mock humankind, had etched across it a permanent sneer. He turned glowing, green eyes upon the travelers.

"We're not trying to capture that," Danae muttered to Culduin.

Culduin drew her close and spoke into her ear. "Be brave."

"You!" echoed a deep and commanding voice. "State your business in my hall of sacrifice!"

Although the voice Danae heard was as loud as a bellow, the creature expended no more effort to utter the words than if he spoke under his breath.

"I come to make sacrifice to the mighty Queldurik," Praesidio responded, his own voice loud but measured.

The creature raised his hand and gestured into the unseen darkness, and the grinding and screeching of metal and gears sliced the air. From above, a long bridge descended on chains and pulleys.

The fiendish lord scrutinized them wordlessly from under a crinkled brow while they waited for the descending bridge. Out of the shadowy, smoke-filled recesses of the altar platform, a smaller fiend scuttled; one very much like the fell priest in body, yet very unlike it in its craven scrabbling as it approached the superior denizen of darkness. The two apparitions conversed in a hissing language devoid of any familiar word. They both turned their eyes upon Praesidio and his sacrifices.

The prickling sensation that Danae felt in the narthex of the temple washed over her again, but this time it felt more like thousands of piercing wounds. She bit back a cry.

The taller fiend waved the smaller servant off. After a quick bow, the lesser creature dissipated in a cloud of vapor.

The suspension bridge that would convey worshipers over the sacrifice fires had nearly reached its position, when the great fiend again gestured, and the bridge ground to a halt. Still, nearly a half-dozen feet of empty air stretched between the planks and the edges of the moat. The fiend's eyes flared with bright light. He reached behind his back and pulled a massive sword from a scabbard strapped between his wings.

The weapon slid out of the sheath with a ring akin to the sound of a wet finger drawn over the lip of fine crystal. Danae's eyes widened. The sword's blade, clear and gleaming, shimmered red and orange in the firelight of the yawning pit before them. The fiend leveled the blade, pointing it at Praesidio.

"We know Elgadrim when we smell it, you rat!" the beast snarled with a grin that revealed pointed teeth. "I cannot imagine what you desire in coming before me, but you had better hope it is to treat with me to offer homage to Queldurik, or death will come to you in a slow and mind-breaking way!"

"I cannot imagine what you mean," Praesidio said. "My sacrifices are elfkind and Radromirian, not Elgadrim."

A bead of sweat ran down Danae's jaw. Could Praesidio truly hope the ruse still held?

Her disguised mentor reached out with imploring hands. "If you would complete the lowering of the bridge, I might convey my offering."

A nagging threat emanated like a stench from the far recesses of the chamber. Faint clicks—perhaps claws or toenails—reached her ears through the lower thrum of flame. She threw herself into Culduin's arms.

"What is it? This is no time to lose heart," Culduin said.

"No, it's not that." Creo permit that her appearance of quailing would mask their conversation. "There are more creatures in this hall. Do you see them?"

Culduin wrapped his arms around Danae's shoulders and squinted into the distance. "I do. But I also cannot fail to recognize the sword that villain points at us is the very Sword we have come to recover."

Her heart thumped in an erratic beat. So there it was, the wondrous item they had come so far to attain, in the hands of the worst possible person who could have it. Hopefully Praesidio had drawn closer to a clear plan of action while she and Culduin whispered. The encroaching creatures would complicate matters the longer Praesidio dallied.

"Your pathetic sense of nobility makes you a laughable liar!" the fiend cackled back at Praesidio. "I shall enjoy making a sacrifice of your little helpers, though as for you, I shall probably feed you to my hounds!"

The disguised knight of the Elgadrim stretched taller, but remained silent.

Would he do nothing? Danae steeled herself. *This is it. I can't give this fiend the advantage of the first move. One chance to get that Sword, or less, I'd imagine.* She squeezed Culduin's shoulders, stepped back a pace, and sprang from his side. A running leap launched her for the dangling bridge. For a moment, she hung in the air, the sweltering heat of the sacrifice pit buffeting the breath from her lungs. Her spring had not been high enough . . .

With a last desperate stretch of her fingers, she caught the suspension chain of the bridge. She swung her body around with the momentum of her leap and tumbled upon the surface of the rocking planks.

Culduin bolted after her, yelping a horrified cry, only to be caught by Praesidio. Danae glanced over her shoulder to see Praesidio grappling Culduin's shoulders, the Elvish words they exchanged too quick and low for her comprehension. Her business stood on the other side of the moat, however, so she heaved a breath and faced the fiend.

Slowly, the enemy turned to regard her, and Danae's stomach felt as though it might drop from her body at any moment.

"What are you doing, little fool?" He stared into her eyes, his own aglow with white-hot light.

A sensation of probing pressure enveloped Danae's skull.

"Ahhhhh. Now I see. You are on an errand, one you dare not allow to fail."

Searing pain grew in her head with every word the fiend spoke, and Danae pressed the heels of her hands against her temples. *Look away. I just want to look away.* Her muscles refused the desire and remained locked in place.

"You have known from the beginning that it was foolishness! And yet, in idealistic hope, you took up with this deceiver." The fiend cast his glance briefly to Praesidio. "A man so full of promises."

Sweat poured down Danae's back. She squirmed. No amount of distance she could put between herself and her assailant seemed great enough. The depths of her soul felt soiled by the fiend's pressing intrusion.

She wished she could snap back a scathing retort. Somehow, though, neither running nor insulting seemed very wise.

"But how do you know any of this will help your father at all?"

The creature's voice softened. "Is there not even a greater chance you have been sorely misused ... taken advantage of?"

A sharp twinge in her gut and the constriction in her throat warned Danae she hovered on the brink of vomiting, though she could not tell if this was due to his pressing words, her own fear, or the relentless pounding in her head. Did she really have any solid evidence Praesidio would help her father once this task was complete? All along she had gone on his word.

What had transpired in Praesidio and Archadion's long discourse without her, back when they set the quest into motion? Could she have possibly been swindled? Bid to reclaim this coveted sword, with no real guarantee the task was in any way connected to her father's recovery? The more she worried over it, the more she discovered the Elgadrim's obligation in the arrangement was unnervingly nebulous. Perhaps Praesidio would allow her to risk life and limb to recover this weapon, wrest it from her and leave her with no antidote for her father.

She glanced back toward her traveling companions. The old man braced his arm across Culduin's chest. The elf maintained a furrowed stare at her, his lips drawn into a grimace and his eyes brimming with tears. Her mind swam with rampaging fears, ancient wisdom from *The Tree*, and hot emotion.

"Could he possibly have your best interest in mind?" the fiend's voice continued, now low and sonorous, his tone like the voice of a lover who woos his beloved. "Why does he withhold good things, even the person you desire most?"

The fiend's violation of parts of her mind she had not dared to explore brought the heat of a flush to her cheeks. She clapped her hands to her forehead.

A furious diatribe to unleash on the faithless Praesidio assembled in her mind like ranks of soldiers lining up for the charge. Maybe Praesidio meant for her to face the fiend alone. But why? For every angry outburst Danae entertained, a placid voice within her spoke calming, wordless comfort, and she wrestled miserably between the two as she cowered on the long bridge.

No more accusations. No more confusion.

She pressed her throbbing forehead on the planks beneath her and uttered, "Creo, give me clarity. I have truly reached both the end of what I know. I need you to unravel this. Let me do your will, not for anyone's sake but yours."

"Come, now," the minion of darkness continued in his syrupy, seductive tone, "Has not this imposter of a guide indeed led you away from the only real power you ever had, your magic? He saw you were too much like him . . . too much of an adversary, and thus sought to strip you of this! How many times did he forbid you to employ your gift? How dare he hide behind the thin excuse that casting spells would bring oppression?"

Stop yammering so I can listen. Danae shielded herself behind her arms. *I can't make any choices on my own here. My will is wayward.*

Somehow, the fiend delivered his accusations with the gentleness of a fond stroke of the hair. "Has your magic not always come to your aid in times of danger? It is not too late. You can regain what he has tried to take from you. Master your own destiny!"

Master her own destiny? Had not her attempts at wresting control of her life made a mess of her situation at home? Every spell she cast, every intervention she planned, brought pain and trouble to those she loved. Papa's stabbing. Her family driven from their lifelong home. What else had she lacked the wisdom to see?

The more Danae pondered the fiend's lure, the more his words crowed as brazenly as trumpets played out of tune. The caressing tone of his voice turned harsher than the rake of claws. The powers she wielded were not her own, and she could never claim them in an effort to exalt herself. Submission to Creo, and Creo alone, was the only answer. Not to Praesidio, not even to the needs of Papa and her family.

The time to speak had come. Danae drew a deep breath and slowly rose. "All this time, I told myself I acted on the behalf of others, but it was self-deception. It was my fear of losing the ones I love that drove me, my desire to hold them tight that plunged me into desperate prayers in the dark of the night. Creo is the commander of pure power, of which I may be a vessel, but not the origin." She lifted her chin. "Through Creo's eyes, I now see his will is above all, and even if he decides to take from me everything I have ever cared about, I must trust that in his goodness he has done what serves the greater benefit of all. Enough lies!"

The fiend snarled and flinched as though strafed with an explosion of glass. "I will not have one of his infernal mouthpieces in my temple!" he growled. "If you will not see wisdom, then die in your folly!" He gripped the greatsword in both clawed hands, and with wide swing, he sliced one of the chains that held the bridge, as easily as he might have cut a stalk of wheat. The bridge rocked and tilted. Danae lost her footing and slid toward the drooping corner.

"Go!" Praesidio bellowed at Culduin, pulling his arm from the elf's chest.

Culduin burst forward like a racehorse from the starting gate. Copper hair streaming behind him, he launched himself toward the bridge.

Danae scrabbled with feet and fingers, and her toe found a gap between planks. She ceased sliding. When Culduin landed upon the bridge, it bucked again. His pounding footfalls further destabilized the crossing, so Danae held on, eyes squeezed shut. An iron clamp on her wrist snapped her eyes open again.

Culduin bent over her, fist clenched around her wrist. "Come on!"

Teeth clenched in iron determination, Danae nodded and rose. She lunged for the altar platform, though Culduin thrust his weight for Praesidio's end of the bridge. A tug of war frustrated Danae's progress. She dug into the planks with her toes and leaned forward, but Culduin's grip clenched unrelenting. Her over-the-shoulder gaze locked with his.

"Help me," she said.

Culduin's throat tensed in a hard swallow. For a moment, his eyes widened, and the furrow if his brow spoke of inner conflict. He clenched his teeth, but after a slow breath through his nostrils he said, "To the end."

They turned to face their enemy together.

38

CREO'S WILL

A laugh erupted from the fiend's black lips. He swung the Sword of the Patron around and cleaved another chain. The end of the bridge tipped to spill its burden into the chasm filled with hungry flames below.

Danae thrust against the planks beneath her feet, but the severed bridge retreated from the force and lent her little momentum. She strained her fingers for the lip of the platform. The onyx stone remained far out of reach. Culduin's grip brushed the lip of the platform, but not enough to catch hold. Down they both plunged.

The fiend reared back his head and cackled. "Burn, little ones, burn . . . " The roar of the flames in the depths engulfed any further words he might have uttered.

A bed of fire rushed toward her. A scream ripped from her throat. "Creo, preserve us!" Danae wailed. *The only fitting words for a last breath.*

The heat around her swelled to skin-broiling intensity. The air undulated and warped. She could not breathe, only brace herself for both impact and the inevitable horror of an agonizing death by flame.

The soles of her shoes met the topmost tongues, but just when the sacrifice fires should have reached up and consumed her, they instead retreated, curling away to empty a wide ring of ash, blackened wood, and charred bones. Danae crashed into the silt with a puff and a crunch.

The impact rattled every tooth in her head and every joint of her members. The world around her spun. The heat still oppressed, but now from a distance. The roar at the bottom of the pit overwhelmed her ears to the point of throbbing in a dull, indistinct rumble.

From somewhere within the muffled drone around her, scraping and crunching reached her ears. She lifted a leaden head from the ground and opened her eyes. Debris stung them and they watered. Through the blur of tears, through the darkness of smoke, Culduin slogged toward her, thigh deep in the charred refuse of countless years of sacrifice.

He flopped beside her and leaned to her ear. "You all right?"

Danae coughed. "I think so." She spat a clod of wet soot from her mouth.

Her voice scarcely overcame the continual throb of flames that crackled at a five-yard radius from them. The inferno lashed furiously all around, as if tethered from flooding over the fuel beneath Danae and Culduin.

"What happened?" Culduin surveyed the clearing nestled within the ring of flames.

Danae shook her head. "Not sure. Answered prayer? If screaming in desperation counts."

"How do we get out?"

After a few more blinks to clear her vision, Danae considered the three-story drop from the lip of the chasm. At least the fiend was out of sight. Their little oasis of extinguished threat offered little in the way of comfort, however, for a towering bank of flames interposed between themselves and the pit's sheer walls. There would be no climbing out. Even as Danae watched the fire, it seemed to creep, if only by inches, back into the circle of extinguished fuel, reaching greedy fingers in between cracked timbers and bones. Her heart wrenched. What good was it to be spared incineration only to wait it out and eventually either roast or starve? Creo must have intended something her addled mind could not grasp.

Culduin closed his eyes. "*Hele p'avignirre positha uvennet dher gaeth.*" The Elvish words trickled from his lips in a slow stream devoid of inflection.

Avignirre. Why did the word prick Danae like a barb in the recesses of her memory? *Avignirre.* It insisted to be heard, echoing in Danae's mind long after he had closed his lips.

"Culduin, what did you say?"

He opened his eyes again and stared into the flames.

Danae shook his shoulder. "*Avignerre.* What does it mean? I think I know it."

The elf frowned at her. "What does it matter?"

"Stop it. Creo didn't restrain these flames just to watch us die more slowly! Translate the word!"

"It means 'phoenix.' I said, 'Only a phoenix might rise from such.'" Culduin again fixated upon the fiery walls around them.

Recognition smacked into Danae like a sudden torrent. "In my journal!"

Perhaps Culduin could not hear her over the constant, ear-stopping thrum, since he maintained his catatonic vigil over the fires. Or perhaps he had chosen not to care what she said, but it mattered little.

"I copied an Utterance from *The Tree* that uses that word. I never managed to translate the whole—" Danae twisted and writhed to pull her pack off her shoulders. She rummaged with graphite-black hands through the contents to produce the book. She flipped back and forth through the pages with trembling fingers. Where was it? She could picture her own script and the very lines she had once used to pen it, so how did it now elude her?

In the meantime, her eyes flicked toward the inferno. Had the ring of fire crept closer?

She finally alighted upon the page she sought, and thrust the open book at Culduin. "Most of these words are like Elvish, right? Tell me what this says!" She jabbed her finger at the words on the vellum.

"*Ellenet, d' p'avignirre dher pa cendraen, ellenet i volet,*" Culduin muttered. "'Rise, like the phoenix from the ashes, rise and soar.'" His eyes lost some of their haunted look. "What does it mean?"

"Well, in Creo's word, the servant who spoke it flew—"

Culduin cupped Danae's face in his hands. His usual sparkle returned. "Use it now! You must."

The cold grip of risk twisted Danae's insides. "Use it?" She sputtered. "I don't know. . ."

"Have you forgotten what you just said to me?" Culduin swung a wild gesture to their circle of ash. "What questions remain?"

"I'm not. . . like those people in *The Tree* that used this Utterance." She lowered her eyes, since Culduin's grip would not permit her to drop her chin.

He ducked into the path of her gaze and pressed his forehead to hers. "It is time to ask yourself, not what you know, Danae Baledric, but what you believe."

He released her and stepped back.

Whatever despair Culduin had shaken slithered into Danae's marrow and chilled her despite the encroaching flames. Her failure in calling upon Creo's name when she confronted the huntsman mocked her from a casket within her memory, until now sealed. What if she failed again, when both their lives so desperately depended upon it?

But no, it was not her task to fail or fulfill. It was Creo's power to be wielded through her, at his bidding and in his sovereignty. She bowed her head and waited.

The first words of the Utterance drifted on the undulating air. Who had spoken them? Heaven and earth, she had! The remainder faltered their way through her trembling jaw. The walls of fire around her blurred. The inexorable pull of gravity loosened its hold on her, and the crumbling wood, the soot, and the shards of brittle bones slipped away as her weightless body rose into the air. A surge of power rushed through her and made her dizzy. Beneath the vertigo, however, another sensation emerged. Not the soiled, unsavory residue Danae had always known after calling upon incantations, but a sense of a crisp breeze over the face of new snow. It swept through her soul. Clean. So this was the nature of power as it was meant to be, not power stolen and warped by lesser beings.

She lowered to the chasm floor again, shouldered her pack, and nodded to Culduin. "Let's get out of here." She wrapped her arms around Culduin's chest and concentrated upon the ascent. He slipped free of the mire, and they rose together. As soon as his feet cleared the surface, the orange tendrils of flames swarmed back over their island of mercy. They shot upward and spared Culduin's boots the assault.

He's so heavy. Danae gritted her teeth through the strain on her healing arm.

They reached the halfway point to escaping the chasm's depth, and Culduin jerked a thumb toward the wall behind them. Danae slowed. He gestured again, with greater vigor. She bent her will upon reaching the wall, rather than the lip, and the Utterance flight complied. She pressed them both to the smoothly-hewn stone, and Culduin beckoned her. Awkward strain though it was, she bent an ear to him.

"We need a plan," he whispered.

"Can it be quick?" Danae groaned. "I don't know how much—"

The body of a hound of Queldurik plummeted over the far edge of the moat, the creature's side riven and smoking. Danae averted her glance from its plunge into the fire.

"Praesidio," Danae breathed. She eased her hovering flight farther toward the lip of the pit.

"Careful," Culduin mouthed. He nodded toward the altar platform.

Danae's heart thundered faster with each subsequent beat as she inched her way up. The closer she drew to the top the more sounds emerged from drone of fire: the clicking of clawed feet, the snarls of what sounded like a pack of canines, and the tread of boots.

Over the lip of the abyss, Danae caught sight of Praesidio. No longer shrouded by his Tebalese disguise, the old knight of the Elgadrim held the Sword of the Sacred Fire aloft, its blue-white light enrobing him in a cool glow that defied the orange illumination of the sacrifice chamber. His Phoenix talisman glowed with a matching radiance.

A circle of ten hounds growled just outside the pool of light the sword cast. Though the beasts' hackles bristled in jagged ridges down their backs, their darting glances over their shoulders betrayed their hesitancy.

A guttural voice snapped from somewhere behind Danae, far too close for her taste. "Kill the Elgadrim wretch, you mongrels!" the fiend commanded.

Danae sunk a fathom lower into the pit. She whispered to Culduin, "There are too many of them. If they get brave, Praesidio won't last."

"The bridge," Culduin replied. "If we could push it up. . . "

Danae's arms burned. The spinning sensation in her head blurred her vision. None of it mattered. "We'll have to give it a try. I don't think I have much more of this in me." She focused only upon the teeming sensation in her head and flesh, which seemed to embody the power that held them aloft. She willed them to drift to the underside of the dangling bridge.

Culduin placed his palms against the smooth planks, settled into the push, and nodded.

With a lung-emptying exhale, Danae bade her gift of flight for a quick burst forward and up. How mercilessly the heavy bridge seared her muscles, and how it pressed upon her mind like the crushing weight of the deep. Her stomach lurched, sweat poured down her back, and her head pounded as though it would burst, yet they brought the bridge toward level. Judging by the salty tang emanating from Culduin's skin, the strain was taking its toll on him as well.

Danae glanced back and forth over the moat. On the central

island, the fiend stood near the altar, his muscle-banded forearms folded across his chest. His eyes widened and his mouth dropped open.

On the far side, Praesidio fended off the attacks of one hound after another, felling those that came within his reach in a single stroke. He spun and slashed in a blur of speed. Carcasses lay strewn around his feet. Praesidio spared only the quickest glance toward the bridge, and before the structure had risen to fully level, he turned and broke from his combatants to pound for the crossing.

Still three hounds followed murderously after. Praesidio's weight crashed onto the bridge and jabbed Danae with new body-wracking stabs of pain with every footfall. The hounds that pursued him onto the crossing compounded the agony.

Just a couple more moments. Danae sucked fast breaths through her nose.

Once Praesidio lunged for the altar platform, Danae surged to the side. The bridge plummeted down again. Two hounds yelped and disappeared into the depths, while one made the leap for the island and slunk, craven, behind his master.

In a final expulsion of will, she flung herself and Culduin for the surface of the platform, and they sprawled upon the ground. Surely the force of the Utterance would have flayed her from within had she tried to sustain it another moment.

Trembling wracked her body. Still, she needed to rise or else face her slaughter. At the edge of her vision, the dark form of the fiend approached, his strides slow and steady. As she staggered to her feet, another wave of nausea swept over her, and swimming tunnel vision threatened to drag her back to the ground.

Praesidio cast off Danae and Culduin's weaponry, leveled a piercing gaze at the fiend, and burst into a loud song. His sword flared with blinding, blue-green light. A pulse of energy burst forth from his outstretched blade and smote directly upon the greatsword in the fiend's hands. Praesidio's assault enveloped the Sword of the Patron in its glow, and vapor curled from its surface.

The fiend shrieked and shook the sword from his hands. It clattered to the stone floor, shards of ice crackling from its surface. Wisps of mist trailed from the weapon, now burning cold.

"Very well, have it your way," the fiend declared. "You may find the power of Darkness a much less agreeable way to die. No infidel dog shall profane any temple presided over by Ba-al Zechmaat!"

A cyclone of green flame swept from Ba-al Zechmaat's hands and careened toward Praesidio, though the old sage swept it aside with a pearlescent wave of Creo's might.

Danae stood agape until Culduin's voice cut into her stupor.

"Danae! Grab your weapons!"

The remaining Hound of Queldurik barreled from behind his master in a rabid flash of teeth and claws. Culduin swept his sword from amidst the pile Praesidio had dropped and brought it around to slice a blood-flinging wound across the hound's shoulder.

The hound stood between Danae and her weapons. She stayed rooted. Better than weapons of the world was the might of Creo. She dredged her memory for an appropriate Utterance from *The Tree*, then pointed a shaking finger at the beast. "*Selir lumintannat.*"

Her hand twitched with a little recoil as a bolt of lightning shot forth. It sizzled across the black flesh of the hound, and the creature yelped. Danae's tight jaw relinquished a smile. *That's so much better than having to touch the target.*

With a jolt of electricity here, a biting carpet of sparks there, Danae combated the beast with not her own might, but the will of her Maker. Creo's vigor careened through her flesh with each summons of power, and the last vestiges of unwholesome residue upon her soul vanished.

Each of the beast's attacks became more frenzied than the last as it snapped, whirled, bit, and raked. It reeled back and forth between Culduin's sword slashes and Danae's divine assaults. The hound hunkered down, thrust its hind legs, and bounded with a gaping maw for Danae. She threw an arm across her face.

Culduin dove into the enemy's path. The length of his blade sunk into the hound's chest. The beast's howl petered out to a gurgle, and it crashed to the platform, finally motionless.

Danae sank to her knees and gasped for breath, yet she lifted her eyes and surveyed the platform. How was Praesidio faring if only one of Ba-al Zechmaat's hounds had proven so staunch a challenge?

The fiend lord and the knight's battle raged on. Shockwaves from both the combatants' discharges of might buffeted Danae, and the flashes and flares dazzled her eyes. Divine power collided in every color of the spectrum. The floor trembled. High-pitched cracks and heart-vibrating rumbles shook the air. She scuttled to the corner of one of the colossi's pedestals for cover. Culduin huddled in behind her.

In a guttural outpouring of harsh words, Ba-al Zechmaat reached his clawed hands for the ceiling. A roaring pillar of fire blasted down from the heavens. Praesidio dove aside, though the flames singed the hem of his robe. He answered the fiend's attack by calling a wall of ice to erupt from the floor. A few backpedaling steps pulled Zechmaat clear.

The fiend swept his hand before him to strafe his opponent with a shower of tiny meteorites, but Praesidio shoved his hands before him. The stony pelting abated as an unseen force hurled Zechmaat across the platform. For every tactic one combatant threw, the other had an answer of equal fury.

Culduin gripped her shoulder. "Praesidio needs our help."

"Are you crazy?" Danae gaped. "What can we do? We'll be reduced to a vapor!"

"Perhaps, but shall we cower here and say we did nothing?"

Danae scowled. Culduin was right. "We'd better use our heads. My little shocks are no use over there. My daggers even less so."

"Trickery could serve us better than might."

Danae wrung her hands, her eyes captivated by the warfare before her, but her mind churning in search of an escape for her mentor.

Praesidio threw a translucent shield up before him, barely in time to deflect a glob of molten fury Ba-al Zechmaat flung toward him. The knight's shoulders sagged as he held the barrier steady. His chest heaved under smoking robes. His ashen complexion looked like the mask of the dead.

At least the fiend's open gashes and jerky movements painted him as battle-weary as her friend. One of the fiend's wings hung limp, and white bone poked from a kink in its structure. His many wounds oozed with a greenish-black slime. Longer inspection revealed the edges of these gashes writhed like a pile of slick snakes, intent on weaving the otherworldly flesh back together. The light of his eyes was dim, the expression on his face drooping and hateful.

Danae's focus slid past the fight and locked upon the long tatters of chains that had fallen to the floor when the fiend cut the bridge loose. She grabbed Culduin's arm. His gaze joined hers.

*H*eavy lengths of chain in hand, Danae crept one halting step at a time in a wide circle around the platform that would eventually bring her up behind Ba-al Zechmaat. Both the fiend and Praesidio staggered about in what had deteriorated into a drunken brawl of lassitude. The two warriors swung at one another with mundane weapons of claw and staff.

The fiend's nails ripped across Praesidio's chest. Danae winced. She cowered when a blow from Praesidio's staff threatened to spin the villain toward her. The sound of footfalls gaining upon her drew her glance. Culduin skulked up behind her, his hands laden with loops of chain of his own. His nod and narrow eyes urged her on.

While the fiend wound up another punch, Danae and Culduin dashed around his legs, wrapping him in tangled loops of chain. Culduin pulled a lasso of the iron links around the damaged wing. The villain roared as the chain yanked tight.

The fiend slashed with his gnarled hand, catching Danae in the ribs and sending her tumbling across the platform. She skidded to a stop, within just a few strides of the Sword of the Patron. She scrambled to her feet and grabbed the ice-covered greatsword in a fold of her cloak.

"Let's go!"

After one more yank to tighten the chains, Culduin sprang after her. He hauled Praesidio along by the arm.

Danae stole a glance back while they ran.

Ba-al Zechmaat took a long stride after them, but jerked to a halt as the entangling chains snapped taut with a shudder. He wheeled and glared down their length to where the chains were knotted and clamped to a pair of sacrifice idols.

Danae skidded to a stop by a tall, carven lever that stuck out of the floor. She threw all her weight against it. The air erupted into the screech of metal against metal. Danae covered her mouth with her hand as the chains around the struggling fiend tugged him toward the sacrifice pit. The ring of sacrifice idols ground along steel tracks that ended deep in the midst of the flames fanned for Queldurik's sake.

Ba-al Zechmaat's writhing only succeeded in knocking him to the floor, and onward the chains dragged him, until the unrelenting march of the idols towed him over the lip of the chasm. Once Ba-al Zechmaat's last clawed hand slipped over the precipice, Danae turned to follow her comrades toward the rear edge of the platform.

She fell in beside Praesidio and Culduin, who glared around the chamber. The elf snorted. "For all we have conquered, shall we lose it, marooned on this island?"

"Maybe there's another bridge?" Danae asked.

"Not that I can see." Culduin swept a swift gesture around the chamber.

The sound of running feet and cries of alarm echoed faintly from somewhere outside the sacrifice chamber.

"Let us check the opposite side of the platform, beyond the colossi," Praesidio said between haggard gulps of air. He hung on his staff.

An unwelcome prickle of tears sprang to Danae's eyes. Would Praesidio even have the strength to flee if indeed there were a way off this platform? She took his arm to prop him. A smile warmed his weary eyes.

They turned for the massive black sculptures that rose from the island of rock, Culduin in the lead despite a quick halt to scoop up their equipment, Danae and Praesidio following at a quick shuffle. With each step they took, the old sage's weight upon her lessened, if only a little.

Indeed, on the opposite side of the circular platform, Danae spied another exit from the chamber, though it lay on the far side of the twenty-foot-wide moat of flames. The sounds of shouts and footfalls grew, and the air throbbed with the infuriated roars of the fiend-lord. Danae scanned the area. *Creo, show us the way of escape!*

Her attention snagged on the support beams that braced the ceiling over the moat. "Look!" She pointed high above them. "If I can get my grappling hook around those cross-beams, do you think we could swing over?"

"Did we not just *fly* from the chasm?" Culduin replied.

"Yes." Danae hesitated. "But I don't think I could manage it again so soon."

"Wait," Praesidio blurted, eyes wide and jaw slack. "You . . . flew? We shall need to discuss that. Later. For now, the grappling hook it will have to be."

Danae pulled out her coil of hempen rope. She swirled the grapple beside her until the metal hook sang in a whir of motion. She let the hook fly. It clanked noisily off the beams and clattered to the floor.

"Do not let it shake you. Try again!" Culduin peeked around the statues, then looked up at the beams.

Danae groaned. She hurriedly re-gathered the rope and readied another toss. The hook sprang from her hand, arced high, and landed with a satisfying clunk around the beam. She gripped the line in her hands and readied herself to make the swing.

"Wait!" Culduin called. He shrugged off his pack. On one knee, he tied the satchel to the bottom end of the rope. "It will never swing back all the way unweighted."

"Good thinking, Culduin." Praesidio said. "Now Danae, you first!" A distant crash announced the entry doors of the Chamber of Sacrifice flying open. Danae clutched the Sword under one arm and launched herself over the pit to land on the opposite side, albeit awkwardly owing to her burden. Culduin and Praesidio followed suit. After reclaiming Culduin's equipment, they retreated from the chamber in a frenzied dash. Ba-al Zechmaat's curses and oaths faded as they ran.

"You realize . . . the fires will not harm him," Praesidio said.

"What?" Danae shrieked. "The chains and the pit's depth will at least slow him down, right?"

"Yes, yes," Praesidio said. "But our time of reprieve will be short."

39

UNLIKELY HELP

*C*ulduin clutched the hilt of his drawn blade as he led the ducking, dodging retreat through the dim back hallways of Queldurik's temple. The shouts and confusion they left behind in the sacrifice chamber faded. He skidded to a stop at a juncture between hallways and peered around the corner. Two red-clad figures shuffled toward him, the words of their conversation too soft to translate, but worried in tone.

Culduin held his hand up behind him. Praesidio and Danae's footfalls came to a halt.

"Two priests coming," Culduin whispered.

Praesidio tried a door a few steps back. It eased open. The old sage poked his head inside, beckoned the group, and slid through. With a light clasp upon Danae's elbow, Culduin ushered Danae after Praesidio, then surveyed the hallway once more. Only the flicker of torches in their sconces moved behind them. He ducked through the door as well.

The room scarcely held them all, being long enough only for the kneeler against the left wall. They huddled in breathless silence as footsteps grew in the distance, then padded past, amidst utterances of words like "sacrifice chamber" and "trouble." Culduin's patchy Tebalese lost some of the context, but what he did understand painted a clear enough image.

Praesidio wriggled and jostled to free his blanket from his pack. He handed it to Danae. "Wrap the Sword, Danae."

All the ruffling of fabric seemed intolerably loud in the stifling little space. A pity they had not managed to escape with the scabbard to the cumbersome weapon, for its exotic appearance would surely draw attention should someone spy them. Culduin strained his ears past the rustling for further commotion in the hall. His muscles twitched with the need to retreat. Once the prayer closet and the hallway outside had grown fully silent again, Praesidio nodded to the door.

They ran through hallways, but slowed to inspect those that lay beyond turns or doors. Without encountering more priests nor hearing pursuit, the group finally burst from an exit that spilled them into the alley behind the temple.

Culduin faced Danae and Praesidio. "Now what? It will not be long before they have rescued the demon from the pit, I would wager."

"Find another place to hide and plan," Danae said.

She slipped into the lead, Sword cradled across her body, her posture low and catlike as she skulked forward on noiseless, swift strides. Culduin mimicked her, and Praesidio ambled behind. Culduin winced every time the man's staff hit the pavement, but it could not be helped. It was a wonder the aged knight pressed on at all.

When they had gotten a scant two blocks from the temple, a clamor of bells pealed in the night, nearly thrusting Culduin out of his skin. His glance whirled back to the black spires, still far too close, silhouetted against the night sky.

"Those don't sound like vespers," Danae said, a tremor in her voice.

"More like an alarm," Praesidio responded.

A comforting thought. Culduin gritted his teeth. "More than just priests are going to be casting probing gazes to the streets. A hiding place is imperative."

Danae pointed up the narrow road. "I think that's a stable ahead. Better than a tavern or other public place, if you ask me."

They scurried for the shadow of the stable wall, rounded the barn, and glanced through every window along the way. Only horses, no stable hands in sight. They dashed through the cover of the carriage run, but Danae hesitated at the door.

"Good enough?" she whispered.

Culduin simply nodded. Danae blew a pent-up breath, then led the group into the tall stone building to pile into an empty stall. The horses dozed in the other boxes, regarding the group with no more than a snort or a tossed head.

Danae gulped for breath. "The entire priesthood . . . maybe Ba-al Zechmaat himself . . . is going to scour this city for us."

She set her blanket-wrapped burden on the floor.

"And the city gate is locked." Culduin returned Danae's bandoliers. "What chance do we stand of remaining undiscovered until daybreak? Even then the gatekeepers will surely have orders to keep a wary eye. There will be no faking our way through this time."

"I had hoped our escape with the Sword would kick up less of a clamor," Praesidio said. "It complicates matters."

"To say the lea—" The clatter of horse hooves in the corridor cut off Culduin's response.

A voice spoke calming words to the animal that had entered, coupled with the sounds of the horse being unharnessed and tended. The smells of warm leather and horse sweat drifted through the air. A fine fix, to be cornered in a ten-foot box.

Culduin rubbed his brow. *A simple stable hand should present little challenge in neutralizing, right? It would be a shame for an uninvolved civilian to lose his life over our need for secrecy.* But a prisoner left behind could eventually talk. Culduin settled into a spring-ready crouch, sword in hand, but Danae pressed a hand on his thigh.

Footsteps drew closer to the door.

He cocked a brow at Danae, but she simply shook her head. He turned his unspoken question to Praesidio, who had drawn his hood low over his face so only his lips and chin still showed. The old sage pulled his cloak tight about him and tucked his talisman into his tunic. He pushed the Sword of the Patron under the straw bedding with his foot.

Before Culduin could glean Praesidio's intent, the door of the stall flew open, and outside it stood a lean Tebalese man. He gaped at them, his gaze lingering on Danae last and longest.

"Sh-shamir?" Danae tipped back and plunked on her rear. "How in the world?"

"The hair color under all that grime is not common to Radromirians, is it madam?" the Tebalese man said, thankfully in the Western tongue. "You have come a long way in the past few months, mistress, since I last picked you up in my sleigh!"

How in the world, indeed. What connection did Danae have with a Tebalese stablehand? "You know this man?" Culduin furrowed his brow.

"This isn't the right time to explain." Danae held out open palms to the stablehand. "Please, we have no time. You've done me one favor already, and I'm loath to ask for another, but please. Let us go. You never saw us! I'll find some way to reward you."

"Reward me?" Shamir shrugged. "There is nothing of this world you could offer me that would lessen the burden of my days, unless you could devise an ending to slavery in Tebal." He scuffed a foot on the packed clay floor of the stall.

"Did you . . . lose your position in Radromir?" Danae asked.

Shamir shook his head. "My master fell in battle, so I've been bequeathed to his vain daughter. I much preferred my post on the desolate road in your country than my lot in life here."

Culduin huffed. Had Danae not already said they had no time? He rose. "Will you release us, horseman?" Culduin pressed.

In the distance, the temple gongs sounded again. Culduin flicked his tongue over his lip and tasted the salty tang of sweat.

"The temple alarm sounds, and that worries you, elf?" Shamir narrowed his eyes. "Perhaps helping you is more complicated than I thought."

Danae interposed her small frame between Culduin and Shamir. "I'm begging you, Shamir. Is there some way out of the city besides the main gate?" She layered a doe-eyed look of vulnerability on the stablehand.

Culduin ground his teeth, but waited for Shamir's response.

"Have you committed some crime?" Shamir asked, but then he held up his hands. "No, never mind. The less I know about your troubles, the less I can tell."

"I will say this," Danae replied. "Our only offense is against the cult of Queldurik."

Shamir brightened. "If that's the case, then I'm happy to aid you. I can do better than let you go. I believe I can show you a place where you might escape the city unnoticed."

"Can you show us right now?" Praesidio asked.

Shamir's eyebrows shot up. "So, you do talk, stranger. Give me just a few minutes. You can all hide in the carriage until I have a fresh horse hitched."

Praesidio placed a hand on Danae's shoulder. "You trust this man?"

"More than anyone else we might meet within Garash's walls," Danae replied.

A bitter laugh escaped Culduin's lips. "That says little."

Danae folded her arms. "We don't have many options."

Culduin sighed. "Lead the way, Shamir. You have our advance thanks for your willingness."

Danae took a step after Shamir, though Praesidio grabbed her sleeve and jerked his head toward the straw on the floor. Gasping, Danae clapped her hands over her mouth, then squatted to collect the bundle she had nearly left behind.

Tragic misstep averted, the group stole after Shamir to the carriage house, where he opened the side door to a plush vehicle. They bustled inside.

Eyebrow cocked, Shamir said, "I shan't be long."

He shut the door after them.

The next handful of minutes passed characterized by the sounds of hooves, jingling buckles, creaking leather, and quiet words from Shamir's lips. Culduin narrowed his eyes and tipped his ear toward the door.

Danae patted Culduin's shoulder. "He's just talking to the horses. Try to take a breath or two."

The carriage rolled a bit when Shamir hitched the animal to the vehicle, and then it rocked as he climbed into the driver's seat in front.

Shamir leaned down to the carriage's front window. "Ready? Whatever you do, stay down. The streets are growing a little busy."

The carriage rattled over the cobblestones, and the thick, crimson velvet curtains over the windows ensured the cramped travelers had no way of marking where Shamir bore them. Only the occasional slice of lamplight snuck through the slits between the panels. Culduin crouched shoulder-to-shoulder with Danae, and their proximity conveyed her continual trembling into Culduin's flesh. He wrapped an arm around her.

"Almost free, dear one," he murmured.

Danae cast him a wan smile and leaned into Culduin's clasp. For a few blissful, worrisome moments, Culduin rested his cheek atop her head.

Shamir drove the horse through the streets at a brisk trot for minutes that stretched beyond counting. The clink of weapon and armor beyond the carriage walls sent Culduin's hand to his hilt, but when the vehicle maintained a steady momentum, he relaxed his grip. A little.

Finally, Shamir called a firm "whoa" to the beast that drew them along, and the carriage wobbled as he jumped from his seat. He swung the door wide. "This is as far as I can take you, and you must be swift from here. There were many guards and several priests roving the streets near the Temple."

Culduin saw Praesidio and Danae from the vehicle first, then crept out himself, wary as a hare. Shamir had borne them to the city's edge, near a very small gatehouse that stood unmanned. Iron gates blocked the dark tunnel through the wall.

The fringe neighborhood around them resembled a cluster of rotten and crumbling molars concealed behind a meticulously polished smile. In contrast to the opulent business and temple district of Garash, the outskirts offered refuse and debris in every corner, and rats skittered between the heaps. Far down the street, three ragged beggars hunched over a fire built in the middle of the street. They cast numb glances in the direction of the carriage, but soon turned back to rubbing bare hands over the meager flames.

Shamir trotted to the gate and tugged at the chain around the rusted bars. He gasped. The gate creaked on its hinges, but a shiny lock swung in the center of the chain. "Locked?" he said. "For so long this gate has gone unnoticed."

"Why should we believe you?" Culduin growled. "If you have cornered us in this slum—"

Shamir flushed, and sweat beaded on his brow. "I've done what I can. Until now, this gate has been disregarded, and only a broken lock hung upon the chain."

"Please, Culduin, don't jump to conclusions." Danae said. "I'm as guilty as anyone of holding Tebalese people in suspicion just because of where they were born. But I might be able to do something about this."

Danae dug through her pack and produced a canvas pouch. She knelt, unfolded the pouch, and selected a long pick. With narrowed eyes, she examined the mechanisms within, then slipped the probe into the keyhole.

Culduin wrung his hands. His heart accelerated from a thump to a gallop.

She switched from one tool to the next, sometimes leaving one wedged in the lock to continue the work with the aid of another.

Shamir paced, and his face took on a sickly pallor as the delay stretched on. "Maybe the opium trade has drawn some notice over here. Why else a lock where there's never been one?"

Praesidio closed his eyes. "The reason does not matter. Creo permit that Danae should show skill with her hands." A dog barked in one of the nearby alleys. They all jumped. "And quickly."

With a surgeon's methodical precision, Danae probed the tumblers of the tiny mechanism. Culduin leaned in. What minute details inside the little keyhole did she see that offered a chance at freedom? She pursed her lips. A bead of sweat ran down her temple. Her fingers twisted her pick an indiscernible fraction.

A spring. A click.

The lock snapped open, and Danae met Culduin's close gaze, grinning in triumph. He caught her in a brisk hug.

When he released her, Danae turned to Shamir and clasped the horseman's arm. "Twice now you've come to my aid, and I want to return the favor. Come with us."

Shamir sucked a gasp. In the distance, the temple chimes sounded again, and he turned the direction from which the sound came. His shoulders slumped. "Alas, this is not my time, for runaway slaves seldom make it far in this country. I won't further endanger your escape. Now, go. If I linger any longer, I'll be late for my mistress, and that will mean trouble." The lean horseman sprang again to his seat. "Freedom will come to me someday, even if I find it only in death. For now, I must serve my earthly master." He wheeled the carriage in a wide circle and trotted off into the darkness.

Culduin lingered in the entryway to the tunnel while Praesidio trundled through. Danae's glance remained fixed the direction Shamir had departed.

"Come," Culduin whispered. "You must."

Eyes glassy, Danae trudged to the tunnel. "You're right. Let's go."

They shuffled through the dark of the portal to discover the gate on the opposite side hung crookedly on one hinge. Thick cobwebs stretched between rusty and peeling bars. Culduin dashed back to the city end of the gatehouse and reset the lock just as they had found it. How frail even a stout lock seemed against the fury they had stoked to flame.

40

INTO THE OPEN

*D*anae, Culduin, and Praesidio stood with their backs pressed to the outside of Garash's wall, optimizing the cover the dilapidated gatehouse and surrounding brambles offered. The slope of the plateau that stretched between them and the clustered structures of Garash's outlying homesteads was open and barren. Danae hugged the Sword bundle closer to her chest and glanced up the ramparts. A guard stood behind the parapet, polearm in hand, less than two furlongs away.

"What are we going to do about him?" Danae whispered. "He's going to see us if we try the slope."

Culduin reached for his bow. Praesidio stayed the elf's hand. "And neither should we leave a trail of bodies if we can at all avoid it."

Danae pursed her lips. "What about the Utterance that casts the recipient into a slumber? Would that work?"

"If it is Creo's will you should use it," Praesidio replied.

"What if it's not?"

"Then he will not grant the request. Better to be sure the choice aligns with his will first, whenever possible, rather than grieve him with constant, unmeditated Utterances."

Danae's stomach roiled. "I don't understand."

Praesidio patted her shoulder. "We shall amend that in time." He closed his eyes and breathed deeply for a dozen breaths.

"We cannot linger here." Culduin began to squirm.

The old sage's eyes opened again. "Use your Utterance, Danae. Culduin is right."

Danae fumbled for *The Tree* and sought the correct page with trembling hands. How faint and small the words were in the moonlight. She pointed at the guard. "*Recaltherrinne, ulsto i entevet.*"

For a moment, the guard watched on, unchanged. Fire surged through Danae's neck and skull.

The soldier swayed on his feet and dropped.

"Great work!" Culduin beamed.

Danae shrugged. "It's not me."

"Later," Praesidio cut in. "Run."

They barreled down the slope and into the cover of the twisting streets of the outer city, but soon left even the outskirts behind. By the time the moon approached its zenith, fiery protest raged through Danae's legs and lungs, and the weight of the massive Sword of the Patron dragged on her arms. Praesidio and Culduin ran a half-dozen strides ahead of her, and a deepening haze of fog that crept into her vision obscured the narrow focus she struggled to maintain on them. She stumbled with a high-pitched gasp.

Culduin halted and turned back for her. "May I take on your burden?"

"Please." She handed the sword to the tall elf. As it passed from her grasp, it was as if a weight far greater than the poundage of the Sword lifted with it. She stood straighter.

Culduin cast a dark glance at the weapon in his hands, and a shudder ran through his body. He gripped it with banded knuckles, clamped his lips tight, and turned in dogged pursuit of Praesidio.

They ran through the vastness of the tundra. The stars grew brighter, and the moon turned from its ascent to pursue the horizon. Danae staggered to a halt and placed her hands on her knees, her chest heaving as though there was not enough air in all of Tebal to satisfy her burning lungs. Her stomach threatened to turn inside-out.

Praesidio and Culduin rounded back to her. Praesidio shook his head. "I am sorry this is so grueling, Danae. But surely you see—"

"I . . . can't." Danae panted. "Not another stride."

Culduin looked over his shoulder. "There is no safety in this barren countryside." Deep breaths broke his words only slightly. "Once the Tebalese determine our heading, surely they will pursue us on horseback and overtake us with little effort."

Praesidio breathed only a fraction more heavily than Culduin.

Am I the only one here who is worn out? Danae shook her head. *We all just nearly died, Praesidio fought off some monster from the underworld, and I'm the only one who seems winded.*

Praesidio squinted the same direction as Culduin. "We shall find no cover until we reach Quel Mahaar. We must resume the pace."

Run more? Tonight? Danae groaned. Did Praesidio intend to run, non-stop, all the way back to the canyon? It had taken days to cover the distance between it and Garash at a steady march.

Praesidio stepped to Danae's side. "Let us take a moment to ask Creo to renew Danae's strength, for she has not the endurance of the Elves."

Placing his hand upon her forehead, Praesidio chanted a musical Utterance, and a cooling wave passed through her, starting at his fingertips and trickling its way to her extremities. Every ache, pain, and protest of weariness washed from her body.

Danae took her first relaxed breath since they arrived in Garash. "So, does this mean every trouble I've got is easily met with the right Utterance?"

Praesidio shook his head. "We are under extenuating circum-stances at the moment. You will see Creo's hand working through his creation in more mundane ways once you return to everyday concerns."

Her stare locked onto Praesidio's tattered robes, the flesh beneath the rents in the fabric clearly whole, and she rubbed her eyes. "Did Creo shield you from wounds throughout that combat?"

"Had that been his will, how grateful this old servant would have been to avoid the pain. But no, the Maker wounds and mends when he deems it needful. You know this to be true in your own experience, do you not?"

Danae smirked and pressed a hand to her ribcage. "It's easy to forget. So many parts of my journey already seem distant, like ink that's fading from the page."

Culduin turned to face her as well. "There are yet refrains to sing in this song, though I can hear a soaring ending on the very wind. It rides to us with the distant smell of spring."

"Well, we've gotten this far, and that's something right there, isn't it?" She reached for Culduin's hand and squeezed it. Without letting go, she intercepted her mentor's gaze again. "If I may ask, how long do you think it will take to deliver the Sword and see me on my way back to Radromir?"

A gentle smile creased the corners of Praesidio's eyes. Always, those gray eyes pierced Danae to the marrow. "I would tell you not to worry, but I know you well enough now to realize such a request is futile. Fear not, my people and I will ready you to return to your father with all the haste we can muster, though I doubt that will be speed enough for your taste, Danae."

"May patience be one of the lessons you teach me. I get the feeling I have an awful lot to learn."

"That you do. But what matters is that you are willing. Welcome to the fold of Creo's devoted, young one."

Danae's lips broke into a grin. Belonging. Purpose. Here were goals worth clasping tight. She shook out her limbs and tightened her pack.

Culduin smoothed a tendril out of her eyes. "It looks like you have the needed pace back in your legs."

Danae breathed deep of the cold, early-morning air. She did indeed have a lightness of limb like never before in her memory. She squared her shoulders and lifted her chin in defiance of the unending flatness of Tebal, against all she so recently despaired of being impossible. "I do. Hand me the Sword, Culduin. One step at a time, I'm ready to run to the finish."

ABOUT THE AUTHOR

Geek flag flyer, nerd herder, and eternal dreamer--these are some of the things Rebecca P. Minor has been called, and she won't deny any of them. She is a full-time freelance artist, specializing in the cute, the drawn, and the imaginary. When she's not making character art, she's writing fantasy novels in the sword-and-sorcery vein. Rebecca is also the founder of the Realm Makers Conference, where a couple hundred of her most awesome friends gather annually. She's taking commissions for character art, graphic novels, children's book illustration and interior art for fantasy and gaming. (As well as polymer clay fantasy creature figurines.) Follow her exploits at www.rebeccapminor.com or on your social media platform of choice.

Finally, brothers and sisters, whatever is true, whatever is noble, whatever is right, whatever is pure, whatever is lovely, whatever is admirable—if anything is excellent or praiseworthy—think about such things.

www.ingramcontent.com/pod-product-compliance
Lightning Source LLC
Chambersburg PA
CBHW051318250626
47155CB00007B/2374